CROWLEY
The Ravensblack Affair

PANDEMIC PRESS

Authors note.

This is a work of fiction. Whatever Aleister Crowley was in life, he won't be found in this story. As a writer of fiction I make things up, I ignore facts and I twist the truth. I do all this for the sake of entertainment. So while this may not be the Crowley that you have heard about I do hope that you will want to find out more about my version, to follow him on his adventures, and maybe even grow to like him a little bit.

Although you shouldn't. Not really.

Eddie Skelson 2015

Part 1

London, 1921

It wasn't the frenzied pounding upon his front door that finally roused Crowley from his stupor. The muffled thuds and thumps had been cunningly translated into the dream-state he was experiencing inside his drug-fuelled imagination.

His subconscious, powered by the opium he had taken at the start of the ritual, had placed him upon the prow of a large ship of which he assumed, given the splendid uniform he wore, he was the captain. The great vessel, an elegant construction of dark timber and majestic sails, gently heaved up and down, caressing the waves as it ploughed on and through a vast azure ocean, and as it moved, the sail, tied by a short length of thick rope, repeatedly swung out, only to be sharply pulled back, banging against the mast.

It was this simple illusion that masked the urgency of the knocks upon his front door. So while the *'thump thump thump'* sounded, Crowley the Captain continued to look out at the expanse lazily swelling before him, seeking the answers required to pull himself out of the financial immurement he found himself in presently.

Opium was just one of a number of elements required for the ritual, a simple spell that induced the vivid dream-state in which, Crowley hoped, it would be revealed to him how he could redress the problem of fortune, or rather the lack thereof. The many other ingredients and various totems which had been required had in their own right helped to further reduce his already meagre funds, and as his eyes fluttered open, signalling his return to the real world, Crowley frowned with confusion and disappointment

His vision shifted, from filtered by a heavy blur to stunning sharp relief as his consciousness surged to the surface, eager to be in control once again, and once his faculties were restored, Crowley began to mentally investigate what he had observed.

The whole episode had consisted of him mostly staring out to sea, he thought, with only the occasional dolphin, leaping through foam that crashed against the keel, breaking up what had been a singularly monotonous journey of the mind. No arcane or eldritch symbols had been seen, no creatures of prophecy, or even popular in occult lore.

Just dolphins. Permanently happy-looking dolphins who were pissing about for no good reason other than their own entertainment.

'*What the bloody hell did all that mean?*' he thought, utterly puzzled. He massaged his temples with strong fingers.

Because the pounding noise had been so effectively masked by his subconscious Crowley didn't realise that it was the *absence* of knocks that had brought him back. Back to the dimly lit library of his Mayfair home. At the moment of his awakening however, all was quiet and so he remained oblivious to it.

Crowley felt a mild depression beginning to creep into his mood, fuel for the infernal, organic bitterness machine powering his perpetual, seething resentment at not getting his own way.

He had decided to perform his spell in the library, the conceit being that it would help to stimulate his mind. Being surrounded by so many eldritch tomes and scripts of ancient lore surely had to help, and he was a fan of ambience, so long as it was comfortable ambience.

He had read every book he owned, each and every page of the thousand or so scripts had been committed to his incredible memory. A memory so powerful that an elephant would drop its hand, flip the table and walk off were it to go toe to toe with him. But this amazing talent was tempered by his astonishing lack of organisational skill. Because organisation required effort and Crowley had no time for effort; he was far too busy to be involved in such a thing.

Instead, his mind was hoarders wet dream of unsorted information. It was a cubby-hole of coats, boxes and spare parts for household appliances, it was a loft of all the stuff that was too precious to throw away but not so interesting that it had to be kept in view of anyone. But really, the most important reason for choosing to perform rituals in the library was that it was warm in there.

Winter had arrived early to Southern England, and due to his recent travels, he hadn't made preparations for coal to be delivered. Having no maid in the house was also proving to be difficult, but as his finances were in a somewhat turbulent state there were certain things that had to be shelved, at least for the time being. So his mood, a shade lighter than black at the best of times, had become so dark of late that Crowley felt as though he carried with him his own personal weather system, whose outlook was frequently grim with occasional outbreaks of despondent.

Lighting in the house was for the most part by gas lamp, but the library was also home to a small log fire and it was from this Crowley obtained most of his heat. Associates had questioned the wisdom of having an open fire in a room that was basically coated wall to wall with paper so dry that a burning look might set it alight, but Crowley dismissed these concerns as nonsense. The fire took the chill out of the air and made it the warmest room in the house, even compared to the living room with its huge, but rarely lit hearth.

Crowley grunted as he rose awkwardly from his plush but well-worn rocker. His mouth was dry and in the gloom of the lamplight he looked about for a pitcher.

He always brought a supply of water into the library before commencing any ritual. It was practical for both health reasons and just in case his know-it-all associates should turn out to be right and he awoke to a blazing room. Demons he could stomach, snooty unholier-than-thou arseholes he could not.

As he walked towards the bureau on which his refreshment was situated a loud and determined stream of bangs sounded, they seemed to be coming from somewhere towards the rear of the house. Crowley's eyebrows tightened as a moment of recollection brought to his mind the great ship he had only moments ago been sailing upon.

'Bangs? Doors?'

He shrugged the thought away, or at least tried to. 'There are no doors on boats. Or are there?'

He wasn't sure if boats had doors.

'Surely they have doors? They probably have them but don't call them doors. What does one call a boat-door? Probably the Poop-Hole or something equally incomprehensible...'

The thought became lodged in his head. This often happened to him. Inane or random ideas, propositions or questions become lodged in his mind until an answer satisfied them. It was occasionally useful but usually just annoying. He blinked the question away, which took some effort and which thereby further annoyed him.

He had no idea of the time but he surmised that it must be late in the evening at the very least.

'Fuck em,' he thought and chose to ignore the knocks. He only ever enjoyed opening the door if he was expecting a parcel, other than that nothing pleasant ever came from answering the front door, and besides, the question of what the doors on a boat might be called had upset his karma.

After a few moments, the banging stopped and Crowley felt justified in his ignorance.

Unfortunately, as he reached the bureau and gripped the handle of the pitcher, furious knocking broke out once again.

'Damned Persistent bleeders!' he snapped.

He thought his name was being called but it was hard to say for sure. The doors to the house were thick, the frames strong, and all of the windows were barred on the inside. Security, and to some extent sound reduction, were important to Crowley, not least of all because the amount of drugs he took during some rituals would leave him utterly without consciousness, thus also leaving him at the whim of anyone, or *anything*, that might breach the house.

He took a swill of cold water and it chilled his teeth, raising his awareness a little more.

'*Check the circle*,' a mental tap on his shoulder reminded him to observe that all was well in the room before he did anything else. Things looked fine, the oil lamp glowed, his chalk pentacle that almost reached each wall was unbroken, the offering dish on a small table to the side of his chair was clear of contents. Business had, it appeared, been as usual.

As he had dawdled at the bureau the thumping had moved from the rear door to one of the windows, and if anything, was more insistent. There were numerous candles haphazardly placed about the library. Crowley picked one up and foraged in his dressing gown pockets for matches. Producing a box and extracting a slim white stick, he struck a flame and carefully lit the wick, hands steady.

The effects of most drugs had almost no impact upon him once he was free of the enhanced state they allowed him to experience. He had witnessed many of his colleagues and followers suffer greatly. Usually from nervousness and a deep lethargy, after what he felt was the smallest dose of narcotics. *He* was made of sterner stuff.

Crowley understood that lighting the large house could be easier than using gaslights and candles, but he had no truck with electricity. He didn't trust it. It was like having wild magic constrained to thin cables and boxes.

You didn't keep wild magic locked away like that. At some point it would get out, and then you would be sorry.

He tightened the belt of his dressing gown—under this he was naked other than his calfskin slippers—and made his way out of the warm library and into the cold and unlit hall. This in turn led to the kitchen, the source of the bloody irritating window thumper.

The candle held before him cast shadows across wall-mounted paintings and curios, sat gathering dust on cabinet tops and behind little glass panes. Halfway down the hall was a large mirror, and as he passed Crowley couldn't help but take a glance.

With the eerie light cast by the candle he fancied that the figure in the mirror looked a little ghoulish. Deep shadows further recessed his hooded eyes and brought his smooth, hairless dome into sharp relief. He smiled at his reflection but wasn't very impressed with what smiled back. He replaced the smile with a grimace, which felt more appropriate. His stature was imposing despite him being garbed in only his comfortable dressing gown.

'Enough to break the confidence of anyone at the door, should they be up to some mischief,' he thought, but Crowley decided to pick up a shotgun that was hung on the wall, just in case.

The gun wasn't loaded—even he wasn't that reckless—but if meddling with the country's most infamous occultist didn't do the job then the threat of a twelve-gauge shotgun, that he had christened Patricia, was usually sufficient to deter thoughts of pushing one's luck at Crowley's door.

'It might be the police,' he thought.

Which was a reasonable assumption, but as far as he was aware he had no warrants associated with his name at the moment, so he wasn't entirely sure what he might have done *lately* that would require them to beat upon his door at this time of night. He also wondered what time it might actually be.

He never wore a wristwatch or carried any kind of timepiece. Time was another thing, that like electricity, Crowley found to be extremely unreliable and wholly suspect.

He considered that chances were the person knocking could simply be some outraged Christian, Jew, or other flavour of holy man, who wanted to vent his spleen. But those chaps were usually courteous enough to make an appointment, or at least have the decency to rant in the afternoon.

Whatever the case, he was resigned to the fact that the matter wouldn't be resolved by dithering in a hall. He marched on with the shotgun, it was broken over his arm but he didn't bother to load it. Guns didn't kill people. People with guns killed people and the beauty of Patricia was that she doubled up as a rather splendid club.

There was a small room which split the hall from the kitchen, it was here that Crowley kept his mountaineering gear. It hadn't been used in a few years and had become what he thought of as 'a bit of a mess'. Negotiating this area at night was never easy, it was also far from easy in daylight. By his nature he was not an orderly man and so had piled the equipment haphazardly with no thought to how it would affect his access to and from the kitchen. He had found himself tripping on various pieces of tackle and canvas of late, which had slumped out from the piles, and although he cautiously stepped over any obvious shadowy lumps he still managed to stub his toe on a metal peg weighted down by a coil of thick rope.

'Christ all-fucking-mighty!' he hissed, and hopped the last few steps into the kitchen.

As soon as he entered the room the light of the candle revealed a pink fist engaging in rapid thumps onto the window. The blurred, indistinguishable face of its owner mouthed his name.

'CROWLEY, CROWLEY!' it barked, impatience writ large. 'FOR GODS SAKE MAN, HURRY.'

The window thumper had obviously seen him enter with the candle but failed to cease the annoying knocking until Crowley made his way over to the kitchen door.

This part of the house exited directly into a street which ran behind a long row of large detached houses, and these made up Cromwell Avenue. Crowley's house sat nestled amongst the residences of well-to-do neighbours, who were by now used to angry visitors and the police to his home at odd hours.

He lifted keys from a hook that was fixed to the wall at the side of the door. Placing the candle down onto a work surface but keeping the shotgun comfortably nestled in the crook of his arm, he unlocked it.

Pulling it open revealed a face he knew very well. It was indeed the police. But not just some uniformed bobby; this was Inspector Bryson, a man whom Crowley had not so long ago called, to his face, an 'ineffectual and plebeian arseferret.'

The Inspector climbed down a step when the door began to open and looked up.

'Crowley I need...' he started, and abruptly stopped as he noticed the shotgun.

Crowley looked at it too, then back to Bryson.

'Can't be too careful Inspector,' he said, and gave Bryson a sharks smile.

Bryson ignored the comment and continued, racing the words out. 'I need you to come with me, right now.'

Crowley replied with measured caution.

'Come with you. Why? What have I done?'

'You haven't done anything,' Bryson replied, a little confused, 'I just need you to come with me, immediately,' He climbed back up the step he had retreated down so as to become level with Crowley. He then leaned in and added in a lowered tone, '*Something* has happened.'

'I see!' Crowley replied with faux astonishment, 'I don't suppose you could be a little more vague could you?'

Bryson reddened, his cheeks sucked in, he presented Crowley with a snort of frustration but managed to reign in his temper. His experience of the occultist had taught him that making a person lose one's patience was part of Crowley's well-practiced method of assault and he would be damned if he would fall for it. Not again.

'Look, Crowley, please, could you just come right away.' Bryson paused, as though seeking something deep within him. 'I need your help.'

Finishing the sentence with such words clearly pained Bryson, and Crowley found himself momentarily at a loss for any kind of witty response, sarcastic or otherwise.

'But I'm in my nightclothes,' he said looking down at his slippers.

'It doesn't matter,' Bryson said, 'come as you are. I have a car waiting at the front. Can we go through?' he asked, although he was already pushing past Crowley as he said it.

'Um, yes I suppose so,' Crowley muttered as he stepped aside.

He indicated the direction of the equipment room despite Bryson already being ahead of him. 'You know the way of course.'

Bryson said nothing and continued walking quickly on.

He had made numerous visits to all of Crowley's London residences, usually to question or arrest him with regards to various charges of fraud, blasphemy, breach of the peace, and so many matters of sexual impropriety that he couldn't number them.

He slowed a little when walking through the equipment room, hopping over something on the floor that almost had him tripped, and continued onto the hall at the front of the house. He paused for just a moment to survey the scene in the library. He didn't look back at Crowley but shook his head a little as he walked on.

Crowley followed, snatching up his door keys and wallet from a cabinet. He had to pick up speed to catch Bryson, who he found waiting by the front door. Keys jangled as he fed one into the lock, and on opening the door he could see not one but two black sedans parked outside, both with their lights on and engines running. He was about to place his shotgun in the corner to the side of the door, but Bryson interrupted.

'Bring that,' Bryson said.

'It's not loaded,' Crowley replied.

Bryson answered abruptly. 'I have shells in the car.' He exited the house.

'*Fucking hell.*' Crowley thought.

Part 2

The had been on the road for fifteen minutes although Bryson had begun to think it was possibly a lifetime. He was sat in the front with a constable driving. Crowley complained that he had been *relegated* to sitting on his own in the back. He would have complained if he had been made to sit up front as well, but he felt it was his right to complain at being made to sit in either position. So he did, for most of the trip.

Bryson also made no attempt to explain where they were going and Crowley refused to do anything so vulgar as to ask, but once they had passed Hyde Park and the sedan was pointed towards Kensington he began to suspect where their final destination might be.

Kensington was home to the very top of the wealth table and Crowley had lived in and out of a merely respectable financial zone for last few years. He had on occasion rubbed shoulders with some of the most famous and sometimes notorious wealthy people in London, but he had never achieved the kind of money that they had access to. The kind of money that bought mansions and estates. As fast as he might acquire a tidy sum, he would fritter it away on foreign adventures, on drugs and on his growing collection of 'curios.'

As the sedan emerged from the dark streets of Camden, the houses grew noticeably bigger and were set in grounds that allowed for splendid gardens and ostentatious drives. A shiver of excitement ran through him as it became apparent that they were headed in the direction of the home of a man knew very well.

'*Roman Ravensblack, London's eminent occultist,*' a sneer twisted across Crowley's lips.

'*What a cock the man is, what a charlatan and a posing panderer. What an enormous sponging, sycophantic, attention seeking arsehole.*'

'Wanker,' he unintentionally said out loud.

'What?' Bryson asked, turning to face Crowley.

'Oh, nothing,' Crowley lied, 'just enjoying this strange and possibly hallucinatory moment.'

Bryson scowled and turned back.

If he was being escorted to Ravensblack Hall, by the Inspector, and with a gun, then things were not looking good for Roman. His sneer was replaced with a malevolent grin.

Sure enough the sedan slowed as it approached the stately pile that was formerly the London residence of the Duke of Argyle, now Ravensblack Hall. The exterior of the house was illuminated by a decorative array of gas lights that edged the courtyard, but there was no sign of lighting inside the hall.

A group of constables gathered at the large double gates which were opened to their full extent. A number of vehicles were parked along the road, a country lane that had no other home adjacent to it for a mile either way. Crowley couldn't see any vehicles in the drive but next to the house, in the courtyard, a lone sedan sat at an odd angle with two bicycles propped against it.

Oil lamps were suspended around the area occupied by the police. Some of the constables sat atop the cars, some leaned against the ornate gates and gateposts, but none ventured any further.

As the sedan drew to a stop and the inspector began to exit, all eyes turned towards him.

'They look nervous,' Crowley thought as he climbed out of the vehicle.

'Wait there,' Bryson said, a trifle abruptly for Crowley's liking.

'I most certainly will not,' Crowley retorted and hurried around to the Inspectors side.

He would be damned if he was going to have Bryson pushing him around any further, not unless he produced a warrant.

'I *demand* to know what's going on,' Crowley said.

He lifted his chin and tried to project an imperious image, despite his naked legs and leather slippers.

Bryson stopped and turned to face him. He chewed the situation over for a moment then spoke with his voice lowered.

'OK look, I'm sorry, all right?' he spread his hands in an 'is that better' expression of conciliation, 'things are a little strange here,' he paused and corrected himself, 'things are *very* strange here.'

He cocked his head back, indicating the gathered policemen.

'The lads are very edgy, four of them are missing, inside that house,' his eyes shifted towards the hall.

'Missing inside the house?' Crowley said.

'Two lads went in. They didn't come out. Another two went after them. Same story... except...' Bryson paused and licked his lips.

'*Something* was thrown through the front door.'

Crowley looked towards the Hall again with greater scrutiny, and was surprised that he had missed something so salient. He hadn't realised that the large door at its entrance was wide open. This closer inspection also revealed something else he had missed; it lay just a few feet away from the bottom of the steps leading up to the open doorway. He squinted.

'Is that a head?'

Bryson nodded. 'We think it's Constable Brindley.'

'Oh dear,' Crowley said as though Bryson had just informed him that he had an ill aunt.

The inspector led him to a table near the gates upon which were large plans and sketches, he guessed correctly that they were layouts of the house and its gardens. Maintaining a low and calm tone Bryson explained the situation.

'A call came in to the station. We don't know who it was, but the man was scared, in a panic. He said that Ravensblack had gone mad, that there was something in the house killing everyone. Two of the lads went straight out in a car and while we waited for more cars to come in to the station I sent two more constables out on their bikes.'

'Brindley?' asked Crowley.

'On a bike,' replied Bryson. 'As none of the lads had called back from the phone in the house I decided to bring all of the men I had available. When I got here with Sergeant Reed was when the head came flying out of the door.'

Crowley had noticed the sergeant when he approached the car. He was a burly man with a terrific walrus moustache bulging beneath his nose. He wore his helmet low over his eyes making the growth look more impressive.

On many of his arrests, the sergeant Reed had been present. A beefy hand with sausage fingers would clamp down on Crowley's shoulder while he was excitedly haranguing those who had come to take him to the station. It always shut him up.

Reed rarely said anything, he didn't have to, he was a giant of a man and the weight of his mighty hand was usually enough to calm anyone.

'Has anyone else been to the house since?' Crowley asked.

'No.' Bryson shook his head. 'They are worried that Ravensblack might have a firearm.'

'I see,' Crowley said, '*scared shitless*,' he thought. 'So what do you want me to do?' he asked.

'You know the man, right? He's one of your lot.'

Crowley scoffed. 'One of *my lot*? What exactly is *that* supposed to mean?'

'Come on Crowley. All that devil worship stuff and the'—Bryson dropped to a whisper—'sex orgies. Ravensblack was up to his balls in it... if you know what I mean.'

Crowley fixed his eyes directly on the inspector's. '*Roman Ravensblack*, or should I say *Carlton Bradsworth*, is nothing more than a posturing peddler of second-rate astrology and palm readings. The man is a total fake, a charlatan, and a fraud. I wouldn't trust him to communicate properly with the living, never mind the dead. I have a length of rope that has more arcane talent than that imbecile.'

'How come he's got more money than you then? Bryson couldn't resist the chance to take a dig.

'Because he's also a cunt,' Crowley replied.

Bryson coughed and looked around to see if anyone had heard Crowley's outburst. He gripped the occultists arm and led him a few steps away from the gathered officers.

'All right look, the thing is, he's into all of *that* and he may have gone loopy, right? So maybe you could talk to him. You know, about that... stuff, and calm him down...'

'Can't we just shoot him?' Crowley asked.

'No. We can't just *shoot him.*'

'Why?'

'For a start we don't know who else is in there with him. He also has friends, let's just say *in high places.*'

Crowley snorted. It was typical. If it was *him* that had gone off the deep end they would have blown his head off in a heartbeat.

'What are you going to do then?' Crowley asked.

'*We* are going to go in there and find Ravensblack. Then *you* are going to persuade him to come out, peacefully.'

'I don't fucking think so,' Crowley replied

'Look Crowley. I'll be there, the sarge will be there, and I'll get one of the other lads to come along as well,' Bryson pulled a revolver from his pocket.

'We're all armed and I've got a dozen lads back here that'll come running if there is any nonsense.

'What? Like my head being thrown through the door,' Crowley replied bluntly.

'No more heads through doors, I promise. I need your expertise Crowley,' at this Bryson spotted Crowley's eyebrows lift a fraction. That's where you got to Crowley, in his ego. Bryson immediately altered his tactics.

'No one knows this stuff like you do Crowley, this is your game, *you're* the guvnor when it comes to...' Bryson wasn't really sure what made an occultist the top of his field and searched his memory for anything that sounded vaguely applicable, 'magicological... work...'

Crowley's fingers drummed at the stock of his shotgun.

Deep down he knew he was being played by Bryson. He wanted to reject the man and his outrageous crawling but the feeling was just too good to dismiss.

'What's in it for me?' Crowley asked, his tone underlining his suspicion that Bryson wouldn't care if his head was used as a football.

'The respect and thanks of a grateful constabulary, and of course the people of London,' Bryson said as convincingly as he could.

'Fuck off,' Crowley replied.

'Ten guineas, and I'll make sure the next bit of bother you have ends well.'

'Thirty,' Crowley replied.

'Fifteen, and you can have any one item out of Ravensblack's stash of goodies.'

Crowley stayed silent.

'Come on Crowley, I know how much you love all those old books and scary statues.'

Crowley held out for another few seconds, mostly for appearances. 'Deal,' he said finally. They shook. Everything seemed quite surreal to the pair of them.

'Right then,' Bryson said, inviting reality back into his world, 'let's get to business.' He called to Reed, 'We need another fella, find me a volunteer.'

Reed nodded and squeezed his way into the throng of constables. In a few moments he appeared with a tall, slim lad at his side.

'Constable Lafferty, isn't it son?' Bryson asked.

'Yes sir,' the constable answered as the colour drained from his face.

'Good lad,' said Bryson, he clapped the youth on the shoulder. 'Sergeant Reed, arm this man,' he said and marched towards the drive entrance.

Reed produced a revolver which looked identical to the Inspector's and placed it into the hand of the constable.

From under the huge moustache he advised quietly, 'Lad, if you are going to have an accident with that, have it with Crowley.'

***

The body of constables went silent as the four men stood in line at the entrance to the drive.

'Right,' said Bryson, he looked at Crowley.

'Right,' Crowley replied.

They began walking slowly towards the hall. Gravel crunched under foot but there were no other sounds to be heard. Ahead, the dreadful scene of the constable Brindley's head, still wearing his helmet, became clearer. A small pool of dark blood had formed beneath it and all four could see that the eyes were open, following their progress.

Constable Lafferty stopped. Each of the others took a step and then also paused.

'What is it, lad?' Bryson said.

'Up at the top Sir, the top right window.' Lafferty pointed towards the large windows on the third floor of the hall. 'I thought I saw something'

'What did you see, Constable?' Crowley asked.

'Begging your pardon Mr Crowley Sir, but I'm not sure what I saw, it moved away from the window when I looked up.'

'All right lad, good work,' Bryson said by way of reassurance, 'keep 'em peeled.'

'Yes sir,' Lafferty said nervously.

Bryson slipped Reed a glance. Reeds moustache remained impassive.

Crowley loaded Patricia and snapped the barrel into place. They continued their slow approach towards Brindley's head.

It was when they were approximately six feet away from the head and level with the car that Crowley noticed something else about the house, besides the wide open door. The windows, the door, all of the steps had...

Before he could examine his discovery further, each of them felt a forceful wind, a blast which was cloying and humid washed over them. It carried a stench upon it that caused Constable Lafferty to bend and begin to retch violently. Bryson and Reed each brought up a forearm to cover their nose and mouth

'Dear Lord!' Bryson said, fearful that should he try to say more he too would be bending to the floor.

Crowley grimaced and held his breath. The smell was almost overwhelming to him. Even without inhaling it he could taste the rotten, acrid core. But worse than the sensation the stench induced was the realisation that he had encountered it before.

'Oh shit!' he said, 'we need to run.'

'What?' Bryson asked from behind his cuff, his eyes were awash with tears. But as he turned to face the occultist, Crowley was no longer there.

Bryson looked behind him only to see the back of Crowley as he dashed back towards the gate. His belt had come loose and his dressing gown billowed out around him. Crowley's pale arse rudely caught the moonlight and Bryson, would have grimaced more if it had been possible.

'RUUUUUNNNNNNNNN!' Crowley yelled wildly as he practiced what he preached.

'*Come on lads*, get after him,' Bryson shouted.

Reed grabbed the hapless Constable by the collar and pulled him on.

When Bryson caught up with Crowley, he was leaning with his on his arm against the gatepost, panting.

'What the fuck was that all about?' Bryson demanded.

'We can't go into that house,' Crowley said firmly, not moving from the gatepost but wagging his finger at Bryson. 'Not without proper protection.'

'What do you mean *protection?*' Bryson snarled.

Crowley waved him off, needing to catch his breath.

***

A Black Maria had arrived and rope was produced to cordon off the area. There was also enough tea making equipment to cater for an army. Bryson indicated that Lafferty should go and get a cuppa. He wasn't happy that Crowley had made them run like fools back to the entrance despite being somewhat relieved to have escaped the awful smell.

Feeling like he could now speak properly again, Crowley took the inspector to one side.

'That fool Ravensblack has brought something in, probably through a Gate.'

Bryson thought that Crowley seemed to be talking to himself more than to him as he continued, 'without the right incantations, totems, and sigils, we won't be able to force it back to where it came from.'

'Have you lost your mind?' Bryson asked making no effort to disguise his contempt for the idea, but Crowley wasn't cowed.

'No Inspector, I haven't, but I'll guarantee that Ravensblack has,' he looked towards the hall. 'Do we know how many people were in there besides your lads and Roman?'

Bryson turned to Reed who shook his head a little, 'No sir,' the great moustache uttered.

'Ok, well… we can assume that he was performing a summoning ritual. At the very least he would require two or three others to assist with that.'

Crowley made his way to a table covered with sketches and floor plans of the Hall. A man with considerable foresight Bryson had ordered them to be brought from the records office in the City. Much to the dismay of the office manager who wasn't happy at being bothered out of hours. As it was Reed who had gone to acquire them however very little fuss was actually made.

Bryson and Reed followed Crowley to the table.

'Did you notice the sigils?' Crowley asked.

'Sigils?' Bryson's brow furrowed.

'The markings under each window, on the steps, the sides of the house. I'll bet they go all the way around.' Crowley took a pencil from the table and flipped one of the schematics over. He bent and began to sketch.

When he was done, he stood upright and lifted a nearby oil lamp over the page to illuminate it clearly.

Reed and Bryson leaned in to see what he had produced. On the page Crowley had drawn a shape. To Bryson it looked like a child's drawing of a starfish. In the centre was what appeared to be a circled flame or perhaps an eye?

'What's that?' asked Bryson pointing.

'That's what is painted onto every section of that house that we might reasonably consider a point of exit,' Crowley replied.

'It's an Elder Sign, and you see this?'—he indicated the eye object in the middle—'This tells us that this sigil is required to protect the summoner from many different types of entities. It's a sort of *universal shield.*' Crowley lowered the lamp to the table. 'It also tells us that Roman had no clue what he was going to bring out.'

'Out from where?' asked Bryson.

'FROM THE ABYSS!' Crowley shouted dramatically, causing all heads to turn towards him. 'From the very depths of the *swirling chaos* that is existence outside of the *one* that you think you know Inspector, that you *blindly* assume is all that there may be.'

Crowley lowered his voice but maintained his theatrical delivery, 'From one of many hells, one of very many hells.'

'You have definitely lost your fucking mind,' Bryson said.

'Do you want to go into that house without me and see for yourself?' Crowley replied.

Bryson moved his lips as if to retort but said nothing. He looked down at the sigil. The acidity of the stench from the house still lingered at the back of his throat and caused a mild stir in his gut.

'If you try to enter that house without me Inspector Bryson, I can assure you that poor Brindley's head will have company soon after.'

Bryson could detect no sign that Crowley was mocking him. He'd rather he was. He disliked the man intensely. He was a braggart, a pervert, and a colossal pain in the arse whether in or out of custody. But he grudgingly admitted to himself that the occultist did have some of the standards associated with a gentleman.

When not using a constant stream of foul language he was well-spoken, and obviously very educated. He was also considered a brave man by many, as he had pioneered often. Crowley's mountain-climbing adventures were known across polite society.

He had encountered wild animals in Africa, dangerous indigenous peoples in the Americas and took enough drugs to take down the average bullock.

Bryson knew most of this because Crowley never stopped going on about it whenever he was arrested.

'All right,' Bryson said, deflated. 'What do we need to do?'

Crowley gave a smile and leaned forward to write on the sheet again. He scribbled out what appeared to be a list, tore the section off the schematic, forcing both Reed and Bryson to reach forward to try and stop him but to no avail, and handed it to the Inspector, who looked it over. Upon reading the itinerary, Bryson looked at Crowley with a puzzled expression.

'Why do you need potatoes?' he asked.

Part 3

It took a little over an hour for the constables to return with all of the items on Crowley's list. Both doors at the rear of the Black Maria were swung wide open and the goods placed inside. Meanwhile Crowley began to make a space in which to work.

One of the officers hauled a sack of potatoes up to him. Crowley took it and dragged it in to the van, he then tipped the contents on to the floor.

'Jesus Crowley, what a mess,' Bryson said, looking on from outside, 'they're covered in shit.'

Crowley ignored him and began to push the spuds around with his foot, 'I need more light, get me a light,' he demanded.

Bryson indicated to Reed, who promptly left to get one of the lamps resting on a car roof. Crowley identified suitable potatoes and gathered them up. Reed returned with the lamp and set it just inside the van.

'Thank you, Sergeant,' Crowley said as he took the lamp. Reed grunted.

As it was passed to Crowley the lamp illuminated the pile of goods on the floor of the van. Sticks of chalk, a large bag of salt, a kitchen knife, a small box of sulphur, and various herbs and oils were arranged about the place.

Crowley muttered to himself for a few moments as he ticked off each item against his list. Satisfied, he stepped down from the Maria, brushing earth from his hands.

'Now, Inspector, I need you to send all of your men home,' Crowley said.

'What?' Bryson spluttered.

'I'm afraid we can't have them here. Not with what is going to happen.' Crowley kept his voice unusually low and calm. 'There is already going to be talk about why I was brought along Inspector. At the moment you can smooth this over easily, you know the sort of thing, that I *know* the man, he's gone *insane*, and you wanted me to rationalise with him as one... *professional* to another, that kind of thing.'

'Well, that's why I brought you along Crowley,' Bryson said, 'you're both fucking nutters.'

Crowley ignored this.

'Ah, but you see the situation is much more complicated than that now you see. Roman isn't just insane, although I agree entirely that right at this moment he probably is. No, I'm afraid he is in fact also *possessed*. It is possible that the entity which has him in its grip has also become manifest inside the house.'

Crowley moved a little closer to the inspector so that he could drop his voice to a whisper. 'The supernatural, Bryson. Demons and monsters, do you really want your men, and the ever so excitable public of London want to know what is going on here?' He raised his eyebrows. 'Even if I'm wrong, which I'm not, how are you going to explain bringing me into this 'Hmm?'

Crowley folded his arms and returned to his more usual arrogant tone. 'I can end all this but I need to keep some things secret, for both our sakes.'

Bryson felt he was being pushed into a corner, but Crowley did make a reasonable point about his involvement. He had brought him to the scene with the weak hope of bringing the situation to a close quickly. This now seemed a distant memory. Whatever was going on in the house was beyond his accepted level of strange and weird, and *he* was a Londoner, so the strange and weird was pretty much par for the course. Besides which keeping a lid on a loudmouth like Crowley was paramount.

'All right. I'll send most of 'em back to duty, but Reed, Lafferty, and three others stay,' Bryson said.

Crowley immediately sensed that there would be no compromise on this and as time was of the essence took the offer.

'Very well, that should work, but I must insist that the men who remain park further down the road. As far out of sight of the house as possible.'

Bryson was about to argue this, but Crowley cut him short. 'They will be well within shouting and screaming and bashing with coshes distance should there be problems.'

'What kind of problems could we have?' Bryson asked.

'You recall the running away, shit-scared and very loud shouting we did earlier? That kind.'

Crowley left Bryson with that thought and returned to the back of the Black Maria.

As he watched the broad back of Crowley, as the bald-headed maniac began to do whatever it was he was doing, Bryson seriously considered just slapping him in cuffs and sending him back to the station. But he had come this far and he figured the damage was already done. The idea of setting a thief to catch a thief, or in this case a madman to placate a madman, had seemed reasonable when he had first thought of it but now... He gave a frustrated sniff and set about dispersing his men.

***

As the last of the cars sped away from the scene, leaving only three constables, all smoking, two hundred yards down the road, a grotesque and eerie sound began to emanate from the hall. All heads turned to face it, except for Crowley who continued to work and mutter inside the Black Maria.

'What the bloody hell is that?' Bryson strode to the Maria and demanded the answer from Crowley.

'Just give me a few moments please,' he replied tersely, either ignorant or uncaring of the noise. 'I'm almost done.'

Bryson walked over to Sergeant Reed who stood at the gates. 'Did you see anything, Reed?'

'No Sir,' Reed said. 'Just heard that horrible sound.'

'RIGHT! All done.' Crowley announced cheerfully from behind them. The three police officers turned as he approached them.

Cradled in his arms, Crowley carried a bundle of potatoes, and a faint smell of burned potato skin wafted towards the policemen.

'I want to you to each take two of these.' Crowley indicated the spuds with his nose.

Bryson thought better of asking why and stretched out a hand to pick one but wavered. The potatoes had been cut in half and there was some kind of discolouration to each, but the poor light made it impossible to determine what it was.

'Go on,' Crowley urged, 'it makes no difference which you take.'

Bryson gave him a black look and then plucked two out from the pile. Sergeant Reed followed suit, the half potatoes dwarfed in his huge hands. Lafferty then took two from the middle of the pile, almost causing them to tumble.

'Sorry,' he said.

Crowley manoeuvred the spuds so that he could grab a handful for himself and stuffed them into his dressing gown pockets, letting the rest fall to the floor.

Bryson and Reed remained silent, holding the spuds as though they might explode at any moment.

'Good... right, this is what we do now,' Crowley started but was interrupted by Bryson.

'Wait. What the Hell are these for?' he snapped.

'I'm about to *fucking* tell you,' Crowley retorted. He paused for a moment to regain his composure.

'I have carved into each of these talismanic charms a sigil that will...'

'You've carved a what into what?' Bryson interrupted again.

'A *sigil*,' Crowley hissed, 'a protective rune. I have carved one into each of the talismans...' he sighed, 'into each of the potatoes.'

Crowley pointed to each spud held by the policemen. 'You will also note that I have sealed, with a small flame, herbs into each of the sigils that will help to protect us from the forces at work in the hall.'

In tandem the policemen looked at the faces of the potatoes and a frown rippled across each forehead. Crowley continued.

'Now, the sigils will not protect us from any physical attack by merely being in our possession, they are effective only against spiritual assaults. But once we have located Roman, if we can press the face of the talismans against his body, against his skin, the sigils should transpose a copy of the binding marks onto him and force the presence that has him back into its realm.'

Bryson lifted his gaze from the face of his potato, which to him just looked as though it had been badly burned, and stared at Crowley blankly.

He wanted to punch the grinning, wild-eyed, pompous, lecherous freak squarely on his nose. He wanted to arrest him, throw him into a cell, and forget that he was there for a week or two. The thought, as it danced around his mind, actually gave him a warm and comfortable feeling, but the strange, awful sound began to rise from Ravensblack Hall again and his momentary fantasy of Crowley's face, pressed up against the bars of a cell in Wandsworth nick, abruptly faded.

'Is that it?' Bryson asked.

'Yes,' said Crowley nodding, 'pretty much'.

Bryson snorted his displeasure.

'Fuck it. Let's go then.'

He turned and walked through the gate, still holding his potatoes as though they might suddenly detonate.

Reed followed immediately behind, putting his spuds into his pockets, choosing instead to hold his baton in one hand and a pistol in the other. Lafferty walked to Reed's side trying to make out the symbols carved into the flesh of his mystical weapons.

Crowley joined them, and like Reed he placed his potatoes into his pockets so that his hands were free, allowing him to tighten the belt on his dressing gown. This done, he quickly took them out again, gripping the spuds tightly.

After they had taken no more than a half dozen steps, every light inside the hall sprang into life and the eerie sound became a ghastly wail.

Part 4

The view of the Chippingdon Estate, from under the canopy of the veranda, was quite breath-taking, Crowley thought as he lifted the cup of hot tea to his lips. And beyond the estate, a good six miles or so, Mount Eranjuana rose splendidly into a cloudless sky. A striking backdrop to the little piece of England that had been transposed onto this patch of African soil.

His aim was to be atop the peak that reached up to the heavens within two weeks, not simply to climb her, but to climb her North face, a feat that no other man in living memory had achieved.

He felt good, strong, and he certainly needed to be strong, as Eranjuana had claimed five souls in the last two years. She had defeated dozens of teams and partnerships and tolerated nothing less than the most excellent climbers.

He would succeed. He would take her, wrestle with whatever she threw at him, emerge victorious, and following that he would eat a good many free dinners off the back of the adventure, of this he was certain. He sipped his tea.

He had expected the rich flavour of the Assam to flood over his palate, but instead there was more of a coppery tang to it, as though the water had been dredged from a corroded metal basin.

Crowley frowned. He squinted.

'*This perfect morning?*' he thought.

Ahead the image of one of his greatest achievements... he glanced around. The veranda was empty, yet...

'It *would* his be his greatest achievement,' he thought. Hadn't he *already* climbed Eranjuana? Had he not already dined on those fabulous free dinners?

He had been in his twenties when he had conquered her peak and now he was a man of...

He blinked as both the veranda and the view warped in front of him. Tt was as though the world was somehow being stretched and twisted.

'Oh shit,' he said.

He looked down at the cup. There was no Assam in there, only blood. Watery, crimson blood. He looked back towards the mountain. It seemed bigger... no, it seemed closer.

'Fuck,' Crowley said

He placed his cup down onto the table, it trembled in its saucer. He stood. The scene around him was slowly fading from his view, except for

Eranjuana. She was getting bigger, looming in front him, she was coming on, coming to sit her fat millennia-old granite arse upon him.

This was a nightmare.

He needed to wake up. He pinched the back of his wrist.

'Ow!' he grimaced.

Nothing changed, except now his skin felt sore where he had squeezed at it, which was just super. That, and Eranjuana was now bearing down upon him like a speeding locomotive, her vast bulk filled his sight and she roared, she roared like a thousand tigers.

It was as the cyclopean mass leaned impossibly over him, as though Eranjuana was some stone beast whose great maw would open and swallow him, that Crowley saw that she had a moustache. A great furry thing that stretched across her impossible girth. The huge maw he had initially only imagined actually opened, and spoke.

'Crowley, you cowardly shite. Wake up. Wake up, you bastard.'

'*Oh,*' Crowley thought. '*Right… I see.*'

His eyes fluttered open fully to reveal what could be seen of sergeant Reed's face, that was to say his moustache bristling angrily at him.

The Sergeant's powerful hands were gripping his dressing gown at the collar. Crowley realised that his head and shoulders were lifted a few inches off the floor where he lay.

'Come on Crowley, get your bloody act together,' Reed barked, and seeing Crowley's eyes open, in surprise, he released his grip letting the occultist drop to the floor and banging his head.

'Fuck's sake man,' Crowley shouted. He rubbed at his bruised head as he brought himself up to sitting.

'What happened?' he asked as he took in the scene. He guessed that they were in the foyer of the hall.

'You fainted,' the voice belonged to Bryson.

'No I didn't,' Crowley snorted. He realised that he obviously had.

'It was an attack,' he spat out the words, tightened his gown belt, and then assumed his more typical aloof posture. 'Something in the house assaulted me through my psychic channels. I am extremely sensitive to emanations of a supernatural nature. Such an assault can overload my senses and force a short period of catatonia.'

He brushed imaginary dust from sleeve of his gown and glared at Bryson, daring him to contradict his explanation.

'Well, it looked like you fainted,' Bryson said evenly, and pointed towards the large doors which Crowley hadn't noticed due to his attention being on the Reed and the inspector, 'when you saw that.'

Crowley turned a little and realised he was seeing them for a second time. He caught a gasp on the edge of his teeth. This time he didn't faint.

The doors were impressively sized, and Crowley knew that they led into a very large room. He had visited the hall a few times, before Roman had purchased it, for parties and grand balls.

'*Good times,*' he thought briefly, then shepherded the thought back to its pen where it could wait for a more suitable occasion.

He knew that the room beyond was big and was used as a dining hall on occasion, and usually the doors glistened with a polished sheen administered by dutiful maids, but now they were darkened by a wash of blood. Their entire surface was coated; not a square inch had been missed.

As macabre an image as that presented, it wasn't that which had forced Crowley deep into the safety of an old and comforting memory. The blood-coated doors were a canvas and onto them a large and complex circle of lines and runes had been realised by a finger drawn through the mess. The artist had created a Summoning Circle, and Crowley now knew exactly what had been called in to this world.

It occurred to him that his hands were empty.

'Where are my potatoes?' he said without any attempt to hide the anxiety in his voice.

Lafferty stepped forward and handed back to Crowley the potatoes that had fallen from his grip when he collapsed. The young officer looked pale.

Crowley surmised that as soon as he had stepped into the foyer he had seen the circle and hit the deck. He thought it must have given the lad a hell of a fright to see him go down like that, but Crowley felt he had good reason to have lost it for a moment. He had encountered this particular scene before, and the aftermath had been... messy.

'Thank you Constable,' Crowley said, and tried to offer a comforting smile. This only made him look a little insane to the plainly terrified young man, but somehow Lafferty found his voice as he handed over Crowley's half-potatoes.

'What's be'ind there, Sir, be'ind those doors?' Lafferty asked.

Crowley looked over to them and his dark eyebrows knitted together.

'Nothing good Constable, I'm afraid, nothing good.' He turned to Bryson. 'I've got good news and bad news.'

The Inspector said nothing, indicating that Crowley should just get on with whatever he had to say.

'The symbol on that door'—Crowley pointed towards the gory circle—'indicates that Roman was trying to contact something very, very powerful, a creature that... I have some experience of.'

Crowley couldn't disguise the shudder that ran through him, and the Inspector's already concerned expression darkened.

Bryson considered Crowley to be a tremendous liar, an absolute master of bullshit, but for all of his bravado, sarcasm, and crass indifference to what was expected in polite society, Bryson knew that the man didn't scare easily. Would he retreat in haste to save his own skin? Yes, definitely, but that wasn't entirely the same as cowardice.

Crowley had fainted, that was clear despite his hocus pocus explanation. As soon as he had seen the door, he had swooned like some overheated damsel, but this only exacerbated Bryson's suspicion and self-disgust that he had made a mistake in bringing him. Insisting they attempt to solve this situation alone had been foolhardy, involving Crowley a serious error of his judgment. He thought that it might be time to perform an orderly withdrawal and admit that he had been wrong.

Suddenly, the huge entrance doors swung together with incredible force, making a terrific *THUMP* as they slammed shut. The four turned as one at the sound. Lafferty let out small yelp, and just as violently as the front doors had closed, the lights, that up until now burned so brightly, extinguished themselves instantly. The whole house was plunged into darkness, except in the foyer where they stood. Here there was a single source of light.

The circle upon the door glowed faintly. A pale green effervescence shone from within the lines and sigils drawn into the congealing blood. Their own breathing was the only sound that could be heard as each man stood as still and as silent as was possible, until finally Crowley spoke.

'Tits,' he said.

'What's happening, Crowley?' Bryson rasped.

There was a sound of movement. Little noises as Crowley fished into the generous pockets of his gown. A moment later, the scratch of a match being struck was heard and a small yellow light appeared illuminating Crowley's face.

Lafferty gasped.

'Keep it tight, Lafferty,' Bryson hissed between clenched teeth.

'S... sorry Guv...' Lafferty replied.

'What *IS* happening Crowley, what the hell is going on?' Bryson asked again.

'Just a second, Inspector,' Crowley said.

The little flame bobbed away from the trio as Crowley made his way across the room. The light rose, briefly revealing something metallic, and then a slightly stronger light appeared as a candle was lit. Crowley repeated this with the two other candles in the holder and the dark receded a little.

'I believe there is another candelabra to the right of you, Sergeant Reed. You are still stood by the mahogany dresser, yes?'

'Aye,' Reed replied.

He hadn't moved from his spot since waking Crowley. The occultist immediately started forward at the sound of Reed's gruff reply. A few moments later he handed the sergeant the second candelabra.

'Don't any of you rich bastards ever consider electric lights?' Bryson asked.

'It's not to be trusted,' Crowley warned.

The foyer once again had light, albeit subdued, and Crowley noted that the glow from the door faded away. He took a quick look at each of his reluctant comrades, and while Reed's expression was impossible to decipher, buried as it was under his low brim and huge moustache, both Lafferty and Bryson were clearly on edge. He cleared his throat.

'Gentlemen, what we are dealing with is not one of the greater demons or Old Ones, but a powerful force nonetheless...'

'How do you mean?' Bryson said.

'*Christ almighty, Bryson,*' Crowley shouted in frustration, 'that was my opener... I'm about to tell you...'

He issued a '*coh*' sound as he shook his head, cleared his throat once again, and continued.

'Roman was attempting to summon a very powerful entity that is known by many names, but for now we shall refer to him as Nyarlathotep. This creature is...'

'Niall what oh what?' Bryson asked.

'NILE ARTH O' TEPP,' Crowley repeated, slowly. 'Look if you are going to stop me every time I say something you don't understand, we will never leave this place, all right?'

Bryson scowled in the half-light but remained silent.

'*Nyarlathotep,* is an Old One, a sort of god but not quite up there with the big boys. He is considered, by most privileged to know of the eldritch and esoteric lore, to be an emissary of sorts, passing on messages and supplying visions for the other gods who cannot manifest on Earth.'

Crowley made subtle hand gestures, cast his eyes beyond his actual audience and projected his voice as though speaking to a packed theatre or lecture hall.

'Now, while this puts him in a very powerful position, this entity harbours a great resentment at basically being an errand boy, and it doesn't take to kindly to being summoned without good cause. Especially by some trumped-up, fart-sucking, shit bag like Roman Ravensblack.'

The last he spoke with more typical malice.

Crowley scanned his audience. He had expected questions, accusations of poppycock, balderdash, and absolute horseshit, but none came. Even Bryson was content to let him continue.

'It appears that Ravensblack foolishly attempted to bring Nyarlathotep *into* the house. This particular old One has many forms but even *dickhead* would know that allowing this creature to manifest physically would almost certainly result in... well, let's say unpleasantness.'

'You think that a door soaked in someone's blood, my missing officers, and one of my lads having his head removed isn't unpleasant, Crowley?' Bryson said in a dangerous, low tone.

'Of course it's unpleasant,' Crowley quickly added. 'It's ghastly, but should Nyarlathotep actually manifest it would have been possible, without considerable defences being in place, that he could break through the protective runes that have been placed around the house.' He raised his eyebrows at Bryson, 'You recall the markings on the door and steps?'

Bryson nodded.

'Some in the trade might call them over the top, but in fact it seems that Ravensblack at least had the wit to make sure that what came through couldn't get out.'

Bryson held up a hand to stop Crowley at that point. A question had crossed his mind. 'Crowley, would I be right in suggesting, given where I think you are going with this, that if myself and Sergeant Reed tried to bash open that door we would be wasting our time and energy?

'I would imagine so,' Crowley replied.

Bryson looked towards Reed who nodded and handed his candelabra to Lafferty.

They strode to the door and after unsuccessfully trying the handle began to barge at it with their shoulders. About a minute's exertion passed until the men returned to their original spots with expressions of defeat and defiance towards Crowley that he might make some sarcastic comment. Crowley said nothing and ensured his expression remained neutral. He didn't fancy having a good kicking at this moment in time.

'So now what?' Bryson asked. 'Why is nothing happening?'

Crowley fixed the inspector with a gaze so focused that, to his surprise, Bryson found himself transfixed. Had there been a fire in his shoes the Inspector was sure he couldn't have budged. It unnerved him a little.

'I believe, Inspector,' Crowley said, back to his pompous, rhetorical style, 'that the reason nothing has happened to us thus far is because, as with all big surprises, preparations have to be made.'

As soon as the last words left his mouth, the bloodied double doors, that led further into the hall, slowly began to swing open.

The men turned their heads as one towards the dark portal revealed, leading into the next room.

'Ah,' said Crowley. 'Looks like it's show time.'

It was Reed who moved towards the doorway first. He had retrieved the candelabra from Lafferty and held it in a meaty fist. It cast the big man in an orange light that danced shadows across his formidable moustache.

Crowley also noted for the first time that the sergeant had elected to pocket his rune-inscribed potatoes and instead gripped his service pistol. The business end pointed into the gloom ahead.

Bryson looked to Crowley suggesting that he follow on, and Crowley raised his eyebrows. Bryson sneered, shook his head a little, then followed after his man. *Now* Crowley moved.

With two bodies up front and Lafferty behind, he felt that any potential ambush was covered by a selection of better targets than himself.

In Crowley's mind, self-preservation was a noble art. The sort of art you needed to be very good at if you were to pass it on to future generations.

The candles didn't produce enough radiance to illuminate more than a third of the room they had entered, but the horror within was immediately apparent. The long dining table that could seat up to thirty guests was immediately visible, or at least the first six or seven feet of it.

Sat at the table and dressed in the chic finery of the London crowd that flocked to Ravensblack's brand of occult titillation and the promise of wanton sexual activity, were some of the guests of this evening's performance.

On the table were place settings for the evening's main meal, not yet served. The candlelight flickered and waved, and as it did so it would occasionally emphasise that the guest's clothes were soaked in blood and that each was missing their head.

'Christ almighty,' Bryson whispered, peering at the scene from the side of Reed's arm.

There was a muffled sound of retching as Lafferty finally released his dinner onto the floor. Crowley took a moment to cast his eyes down at the boy.

'Do it quietly, Constable,' he said although not harshly.

Returning his gaze to the room, Crowley narrowed his eyes and took in what the light wasn't revealing to the others. The walls were daubed with markings, the floor too. He was pleased to see another sigil at his feet, another barrier.

The entity had not attacked them in the hallway as it couldn't get through, that is if it had wanted to. Yet this didn't appear to be the case.

Crowley suspected that what they were up against was more interested in amusing itself with them. At least for the moment. The constable's head tossed out of the door had merely been to get their attention. However, this also presented the fact that *someone*, a person not bound by the spell, the sigils and runes cast, had done the deed.

Crowley's synapses crackled as his mind sent an army of information seeking charges through dusty storerooms of pertinent lore.

'Sergeant Reed,' Crowley said, 'could you be so kind as to move on a little? I need to see fully the situation at this table.'

Reed took a few cautious steps forward. Nothing stirred and no sound could be heard. Again, with his senses on full alert, he moved another couple of feet, carefully making his way down the near side of the table. The light blossomed around the space in which he now stood and Crowley observed that not all of the seats were occupied, although settings were laid out. Some of the glasses at those places contained wine or some other refreshment.

Crowley shuffled forward a little, keeping in line with Reed. There was a scuffled noise to the rear, he froze, but realised it was just Lafferty getting to his feet.

'*This thing is big on heads, it seems,*' Crowley turned this over in his mind, '*spectacle, and heads.*'

It wasn't Nyarlathotep himself, he was now satisfied with that conclusion. If that monster was manifest it would have already turned them inside out. No, clearly Roman had missed the mark. He had attempted to open up a portal somewhere in the house, called on the emissary to give some favour or other. There would have to be a fairly serious sacrifice too; when playing at this level the stakes were considerably higher than some table knocker screwing you for a few shillings.

Whatever it was, Nyarlathotep hadn't played ball.

He had sent *something* though, in return for Ravensblack's time and that of his stupid guests, something quite horrible, and it had come from the Shadow and the Void, that stench... it was a dead giveaway.

Bryson came to Crowley's side.

'Everybody's dead. *Dear Lord*, there must be twenty to thirty people here,' he said quietly.

'Not everybody, Inspector,' Crowley replied.

Reed had taken a few more steps down past the row of corpses, his candles furthering the horror.

'Do you see that some of the chairs are empty, yet there are the signs of someone having sat and dined or drank.'

'You think they're alive?' Bryson asked, hopeful.

'No, not as such. But I do think that they are in the house somewhere, waiting for us.'

'What does that mean?' Bryson asked, genuinely confused.

'It means that we need to be very, very careful.'

'Crowley!' Reed's voice. Sharp and urgent.

Crowley looked at him, checked the room for anything that might be ready to leap out at him, and once satisfied that everything was at a fairly stable state of threatening horror, rather than the level of horror that ripped out throats, made his way towards the sergeant.

He drew up next to Reed. Bryson and Lafferty had followed. The sergeant held his candelabra out over one of the headless guests, so that the very middle of the dining table was visible. For the first time since the lights had gone out Crowley wished the candles were not quite so bright.

A large metal tureen sat squarely in the centre and piled up inside it were the heads, he assumed of the guests. They were sightless, as each appeared to have had its eyes removed. The raw sockets stared without seeing.

Lafferty dropped to his knees once again, but this time Crowley let him be.

'Fuckin' hell,' Reed exclaimed. 'God preserve us, who would do such a thing?'

'Not who, Sergenat, what!' Crowley now became more animated, 'See?' He pointed a finger excitedly, 'see the back of the heads?'

Although both horrified and repulsed, Bryson craned his neck, desperate not to come into contact with the decapitated body sat with its back to him, whose head he might even be observing in the pot at this moment.

'The brain is missing,' Bryson said.

'Removed!' Crowley said, almost triumphantly.

Reed withdrew the light and the heads became a bumpy silhouette.

'Gentlemen, I can confidently advise you that the creature we are dealing with is a Mokoi, best known by those of aboriginal Australian origins,' Crowley finally explained.

'A creature?' Bryson said, 'Crowley are you saying some kind of monster is responsible for all this?'

Bryson couldn't hide his incredulity. Despite the blood, the bodies, the glowing circle, and the lights going out, his sense of rationality clung on to his belief that the only real monsters were men and bloody big tigers.

He placed his potato down onto the side dish of the guest to his right and withdrew his revolver.

'This is madness, Crowley, and you are as insane as whoever is running around this place with a... whatever it is he's using to chop off heads and scoop out brains.'

'You really think that one man managed all of this?' Crowley gestured at the grisly scene.

'Possibly,' Bryson replied, though not convincingly.

'And he had time to run around shutting doors so tight that we are unable to open them and somehow made a pattern inscribed in blood glow with an eerie light?'

Bryson's eyes narrowed. He was quiet for a moment, then shouted, 'Accomplice! The man has an accomplice, maybe more than one.'

He turned fully to face Crowley, 'That's how it is with you lot, isn't it? You have your little followers running around after you, buying in to all the fucking insanity you peddle.'

'Er Guv...' Reed said

'I'll tell you something, Crowley,' Bryson barked, 'when I empty the contents of this pistol into the chest of your *Mokoi*, we'll see just how well monsters handle bullets eh, how about tha... ?'

'GUV!' Reed called out.

Reed's interjection stopped what Bryson realised was becoming a rant. The seargeant pointed his pistol towards the centre of the room on the far side. There, only just visible, was another set of double doors, these Crowley knew would lead into a corridor the servants would use to bring the food and drink to the guests. They would also lead into other rooms, and both upstairs to the bedrooms and down to the cellar.

What had brought Reed's attention to them was that they had slowly swung open as his boss had been grilling Crowley. More importantly, a figure, cloaked in shadow, stood in the middle of the doorway where Reed was aiming his gun.

Bryson raised his pistol towards the shadow, 'Identify yourself,' he ordered.

The figure said nothing. It was tall. Something about the head...
'Light him up, Reed,' Bryson whispered.

Reed lifted the candelabra so that its light would spill into the doorway. Although still not well-illuminated it was clear enough to make out, if not who, then at least what it was. The figure wore the uniform and helmet of a police constable. Bryson *knew* that it had to be one of his lads.

'Identify yourself, officer,' Bryson said again, but the figure remained still and silent.

'Crowley, give me your light,' Bryson said, and Crowley immediately handed it over.

Still training his gun on the shadowed figure, Bryson moved the candelabra forward and as the light joined with that of Reed's, the police constable was revealed.

His whole face was a shocking mess of blood and gore. There was a glint of silver as the handles of forks that had been rammed into his inner jaw reflected in the candle light. The forks gave the officer a new set of teeth formed from the array of pointed tines, while the handles waggled slightly beneath his chin. Along his arms, long, wickedly sharp kitchen knives had been driven through from the underside and their razor edged blades stuck out along their length, forming what could almost be a defensive line of skin-shredding points.

The constable lifted his hands and revealed that more utensils had employed. Two corkscrews had been wound into his hand from the back and now the twisting shafts protruded from his knuckles. The officer clenched his fists and opened his mouth wide to show off his diabolically customised armour and weapons.

None of the men could move such was their horror; even Crowley found himself mortified by the violence that had been done to the man. Suddenly and with athletic agility, the constable leapt from standing onto the table and kicked the tureen with such force that its contents flew out.

Reed and Bryson both raised their arms to protect their faces from the heads that bashed at them. Staggering back from the shock and impact, Bryson fell onto Crowley and the two landed in a heap on the floor. The heads of the guests tumbled about them.

Reed possessed far greater balance, practically tree-like, and withstood the barrage. He brought his pistol down to take a shot at the defiled constable, but as he directed his aim a blade-covered arm swept out and caught him.

Thanks to the thick cloth of his uniform, the knives only slashed down to his shirt cuff, but it had been close and the blow was hard enough to knock the pistol from his hand. It flew into the darkness.

The constable screamed with unnatural fury and Reed saw, close up, the mess of his mouth and the terrifying line of tines. The thing swung again—Reed could no longer think of it as a person, as one of his lads. This time a fist attempted to drive three corkscrews into his face and, once there, to gouge out his flesh, but Reed reacted well. He dodged to his right and the monster's fist flashed past him. He straightened and swung the candelabra with force against the side of its face.

It was a well-placed blow and the constable staggered from the impact. Unfortunately, two of the candles flew from their holder and the room became darker in an instant. Reed backed away, hoping to conserve the one light he had remaining.

When Bryson had fallen, he had dropped his candelabra, but the candles remained fixed into their holders and maintained their flame. Rolling off Crowley, who was in turn pushing at him, Bryson snatched up the candelabra and handed it to Lafferty, who stood rigidly to the side of him. Bryson turned just in time to see Reed's counter against the constable, he raised his pistol and fired three shots at the creature.

In the small room the gunshots sounded like cannon fire and rang heavily in their ears. The light and shadow made it difficult to see movement, and as Bryson attempted to regain his target and unload more bullets he found that the thing was gone.

'Shit, where is he, where is he,' Bryson shouted.

Reed peered into the room hoping to spot either the constable or his pistol, both hopefully.

All he could see were the few headless guests caught in the weak illumination of the candelabra that Lafferty held.

'Bugger,' his moustache said bitterly.

Crowley stepped closer to Bryson.

'You won't hurt him with bullets,' he said, close to Bryson's ear, 'you might annoy him, but you won't hurt him.'

'Yeah, well we'll see won't we?' Bryson replied.

Crowley retorted with uncharacteristic calm. 'Inspector, that man had enough dining utensils stuck in his body to fillet an elephant. Do you really think that having a few holes in him is going to cause him some inconvenience?'

Despite Crowley's warning Bryson continued to scan the room with his pistol held out, ready to fire, but doubts began to surface. Crowley placed his hand carefully upon the inspector's tight grip on the pistol.

Bryson allowed Crowley to push his hand down to his side. Crowley then took the gun and replaced it with one of his half-potatoes.

'This is what you need. The eyes are where you will get him,' Crowley said.

Bryson turned his head to look at Crowley. He couldn't see any trace of mocking or mischief, only concern. Crowley gave him a small, reassuring nod.

Lafferty screamed. The shadows erupted as the candelabra he was holding shook violently. The thing had dropped down upon him from the ceiling and onto him.

Bryson, closest to the lad, rushed forward to try and wrestle the creature off him, but Crowley sprang forwards, gripped his arm with all his strength, and managed to haul him back.

'Be careful man, he's got blades sticking out all over the place!'

Bryson realised that had been just about to try and grab the thing's arms. He would have lost fingers at the very least. Lafferty screamed again and Bryson stepped forward.

This time he grabbed at the tail of the constable's coat and tried to pull him off. Crowley, seeing the plan, joined in and the two pulled as one.

The thing's arms suddenly flailed, releasing the lad, and the combined power of Bryson and Crowley lifted it bodily by its jacket. It let out a terrific wail, its scream bounced off the walls and it shook, vibrated almost, thrashing at the air until it abruptly stopped moving.

Bryson and Crowley hauled at it again and this time the body fell limp and was easily dragged away from Lafferty.

'What... what... is it dead?' Bryson said.

Crowley inched a foot forward and then strained to push the body over with it. He didn't want to be within 'I'm not really dead, ...here, have a face full of knives,' distance. The thing remained still and fixed into an eye, amidst melted flesh, was a potato.

Lafferty sat up.

'I got it with the spud, Sir, in the eye like you said to.'

Part 5

It watched them and it listened. It couldn't understand their language just yet, not fully, but their actions and tone easily translated their fear. Through the eyes of its offerings it had followed the progress of the humans through the house.

The one who was called Bryson appeared to be the leader of the group, but the Mokoi sensed that it was the hairless one who was directing their actions, the *Crowley*. The Crowley had knowledge of the Shadow and the Void, this was clear, and although he was craven and driven by the hope of personal gain and self-preservation, his knowledge protected him. His mind was far too well-guarded against the power of the Mokoi to simply scare him into submission.

The big one was the muscle, he was the true warrior of the group and was called *Reed*. The Mokoi had already determined that the man would also not easily be cowed by its surprises. This human's mind was one of raw and unwavering pragmatism coupled with an unbreakable determination. Whilst the one that was called Bryson had this same frustrating resolve, his thoughts were more open, more malleable, and were it not for the hairless one, the Crowley, supplying him with sufficient will, the Mokoi would have struck at him first to break their collective spirit.

This left the youngest, newly adult, the Mokoi had thought, a stranger to the brutality and horror towards his fellow man that his peers had witnessed.

His mind was fresh, filled with empty spaces in which the Mokoi could enter and grow. He would be like the others who had entered the house before him, blind to everything that they could not imagine and thus easily taken as their minds crawled into retreat at the joyful horror it had shown them.

Yet this had not been the case. The boy-man had somehow found strength inside him that rejected the fear. This was as frustrating as it was disappointing.

The Mokoi had delighted in its work performed upon his puppet man. A brother of some sort, it thought, to the boy-man and Reed as it wore the same clothing, the same warrior garb.

The utensils it had employed upon its body should have been both terror inducing and potentially lethal to those it attacked and yet it had failed. The boy-man had the wit about him to use the arcane defences supplied by the Crowley and now, having proven to himself that he had power against the Mokoi, he would be almost impossible to control.

It flitted through each of the eyes that it had hidden about the house, ensuring the further surprises it had prepared were ready. It was frustrated, though. It would not have much longer in this world as it had expended much of the essence it had gained from the humans that had been gathered at its summoning.

Unless it could extract enough power from these men to break through the barriers that its host had created, it would fall back into the Void. Into the timeless, empty Void from which it had been called. The Mokoi needed their minds, and only through inducing fear and terror could it hope to slip into them and gain the control it needed.

But it didn't need them all. No, it could afford to thin their ranks just a little, it had feasted on the offerings that the Ravensblack had brought and that had been nourishment indeed, so many souls, so many eyes. The Mokoi almost purred at the thought of the hours it had spent ravaging the minds of Roman Ravensblack's guests, but it knew that it had been wanton and reckless, cursed were the creatures of the Void, damned by their own infinite lust for gratification.

It took a moment to look deep into the imprisoned mind of its host. Roman Ravensblack was locked away, deep inside a pit fashioned from his own thoughts. The Mokoi couldn't harm its carrier. All others were available to satiate its pleasure, but its host must remain intact and unhurt.

Should the host die, then the Mokoi would immediately be sucked back through the portal. To keep Roman occupied, it had conjured a world populated with the man's own nightmares. It chuckled as it observed him, running through the city streets chased by large naked women, whose sagging breasts swung against swollen, fat-rippled stomachs.

If they caught him, they would carve out his genitals and swallow them. Before he turned away from Roman's plight, the Mokoi added a little swampy ground up ahead, just to add to the terror.

The group began to move; the eye that it had fixed into the chandelier directly above the table saw them approach the doors through which his puppet had entered. Quickly it moved to the second eye, positioned in the hall. As the men entered, their candles bloomed and pushed back the dark revealing another set of double doors across from them and stairs at either end of the hall, a set that went up and at the opposite end a set that descended into the basement.

The Mokoi licked Roman's lips. 'They will come up,' it thought. They will come up the stairs and its surprises would be waiting for them. 'Only stupid men would venture down into the depths of this house.' The Mokoi stretched Roman's mouth with a wicked grin.

'I say we go down,' Crowley said firmly, 'a summoning of this nature requires a good deal of room, and as ridiculous and pointlessly big as this house is the bedrooms would not be suitable.'

'I don't give a flying fuck if it requires a space the size of Wimbledon Common,' Bryson retorted, 'I am *not* sending my lads down those stairs,'

'But we *need* to find the summoning area,' Crowley insisted, his voice raised.

'So, go and find it,' Bryson countered raising his voice to match.

'I can't go on my own!' Crowley shouted with an angry growl, dismissing the advice as though Bryson had just suggested he fly out of a window.

'Why, Crowley, scared?' Bryson chided.

'Of course I'm fucking scared.' Crowley was now approaching his limit with the Inspector and his stupid, time-wasting fancies. 'Do you have to share your brain cell between other Inspectors on a minute-by-minute basis? Don't you recall that one of your men just tried to carve up Lafferty with an assortment of kitchenware?'

'No, I haven't forgotten, Crowley. What I am saying is that if we go down those stairs I am concerned that whoever is responsible for this might have something else lined up, perhaps this time with the fucking gardening equipment.' Bryson stepped up close to Crowley. 'There are windows to smash upstairs, windows to jump out of if your man Roman suddenly appears with a shotgun, in the basement there are just very thick walls.'

Inside Crowley's mind the plunger had been pushed down, the crates of TNT that sat above the fragile shell that covered his patience was vaporised in a glorious explosion of anger, indignity and frustration. He wasn't prepared to have this arrogant, pig-headed peeler dictate what should be done in a situation that only he, as a professional in matters of the occult, should. He too stepped forward to directly confront his nemesis. Their faces were so close that only a shadow kept their noses apart.

'You have no idea what awaits you in either direction, Inspector, *but I am telling you* that the solution to this nightmare is in destroying the portal that the thing came through, and that the portal will *not* be upstairs! *Now* if you want to educate me upon matters concerning the summoning of demons and the casting of eldritch spells, if you want to give me your considered opinion on how a man walks around with knives through his arms, corkscrews driven through his knuckles and forks thrust through his jaw, fire away, but if you don't have one, if all you have is a coppers hunch, or some vague fucking life raft in your narrow imagination that you are clinging too, that this is all just the work of some drug crazed, socialite fuck-up, go for it, I'm all ears.'

Reed could see, even in the half-light, Bryson's narrowed eyes and strained neck, taut from the severe clenching of his teeth,. And although Crowley was clearly as furious as Bryson, the Inspector had a gun. He understood that the situation was a single smart comment from Crowley to adding a further casualty to the current tally, Yet, the two only eyed each other in a silent standoff, each far too angry to attempt any further vocal retort.

'Beg pardon, Sirs. I think we're being watched.' It was Lafferty.

All three heads turned to him.

'Up on the top of the frame there, on the picture frame.'

Lafferty pointed at a portrait that depicted a gentleman in well-to-do rustic attire with a red setter at his feet. Now all eyes looked up above it and there, resting on the thick wood of the frame, was a single eye.

Crowley moved around Bryson to get a closer look. The eyeball stared back at him, Crowley felt himself blink, his own eyes attempting to compensate for their fellow organ being unable to perform such a task.

As Bryson stepped up to take a look, Crowley turned and walked down the corridor a little, searching.

The wall was lined with paintings, mostly portraits, and at the opposite end of the hall there was another frame that had a small dark bump that ruined its perfect line.

'Yes, yes,' he said, he turned to the others 'you see, the *eyes*? It's watching us through the eyes. I'll bet they are tucked away on shelves and on fittings. Directed towards where we might go.'

'Rubbish,' Bryson said.

He shook his head and spoke, not directly to Crowley this time, but to Reed and Lafferty as if to elicit their agreement.

'How would someone see through someone else's eyeball, never mind an eyeball that's not located where it should be?'

'That is the whole point, Inspector,' Crowley said, exasperated, 'this is not some *one* this is some *thing*. This is a *Mokoi*, a creature of the Void and the Shadow! It is using the eyes to observe us, to help it prepare!'

Crowley walked back towards the group. He had returned the potato halves to his pockets and tightened the belt of his gown as he approached. He gave Lafferty a glance, his expression one of approval and interest.

'Well spotted, lad, I hadn't even considered what the eyes might be used for, tell me, what made you suggest that it was using them to watch us?'

The heat had almost entirely left Crowley's voice, and he had returned to his milder but still dangerous tone.

'I dunno, Sir, beg pardon but it just seemed sort of obvious,' Lafferty replied earnestly.

'Hmm, interesting,' Crowley murmured.

He returned his attention to Bryson, but no longer spat his words at him. 'I know that this is difficult for you to accept, Bryson, but surely you can now see that what we are dealing with here goes beyond what is normal, at least in your sense of the word.

This is the supernatural. and at its most dangerous, there is an entity about this place whose reason and rationale we can hardly begin to guess at, such is its alien nature to us, but rest assured that what is forefront in its mind is to escape the house.

'And it can't leave because of the signs?' Bryson said, surprising Crowley a little.

'The sigils, yes.' Crowley said, a hint of excitement in his voice. 'Right now I can't explain further, but you must appreciate that there are rules that exist even outside of our natural world. Just as sure as within the constraints of our own laws what goes up must come down, so there are similar, unequivocal constraints working against creatures from other realities than our own. This thing cannot pass through those barriers, it cannot break them itself and it cannot force others to do it, unless it has enough power to protect itself.'

Crowley approached Bryson but this time kept a respectable distance and implored the Inspector rather than bawled.

'You see, if it controlled your mind Inspector, and you touched the sigil, it would still feel the effect of it. A controlled being is an extension of the creature, not something wholly remote.'

'And it needs the power to... act as a buffer?' Bryson said carefully.

'Yes! Exactly.' Crowley exalted. He could see that the Bryson was finally beginning to accept, perhaps not all, but some of what he couldn't imagine. It was a step, small, but a step nonetheless and it would help he was sure.

'Whatever it was Roman offered to Nyarlathotep it was used by the Mokoi to enter our world. Once it was here it infested a host, almost certainly Roman himself.' Crowley swept his hand towards the dining room. 'The guests here would have supplied power for it, but only *limited* power, and every second that an entity from the Shadow and the Void is present in our world, it consumes itself.

It is unnatural to the laws that govern this dimension and therefore is rejected by nature. To maintain its presence the Mokoi requires a constant intake of power to, as you say, *buffer* it, to prevent it from being sucked back into its own world. Further to that Inspector, if its portal, its gateway is closed and it cannot return. In such a circumstance ultimately it will be annihilated!'

'So, if we find this portal that it came through, and destroy it, the thing is dead, *proper* dead,' Bryson said.

'Proper dead, yes.' Crowley replied. Carefully, not wanting to block the Inspectors path towards the light.

'What if we burn the house to the ground?' Bryson said.

'A splendid idea, except for just one thing. If we torch the house, we can't get out and we will burn to death inside it.'

'We could smash the win...'

'The windows won't smash, just like the front door wouldn't open. The creature has used its power to seal them, I assure you.' Crowley nodded slowly which encouraged the inspector to mimic him.

'Right,' Bryson said. He looked at Reed. 'What do you think, Sergeant?'

Reed's moustache stiffened. Deep under the brim of his helmet his recessed eyes twinkled darkly.

'He's talked bollocks since I've known him. He's probably talking bollocks now, but... well... given this whole situation is bollocks, there's a good chance that he would be an authority on it.'

Crowley frowned a little 'Er... thank you sergeant, I think.'

'What about you, son?' Bryson turned to Lafferty, 'you have a right to offer your opinion on this.'

Lafferty's eyebrows raised and he shuffled a little, uncomfortable at being in the spotlight.

'Well Sir, truth be known, I think that Mr C—sorry Sir, *Mr Crowley*— seems to know his stuff, and as soon as I stepped through that front door and Mr Crowley fainted...'

'I was overcome by a psychic paralycentric episode, lad,' Crowley corrected.

'Beg pardon Sir, when Mr Crowley had the psychic... wossname, well I felt something really odd about the place and right from then I reckoned that there was something not normal going on. I mean, obviously the heads and things ain't normal, but *more* not normal, if you follow, Sir.'

Bryson wasn't entirely sure that he did follow, but the intent was clear. The lad was prepared to accept Crowley's suggestion, even Reed seemed to be on board. and as Lafferty had said '*truth be known,*' Crowley did appear to have a grasp on what was going on. Plus the occultist was scared all right, he had admitted as much, but of knives and corkscrews, not ghosts and ghouls. He pursed his lips as he bowed his head in thought.

Finally, Bryson looked up and then around at the men. 'OK. We go downstairs and look for Crowley's portal, *but* if we find nothing, we torch the basement and head for the windows, right?'

Lafferty and Reed nodded in agreement, but Crowley remained still, his lips tightly sealed. He wondered if the eyes would still be watching as they all died in burning, screaming agony should they fail to locate the gateway.

Part 6

If the Mokoi could have made the eyeball blink with surprise, it would have. As the group of humans began to descend the stairs to the basement, it let out a piercing scream of rage and frustration. WHY would they descend! It had shown them the figure in the window of the upper floor to lure them, how could they come to the decision that going down into a walled-off portion of the house with only one exit was a good idea!

All of its surprises were on the upper floors, its puppets waited with the markings of the Mokoi's glorious excess, their bodies were carved and decorated with all manner of objects, and it had used entrails and organs to decorate the path that the humans would take. It had imbued a great deal of its power into the remaining bodies and heads to animate them, to turn them into lethal agents of fear and carnage. All wasted, all its art, all its time!

It thought quickly, if they descended unmolested into the basement they might reach the gate, they might reach *him*. Taking the mind of Roman, of any host, came with a price for the Mokoi, some it thoughts would become tainted by the pre-existing beliefs and conceptions of it. This is why the Mokoi would only enter a spell caster when possible, a shaman, or a wizard, humans with a grip on the world beyond theirs. To fully exert its power, the host mind must be able to channel the essence that made all things considered supernatural by these creatures function.

But Roman was weak, a mere acolyte that dressed himself as a sorcerer. The Mokoi had quickly gained the measure of the man as it rifled his thoughts and ransacked his memories. As the horrors that the Mokoi conjured chased Roman's conscious into itself it took the human's body and began to work its way through the guests.

By the time the warrior men had come to the house, the Mokoi had extracted enough of the essence that the guests contained, a disappointingly small amount, and had used much of it to make them its puppets. Its energy was now at a premium.

Keeping the doors and windows sealed took power, affecting the lights, the winds, the doors and all of the theatrics sucked its pool of energy away. Soon the inescapable draw of the portal would overcome the resistance that the essence gave the Mokoi and begin to draw it back into the Shadow and the Void. Worse, if the humans actually made it to the gate, if the hairless one, the Crowley, managed to close the gate, it would be doomed, ended utterly.

It had hoped to have a little more entertainment, it had hoped to savour the fear of the humans before it eviscerated them and took its trophies. Now it had to move quickly, it had to kill them.

Bryson, at the head of the group, began to move down the stairs and the others followed. He paused for a moment and turned his head to face Crowley, still in his position between Reed and Lafferty. 'How come we aren't removing the eyes, if they can *see* us? Should we go back and shift them?'

'No.' Crowley replied. 'We should take care to touch nothing organic where possible. The power of the Mokoi will feed through it. I'm not sure what strength it has, but it's possible that contact will allow it to look directly into your mind. They are creatures that feed on fear and paranoia, they enter our thoughts and seek out the things that give us nightmares, then deliver them back to us tenfold.'

As Crowley finished talking the house vibrated as a high-pitched wail coursed through the walls. As one, the group flinched. Even Reed took one step back up the stairs forcing Crowley to back up into Lafferty in a domino effect.

'Jesus!' Bryson exclaimed, 'that bloody noise again.'

'Different,' Crowley said, 'it's angry. When we approached the house, it was not the same. I suspect the Mokoi is running out of time and we are pissing it off. Perhaps the officer was its only puppet, or it's upset that we know about the eyes... I don't know.'

Bryson said nothing. He flicked his eyes to Reed, and the sergeant offered a small nod. Bryson continued down the stairs. There were paintings on the walls here too. The staircase was well-kept and was clearly considered part of the house where a guest might visit.

Bryson had been into a number of these big houses in the course of his duties. The basements of most were just wine cellars. Vast spaces committed to storing dust-coated vintage bottles, barrels, and occasionally the decorations and furniture that the owners had grown bored of. He hoped there weren't safari trophies. They scared the shit out him. He had experienced quite enough of heads that were unattached to bodies for one night.

'What's down here, Crowley?' Bryson asked as he took a few more cautious steps.

'Roman will have a fairly large open space where the guests would gather. The creature he was attempting to contact, Nyarlathotep, doesn't have any specific ritual that I know of. Usually it contacts you rather than you it...' Crowley shuddered as a memory, long shuttered away, tapped upon the door it was locked behind.

'Mr Crowley, Sir,' Lafferty whispered from behind his ear.

'Yes, Lafferty?' Crowley replied.

'If this thing, this Mokoi, is so powerful like, why doesn't it just attack us?'

'It can't,' Crowley answered, he found that he was keen to talk to the lad, something about him raised Crowley's curiosity.

'I'm sure it would love to but the fact is that it simply can't. Mokoi are creatures who seem to have a need to employ a certain artistry in their work. I first became aware of them in Australia. They would be found inhabiting the body of a shaman who had probably spent a little too long walking in what they call the Dreamtime, and out of his gourd on narcotics of course. The shaman, under the control of the Mokoi, would begin to spread fear amongst its tribe, feeding on the terror it created.'

'Blimey,' Lafferty said.

'Indeed,' said Crowley. 'I believe that such creatures may have also been found in the South America's where violence, fear, and sacrifice were rife throughout the civilisations that existed there.'

Crowley turned to face Lafferty fully, stopping him on the stairs, realising that he had a willing audience, even if it consisted of only one person and he was in considerable peril, he couldn't help but begin to show off his knowledge.

'You may be aware of stories of the conquistadors raging mercilessly through that continent, but let me assure you that those men encountered more than hapless natives and ignorant superstition.'

He watched as the constable's eyes widened. '*He accepts*,' Crowley thought. Lafferty was clearly open to the idea that there was more to the world he lived in that what the priests and politicians told him there was.

'Don't let this thing scare you into doing something that deep down you think is a bad idea, lad,' Crowley advised solemnly.

'Yessir,' Lafferty replied, nodding.

'Crowley, are you coming?' Bryson snapped.

'Right behind you, Inspector,' Crowley said jovially, and nimbly advanced down the stairs with Lafferty in pursuit.

Bryson had reached the bottom of the stairway. He took the candelabra from Reed and held it before him.

He hadn't known what to expect, a lake of blood, piles of intestines, undead creatures staggering towards him, Jack the Ripper, but there was nothing of that sort revealed by the candlelight.

There were benches, rows of them, and tidily folded and equally spaced atop them were robes, folded into thick squares. The walls were painted, more portraits and a few landscapes hung upon them. There were compact serving units on wheels, and on top of them were bottles of wine, glasses, selections of cheese, and biscuits.

'Crowley?' Bryson called out.

Crowley came down and squeezed past Reed to take a look.

'*How typical,*' he thought as he took in the scene. This is what he hated most about Roman. The occult to him was a business venture, a jolly for his well-to-do friends and those that crawled inside his social circle. Throwing his usual caution to the wind, Crowley stepped forward.

'Lift the lights, if you would be so kind, Inspector,' Crowley asked.

Bryson held the candelabra higher and stepped to Crowley's side. The orange glow spilled onto the walls at either end and at one, the furthest double doors, larger and more ornate than those upstairs, became apparent.

'Through those,' Crowley said and pointed to them with his forefinger.

Bryson noticed that in the same hand was one of the potatoes. While still holding the candelabra aloft, he put his pistol into his pocket and pulled out his own half-spud. He consciously reeled against it but something pulled at his instincts and overcame his distaste for the occultists mumbo-jumbo.

Crowley began to move forward and because of this Bryson could see that the man was clearly under the influence of his own desires.

He suspected that Crowley wanted to *know*. He *had* to know, in fact. Jealousy? Bryson couldn't be sure, but Crowley's enmity towards Roman didn't derive purely from what the man had, respect, fame, friends, but what he could do. Despite the senior occultists claim that Roman was just a crook, he obviously had some talent.

As they approached the doors, Bryson marvelled at the intricate carving that formed them. They were totally out of place, set as they were between cleanly painted manila walls. They were old things, with deep recesses that swallowed the light. The raised images the candlelight exposed from the shadows were terrible and unnerving. Bryson fancied that they moved somehow, that the strangely organic patterns shifted and coiled inside each other.

'More bloody doors.' It was Reed. He drew up to Bryson's side and let out a deep puff of breath. It was getting a bit much. Reed didn't mind a bit of rough stuff, he was no bully, certainly not a braggart, but he knew that he was a big man, imposing as Bryson often told him, and was very capable of using his size and strength to calm matters. This was often by the application of a fist or when required a steel-toe-capped size-twelve boot. More popular though was to engage *His Majesty's Pleasure* upon those who resisted arrest, his trusty baton. Slinking around dark houses, jumping at sudden knocks and shrieks wasn't for him.

He didn't care for Crowley either, him and his weird lifestyle. The man was just another in a long line of privileged, preening dandies that

Reed found himself dragging out of knocking shops, taverns, and gutters. He just wanted to punch something very hard and then arrest it. Although the order wasn't crucial.

'I suspect that these are the last we will need to encounter, Sergeant,' Crowley said. 'And they are not just any old doors, these are *very* old doors, ancient in fact.'

Crowley moved closer and each of the men kept time with him but a step behind.

As he closed on them, Crowley recognised much of the bas-relief and was truly shocked at what he saw.

'Good god. Hastur!' he said with a mix of awe and trepidation.

'What's Hastur?' asked Bryson.

'Bad,' Crowley replied. 'Very bad.'

He moved the candelabra around the door to take in as much of their form as he could. As the angle of the shadows changed it seemed that the strange carvings almost seethed from the wood.

When he was done he stepped back.

'What *were* you up to, Roman?' He had meant to say it to himself but realised that he had spoken out loud.

'Problem?' Bryson said.

'Perhaps,' Crowley replied quietly and as if to match his whispered response the atmosphere became still and silent. He turned to Bryson.

'Whatever has Roman will be behind this door, this is the entrance to his ritual room, and past here things will become even stranger than you have experienced so far.'

'Will he be armed?' asked Bryson.

'He won't need to be,' said Crowley, 'but possibly.' He turned back to the door and sought out a handle or something that looked as though it might cause them to open. There was nothing obvious. 'I'm not sure how this...'

There was a sound of thumps. Movement on the stairs, more than one person and at speed. As one, Bryson, Lafferty, and Reed turned, but Crowley continued to scan the door.

'Crowley! Reed shouted, 'behind us!'

'Yes, yes,' Crowley said without taking his attention from the eldritch patterns 'I'm afraid you will have to deal with that, I'm going to be busy.'

Crowley sat and placed his legs into a lotus position.

'WHAT THE FUCK ARE YOU DOING?' Bryson shouted in disbelief.

'The door will require a ritual to open. I need to prepare, try not to be too noisy, it's distracting,' Crowley replied with irritating calm.

'GUV!' Reed shouted.

From the gloom, a figure staggered towards them.

Part 7

The Mokoi reacted to the unexpected turn of events quickly. Two of its puppets were on the first floor where it had expected the party to go. It focused its thoughts upon them and gave them their commands. They twitched, arms and shoulders spasmed, their mouths opened and closed as the power of the Mokoi flooded into them. They began to move, slowly at first but then gained balance and strength as the Mokoi filled them with its essence. They transformed from shambling, ruined corpses to agile agents of its will.

In the dining room, the headless guests—each had been marked by the Mokoi with its sigil, a spiral, carved into the back of their necks—began to move. Its power reached into them and the bodies began to stand. A pantomime followed as the decapitated followers of Roman Ravensblack wandered about the room looking for heads and eyes. Any head would do, any eye was fine. The Mokoi could not give the bodies vision without them, humans were awkward like that even when dead.

The guests that found both head and eye assembled them as best they could, pressing the organs into empty sockets. The Mokoi fumed as some clumsily pressed too hard and the eyeball squelched between their fingers, others didn't secure the eyeballs properly and they dropped to the floor only to be trodden upon, if not by other guests then by themselves as they tried to locate them. It was a shambles and most of the eyes were lost to such mishaps within a few minutes.

The bodies of the officers were by and large intact, although the Mokoi had entertained itself before they had died. It had managed to resist taking their eyes, but as it had waited for the others to arrive it had skinned them both, and then dressed them back in their uniforms. The eyes that it had spared bulged out of what was left of their faces.

Recipients of most of the Mokoi's power, the officers were able to seek out the eyeballs and try to assist the headless guests.

They repositioned eyes that were in backwards or looking up or down so that the Mokoi could finally guide them. The guests that held heads gripped by hands on the end of outstretched arms now formed a line at the door that snaked around the table. It was difficult, very difficult for the Mokoi to control so many at once. Their movement would be poor, their reactions slow, but they would at least cause problems for the humans as the warrior men, the *policemen*—it knew this now as it had procured the information from Roman—went about their business.

Once they had sight, and the heads communicated with the bodies through the Mokoi's power, the guests could carry out their simple instruction. Kill anyone who wasn't already dead.

They began to move, one unsteady step in front of another. The skinless officers moved up and down the line, keeping them in order like ghastly supervisors. Their teeth chattered, but no voice came through them, instead when urging the guests to move the little enamel slabs clicked together faster. The grotesque conga line moved through the hall and began to descend into the basement.

***

'GUV!' Reed bellowed.

Bryson turned on the spot and saw the gory head, one eye staring out from a socket surrounded by raw meat. Holding the head was a hand and that hand was connected to the arm of what once must have been a lady with a generous bosom. The head had a beard. Bryson deduced that somewhere along the line a mistake had been made.

'You've got to be fucking kidding,' he said.

The sounds of awkward footsteps could be heard and more suspended heads came forward.

They stared at the group with ill-fitted eyes. Bryson could see that each animated body held a weapon in its other hand, a knife in most but some carried spoons. Probably not as intended by the Mokoi.

Reed risked a look back to Crowley. He could see that his eyes were shut, he was mouthing words, and his arms were raised and unmoving. Crowley couldn't just open that door, he thought, just like the door upstairs, just like the windows, if the old bastard was right that was. It needed a ritual, he had said, *a spell.*

'Ok, lads.' Bryson said, his voice firm, strong. 'We have to keep this lot away from Crowley. More importantly we have to keep them away from us.'

He glanced at each of his colleagues. Neither said anything but both nodded. Reed had placed his candelabra on the floor and had his pistol pointed at the first figure that had appeared. His other hand was a clenched fist that looked like it had the stopping power of an anvil.

Lafferty still held the other candelabra with his left hand, and in his right was a potato half. Bryson decided to meet them halfway, he drew out his pistol and kept one of the potatoes ready. His looked a little squashed and he wondered if it would make a difference.

'Just say when, Guv,' Reed said in a tone that often made armed men decide to put their knives and clubs away and go home for an early night.

'You OK, Lafferty?' Bryson said.

The horrors were close now, close enough for him to see their spinal columns showing from their neck.

'Ready, boss,' he said.

Bryson took a deep breath. He fired at the head nearest to him, aiming for the eye and his shot was perfect. The man's face was already the thing of nightmares before the bullet struck, but as it tore through the eye and ricocheted around the skull it caused the delicate bones to fragment and explode from its face. Bryson had to look away.

On cue, Reed began to blast at the heads the shambling bodies carried before them. Arms had raised with the knives clutched in their fists ready to swing down onto the officers. But the bullets from Reed's gun were devastating at such close range.

Even when the single eye wasn't hit, the force was sufficient to snatch the head away from the weak grip of the creatures.

'Reloading!' Reed shouted and Bryson, recovering his composure, commenced firing.

The puppets were too slow, too clumsy. The Mokoi knew that its plan of overwhelming the men with them was doomed. Some had already fallen on the stairs and their heads had rolled away. They had begun stabbing blindly at anything in front of them, which meant each other.

The organised line had become a mindless trampling herd and furthermore there seemed to be no way to terrorize these four men. The Mokoi started to become a little afraid. There were very few opportunities to escape the Void and worse, if the Crowley was able to destroy the gate, its very being would be utterly destroyed. It would consume itself as it fought the natural forces of this dimension.

It considered retreating, releasing the useless body of the half-wizard and going back to its grim, desolate existence in the Void, but the thought of another aeon of that life firmed its resolve. The officers it had were its last defence if the door was opened. It must save them, conserve its energy for a final assault by them. If it could take down the Crowley, who they would need to close the gate, then it might also be able to destroy them all.

As Bryson reloaded, Reed once again began to pick off the oncoming bodies. Some of them, although they could no longer see through losing their eye or the whole head, managed to stumble forward and were slashing up and down with their knives and spoons.

Nimbly, Lafferty dodged between them, cautious not to get in the way of Reed's line of fire, and pressed his potato against the exposed flesh of their necks.

The effect was instant. The meat around the potato steamed and boiled and the body shook violently, then abruptly dropped to the floor.

Suddenly all of the bodies dropped at once. They were still. The only sound that could be heard, after the ringing of Reed and Bryson's thundering shots had ceased in their ears, was a low pitched 'Ommmmmmmmmmm' coming from Crowley.

'Is it over?' Lafferty asked.

Reed walked towards the nearest of the bodies and nudged it with his boot with almost an almost Crowelian level of caution. Nothing happened. He listened. Other than the constant drone of Crowley reverberating around the room, it was still. No thumps upon the stairs. No shuffling feet.

'I think this bit is,' Reed replied. 'Guv?'

Bryson approached him and looked around the basement as far as the candlelight allowed.

'Why did they stop?' he asked of no one in particular. Lafferty risked a look back at Crowley, who didn't appear to have moved an inch during the commotion, and then stepped over a body to stand next to the inspector.

'I reckon that maybe they ran out of whatever it is that was moving 'em boss,' he said it with confidence. 'Mr C, he said that they was powered by this thing but that it only had so much to use, y'know like if you turn up the light on an oil lamp the oil gets used quicker. So maybe all this'— he swept his hand about the room to indicate the sprawled corpses— 'used up too much power. Maybe it's knackered. Beggin' yer pardon.'

'The lad is right.' It was Crowley. All three spun in surprise.

Reed's finger was a hair from squeezing the trigger. Bryson, once he got over the shock, scowled. Lafferty beamed.

'Crowley,' Bryson said. 'For God's sake man, I nearly had a fucking heart attack.'

'Apologies, Inspector. I didn't think you had such a sensitive disposition,' Crowley said, the sarcasm plain.

Despite his tone, Crowley had not meant to cause offence but he saw that his remark had somehow bit deep into the inspector. The mess of bodies, the destroyed heads of so many people, this had all clearly affected Bryson more than he cared to let on, and Crowley actually felt a rare sliver of shame slip down his spine.

He believed that he rarely met *good men*, he met men of principle and men of honour, but this didn't necessarily mean that they were *good*. Principled and honourable men had ordered thousands to march to their deaths in war. *Good* men would have seen the madness in that and stopped it. He decided to press on and let the comment be buried by his next statement.

'The lad probably has the measure of the thing. A creature like the Mokoi is very dangerous, anything that can animate bodies, control minds, or even throw a plate across a room is tremendously powerful, but that power comes at a price. The more it exercises its abilities, the greater the drain on its energy.'

'So, is it dead?' asked Bryson

'No... sadly no. It will be conserving what it has remaining. This was a desperate act, I think. It hoped to keep me from breaking the spell that sealed the door.'

'And did you break it? The spell?' Lafferty asked.

'I bloody well hope so. My calves are killing me...' Crowley turned and pushed at the doors.

Part 8

The stench was overpowering. This time, all of the men staggered back as it washed over them, even Crowley, who had thought that his nose had become accustomed to even the most rank and fetid fragrances of the Void, found himself close to heaving.

'Dear Lord, dear Lord...' Bryson mumbled, jacket sleeve clamped over his mouth. Lafferty, already drained of breakfast and dinner, retched only saliva and bile while Reed turned away, struggling to maintain his usual granite composure.

A few seconds passed before Crowley wiped tears from his eyes and announced with as much dignity as he could muster, 'Get those potatoes out, lads.'

They all obliged his command. Even Reed, once he had ensured that his pistol was fully loaded, took the spud he had abandoned to his pocket back into his fist.

Now that the doors were open and the initial blast of the stench had been diluted in the less contaminated air of the basement, it became clear that there were oil lamps inside that had reminded alight, '*or perhaps they have just been re-lit,*' Crowley considered.

The space ahead was more a cave than a room. The floor, walls, and ceiling were uncovered, untreated earth, the actual foundation of the house. At the far end of it was what could only be an altar; the lights were strong enough to reveal most of the details. Upon the altar were bowls containing, what exactly Crowley couldn't be sure, but he was willing to bet that it wasn't assorted fruits.

An obligatory protective circle had been stencilled around it to a diameter of about six feet and, at the rear of the altar were two large burgundy curtains with a gold trim through the middle and down the edges. Expensive stuff.

They were closed together, as behind them, Crowley thought, there would be the high priest's preparation room which he suspected, if a creature or person were really shit at hiding, is where one would go when men armed with existence-threatening potatoes were approaching.

The more unnerving elements of the room were to be found along the walls, upon shelves that had been fixed to carry the oil lanterns. The remaining eyes of the guests stared at them.

'Behind the curtains, gentlemen. That is where it will be,' Crowley said confidently.

'What do we do?' Lafferty asked.

Crowley was silent. He hadn't actually thought this far ahead. Dealing with the sigils, the doorway, and being as patronising as he felt he was able had been simple enough, he merely fell back on the knowledge that he had accumulated over the years and his experiences on his travels. But he had never actually come face to face with a Mokoi, not this close at least.

Crowley had always preferred to think of himself as an acquirer of knowledge, and an acquirer of the odd relic that he could knock out for a few quid to the London condescenti. He genuinely thought that what he had here, upon arriving at the house, was the opportunity to nab a few of Roman's juicier items, make the man look like a cock and even possibly get the police to burn his hall down to the ground based on a few well phrased lies.

But that had all been based on his belief that Roman Ravensblack had less ability to actually perform a ritual than an otter had of knitting a pullover. He knew it wasn't bravery that had allowed him to venture so deep into this situation, it was the belief that of the three men with him he could probably run faster than at least one of them.

'Mr Crowley?' Lafferty enquired.

'Yes.' Crowley replied and nodded his head, trying to give the impression that the question had already been answered.

'Come on Crowley, what do we do? Do we charge at it? Rip down the curtains... what?' Bryson said.

Reed twisted his head a little to get a look a better look at Crowley, who in turn saw the plain accusation of fuckwittery directed at him via the sergeant's moustache. The seconds were now ticking by at double step for Crowley and a cold sweat began to rise across his skin. He hadn't a clue.

The portal, he guessed, must be behind the curtain also. You couldn't see or sense them until you were very close, only the smell that poured through from the realm beyond gave any clue of its presence from a distance. He could deal with that. He knew how to shut a gate to the Void; it was practically occultist training page one, if you are able to let it in, be twice as certain that you can shut it out.

He had at first thought the obvious solution would be to shoot, stab, or in some way or other render Roman dead; then the Mokoi would have to flee the body, but a memory came to him. If you killed the host of the Mokoi, it would use the person's life-essence generated as the soul departed to enter another host, if there was one close by. As he wrestled with this, a memory, drawn from a conversation with a shaman, who had gotten blind drunk with him at a bar in Adelaide, rushed to the surface.

'BANJOS!' Crowley announced. We need a Banjo!'

The three men stared, mouths open despite the cloying odour from the cave getting into their throats.

'A banjo?' Bryson echoed. 'What the fuck do you need a banjo for? Are you planning to strum it to death?'

'What?' Crowley replied, 'what *are* you wittering on about?'

'What are *YOU* wittering on about?' Bryson countered.

'A *proxy*, another host. We need something for the Mokoi to enter when we force it from Roman. It can't survive for more than a few seconds without a host. In Australia, shamans would use a Banjo frog. They would ensure that their bodies were sufficiently rune-inscribed and then lure out the Mokoi, with no suitable human to infest, it would have to inhabit the first living thing it could find... the BANJO FROG!'

Crowley looked upon the men with an air of triumph.

'Do you have one?' Bryson asked coolly.

'What?'

Do you have a Banjo frog about your person?

'Of course I don't have a banjo frog about my person. I'm a master of the occult, not a fucking stage magician.' Crowley eyed Bryson as though the inspector were the lowest form of pond life.

'What I'm saying is that we need to make sure that when we force out the Mokoi, we have something for it to enter into.'

'Like what?' Bryson asked, unaffected by Crowley's intimidating tone.

'Like... a... receptacle of some kind.'

Bryson shook his head and turned away. Ahead the curtain remained drawn.

'Sergeant Reed,' Bryson said forcefully and without turning back to the scene.

'Yes Guv,' Reed replied.

'Would you be so kind as to order whoever is behind that curtain to surrender or you will commence firing into the curtains?'

'No!' Crowley grasped Bryson's shoulder, at which the inspector spun to face him.

'Sergeant Reed, should Mr Crowley attempt to interfere in this arrest, you are given full leave to shoot him too.'

'Right, Guv,' Reed replied.

Crowley spluttered, his exasperation turning his face crimson.

'Look, Inspector, you can't just shoot this thing. All you will do is kill Roman, which I agree has some merit, but I have just explained that the Mokoi will seek a new host, and the only living things available right now are us!'

Bryson once again squared up to Crowley. His own officers trying to kill them, headless assailants, eyeballs that spied on him, and now Australian frogs that would trap demons or ghosts or whatever it was that the perverted lunatic in front of him was claiming was too much.

'No. You look, Crowley. I've had my fill of this. All of it. Our guns made short work those headless bastards, so I'm fairly certain that you are underestimating the power a bullet has over your supernatural friends, therefore unless you can come up with a better idea in five seconds, my plan takes precedence over your potatoes. Got it?'

Crowley stood rigid with suppressed fury. He wasn't sure what the Mokoi could do, surrounded as it was, its minions seemingly disabled, its power now running out along with its time in this dimension, but there would be *something*. His mind sped through his vast banks of demonic lore.

The Mokoi could not summon other creatures; they were strong but not that strong. They couldn't turn into giant bubbling messes of insane violent flesh, strung with organs that snapped with vicious teeth (what fun that particular encounter had been), and they couldn't control more than one living person at a time. He had missed something, he was sure.

Something Bryson had said pushed at the back of his thoughts.

'*Come on, you know what it is, Crowley,*' a version of his own voice but even more smug and condescending wheedling and whiney, '*this is your arse, best to remember.*'

What happened next blurred from one scene into the next for Crowley.

Bryson was staring directly at him. He was mouthing words but Crowley had no idea what they were because his mind had finally fished out the missing information and presented it as a question.

'*Bryson's other officers, where were they?*'

The explosive retort of a firearm. Reed's pistol firing shook his thoughts and both he and Bryson ducked and stepped back, away from the sound.

Bryson looked towards the source and saw Lafferty apparently fighting with Reed. The slightly built lad had a hold of Reed's huge fist, the one holding the pistol. Caught off guard, and unbalanced with the surprise Reed had been spun away from the opening to the ritual room and now faced back into the basement. Lafferty was forcing Reed to fire by squeezing the sergeant's fingers with his own.

Crowley didn't look to where the sound had come from, but to where the bullets had struck. Lafferty had managed to extract three shots with his sudden assault on Reed and they had all vanished into the gloom except for one. This had struck the skinless cheekbone of what remained of a man in police uniform.

Reed had been totally unprepared for Lafferty's sudden action, he had been focused on the curtain ahead and the orders of his boss and the young constable had managed to swing his thick arm with ridiculous ease.

He had recovered quickly, however. He wasn't a man who was shocked or surprised for long, and his reaction time was impressive for a man of such solid build. Had he not seen the destination of the second bullet, seen it explode the side of the ruined face with chattering teeth that was creeping out of the darkness he could have easily thrown Lafferty aside. Instead he allowed the lad to squeeze the trigger once more, but unfortunately the shot went wide and the thing advanced.

In the moment before he acted, Lafferty had been about to approach his boss, to plea on the side of Crowley.

He couldn't explain to the guvnor why he believed the infamous Mr Crowley so fully, but neither could he explain all of the strange occurrences, dreams, and visions he had experienced since he was a child.

He had to make the guvnor listen; he had to do his best to help Mr Crowley and thereby help them all.

It was then that he had seen the thing emerge from the shadows. It had spied its chance: The group was arguing, their attention was on each other or on the curtain where the Mokoi was waiting.

Catching sight of the assault Lafferty had dropped his spuds, grasped Reed's hand and whirled the big man's arm around without thought of any consequence. His instincts had overridden his usual deference and caution.

Despite the threat coming from the direction of Reed and Lafferty, the thing appeared to take no notice of them, even when half of its face was blasted away, and it went straight for the occultist. In a panic, Crowley stepped further back, into the ritual room.

Bryson had still not caught up with what was happening. His first thought was that the lad had been taken over, just as the guests had been, that he was attacking Reed, trying to use the sergeant's gun to kill him and Crowley. He raised his own pistol and aimed it at his struggling officers. His finger tightened on the trigger. Lafferty's head was visible above the arm of Reed.

But what if it was Reed? What if the lad was trying to stop the sergeant, fighting the big man to stop him shooting at him and Crowley? He hesitated; Reed was the bigger, easier target, and if it was him the Mokoi had control of then they were fucked. If it was Lafferty, could Reed gain control over the boy before one of those shots ripped into its target? The thing upstairs had been fast, strong, maybe...

Bryson's pistol wavered in the air before him.

If the old bastard was right, if this thing got out of the house, what would happen? It fed on fear and terror, Crowley had said. Could he risk shooting the wrong person? Bryson let out a roar of frustration as he prepared to shoot both of his men.

Crowley had no powers, no magic to save him. Everyday people, who's only understanding of the supernatural was fairy stories, believed that spells were cast with a few magic words.

They didn't realise that time and resources had to be expended to manipulate the fundamental properties of the universe and twist them to your bidding. It was said that truly powerful entities could alter the Essence that lay at the very centre of it all that way, that they could do it at will, but that the exact same power prevented them from setting foot into this reality, as they would be annihilated instantly. A collision of forces equal in energy.

Those entities were the gods, recipients of the most awesome gifts of power but equally impotent in using it in the domains they most desired to reign over. Crowley wasn't surprised that they were always pissed off.

The scene had unfolded in the blink of an eye but if Crowley did have a gift or talent that was possibly of unnatural origin, it was for quick thinking where his own skin was concerned.

He surmised that Lafferty must have seen the thing, grasped Reed's hand as it gripped the pistol, and then whirled the man's arm around so he could to shoot at it. Bryson would have caught only the struggle, must be thinking that one of them was under the Mokoi's control. It was a fair assumption, and in fact, Crowley also had this suspicion for a second. The Mokoi would always seek out those who manipulated the essence, wizards, shamans, witches would be its first choice, but second to that might be those who have the ability, but not the knowledge to use it, and Lafferty...

Crowley quickly dismissed that thought. Bryson was about to make a terrible error of judgment and had to be stopped. He knew that he would also have to save his own life this time, as his retinue of guardians were too busy trying to kill each other. The skinless creature was charging towards him; it would come behind the already occupied Bryson and then leap at him. It would tear his face off with those horribly white teeth. Crowley charged at it.

He had backed away enough to require three powerful strides to get to Bryson. As he reached the Inspector, he shoulder charged him with all his strength. Bryson's pistol boomed as it flew from his hand, the shock of Crowley's impact shaking him to his core. The two men lost all balance. Bryson impacted squarely on the skinless officer and Crowley in turn collapsed on top of the inspector.

All three fell to the floor, and the creature's chest, more fragile without its elastic, shock-absorbing cover of skin, collapsed under the weight.

Crowley rolled to the side. Bryson looked into the strained eyes of the creature and stopped thinking. Thinking would have slowed him down and so instinct took over. He lifted his head and bought it squarely, brutally down onto the face of the thing. Without lips to protect them, its teeth caved from the blow. Bryson got to his knees, straddling the writhing body and pinning its arms. He pushed his thumbs into its eyes. The ease with which they sank deep into the sockets surprised him, and he felt a nauseating squelch as the orbs popped under the pressure.

As the creature had gone down under Crowley and Bryson, Reed and Lafferty had got the measure of their own situation. Lafferty released his grip on the sergeant's hand. He had planned to run to the aid of the guvnor and Crowley, but as he started towards them Reed shouted out. 'There's another lad, *ahead!*'

The report of the pistol filled the room once again. Reed had fired at a figure that had appeared on the very edge of the circle of light, but it had vanished before he could take another shot. Lafferty now had time to pull out his own pistol.

'Cover me, lad, I need to reload.'

Without waiting for Lafferty to respond—he now had complete confidence in the young constable—Reed swiftly and with a practiced hand added bullets to the empty chambers.

Lafferty risked a glance towards the others, and he could see Bryson atop the thing. The inspector seemed to be in control of the situation, and as he returned his observation to the dimly lit corner of the room the second of the skinned policemen leapt into view.

Lafferty began to fire at it, and in a moment his shots were joined by those of Reed. The thing's body twitched in the air as the barrage of the two pistols tore into it.

Lafferty only managed two hits, but every one of Reed's bullets struck true. He had fired in an almost vertical line from thing's chest to its head and his final shot joined with that of Lafferty, two bullets entered into its skull at the same moment. Its head exploded and the creature dropped onto the floor.

Despite Bryson crushing its eyes the creature bucked underneath him and its bare teeth snapped as it shook its head violently from side to side. Crowley crawled forward; the potatoes had fallen out of his dressing gown pockets when he had collided with the inspector.

He snatched one up and shouted.

'Bryson, take this, quickly!'

Spittle flew from the inspector's clenched teeth as he used all of his strength to maintain the grip he had on the thing's skull. He snapped his head around and saw Crowley, his hand outstretched, half a singed potato clutched in his grasp.

'Take it, man, take it!' Crowley screamed at him. Bryson didn't hesitate; he pulled his thumbs out from the thing's head, beyond feeling any revulsion at the slurping noise it made. He reached back with a bloodied hand and took the spud. As soon as he had the rune-inscribed tuber in his hand, he swung it down onto the forehead of the monster, raw muscles that covered the skull snapped as heat burned at them. The thing gave a final lurch and then sagged beneath him.

Part 9

'Dear Lord', Bryson gasped, his thoughts returned to him and he looked towards where he had seen Lafferty and Reed apparently fighting. They were both approaching.

'There was another,' Reed's moustache said grimly.

'Is it dead? Bryson asked

'As dead as things seem to get here,' Reed replied.

Bryson, energy spent and adrenalin beginning to cloy in his muscles, rose to his feet accompanied by small gasps as if he were an old man. He stepped away from the skinless thing on the floor and turned to Crowley.

'Thank you,' he said, the sentiment was painfully genuine.

Crowley nodded. It was then that he saw the orange glow of flames licking at the walls and the stairs. 'Oh shit, look, the fucking basements on fire.'

The group turned and could see that Crowley was perfectly correct. An oil lantern must have been hit by a bullet or been knocked over by the creatures, but whatever the cause the fact was that the oil had started a blaze which had caught as they had fought.

Reed marched over to it and removed his jacket as he went, Lafferty followed and began to do the same. At first Reed tried to swat down the flames but the oil immediately adhered to his jacket and it too began to burn. Lafferty attempted to stamp down on smaller patches to put them out, but to no avail. The fire continued to spread, it climbed the stairs and a thick pall of smoke started to fill the chamber.

'We aren't stopping this, Guv,' Reed bellowed.

Bryson turned back to Crowley. 'Will this do it? We've hurt it, you said it would be weak. We've killed its soldiers, can it get out now?

'I'm not sure,' Crowley said and then shook his head, 'if it can stay alive, keep Roman alive long enough for the fire to destroy some of the sigils, then it could still escape.

'What do we do?' Bryson asked. Crowley closed his eyes and let his head down, his chin almost touching his chest. He said something, but Bryson couldn't quite catch it. Reed and Lafferty were still trying to control the fire, noisily stamping and slapping at it with their jackets.

'What? What did you say, Crowley?'

Crowley looked up and his eyes bore in to the inspector. The resolve in them was clear.

'You need to run, get the lads out. I'll take care of this.'

'What about you?' Bryson asked.

'I'll be alright,' Crowley replied. 'You thought I might be a magician, Inspector, don't you think I have a few tricks up my sleeve?'

Before he could reply, Bryson gasped as the curtain in the ritual room was ripped down from within. Seeing the inspector's expression, Crowley whirled around and there, in his high priest robes, covered from head to toe in blood, was Roman Ravensblack.

'Well, well,' said Crowley. 'I was beginning to wonder when you would finally show up.'

Bryson looked about the floor for a weapon. He snatched up a knife that one of the headless attackers had been carrying and stepped to Crowley's side. Crowley looked at the knife.

'No,' Crowley ordered. 'If you kill Roman, it will just go for one of you lot.'

'Not you?' Bryson said.

'No, I'm... protected, it would be too much work and it doesn't have a lot of time. It will go for the boy, most likely.'

Bryson didn't question this. He looked back to the two officers who were clearly losing the fight against the blaze.

'You need to get up those stairs before it's too late,' Crowley said, and as he did so Roman moved slowly towards him. The man's eyes were pitch black orbs of malevolence, and in his hand he carried an ornately decorated knife with a savage blade.

Crowley recognised it instantly. It was a Blade of the Abyss. Not as powerful as a Khopesh but still not something to trifle with.

'*Worth a few quid that,*' he thought.

It was hard to see the real Roman under gore-caked hair, and the pitch black eyes commanded attention away from the aquiline features that brought him so much attention from wealthy, but mind-numbingly bored and frustrated ladies that flocked to his dark allure.

Crowley stepped forward, back into the ritual room. Roman snarled at him like a wild dog, then produced a grin that revealed the man's perfect white teeth, made brighter against the blackened blood that smeared his face.

It wanted to finish them. It had saved its final energy to destroy them, but the fire was yet another in a sequence of events that had not gone the Mokoi's way.

But if it could take the boy, and finish off the others or just let them roast, it might be able to escape when the fire brought down the protective barriers that its host had put up around the house.

All it had to do was get past these two, the Crowley and the Chief. It would carve up the hairless one and then let the Chief destroy its host. It would be free then, only for a few moments, but it would be enough to enter the boy and escape up the stairs. If it was the first to the top, it could keep the others down, make them choke on the fumes and burn, they would *BURN*.

'Time for you to go, Inspector,' Crowley said.

Bryson stared at the slowly advancing figure of Ravensblack. There was nothing human in those eyes; the way it slowly rotated the vicious looking knife was evidence of its intent.

Somehow, despite trying to resist the feeling, he knew that he and the lads would be no match for it. They had handled its remote agents, the staggering, awkward zombies, but this was the creature itself.

'Can you stop it, Crowley, are you certain?'

'Piece of cake,' Crowley replied. 'Oh and when you leave, I noticed that Roman has a model of a large sailing vessel, just behind the main doors in the foyer. I want it.'

'What?' Bryson asked, confused.

'You said that I could have anything that I chose from Roman's inventory. I want that.' Crowley said firmly.

No wiser, Bryson nodded and made to leave. As he turned Crowley unbelted his robe and shrugged his shoulders. The gown fell to the floor revealing him in all of his naked glory. Bryson's jaw went slack.

He stared longer than he wanted to at Crowley's naked body. The man was big. He carried a good amount of weight but he wasn't corpulent, rather he had considerable brawn. What was most striking though was his skin, the man was simply covered in tattoos.

Some appeared to be lush, colourful landscapes, others sigils and runes like the ones he had indicated to them as they had trekked through the house. There were unintelligible words, strange lines with confusing angles, bizarre creatures and on his shoulder, just below a crimson heart, the word 'Sue.'

How strange such a simple symbol and remarkably ordinary name seemed amongst all of the chaos and insanity that was imprinted onto his body.

'*Is that what he means by protected?*' Bryson thought.

'GUV!' Reed shouted. 'The stairs!'

Bryson looked. The flames were now filling the lower portion of the stairwell and threatened to surround Lafferty and Reed at the bottom.

'Good luck,' he said to Crowley and then ran over to them.

'Sir, if we don't go now we won't get to the top of those stairs without being on fire ourselves,' Reed said as Bryson neared.

'We are going now,' Bryson replied. 'Lafferty, get up those stairs.'

'What about Mr Crowley, sir?' Lafferty looked over to the ritual room entrance and saw Crowley, naked, closing the doors to the ritual room.

'Mr Crowley!' he shouted and started towards him. Bryson caught his shoulder and hauled him back.

'Lafferty, get up those fucking stairs lad, and that's an order,' Bryson shouted into his constable's face, he could see the genuine look of horror in his eyes, horror at leaving Crowley behind. 'The longer you take to go, the worse the situation for myself and Reed, got it?'

Tears began to stream from Lafferty's eyes, and Bryson understood that it was not the effects of the smoke that boiled around them.

'Yes sir,' Lafferty said quietly. He turned and leapt as far as he could up the stairs, disappearing into the flames.

'After you, Guv,' Reed said.

Bryson nodded and jumped. Reed followed but not before he had looked back towards the closed doors of the ritual room.

'Give it hell, you weird bastard,' his moustache whispered. Reed launched himself into the flames.

***

The three officers held their breath and covered their faces as they barrelled up the stairway. They were fortunate that the fire had only reached the first few feet of the staircase, and other than the smell of singed hair there had been no other effects of running through it.

'Out,' Bryson said at the top, 'hopefully Crowley was right about its power and it can't keep the doors sealed.'

'Shouldn't we try to put the fire out?' Lafferty said.

Bryson considered it for just a moment. They could fetch water, pour it into the basement and try to douse the flames. He wasn't sure it would be enough though, the smoke, the heat, it was possible that they might be able to get Crowley out, but then what about the thing, what if it had control of him? 'It would go for the boy,' Crowley had said.

'No,' Bryson replied. He placed a hand on Lafferty's shoulder. 'We let it burn, this whole place. It's what Crowley wanted.'

Lafferty made no attempt to hide his sobs, and Reed placed his hand on the boy's back to guide him from the top of the stairs. The view below looked like the entrance to hell. 'Come on lad, this isn't over yet,' Reed said.

They quickly passed through the hall and the now empty dining area. When they reached the foyer, Bryson saw the model ship that Crowley had told him he wanted, his reward. It was sat on top of an expensive-looking polished cabinet. The ship was beautifully crafted, complete with intricate rigging and genuine canvas sails at full mast. Bryson took it from its plinth and tucked it under his arm as carefully as he could. He saw that both Reed and Lafferty were looking at him quizzically.

'Don't ask,' he said.

They made for the door, and Reed turned the handle. It opened up into the cool night air.

'Right. Now we run.' Bryson said and began the exodus.

The three charged across the gravel of the courtyard and back towards where their vehicles and fellow officers awaited them. When they reached the main gate, Bryson looked back towards the house. There was no sign of flames just yet, no smoke.

He would need to delay the other officers, make sure that the fire had chance to really take control of the building.

'We need to ensure that no one goes near that place until it's a pile of charcoal and cinders,' Bryson said, he looked in turn at Reed and Lafferty.

'Yes Guv,' they replied.

Bryson walked quickly to his sedan, pulled open the rear door and carefully placed the sailing boat, Crowley's strange treasure, onto the seat.

Reed sat with Lafferty on the footplate of the Black Maria; the sergeant had his arm around the boy who was crying into a handkerchief one of the other officers had given him. They had come running up the road when they had seen their colleagues emerge from the hall.

Bryson began to formulate his story. Roman Ravensblack had gone insane, killed his guests, and murdered the officers that had come to their aid. That was so close to the truth as to be easily told. Then the maniac had then set fire to the building, which unfortunately he and his officers had been too late to put out. Mr Crowley had offered to assist them as he knew Ravensblack, but he too had unfortunately... No, he wouldn't mention Crowley at all. The other officers had seen him, but he could say that Crowley had fled the scene. Anyone would believe that.

Bryson had a strong suspicion that when they were finally able to search through the wreckage of the house, when they accounted for all of those poor souls who had been horribly murdered, that Crowley's body wouldn't be found. He couldn't say why, but the idea was impossible to ignore.

Crowley may not have been able to leave by the door, but there was a gate of sorts in that house, and he wondered if perhaps London's most notorious occultist had figured out an escape route, one that involved pathways he couldn't hope to comprehend.

Self-preservation, it was the core of the man. Bryson suspected that it was *inscribed* upon his very skin, amongst those illustrations and alien words that were some sort of arcane armour.

It boiled down to this, would a man like Crowley really sacrifice himself to save a bunch of coppers?

He looked at the model boat the occultist had demanded as his prize and thought that it was possible, very possible that Aleister Crowley would soon be coming back to claim it.

Mad Dogs and Englishmen

Part 1

London, 1921

The docks were never quiet or still, and for as long as Bryson had lived within its borders he had understood that no part of the city of London ever truly slept. It was, if you were to believe the poets, a living machine, and no great leap of faith was needed for Bryson to understand how they might come to such a conclusion. London was the both the heart and engine of the United Kingdom and the dockyards he walked through were a part of how it fed its diverse provinces.

Merchant vessels were disgorging their holds right. Food, minerals, livestock and immigrants flooded on to the quayside, all to feed the persistent demands of commerce. Bryson could advance the metaphor on to the people, for the inhabitants of the capital were both blood and oil, they scurried through its streets, its grime-coated arteries, carrying goods, trading them, selling and sometimes stealing. The method didn't matter, the city had no interest in how its commodities were moved from person to person or from place to place, whether legally or illegally. All that mattered was the constant transfer, the endless cycle, in and out, bought and sold. People willingly went into its heart and London took what they offered up to it, in return it pumped out the money they so desperately wanted.

Bryson lived and worked inside city's nervous system, his domain was where the actions and reactions of the body politic took place. He patrolled and investigated and fought against diseases that ate at it, parasites attempting to drain all that was good and honest from their host. Not that there was too much goodness of late, and because of this the he rarely noticed the money. All he saw was the blood and shit that splashed against the walls of homes and spilled onto the streets as the system, which at first seemed so robust, broke down as forces conspired against it. London was a machine engaged in orchestrating its own destruction.

It was seven in the morning when he had arrived at the dockside. Already a crowd had gathered around the area of the wharf his constables were attempting to keep clear. Bryson strode through them, nudging aside dockhands, storekeepers and ladies whose trade was in demand even at this early hour. Some turned as they were moved aside, ready to take issue with being forced from their observation point, but when they caught a look of the clean and pressed attire, the shaven face and resolute steel-grey eyes they just shuffled into another position.

As he reached the front of the crowd Bryson was pleased to see Reed at the centre of it all. The sergeant stood like a rock that dared the waves to crash against him. He gripped a baton in his huge fist, the business end resting in his palm. Constables, six in all formed a semi-circle around the entrance to one of the warehouses that lined this section of the docks. As he passed through the crowd one of the policemen looked sharply in his direction but then brought a hand to his helmet in salute. Bryson nodded and continued to Sergeant Reed.

'Morning Sergeant.' Bryson called as he approached. Reed turned, lifted the baton from his palm and tapped the end onto the brim of his helmet, which as always was set low, obfuscating his eyes. His moustache, on fine form for a mild spring morning, added to the solid and intimidating presence that Reed employed to keep the peace.

'Morning Inspector,' the sergeant replied

'What do we have?' Bryson looked towards the large, filthy doors of the warehouse that were opened a little, about two feet of space offered between them.

'Nasty business, Sir.' Reed said. He shouted out to his constables, 'Keep 'em orderly lads, any nonsense and you give them some of His Majesty's Pleasure.' To emphasise the point he performed a dextrous twirl of his Baton. Then, satisfied that his officers were resolute, he ushered Bryson into the warehouse.

As he stepped through the gap and into the building, Bryson immediately became aware of a faint but acrid stench that hung in the air about them. He gave a pronounced sniff then looked to Reed. He said nothing but the Sergeant understood the question Bryson had asked using only his eyebrows. Reed nodded.

The warehouses along this section of the docks were mostly for the storage and movement of household and industrial goods rather than food.

It was from these towering, fragile looking constructs of weather beaten, warped timber that the exports of Britain's empire came from afar, to be sorted and then sent out across its green and pleasant land. Furniture, textiles, works of art and cultural pieces came from artisans across the known world. Even animals were temporarily stored here, tigers, elephants, tropical birds and fine horses.

As Bryson was guided through the maze of large, stacked crates that threatened to crash down upon them, he saw stencilled imprints that declared the port of origin of each box, Jamaica, China, Peru, and Brazil. They were only places on a map to him, fantasy lands with strange names and stranger cultures, not the kind of thing he was interested in, it was of the sort of thing that *he* would like though. Bryson quickly dismissed thoughts of Crowley, thinking of anything even related to him quickly escalated to darker thoughts of Ravensblack Hall, and that was something he didn't need on his mind whilst at a crime scene.

As he turned the final corner of the narrow street, created by the walls of wooden boxes, Bryson found himself at the very centre of the warehouse. It was clear of crates to a distance of about twenty feet and in the centre a great circle had been drawn in chalk upon the floor.

Bryson wasn't at all surprised that the circle contained various sigils and runes, in fact not seeing evidence of occult iconography within circles was what seemed odd to him these days. Not all of the scrawls were visible though as blood, drained from the bodies six men suspended by their feet from the thick support beams crossing above their heads, obscured a good deal of them.

Each man was naked, each bore the marks of being wounded by a knife or similar object, but the most evident injury was a large rent in each of their stomachs. Entrails hung down from the gaping holes slick with blood.

'Dear Lord...' Bryson said.

He stared silently at the awful scene and took in the appearance of the men.

All were black-skinned, slim, *skinny* he thought, they also looked young, perhaps in their late teens or early twenties.

Reed chose his moment carefully, not wanting to interrupt the Guvnor's train of thought, waiting until Bryson looked down and shook his head before taking the opportunity to speak.

'They were discovered at just gone six this morning Guv, one of the local men who does some fetchin' and carryin' for the bloke who owns this operation. He says he came by to pick up some stuff he was supposed to be taking off to Norwich today.'

'Where's he now?' Bryson asked.

'I sent him back to the station with the lads that first came by the place, they were a bit shook up so I thought it best. Apparently the gent came running up to 'em as they were patrolling the dock, the usual beat for them, and the fella was shouting that there had been bloody murder. He brings 'em to the door, wouldn't go in, and this what the lads found.'

'Bloody murder indeed,' Bryson said.

'That's one of them sodding circles ain't it boss?'

Bryson sighed. 'Yes, I think it is Reed, I do believe it is.'

'Do you want to me to fetch him?'

'No,' Bryson said and let out another, heavier sigh. 'I'll go. You keep this place locked down, I don't anyone near it until I get back. Meanwhile do we have any more officers available? Lafferty?'

'I sent one of the lads to get a few of the others out of bed, Lafferty will be one of them.' Reed answered.

'Good, good,' Bryson said quietly. 'Right, I'll go and get Crowley.' He turned to leave but stopped as Reed spoke.

'Do you think it's that thing again boss, the Mokoi? Crowley said it couldn't be killed unless it was stuck here, and he took it back into that…gate didn't he?'

Bryson had considered this as he had stared at the blood, the circle and the dripping entrails.

'No, I don't think so, if there were eyeballs draped about the place, heads on sticks, maybe, but I think this is something else.'

Reed's moustache twitched in agreement.

Bryson felt a chill as he drove towards Mayfair. The last time he had sought the assistance of Aleister Crowley it had resulted in a night of horrors he only wished to forget, and yet here he was again, leaving a crime scene that was more akin to an abattoir and about to elicit the aid of a man he should probably be arresting, all things being equal.

As he drove he observed people going about their business, hard-working for the most part, certainly undeserving of being mauled and mutilated by godforsaken creatures even if their trade was dishonest.

Well, perhaps the child rapists… he thought.

Crowley's home, this one at least, was in a very salubrious part of Mayfair. It was very difficult to arrest people who lived in such districts and nigh-on impossible to drag them in front of a judge. Connections. Bryson tapped sharply at the steering wheel as deeply buried frustrations briefly rose to the surface. It was all about connections.

All of these wealthy people had some form of contact with other equally wealthy people, and all of them led two lives. One the upstanding and decent member of society, the driven and determined entrepreneur or perhaps an heir to some landed dynasty who upholds the family chivalric code, and then the other life, the bigamist, sexual deviant, pornographer, murderer, occultist…

Except it isn't a second life for Crowley is it? Bryson pondered, *the arrogant bastard does it all right out there, bold as you please, doesn't give a tuppeny fuck*

He didn't want to like Crowley and had made it a point of principle to avoid him unless it was in an official capacity. He avoided him because there was something about him that undermined your resolve. He was smart, no doubting that, Bryson guessed that he was probably educated at

Cambridge or some other such rich man's school, he had some balls, Ravensblack Hall had showed him what Crowley was capable of when he was in a corner.

He caught himself, he often did when disparaging Crowley because just to say 'when cornered' wasn't fair. Crowley could just as easily have run up those stairs with them and instead he had shut himself in with the thing, stark bollock naked if you please, so no, not a coward, not really.

And besides he… and there it was, finding yourself making excuses for him. *Crowley isn't even here and he's chipping away at me.*

Bryson scowled and turned his thoughts to the case, *Six men, all ages but mostly young,* he guessed, *eighteen to twenty-five, suspended by what looked to be standard cargo rope and with their guts cut open…torn open?*

His first suspicion would have been a message from a rival gang, the foreigners seemed to relish chopping bits off each other whereas the London lads usually just gave you a clout or perhaps broke a few bones. In very rare cases a snitch or some boss whose tenure had come to an end might be found floating in the Thames. Dead was dead of course but the manner in which a person arrived at said state was important, and strung up and gutted like a pig wasn't cricket. *Not even a sport,* Bryson thought.

Groups of dead people, ritual murder and Aleister Crowley. Bryson shuddered, the whole thing had 'further bloodbath to follow,' written all over it.

***

Although expensive and certainly not small, Crowley's house was remarkably plain compared to the others that formed the row of which it was a part. One side was detached and it was through the narrow gap between the two houses that Bryson had run to the back of Crowley's house on that fateful night, to bang the bloody hell out of his kitchen door and wake the drug addled bastard up.

Considering who they had for a neighbour Bryson was genuinely surprised that he had never been contacted by one of them with a complaint. Too scared? Possibly, Crowley didn't try to play his reputation down, quite the opposite, the man fell short of wearing a billboard with 'I'm a friend of Satan,' scrawled on it, but only just.

He was a gentleman, Bryson supposed, of sorts, swore a lot though. Bryson appreciated that he too was perhaps over-fond of the vernacular but Crowley had a special way of swearing that he didn't like. It was mean and witty and always designed to make everyone else in the room think you were some kind of twat when he started on you.

Crowley did with language what bare knuckle boxers did with razors in their hair. It was never a fair fight and it was always dirty.

He pulled up outside the house and looked up at the windows. All had drawn curtains but the light of an oil lamp blazed behind one of them. Bryson exited the vehicle and climbed the steps to Crowley's door as he had done three months ago, with mixed emotions coursing through him, feelings of both annoyance and damned bloody annoyance.

He had been prepared for and expecting any number of things to happen when and if Crowley opened his front door. A torrent of foul language at a volume sufficient to wake most of the street, cynical and snide comments upon his ability as an officer of the law, a tirade of self-righteous grandstanding designed to cajole him into offering some kind of extra payment, beyond the fifteen guineas they had agreed upon at the scene of the Ravensblack affair. What he had not expected was the door to be answered by Constable Lafferty.

'Oh… Morning Inspector Bryson,' Lafferty said, failing to disguise his surprise at seeing his boss, to the extent that he neglected to close his mouth after saying his name. He stood in the doorway with his jaw hanging like peeling wallpaper.

'What the bloody hell?' Bryson matched Lafferty's incredulity and raised it, all in, no table limit. His jaw clamped shut. Tight. His eyes blazed with a fusion of anger and disgust, and the tightly clamped jaw ground his teeth as though he were worrying at a length of steel.

'Er… well, you best come in Inspector, Mr Crowley's…' Lafferty stammered through his welcome and explanation but Bryson caught none of it. His mind whirled with awful possibilities. What had Crowley done to this boy, was it some perverse sexual exploitation, what vile practice?

Not knowing if Lafferty had finished talking or not Bryson launched forward, storming past him and into the house. He made straight for the Library, he had seen Crowley's magical circle in there the last time he had come, that fateful evening of hell at Ravensblack. He thought the old sodomite would probably be in there now, chanting and whatnot, probably while shoving colossal amounts of drugs up his arse. He had most likely coerced young Lafferty into 'DOING IT FOR HIM!'

His thoughts whirled and raged and when he entered the Library and found it empty of both occult circles and Crowley he bawled at the ceiling. 'CROWLEY! CROWLEY YOU TWISTED BASTARD, WHERE ARE YOU?'

Lafferty had stopped to lock the door before running after the Inspector, and as he entered the Library he raised his palms and spoke in slow, even tones.

'I'm fine Inspector, Mr C ain't done nuffin he oughtn't, I promise.'

Bryson didn't seem to hear and bawled again 'CROWLEY YOU SHIT! GET DOWN HERE NOW!'

'Guv, guv, it's alright honest. Mr Crowley's been educatin' me on all the stuff that's out there, wot we might encounter like.' Lafferty stepped closer and spread his hands a little. 'I'm alright Guv, promise.'

Bryson calmed a little. He could feel the heat of his face and supposed he must be almost purple from his shouting. The lad looked fine, he was properly dressed, and perhaps it looked odd because he had never seen the boy out of uniform.

He took a breath and spoke slowly and with restraint. 'Where…is…Mr…Crowley?'

'He's in bed Guv, usually sleeps until nine.' Lafferty said dropping his hands to his sides.

'And…why are you here?' Bryson asked. He recalled Lafferty had said something about education but nothing more.

'Well Guv, since what happened at Ravensblack Hall, all the strange stuff, well Mr Crowley says I should learn about it, about what else was out there…in the void.'

'In the void…' Bryson echoed.

'Yes, Sir. Mr Crowley reckons that I…well he reckons that I would be pretty good at dealing with such stuff as I'm…well, he says I've got something that means I can handle it, y'know, the 'orribleness of it all.'

Bryson narrowed his eyes "Handle it'? You were on your knees throwing up for the first thirty minutes.' He knew what he had said was true but nonetheless Bryson felt a sting at picking at the lad. He had been incredibly brave in that house, heroic even.

Lafferty reddened and his head dropped a little at first, but he lifted it as though pride had reinforced his spinal column.

'Yes Guv, that is a fact, but Mr Crowley says that was only to be expected, first time an all, he says the fact that I didn't end up in Bedlam means I got what it takes to deal with these bleeders…beggin' your pardon Guv.' He was silent for a moment and then added, 'He says you and the Sarge have it too, Guv.'

'Have what exactly Lafferty? What's this maniac been selling you?' Bryson asked with stone-chiselled suspicion.

'Mr Crowley says that most people can't take seeing that sort of stuff, what we saw in the Hall, he says it's screaming and scratching at your eyes and then off to the padded rooms for your everyday bloke, but some people 'ave…'

Lafferty paused to make sure he got the phrase right in his head before he said it, 'minds capable of bearing witness to the vast and timeless void that exists in the darkest corners of what we perceive as a single reality.'

Bryson's jaw closed and once again began to chew at imaginary bars of tempered steel. He believed the lad when he said that Crowley hadn't...harmed him. Lafferty had an almost breathtaking honesty about him. How he ever became a police officer was lost on him. Many coppers were roughnecks, thugs or just plain crooked and in it for what they could grab at the scene. Not all of them, of course, and he was hard on the troops, he knew that. Not so much because they were prone to villainy while in the uniform, but in case they *turned* to villainy while in the uniform.

Discipline. He instilled discipline in his men but he couldn't make them honest.

'Alright. Well, I haven't got a fucking clue what you just said Constable, and I suggest that we have a very long and thorough discussion about what exactly you are doing here.' Bryson sighed, exhaling as much of the heated air he had built up inside him as he could. As it stood, if the lad was sound, and it seemed that despite the strangeness of it all he was, then he was back to where he started. He had to ask for Crowley's help.

Dear Lord... he thought.

'Good Morning Inspector!' Crowley appeared in the doorway. He spoke loudly, and with patently false joy, as though he were greeting people at a wedding. 'How very nice to see you.'

Bryson's eyebrows furrowed as he tried to make Crowley's polite and friendly introduction work in the real world.

'Oh...I'm terribly sorry, slip of the tongue,' Crowley gave a small laugh. 'What I actually meant was WHAT THE HELL DO YOU THINK YOU'RE DOING BAWLING AND SHOUTING IN MY HOME IN THE MIDDLE OF THE FUCKING MORNING?' Crowley thundered, then continued, with a vicious, perfectly enunciated diatribe against the establishment.

'Mr Crowley Sir...' Lafferty offered his raised palms to the angry occultist but the effort was wasted. Crowley wasn't prepared to throw away a perfectly good opportunity to be outraged and indignant at the police.

'Constable Lafferty, I am quite certain that the Inspector will have a satisfactory explanation for his outrageous attitude and gross imposition.' He folded his arms and glared. Bryson jutted his jaw forward in a combative fashion. Crowley didn't intimidate him, no matter how much he wailed and threw his accusations around. Rich men throwing their toys about only made him want to resort to *His Majesty's Pleasure* to help calm them down. Bryson had no doubt whatsoever that Reed would have punched Crowley's lights out the moment he had begun his tirade, but Reed didn't have the concerns of position that an Inspector had to consider. He also had to remember that he had made a couple of promises to Crowley, after Ravensblack Hall, after Crowley had returned.

Bryson was a man of his word and a promise, even to a devious, lecherous freak like Crowley, was a promise he would keep.

'I need your help. We have a situation at the docks.' Bryson said.

'Oh! Splendid! Why didn't you say so? I'll get my hat.' Crowley turned and walked back into the hall.

Bryson made to speak but stopped. Instead he simply watched as Crowley hurried away. He looked at Lafferty, who shrugged. 'He's very…mercurial.' Lafferty offered.

'Did he tell you that?' Bryson asked.

'Yes boss.' Lafferty admitted.

'If that man tells you it's raining,' Bryson jabbed a finger towards the hall, 'make sure he's not just taking a piss on you, right lad?'

'Yessir,' Lafferty replied.

A moment later Crowley reappeared complete with a heavy black coat and dark brown fedora, he also carried a walking cane of polished black wood with a silver top.

'Let us away!' Crowley said with a genuine smile of excitement. 'Tell me the details in the car Inspector.'

He once more turned and disappeared into the hall and as he went called out to Lafferty. 'Come on lad, let's see what you've learned.'

Bryson gave Lafferty a sharp look. 'Yes, let's see what you've learned Constable,' he said through barely-moving lips.

'Right sir,' Lafferty nodded, and had become a little pale. 'After you, Sir, I'll need to lock up.'

Bryson shook his head and followed after Crowley.

Part 2

Bryson expected Crowley to be quiet once he had told him what had been found in the warehouse. He thought that he would sit silently, considering what the mutilated bodies might mean in his world of black magic and weird rituals. Crowley wasn't quiet. He didn't even mention the problem at the docks, instead he set about slandering almost every politician, Royal, luminary and dignitary that could reasonably be considered of note.

Bryson tried to mentally block him out, but the man was incessant. His reserved his most severe attacks for others involved in his own insane belief, particularly those who were attached to any of the so-called 'Orders,' but especially those in the Hermetic Order of the Golden Dawn.

Bryson knew about the Golden Dawn, pretty much everyone did. It wasn't secret or even subtle, much like Crowley in fact. Up until now he had only thought of it as just another excuse for rich people to gather of an evening to fuck each other stupid. He had been fairly certain that all the trappings of black magic and Satanism were just for decoration. Even at Ravensblack's place he had seen tidily folded robes and dinner guests dressed in their finest clothes. He wouldn't have been surprised if there had been a fucking cabaret to follow.

However the heads, the eyes and the walking corpses changed all of that. He shuddered. Crowley continued to unleash his scathing vitriol from the back of the vehicle. He had now moved on to Poets.

The City was fully awake and Bryson knew that the small crowd he had left at the dock would be a mob of onlookers by now. Worse, keeping what was in there out of the public eye would be difficult. It wasn't witnesses who would break the silence, it would be his own officers. Lurid tales of vice and murder sold newspapers, eyewitness recollections entertained those who frequented public houses and who would reward the narrator with frequent ales to keep his throat lubricated.

As horrific a story as it already was, embellishments could be added for effect, and ultimately the seeds of fear would be sown.

Within a few weeks, possibly days, hysteria would spring up from the dark imaginations of those who had heard a version of a version of a version of the events.

Ravensblack had been moneyed, keeping all that shit quiet had been easy. The wealthy buried their lies and secrets under a mountain of gold. Those with power would protect other powerful people just to keep the gates closed. To keep those who toiled for them blind to the unsavoury lives of opulence they enjoyed. But when the poor were taken, when working men and women died violent, unholy death's there was always a reaction, violence met with violence.

There were a lot more struggling workers than there were rich people and Bryson had to keep them calm, he would have to feed lies and half-truths to them. 'Keeping the peace,' he thought with no satisfaction.

'Fucking hell that's a fair old crowd Inspector.' Crowley broke from his rant as the sedan turned onto the main thoroughfare that led to the harbour. Even Bryson was taken by surprise as the mass of people came into view, by his estimate the mob was easily fifteen to twenty deep.

'It's the dock workers,' Bryson said, realising. 'They can't get to work because Reed has the middle of the place sealed off.'

'Reed, eh?' Crowley said. 'Well if they try to break through I wouldn't fancy their chances.' Crowley laughed and nudged Lafferty.

Bryson didn't respond. If they broke the cordon he was fairly certain that Reed would indeed take a good number down, but they would soon have the better of him and his constables. Even the Sergeant couldn't hold a swarm of angry dock workers much longer. He pulled up a short walk from the crowd so as not to be conspicuous, and once parked he turned to face Crowley.

'Right, how long do you think you'll need to be in there? Because that's a restless crowd and it's getting more agitated by the minute.'

Crowley puffed his cheeks and closed his eyes, looking up as though he were working through his monthly accounts. After a moment he returned his gaze to Bryson and adopted the imperious look he wore when trying to appear important.

'Couple of hours I should say.'

'A couple of hours!' Bryson almost croaked the sentence out. 'Crowley you don't have a couple of hours, for God's sake man, that crowd is currently pissed off, and in about twenty minutes it's going to reach the murderous stage.'

'Nonsense,' Crowley snorted.

'Excuse me?' Bryson wasn't in the mood for this, not at all. 'Look Crowley I only came to get you because I promised…'

Crowley climbed out of the car.

Bryson looked at Lafferty who tried to make himself invisible using the power of embarrassment.

'JESUS!' Bryson shouted, slamming the palms of his hands onto the steering wheel. He got out of the car and ran to Crowley.

'What are you doing?' he snarled, careful not to raise his voice too loud lest he caught the attention of the crowd.

'I'm going to investigate the scene,' Crowley replied as though the Inspector had just asked him what time it was.

'You won't have time, this lot are going to go off and soon.' Bryson insisted.

Crowley stopped and faced the Inspector. 'Do you know why that crowd is there Inspector?'

'What?' Bryson asked.

'Why are they there, why haven't they left the scene?'

'Because they want to go to work you fucking imbecile, and because they want to know what's going on.'

'Correct on both points, not the imbecile bit though, which I'm going to let go because you are clearly having one of your moments.'

Before Bryson could advise him that he was going to punch his teeth in Crowley removed his hat and gripped the Inspectors arm.

'Don't worry, I'll take care of it, you just wait here and when people ask you anything just nod and say yes.' Crowley gave him a friendly slap on the arm and walked into to the crowd before Bryson could think to stop him.

It didn't take long. Minutes? Possibly only a minute. Whatever the time scale, Bryson couldn't believe the speed at which people began to disperse from the area.

No one stopped to ask him questions, they simply hurried by, some looked back as they went but none stopped. Bryson would swear, when asked, that he had seen a ripple of heads as they turned to face each other in the crowd. Around it went, a little shockwave of information being passed from mouth to ear and at the epicentre of it all was the great liar himself.

With the crowd thinned to just a handful of the most resilient, and from the looks of it, most debased of the onlookers Bryson strode quickly to Crowley's side. A confused-looking Constable was approaching the occultist, ready to halt him, as Bryson caught up.

'It's alright lad, he's with me,' Bryson said.

'Right you are, Sir,' the constable replied, and as the two were about to continue towards Reed asked quietly, 'Is it true, Sir?'

Bryson stopped. 'Is what true Constable?'

'About the plague Sir...that the plague has done for some lads in there.' The nervousness in the officer's voice was plain.

Bryson glanced at Crowley and then back to the Constable. 'Nothing certain yet lad, just make sure that people keep their distance while we check it out.'

'Yessir,' The constable replied and quickly returned to his station. A little further away than his station.

Reed walked over.

'Plague, Sir?' Reed's moustache enquired.

'Crowley,' Bryson replied by way of explanation.

'I see, Sir.' The moustache scrutinised Crowley, then turned and led them into the warehouse.

Inside Bryson watched without interruption as Crowley studied the scene, spending a few moments examining each of the symbols contained within a narrow channel. It followed the circumference up to a spot on the eastern point of the circle. Here there was a very definite gap.

Crowley didn't appear to be very interested in the poor fellows that were lightly swinging above it, and to his surprise within five or six minutes he announced to Bryson, 'Right, all done.'

'What, already? Done?' Bryson asked.

'Yes. I think I have the measure of it,' Crowley replied

'But you've barely been here five minutes, you said you would be a couple of hours.' Bryson pointed to the suspended corpses. 'You haven't even examined the bodies.'

'Why on earth would I want to go poking around dead people?' Crowley gave Bryson a disgusted look, 'I'm not a coroner.'

'But…aren't you looking for…tell-tale signs of…whatever did this? Bryson realised he was grasping here, he had assumed that the bodies would be important as a clue, because they should be. That's how coppering worked, everything was a clue, the whole scene, and everything had to be checked and noted and checked again. You had to knock on doors, pressure witnesses and call in favours.

'A man did this, Inspector. Well, men,' Crowley stated.

'Like a gang? It's a gang thing?'

'Kind of. I suppose. But not the sort of gang you're used to dealing with, of course,' Crowley pointed to the circle.

'That isn't a summoning circle, so whoever did this wasn't trying to bring anything through the Shadow and Void. It's an offering.' He indicated the bodies. 'Those young men were sacrificed to the God of the people that made the circle. I shouldn't worry about it,' he said and made to leave.

Bryson caught Crowley's arm as was about to pass.

'Shouldn't worry about it!' Bryson spat the words out. 'This is wholesale murder, butchery in the heart of the Capital, man, when this gets out there will be riots, that is, of course, once the riots over the make-believe plague you've started have finished.'

'Poppycock,' Crowley replied. 'Just say it's a turf war or something. The usual gang stuff, no one's hurt by a little cover up.'

'No one's hurt!' Bryson released Crowley's arm and pointed up, 'What about those poor sods eh?'

Crowley sighed, as though the stress of being vague and unhelpful was tiring him, 'They weren't murdered inspector, they were willing participants.'

Bryson's jaw went slack.

'This is a cult that operates across the world, well at least in most of the places where civilisation hasn't quite caught up to the nineteenth century.

Granted it's odd to see them at work in so modern a place...and so publicly, but the ritual is fairly innocuous, it's just topping up favours with their God. A bit like throwing coins into the collection box really.'

Bryson searched Crowley's expression for any sign at all that his apparent indifference to the deaths of the men was anything other than genuine, but he could see nothing.

'You're a monster.' Bryson said quietly.

'Nonsense,' Crowley replied. 'I'm a professional. I'm a surgeon examining a tumour. Those boys couldn't have been happier to die, and if you or I were here to try and stop them they would have cut off our heads and decorated the harbour with our innards. So fuck them and fuck your judgmental attitude inspector. Now, I'm going for breakfast and I sincerely hope that I won't be paying for it.'

Bryson glared at Crowley for a moment. Once again thoughts of employing *His Majesty's Pleasure* briefly floated across his conscience but then receded as the coppering portion of his brain kicked in, bringing its notepad that recorded all conversations.

''Publicly',' Bryson said.

Crowley had been about to leave but he paused and narrowed his eyes a little. He had tried not to give anything away, tried his best. Normally offering some outlandish statement, designed to shock a person's sensibilities threw most people, but he was quickly learning that Bryson wasn't as dense as most.

'Excuse me?' Crowley said.

'You said that these things usually only happened...I don't know where, but not here, right? Not places like London and not *publicly*. So what's the story, this isn't right is it Crowley? This isn't just coins in the collection box is it, you slippery bastard?'

Crowley was quiet. He didn't like to be quiet. When struggling for an answer that would extricate him from any possible involvement or repercussions in a matter he would normally continue talking, delivering a broadside of non-information to the recipient until boredom or confusion had the better of them, and he could continue on his way.

Bryson's stare bored into him and Crowley understood that he was being read by a man whose job it was to detect lies and falsehoods, half-truths and all of the other weapons usually at his disposal.

'It's complicated.' Crowley replied, finally.

'Complicated how, Crowley?' Bryson leaned in a little closer and lowered his voice. 'And if you skirt towards the phrase, 'you wouldn't understand,' I'll make sure you spend the next few hours swinging up there with 'em.' His eyes flicked towards the victims.

His eyebrows raised just a little, in what Crowley knew to be the Inspector's '*I'm not joking*,' expression.

Crowley lifted his chin a little as though he was about to express defiance, but did briefly look to the swinging corpses.

'Well then,' Crowley's tongue moved across the inside of his lips, 'look, this isn't the place. My little distraction won't keep for long and I'm sure it will be easier to clear the area without me tootling around, so why don't we meet at lunchtime and I'll see what information I have on these fellows…from my library.

Bryson nodded slowly, 'Right, lunchtime. At the nick.'

What? Fuck no. I'm not sitting in that dungeon you call a police station, not without a warrant anyway.' Crowley's indignance was clearly genuine, and Bryson decided to slacken the line a little.

'Where then?'

'The British Museum,' Crowley replied

'Why?'

'Because of your interest in Seventeenth Century embroidery Inspector,' Crowley replied testily.

Bryson's frown. 'I'm not interested in any kind of embroidery what do you…oh I see, very good Crowley, tell you what why don't we meet at the Albert Hall as you appear to have an interest in being punched in the head.'

Crowley pursed his lips. 'The British Museum, at one. Egyptian display. You may as well bring the other two, they might learn something.'

Bryson allowed himself the smallest of smiles. 'One o' clock. I'll be there. Don't be late.'

Crowley said nothing and walked out of the warehouse. In the ten minutes or so he had been inside a crowd had begun to gather again, but not as many people were gawping as there had been previously. Reed watched him exit the building and indicated to one of his constables that Crowley should be escorted safely away.

As Crowley moved through the gathered people, ignoring questions, the constable giving people warning looks, Reed's moustache twitched.

'Nasty business,' it said.

Part 3

Bryson arrived early at the museum, only to be surprised that Crowley was already there. He was easy to spot as he had not entered the building, and was instead a few feet away from the large open doors and was engaged in a slanging match with a slightly built, aged man, in a dark brown woollen suit. Visitors to the museum looked on curiously but didn't stop as there was quite a queue for entry.

Bryson looked to Reed and Lafferty who were sat in the back of the sedan. 'Do you think there is anyone he doesn't fall out with?'

Neither man replied. Their agreement was tacit in their silence.

Climbing out of the Sedan Bryson could hear Crowley's voice above the collected chatter of the museum guests waiting to enter, and the general noise of London that filled the rest of the available space. Bryson was actually curious to find out what Crowley was creating a scene over this time, what possible slight the British Museum had caused him, or what the pale fellow in the wool suit had said or done, or implied or more likely Crowley had inferred, to give him cause for the altercation.

Probably asked the time, Bryson thought.

'Ahh, Inspector!' Crowley called out as he caught sight of the police officers making their way up the short flight of steps towards him. He was smiling broadly Bryson noted, the smile appearing the moment Crowley had noticed them, spreading across the occultist's face like a pool of syrup pouring onto the floor. He and his boys were the clearly the cavalry.

'What's going on, Crowley?' Bryson asked.

Crowley almost danced down the few steps between them and upon reaching the inspector stood at his side and pointed at the wool suited gentleman.

'Would you be so kind as to explain to this oaf that I am here today upon police business, and that any matters concerning previous incidents here are void.'

Bryson looked to the old man who was clutching a large leather bound book to his chest.

Close up he was quite a striking fellow, gaunt in appearance and short, no more than five feet tall, and as they had argued Crowley had towered over the man. He wore small round glasses with gold frames and they sat upon a chiselled roman nose. His gaze towards Crowley was baleful, thin lips tightly pressed together. The book he gripped looked old and valuable. Bryson thought that were the man able to commit murder on the steps of the British Museum the book would be used to beat Crowley to death.

'What previous matters Crowley?' Bryson asked with a hint of resignation in his voice. He had already conjured up a number of incidents that Crowley could have been involved in at a Museum.

'Misunderstandings,' Crowley replied with a politician's skill at delivering a quick and entirely empty response.

The wool-suited gentlemen began to approach them. He didn't prance down the steps as Crowley had done, instead walking with an austere gait. Bryson's first impression was that this small man, in his gold-rimmed glasses and comfortable but presentable attire was someone who was used to dealing with men like Crowley. If there were other men like Crowley.

'Good day to you, officer.' The old man thrust a hand forward towards Bryson who took it instinctively. They shook, brief, professional, firm, after which he returned to his holding fast of the leather tome.

'Good afternoon, Sir,' Bryson replied. 'I'm Inspector Bryson of the Met and these are my colleagues Sergeant Reed and Constable Lafferty.' Lafferty and Reed both touched the brims of their helmets. 'It appears you are already familiar with Mr Crowley.'

'Yes. I am indeed.' He didn't look at Crowley 'My name is Professor Algernon Kurt-Braithwaite and I am the Curator of the Museum, and if you are not here to arrest me, Inspector, please do call me Professor Braithwaite.'

'Good to meet you Professor Braithwaite and no, I'm certainly not here to arrest you, actually I'm here to meet with Mr Crowley.

'Meet with Mr Crowley, here, at the British Museum?' Braithwaite replied, suspicion evident, and this time he did allow a brief flick of his eyes towards Crowley.

'Indeed,' Bryson replied.

'Inspector are you aware of the…character of Mr Crowley, that is to say his interests and persuasions?' Braithwaite asked politely.

'If you mean do I know that Mr Crowley has somewhat unusual beliefs, and that elements of his moral character have been called in to question then yes I am, I am very aware,' Bryson replied.

He understood that he was dealing with a smart man. A clever man. He hadn't slandered Crowley for example, he had only asked if he was aware of his interests and persuasions, no opinion had been offered. Truly smart men never told you how smart they were, unlike Crowley who, smart as he was couldn't wait to show off and point out anything clever he might have had a hand in. It was much the same way with men who were very good in a fight, they never told you that they were strong and fast and agile, you just woke up with a crowd staring at you.

'Perhaps then, Inspector, you will understand why, as a matter of principle Mr Crowley has, for a long time now, been barred from this, one of his Majesty's most important institutions.'

'Barred, you say,' Bryson said. He still wasn't sure where to go with this man. His instinct alone told him that Braithwaite would not be cowed or bullied, something about the wrought iron gaze he maintained suggested that he had seen things that perhaps were not meant to be seen and then he had looked again, just to be sure. He could probably just barge in he supposed, ignore any protests, but the fact was that he didn't yet know why he needed to be here. Crowley had sprung this upon him and...

Have I been played? he suddenly thought. *Has that bastard done me up?*

Bryson's mind produced the facts and assembled them into a theory. *He's obviously not welcome here, he knows he has some information I need...no...that I think I need, because he made me think that I wanted it by pretending that I didn't need it....* His thoughts reeled. *I've been cunted!*

'Yes Inspector. We felt it was required to exclude Mr Crowley from the museum following numerous attempts by him to enter areas that are not permitted to members of the public. We also suspect that attempts have been made to leave the premises with items about his person that are the property of His Majesty and the British public.'

'Bollocks,' Crowley said, leaning in towards Braithwaite. 'Why don't you tell him what those private areas contain and where those items came from in the first place, you pernicious little toad.'

'Crowley!' Bryson snapped and to his surprise Crowley retreated.

'He is also renowned for gratuitously insulting academics, clergymen and officials both within and without these walls.' Braithwaite added.

'Well, I can certainly believe every word of that Professor Braithwaite.' Crowley made to chip in, no doubt with some forceful and abuse-laden torrent but Bryson held up a hand which halted him.

'However, the unfortunate fact of the matter is that Mr Crowley is currently assisting us with a very serious situation, and it is important that we gain access to the Museum. Rest assured that I will be observing any and all of Mr Crowley's movements and Sergeant Reed will make sure that he is polite and gracious to any person, or persons, that are unlucky enough to have to speak to him.'

Braithwaite looked at the Sergeant. A bony finger pushed up his spectacles although they had no chance of slipping from his commanding nose.

Reed's moustache acknowledged that he was prepared to help Crowley remember that he was a guest of the museum by whatever means necessary should it be required.

'Very well. It seems to serve no purpose to stand here upon the steps, creating an exhibition for our guests who have a genuine desire to explore the knowledge within.' He turned his attention to Crowley. 'You may enter, Mr Crowley, so long as it is understood that you,' he turned back to Bryson, 'personally shoulder all responsibility for him whilst he is on the premises Inspector.'

'Understood,' Bryson replied gravely.

Braithwaite flicked his gaze over each of the men then turned and walked up the steps. 'Follow me, I'll let you through.'

As they ascended Bryson kept pace with the Professor. He could hear Crowley muttering, probably slandering Braithwaite to the entirely uninterested officers either side of him.

'May I ask what the book is?' Bryson asked, his interest genuine.

'It is the Germanus Theologoram, an early Seventeenth Century collection of biographies of German theologians.' Braithwaite replied. 'I don't particularly like Germans and was considering using it to beat Mr Crowley to a pulp if he tried to gain entry by force.'

'Oh, I see,' Bryson replied. 'I don't suppose you'd be prepared to loan it out at some time would you?'

Braithwaite's thin lips briefly creaked into a narrow smile.

Bryson couldn't help but be awed by the Museum. As Braithwaite walked them through room after room of staggering examples of archaeological and natural history, he chided himself for not having taken advantage of the benefits that London had. These places were rewards for existing within the machine. Why, after a day of looking at corpses and threatening villains didn't he come to somewhere like this and engage with the history and culture and world that existed outside of the grime and oppression of the City?

He knew why. Because to allow his mind to wander from the job, to allow the wonder and beauty of lives and civilisations long dead to enter his thoughts, would blunt the edge he needed to deal with the lives that were still going on around him.

They passed a room filled with stone carvings, bas-relief and statues from Egypt. Visitors were allowed to stand right up to them, and if they timed it well enough, they could actually reach out and run a hand down the coarse surface without a member of the museum staff spotting them. They could touch something that a person had created thousands of years ago.

Braithwaite appeared to be taking them to the very furthest part of the museum and this involved a good deal of climbing stairs, and taking short detours through inconspicuous side doors. Crowley had spoken to the curator briefly and he was pleased to see, politely. Whatever the exchange concerned, Bryson had heard him mention something that sounded like Cho-Cho. Braithwaite appeared to know exactly what Crowley was talking about. Bryson also thought that Crowley had requested something towards the end of the conversation and that Braithwaite had refused. The old man had slowly shook his head as Crowley had engaged with him over this last part and the occultist, although maintaining his civility as required, had a definite dark look about him when it was over.

They entered another of the smaller rooms in which the museum held artefacts of a smaller nature and from the lesser-known areas of the world. There were a few nameplates here and there but these gave very scant information on what the objects they were associated with were for or represented. Many were prefixed with Tibetan or Burmese as their indication of origin.

Braithwaite stopped in the middle of the room and then walked towards the wall to the right of him. He paused by a wooden stand that bore a head carved from a solid block of stone, the Inspector assumed it represented some aboriginal King or other ancient person of note. He turned to Crowley.

'Are you absolutely sure about this, Crowley?' Braithwaite asked.

Bryson noted there was no 'Mr' now, he was simply Crowley, and clearly the gentlemanly reference to him was for the public to see and to allow him to maintain some distance socially. The Professor knew Crowley far more than as just an annoyance in the work place.

'I promise you Algernon, these men can be trusted and they have what it takes. I've witnessed it with my own eyes.'

Braithwaite was still for a moment. He then reached inside the collar of his shirt, no mean feat as it was stiff with starch, and produced a chain upon which was a single ornate key. He slipped the loop over his head and reached behind the stone head. After a moment there was an audible click and in the wall immediately ahead of him a faint dark line appeared.

Braithwaite looked around the room, particularly at the entrance. Satisfied that no one was going to wander in he gave the wall a light push with his palm, just to the right of the line that had appeared. Another click and suddenly where there had only been a wall there was now a dark rectangular space. A doorway.

'Quickly if you please gentlemen.' The professor stepped aside to allow them entry, all the while observing the far side of the room in case a tourist stumbled on to this secret. Bryson led the way, followed by Reed and Lafferty. Crowley took up his usual position that gave him the best chance of running away in the event of something unexpected. Braithwaite followed, taking one last glance around and then pulling the secret door to.

It was dark in the room. Crowley struck a match but just as the flame flared up it was immediately blown out by Braithwaite.

'Don't mess about, Crowley,' Braithwaite scolded. 'No naked flames in here.' There was the sound of movement across a wooden floor and another clicking sound. This time instead of a door opening an array of bulbs gently glowed into life revealing the room they stood within. It was equal to the space it was adjacent to except instead of plinths, cabinets and wall hangings there was only shelving, row after row of wooden constructs.

Upon these shelves were boxes of various sizes, some cardboard, some metal, and some wood. All bore a label on the front of them, although from where he stood, Bryson couldn't make out what any of them said, the print was small and typed.

'Before I take you to the items that Mr Crowley has requested I wish to show you something else gentlemen, a little test if you will,' Braithwaite said.

'Really, Braithwaite, I've already explained what they've witnessed, surely that's enough?' Crowley responded testily and Bryson detected a hint of something rare in Crowley, compassion.

'No. I insist,' Braithwaite said firmly. 'A demon, lesser greater or otherwise, doesn't quite cut it where *he* might be concerned. There are sights and then there are *sights* Crowley, they must see the object and according to their reaction I will proceed, or we will conclude this little adventure immediately.'

Crowley puffed. 'Very well.'

'Beg pardon, Mr B.,' Lafferty said, taking a step forward, 'but it ain't gonna be anything' 'orrible is it? Only I've had some lunch and my innards, well, they don't take too kindly to the 'orrible stuff.'

Braithwaite's face wrinkled 'Mr B?' he said.

Crowley muttered, 'It's something he does, just ignore it.'

'Oh I see,' Braithwaite replied in a tone that suggested he didn't see at all. 'Well, Constable, I wouldn't say horrible,' Braithwaite found himself exaggerating the *h* in horrible to make up for Lafferty's total abandonment of it. 'What I wish you to see is…challenging.'

'How many eyes has it got?' Reed asked.

'Er… no eyes, Sergeant, it's a piece of rock,' Braithwaite replied.

Lafferty's shoulders relaxed a little and even Reed appeared to assume a less guarded stance although it was harder to tell with him. The Sergeant's usual position was straight and unmoving, the low brim and huge moustache coupled with his impressive build presented a formidable defensive wall. The statues in the halls of the museum could appear more animated.

'Very well,' Reed's moustache barely twitched.

While Reed and Lafferty appeared to be taking things fairly stoically Bryson had become quite nervous. Within a few minutes this had gone from being a lunchtime meeting, in a very public place, to a clandestine gathering in a secret chamber. Talk was in the air of dark things, tests and sights. He had put his lads through the mill the last time he had involved them with Crowley and he couldn't help but think that it was about to happen all over again.

'Follow me please, gentlemen,' Braithwaite said. He started off down a channel created by the rows of shelves. Bryson noticed that many of the boxes were tightly sealed with straps and in a couple of instances a lock and chain. Halfway across the room the shelves stopped for a distance of about ten feet until the next set of rows continued and here, in the middle, was a large table with a solitary chair. A single bulb was suspended above it providing strong and even light.

'Bear with me just a moment gentlemen, I'll return shortly.' Braithwaite walked to the end of one of the far rows and then disappeared into it.

'What's this all about Crowley?' Bryson hissed.

'Don't worry, you'll be fine.' He looked at Lafferty and Reed. 'You too. I'm confident that you have what it takes.'

'What it takes?' Bryson said.

'Yes, you know, the right stuff, a stiff upper lip, big balls, that kind of thing.'

'Big balls, Crowley?' Bryson repeated.

'Metaphorical big balls of course Inspector.'

Braithwaite reappeared and was carrying one of the larger boxes. It was a plain enough container made from what looked like pine boards. On the front, like all of the other boxes, was a label, and Bryson could see that rather than any words there was just an alphanumeric code. A reference of some sort, he thought, most likely there was a huge ledger somewhere that listed the contents of every box and file in the building. He had a sudden desire to get his hands on that item, should it exist, he had no doubt that many, many unsolved crimes might have clues right here in this room.

The professor carefully laid the box upon the table, it was heavy and he struggled a little to set it down evenly. When done he looked at his guests and placed the palm of his left hand upon the lid.

'Gentlemen, this artefact was discovered in the furthest explored reaches of the Antarctic. I will not go into its history, suffice to say that as with almost all of the items of this type it came to us at great expense, and please understand that I do not mean that any monetary cost was involved. Let me also add that we, despite years of research, don't know what it is. We don't know what it represents or even what it is made of. We know nothing, other than it being a mineral substance that has presumably been fashioned in its appearance by means other than natural. Beyond that we are at a loss.'

'Why do we need to see this?' Bryson asked. 'What's the point of it, is it connected to my case?'

Braithwaite needlessly adjusted his glasses with his bony finger.

'No, at least not directly Inspector. You must understand that I have taken great faith in bringing you here, into this room. I have done so solely based on what Mr Crowley has informed me about you, about all of you. Take note that I don't care much at all for Crowley, neither his attitude nor his activities, but we do share a common interest and a singular desire to ensure that certain forces are kept in check.'

'Forces?' Bryson said.

'If I may Inspector?' Braithwaite said in a cold tone of admonishment at being interrupted. Bryson flushed a little and gave a curt nod.

'You recently experienced a taste of what is out there, what is guessed at and whispered about by the great masses of people, everyday folk who only wish to live out their lives in an ordinary and harmless fashion. Granted Inspector that you deal with the other side of this, the smaller portion of humanity whose goals are perhaps more base, more primal but still, even those people are protected from what lies beyond their reason.' Braithwaite patted the lid of the box.

'When a person like that is presented with something that is alien to their understanding, something that exceeds their capacity to rationalise, something so horrible, so awful, sometimes quite so vast that to try and comprehend it results only in the delicate framework of the mind collapsing. It is because the collapse is from under the weight of the truth that is revealed, their minds will often retreat from it, consciousness and reason seek safety buried away in their minds own subconscious. Madness Inspector! Fear, paranoia, a paralysis of sanity is their defence, however this leaves them open to overt threats and subtle persuasions from the forces I have mentioned.' Braithwaite looked around at each of them.

'What is inside this box is not the forces I am talking about, but I do believe it to be of their world, or at least one of them, and it will I hope, present further evidence of what I have suggested to you. That we are dealing with situations in which what we perceive as the normal rules of our universe, simply do not apply.'

At that he lifted the lid.

Interlude

Ravensblack Hall 3 months earlier

As the doors closed behind him Crowley watched the Mokoi cautiously move around the altar and mirroring its movement he took sideways steps in the opposite direction. Slowly, they circled each other. Roman's face, animated by the demon, licked at its lips, its eyes unblinking.

Crowley could feel the heat the runes patterned upon his skin generated in the presence of a creature of the Shadow and Void. No smoke entered the room, the door was not your average bit of carpentry, but this also meant that no air was coming through either yet. Despite this, he could feel the heat behind the door as the fire raged beyond

Crowley fully understood it was not just the Mokoi that was against the clock.

After they had walked in almost a full circle it was clear to him that the thing was entirely powerless to attack him. He had known from the start, or at least once he had realised the nature of the entity he was dealing with, that his body was fashioned with sufficient wards against it, but until this moment he had not been completely certain of just how totally he was protected.

This being the case there was a chance, slight though it was, that he might not be able to save Roman's skin, but he could save his soul. He just didn't want to.

'Have you picked up any of the language yet?' Crowley asked the creature.

Roman stopped. The Mokoi continued to dextrously twirl the knife in its prisoner's fingers.

'Crowleeeee,' it hissed.

'Very good,' Crowley replied, he knew when these things took possession of a mind they would ransack its memories and as they went through them, seek out anything that would further its cause. It was only natural that they would begin to adapt to the nature of its host's communication.

The Mokoi had been in control of Roman for a good few hours, and while at first English would have been nothing more than a garbled mess of sounds, by now it would probably have the basics at least.

'How is Roman doing? Locked away nice and tight in his own nightmares I expect?'

The creature let out a deep, guttural laugh, like a drain gurgling as air moved through slime and shit.

'I'll take that as a yes.' Crowley said. Roman had a considerable mop of hair, his pretty little face was cloaked in fine blonde locks except these were now for the most part caked in drying blood. At the back, however, his leonine mane had escaped being spattered and Crowley could see that the hairs were lifting a little. Something was drawing them back as though static was attracting them. It had to be the gate.

He still couldn't see the portal but he could certainly sense its presence. It was only a weak gravitational pull upon him but for the Mokoi it would strong and compelling. If the creature was to do anything it would have to be soon, or it would succumb to the gate as the energy it was using to negate the attraction depleted. When that happened the Mokoi would be drawn back into its own world. Now was the time to make a deal.

'You know, you've had quite a bit of fun here but I think we both know this is the end of all that.'

Roman hissed again. 'Crowleeee,' it spat, and the occultist reckoned that to be translated roughly to 'go fuck yourself.'

'Now, now, no need to be hasty. I mean, just because you're going to have to go home it doesn't mean you have to go alone, does it?'

The Mokoi stopped spinning the knife. What it had wanted to do, the moment Crowley opened the door, was open him up. It had wanted to draw Roman's fingers through his guts and suck out each of the sorcerer's eyes. The Crowley positively vibrated with energy, far more than the insipid excuse of a man that it inhabited now. If it could take him, it could feed off him for a long time, it could escape the house as the walls that bore the runes collapsed and would be free to establish its domain on Earth.

Except none of that was possible. The Crowley was completely protected, both mentally and physically. With no puppets to do its bidding, to fight for and defend it, all the Crowley had to do was touch the skin of its host and it would be dismissed from existence.

But it hadn't. Instead the Crowley had kept its distance, it had spoken to the Mokoi of a *deal*, it chewed through Roman's memories, a bargain, an accord. A deal was something that would benefit them both. The Mokoi was intrigued now. The gate almost had it, it could not stay here any longer, but surely the Crowley would also be ended here should he stay? The charms and protections upon its loathsome body couldn't protect it from the elements of its own world.

It would listen to the *deal*. The Crowley might be a greater sorcerer than it had considered, the Crowley might be prepared to help it, perhaps the human was an ally of the Shadow and Void.

'Deeaaaaal, yessss,' the Mokoi said. 'Crowleeee.'

Crowley smiled his shark smile. 'A wise decision my friend, a very wise decision.'

Part 4

Braithwaite reached into the box with both hands. It appeared to Bryson that he struggled with the contents for a moment, his hands were moving inside as though he couldn't quite determine how to grip whatever was in there. Finally, he seized something and withdrew it. The professor had not misled them, it was a piece of rock, but it was no ordinary chunk of granite, marble or basalt or any other typical mineral of the earth. This was apparent immediately as there was a faint glow to its surface. Further to this, the glow was not static, rather it pulsed across the stone in a random fashion.

As its whole came into view, Braithwaite placed it onto the table and all were compelled to look away for a moment, even the professor. It was instinctive, like turning your head from a loud bang or a sudden, dazzling flash of light, but it was not a noise or blinding beam that struck each man.

It was angles.

The lump of rock had been fashioned in some manner, as one might carve a relief or decoration upon the coving of a monument or building. Hands, Bryson assumed it was hands, had chiselled with skill the lines and shapes that separated the carved rock from the raw original, evidenced in that this piece had clearly broken away from some larger whole. But the angles, the angles were all wrong!

No matter how he tried to look at the piece, whether he narrowed his eyes or he tilted his head, blinked repeatedly to clear his vision, Bryson still could not maintain his observation of it. It was though the lines moved in a way that was uncomfortable to his senses. As he tried to follow what to all intents and purposes was a straight line in the work he would get lost, his eyes would ache and he would once again look away from it. He glanced at the others, it was the same for each of them, even Crowley, who did appear to have some measure of resistance and held his gaze longer, still had to look down occasionally.

The professor had only looked at the piece briefly once it had been placed on the table. Now he studied the reactions of the policemen. Bryson caught his eye but Braithwaite gave nothing away in his expression.

'What is it?' Lafferty asked, and all of them looked away from the rock once more. Bryson was grateful that the lad had spoken up as he wasn't sure how long the Professor was going to subject them to this test of his.

'To be perfectly honest with you Constable, we don't know. We have theories, of course, but they're just that, theories. At the moment the best that we can postulate, and again I must stress that I offer only an unsupported opinion, is that it is a piece of masonry, worked upon, the lines are not naturally formed, from a dimension that is presently alien to us.'

'Alien?' Bryson asked. 'Like the Shadow place that Crowley was going on about?'

The professor looked to Crowley with a severe expression of accusation upon his face. Crowley shrugged.

He turned back to Bryson. 'No, at least we think not. This is possibly from a realm that I don't feel comfortable discussing, even here in this protected place, but once I am satisfied that you gentlemen are the kind of people able to deal with such information I will enlighten you.'

To the relief of the group Braithwaite lifted the object and returned it to the box. None of them sought a final inspection of it.

'That is of course unless Crowley has already disgorged every secret we have from his perpetually open mouth by then.'

'No need for that,' Crowley grunted.

'Did we pass, Sir?' Lafferty asked. All eyes turned to him. 'I mean the test, with the rock, did we pass?'

Braithwaite placed the lid onto the box and patted it gently once again. 'Yes, actually you did.' He placed his hands flat on the table and looked at each man in turn. 'Since we first acquired that item it has been revealed to very few, it acts as a kind of litmus test. Anyone who can stand to look at it for more than even a second has something about them, a hardening if you will, their minds are able to not only accept what they are seeing, even though they might be repulsed by it, they can also reason with its existence.'

'Tell them what happens if they can't reason with it.' Crowley chimed in.

Braithwaite's lower lip moved a little, an involuntary twitch of his muscles as he thought through his response.

'Madness,' he said. 'As I mentioned earlier, our minds protect, us or at least that's the aim of our impressively evolved but hardly flawless brain. When faced with something that's beyond the normal, let us say the supernatural, or perhaps a better example would be some horror like a man possessed by a demonic entity that ritualistically murders dozens of people in order to gain their life essence to fuel its existence on this earth.'

Braithwaite paused to check that all were fully aware of what he was referring to. 'The sheer terror that this vision, this situation, would cause to most ordinary people would result in their mind fleeing into itself. They would be cocooned in a world of their own devising until they perceived that the threat had passed, but of course we know that escaping from that world is very difficult. By rights you gentlemen should have run screaming from Ravensblack Hall or crawled into a corner and gibbered like idiots as the nightmare unfolded.

'I was scared,' Lafferty said, with some embarrassment.

'As you should have been!' Braithwaite returned, his voice elevated. 'As any man or woman would be in such a position. Fear is important to us, it is another of our evolutionary mechanisms, and it speeds our thinking, pumps adrenalin into our muscles and prepares us to fight or flee! It is terror that we have to avoid, when we cross from a respectful fear of our enemy and become terrified of it then we are at its mercy.' Braithwaite thumped a fist upon the table.

Bryson was impressed at the man's conviction, he spoke with absolute certainty and commanded their attention. His diminutive size was dwarfed by his character and charisma. The professor paused again and regained his cool composure.

'So in short, this reveals to me that Crowley could well be right about your ability to withstand the horrors and dangers of what we face.'

'Who's 'we'?' Bryson asked.

'Everybody, Inspector. Humanity. You, me, our families and our friends, people and cultures that may be out there that we have not even discovered yet. There is a darkness coming. It seeks to gain entry to this world and to find a way to claim it. It is the task, the duty of people like us to stop it.'

'A darkness?' Bryson said.

'Evil, Inspector. Alien, diabolical and ruthless. The gate at Ravensblack is how they enter our world from theirs.' Braithwaite replied.

'How do we stop them?' Lafferty asked, and Bryson detected no hint of nervousness in his voice now.

'That will be up to you, Constable. If you and your colleagues are prepared to take an oath of secrecy and to commit to fighting this threat with every fibre of you being, if you feel that your integrity is sufficient, then I will see to it that the methods and equipment required are at your disposal.'

'If I may Professor?' Bryson said,

Braithwaite nodded. 'Of course inspector.'

'This is a bit much I think.' He pointed at the box. 'That thing, what happened at Ravensblack Hall and of course the scene at the docks this morning which you have clearly, somehow, been fully appraised of already, I get that it's not normal by any stretch of the imagination, but Professor I deal with incidents that are not normal every single day.

People don't normally murder each other, they don't even normally rob or cheat each other either, and the exception is a handful of miscreants in a city of millions.

'Do any of them walk around without their heads Inspector?' Braithwaite's question was delivered with detachment and not with the dripping sarcasm that Bryson would expect from Crowley.

'No, no they don't, but…' Bryson struggled not just with the words but with the very ideas that were being thrown at him. 'I don't think this is something that I…that we,' he indicated Lafferty and Reed, 'can help with.'

'Inspector, believe me when I say that I understand fully your reticence, were I in your position, and in truth I once was, I too would have reservations and doubts, concerns for my colleagues also. None of this is a problem, in fact it speaks well of your reason and character. You are here today because Crowley believes that there may be something within the museum that could help with your current case. I suggest that you go about that business, get this matter resolved as it is your task at hand and once that is done think upon what I have said.'

Braithwaite looked to each of the men in turn. 'I must of course ask you to keep both the matters we have spoken about today, and the existence of this room and what you have seen here, strictly confidential.'

All heads nodded.

'Crowley, on the grounds that you have for once done the right thing I will leave you to your own recognisance in the museum, but I expect you to neither steal nor deface any of the items here. Believe me when I state that should you breach the trust of this institution or my Order one more time the repercussions will be most unwelcome to you.'

'How very fucking noble of you,' Crowley replied.

Braithwaite ignored him. 'Gentlemen, if you will make your way to the end of the room, where you first entered, I will check that we are clear to exit and then you may begin your investigation. I believe that Mr Crowley will want you to view our relics of Burmese origin.' At this the professor strode back along the aisle they had first walked down. Bryson started to follow but noticed Crowley eyeing the boxed object.

'Don't even think about it, Crowley,' he said quietly but with force.

'I was just checking that the lid was on correctly,' Crowley said, feigning surprise and emotional hurt. He felt a pressure on his back as Reed guided him forwards.

'Move it, Crowley,' Reed uttered from beneath his watchful growth.

When they reached the door they had entered by Bryson noticed there was a small green light above it. Next to this was a similar bulb but with a red coat, this was not illuminated whereas the green light twinkled. He assumed that this must mean the room beyond was clear of the public.

Braithwaite pressed a panel to the right of the door and the 'click' that had been heard earlier sounded again. The professor pulled open the door and ushered the men out. Once they were assembled he pushed the door to, even with his knowledge of its existence Bryson couldn't see any trace of it once it was closed.

'Right gentlemen, good luck with your investigation. I look forward to speaking to you all once again should you be interested in assisting with what I assure you is something that could one day affect us all. Until that time, if I may be of any assistance do not hesitate to contact me.'

He shook the hand of each of the men leaving Crowley to the last. As their hands gripped Braithwaite looked up at the occultist and leaned in a little closer.

'I'm not entirely sure what it is, Crowley, but something is different about you. Something…I can't quite put my finger on.' Braithwaite's eyes searched Crowley's as though trying whip curtains away from a figure hiding behind them. 'However, this feels right to me,' He indicated the policemen with a nod of his head. 'I hope that perhaps we will continue to see you in a new light.'

Crowley also leaned in. 'Don't think for a second that I'm going to suddenly leap into bed with the Templarii, Algernon. I'd sooner go down on Napoleon's corpse.'

Unfazed, Algernon smiled. 'Well, I do have contacts across the globe Crowley, I'll see what I can do.'

The two men released their grip upon each other. Braithwaite bowed slightly toward the group. 'Good day gentlemen,' he said and exited the room.

They stood for a moment in a dazed silence until Crowley clapped his hands together. 'Well, wasn't that exciting?' he smiled and took the Inspector by his elbow. 'So, on with the show. This morning's little escapade, little dark chaps swinging from the rafters, magic circles and buckets and buckets of blood, let's see what we can make of that.' Before Bryson could respond he felt himself being guided towards the nearest corner of the room. The others followed silently behind.

This part of the room was home to a number of glass cabinets at waist height. Inside were various obviously ancient artefacts, simple jewellery such as leather bracelets, rings carved from stone, necklaces with teeth and other bones secured to them and other primitive, decorative items.

'You see all this?' Crowley swept his hand expansively, 'no one comes here to see this.' He turned to face the wall and pointed up to a series of objects that lined upon a shelf that was too high to reach. 'That is what the public really come to see.'

At first glance Bryson wasn't entirely sure what he was seeing but as he squinted he realised that the dark, leathery balls were heads, shrunken heads.

'Dear Lord…' he said.

'Marvellous, aren't they?' Crowley said. 'Not easy to achieve either, you really have to know what you are doing. Get the wrong mix in the pot, a touch too much heat, and all you'll have is a boiled skull.'

'It's obscene,' Bryson retorted

'It's religion,' Crowley countered. 'And more importantly it's the religion of those chaps you found this morning.'

Part 5

Bryson realised that it wasn't hard listening to Crowley, at least if his commentary wasn't directed at you. The man spoke eloquently when he wanted to but steered from language that was not needed for the likes of him and his lads. They weren't stupid, at least Bryson felt that he and his colleagues had enough wit and savvy to engage with those who were perhaps more learned if they were prepared to give them a little time and simple explanation. Crowley appeared to be gracious enough to do this without being asked.

It was also quickly apparent that the occultist's knowledge of history, geography and all aspects of the sciences was vast.

He spoke with absolute confidence of his subject, be it the origins of the religion at hand or the demographics of the land it was situated in. His voice was refined and smooth, almost musical and although he never dropped the clarity that the upper classes employed in their diction it didn't jar in Bryson's ears as so many of them did.

'They are, I'm afraid, entirely cannibalistic in their choice of diet.' Crowley stretched, his heels leaving the floor and used his index finger to point at markings across the forehead of one of the shrilled faces.

'You see this one, see the scars?' He looked over his shoulder, the policemen nodded. 'This chap would have been a Shaman, a sort of head priest to the tribe. It would be his job to administer all of the rites and rituals.'

'Why's his head up there then?' Bryson asked.

'Ah well, you see,' Crowley's heels returned to the floor and he turned to face his audience. It had now swelled in number, a collection of well turned-out ladies and gentlemen had wandered in to the hall as he had been describing the various topographies of Burma and its outlying regions. 'It is also the Shaman's task to ensure that suitable flesh, human flesh is always available.' There were gasps and a horrified 'Oh my' from one of the ladies. No one departed however.

'In the event that no suitable meat was made available the Shaman would be the first to be added to the new austerity menu while the tribe sought out new hunting grounds.

A replacement Shaman would be initiated, headhunted so to speak,' Crowley said and laughed. The crowd stared at him blankly.

'Ah of course, not familiar with the term.' Crowley said, somewhat quickly Bryson thought, as though he had said something he shouldn't, although the Inspector couldn't perceive what it might be.

'I say,' a gentleman's voice from the gathered spectators. 'Excuse me, Sir, but why on earth would these savages partake of human flesh? Surely their locale would be swarming with animals fit for consumption.'

'Why, for their God, Sir!' Crowley said for the benefit of all assembled. 'To appease their deity, by consuming the very essence of mankind and thereupon transmitting their energy to it.' Crowley lowered his head a little and looked up at the audience through his heavily hooded eyes. Bryson knew that this was pure showmanship. Crowley was enjoying himself.

The occultist lowered his voice and spoke in a smooth baritone. 'What you call a demon, they call master, as you worship your Christian God so they are in thrall to creatures that exist out of our time and space. It is through these people that the Outer Gods can gain some small measure of access to our world, and from there they work tirelessly to gain a foothold. Souls is what they seek, ladies and gentlemen, the everlasting essence of mankind, and the conduit of energies beyond our comprehension. The Tcho-Tcho wish to feed our souls to their God.'

'Hah!' the gentlemen replied. 'Bloody savages, bloody barbarians, they just need the bloody army over there, that'll sort them out.' There were muted utterances from the crowd 'hear hear' and 'good show.'

'Charles dear...language.' A woman Bryson presumed to be the gentleman's wife looked a little embarrassed at her husband's stridency. 'I must apologise, my husband is a Colonel for His Majesty's armed forces.' A few more 'good shows' rippled around.

'Not at all, madam,' Crowley replied. 'After all, what kind of a religion would Christianity be if it was based on horrific torture, mass murder, raising the dead and the eating of a person's flesh?'

'Well...quite, indeed,' the lady replied. A few more 'hear hears' and 'good shows' did the rounds but then there was a peculiar quiet as though the crowd were uneasy with what had just been said.

'So there you have it. The Tcho-Tcho tribe of Burma, a singularly sadistic, cannibalistic and utterly devoted race of people who, thank heavens are not at large in London. Our fine city, our jewel in His Majesty's crown.' Crowley took a small bow as the audience immediately and politely applauded. He smiled at Bryson from his bowed position.

With the show over the crowd began to spread out, visiting the other displays in the hall or wandering off into the next section that covered Australian aboriginal peoples.

'Any need for all that Crowley? Bryson asked.

'They're sheep, Inspector. Too stupid to realise that they're only alive so that they can be sheared every now and then, and when they can't produce anything valuable society will eat them,' Crowley replied scornfully.

'Don't you believe in God, Mr Crowley?' Reed's moustache enquired with a low, earnest tone.

'Of course I believe in God, Sergeant,' Crowley snapped, 'I'm no atheist, I'm the opposite. The problem is that I believe in all of the gods, and I know that they're all cunts.'

'Crowley!' Bryson hissed between clenched teeth. He quickly looked around to ensure that there were no women or children in close proximity. 'For God's sake, man, have some sense of propriety.'

'Fuck all that,' Crowley replied. 'But we're done here, I've told you who you are up after so it's up to you now.' He started to leave.

'Where do you think you're going?' Bryson asked. Crowley stopped and looked at him with a frown.

'I'm going home. I've done my bit. These blokes are only human so your guns will do the job this time, you don't need me. Find them, I strongly suggest you shoot them, and there you go.' He gave a mockingly casual salute. 'Ta ta,' he said and continued on his way.

'Want me to stop him, Boss?' Reed asked but Bryson sighed.

'No …no let him go. If he's right, and at the moment I've nothing to get in the way of that supposition, then we're looking for humans and again he's right, finding people in this city is what we're good at.' Bryson took a final look at the row of shrunken heads on the shelf. They were horrible, evil-looking things and he shuddered a little to think of the violence that they might have committed in life. He turned to Lafferty and Reed.

'I want you two back at the station. Start going through the reports of missing persons, recent stuff.'

'Right, Guv,' Lafferty and Reed replied in tandem.

'I'm going to find out what I can about Crowley, Braithwaite and all of this other bullshit.'

'You reckon Mr C is lying Guv, do you think that 'him an' the Professor are up to something?' Lafferty asked, concerned more than suspicious.

'I think they're both full of shit Constable. I think that both of them have their own agenda and somehow we've been dragged into the middle of it, so right now we treat them both with equal contempt. Lafferty I know you think that Crowley's some sort of inspiration, or teacher or…I don't know what, but be careful, tell him nothing, you hear?'

'Right boss, but to be honest he rarely asks anything about, y'know, the job. It's always about dreams and feelings an stuff like that.' Said Lafferty.

Bryson eyed him carefully. There seemed to be no lying, no duplicity in the lad at all. He wasn't sure that this was a good thing.

'Right, well, keep it closed anyway. Got it?'

'Yes Guv.'

'I'll be back at the station later. I'll telephone you in a few hours to see if you have anything.'

'What about a vehicle Guv, you need a lift anywhere?' Reed asked.

'No, thank you. I'm going to walk for a while. I need to think.'

'Right guv,' they replied in unison once again.

Part 6

Once he was out of the museum Bryson headed towards Hyde Park. The weather was grim but mild and a drizzle of rain coated him as he made his way across the city. He barely noticed it. His mind was preoccupied with Braithwaite, with the strange rock, with Ravensblack Hall and the ever-present Crowley.

The occultist had appeared at the station two weeks to the day after Ravensblack Hall had burned to the ground, after the night that had consumed twenty-seven members of London's upper class, twelve of Roman's staff and four of his own men. The great and mysterious Aleister Crowley had returned.

He had been sitting on a chair in the waiting room when Bryson entered the station. He looked different. Perhaps because he was properly dressed in an expensive looking suit, and not a dressing gown. That had been the last apparel he had worn for the whole evening on that dreadful night, until he had removed it of course. No, it hadn't been the suit, it was something else. The weather had been awful since, much worse than today, yet Crowley looked tanned. He had an almost olive tint to his skin and he was grinning like the Cheshire Cat.

Bryson wasn't sure at first if he was pleased to see him. The days following that night had been a living hell for him. The police commission, the press, the government, all of them had been on him like wolves. All wanted explanations, all of them wanted a head to toss to the masses. Fortunately, he had been able to give them Roman's. His body had been located in the basement, untouched by the fire which had been held back by the pair of ornate doors. Other than some blackening by soot they appeared to have been untouched.

Bryson was not at all surprised that those doors had gone missing overnight. His story of the madman's rampage through the house, possibly assisted by members of his cult who had in turn been murdered, had been sufficient.

The press had led with 'Devil Worshipping Maniac Slays Dozens,' the Government appeared to lose interest once there was no evidence that any of the ministers who had been present, there had been there were involved in any of the occult practices that Roman was famous for. They were there purely as guests of other guests, it was claimed. Bryson doubted that very much.

The powers that be in the police commission had been unusual however. He had expected a thorough carpeting from them. Officers lost, civilians massacred, had they fired him on the spot he wouldn't have been the least bit surprised. But this was not the case.

To begin with he was moved to a new branch of the Met that dealt solely with homicide and further to this he found that he was second in command only to the division Chief, a man he had no previous knowledge of and who had apparently served most of his years in Scotland. He had moved down to London purely for this role. His name was Malcom Seymour-Brady, although he was referred to as Chief Brady, in his late sixties, quite striking in appearance, tall, slim and with a fairly unruly mop of snow white hair.

Bryson had been impressed with the man. He had been polite, cordial and quite prepared to see Bryson just 'get on with the good work'. He was particularly interested in the gang scene in London and was prepared to give Bryson all the support he needed to gain intelligence on them. Other small favours had come his way too. A modest pay raise, additional men for his team, although he had not had any say on where these men were to be pooled from, but they seemed like good blokes. All in all the tragedy of Ravensblack Hall had not impinged on his career at all.

Then there was Crowley.

When he had seen Crowley sitting in the waiting room, with his smart suit and was it a tan? Bryson had only one question he wanted an answer too but it wasn't forthcoming.

'Where the hell have you been?' he asked as Crowley almost leapt to his feet, took his hand and shook it enthusiastically.

'Ah Inspector it's a long story,' Crowley replied with a considerable grin, 'which I'm not going to tell you.'

'Why?' Bryson replied

'Come, come Inspector, I can't tell you all of my secrets.'

'You haven't told me any of your secrets,' Bryson countered.

Crowley laughed. 'So true! Still what you don't know can't hurt you.'

He leaned in closer to Bryson and whispered, 'At least not if you are the faster runner eh?' He pulled his head back and laughed again.

Watching Crowley laugh was awful. It seemed so at odds with his usual glowering cynical expression that it was practically demonic. Bryson really thought the man might be quite mad when he saw him like this, which he had on occasion, whenever he had been arrested for some misdemeanour and knew full well that he was going to walk scot free.

'We need to talk, Crowley,' Bryson said quietly. 'Away from here. I need to talk about Ravensblack Hall and what the bloody hell you have been up to since that night. I've had Reed and Lafferty call at your house every day.'

'Yes, sorry about that Inspector. I'm afraid I've been away, of a fashion, and it took a while to get back. Still I'm here now.'

Crowley's huge smile didn't once falter.

He's as happy as a dog with two dicks, Bryson thought. *He can barely contain himself.*

Bryson looked at his watch and saw the hours working against him. 'Look I have a good deal to attend to today but if you are able I'll meet you this evening, around eight?'

'Excellent!' Crowley beamed. 'Let's do that. The Savoy?'

'I think that the Savoy is a bit...' Bryson started but was cut short by Crowley.

'Nonsense, nonsense. The Savoy at eight and it shall be my treat.' At that Crowley turned to leave.

'Crowley,' Bryson said and the occultist turned. 'It's good to see you.'

Crowley's smile faded slightly, he almost looked pained. In that moment Bryson saw whatever wind had been driving his sails drop a little.

'That's kind of you to say Inspector,' Crowley nodded, to himself Bryson thought. 'And I look forward to seeing Reed, and young Lafferty of course.' His smile returned and he left the station.

***

Bryson's destination was 136 Salisbury Avenue or, as it was more popularly known, The Westminster Lodge of Freemasonry. As far as secret societies went the Freemasons ranked high in quality of membership but low in ability to stay secret. The large black letters set on a green paint coated wooden board announced to anybody who was interested that this was their main office. He knew of at least a half dozen high ranking officers and literally dozens of councillors, politicians, doctors...the list went on, who were members.

He had never been asked to join. He wondered if this might change in lieu of his sudden rise in status within the force, although he had still not been given a move up from Inspector, because that seemed to be their modus operandi. As soon as someone gained some measure of influence in a body, it didn't appear to matter which, they were approached. Bryson didn't like it. It was his belief that servants of the public shouldn't be involved in this kind of thing. Whatever this kind of thing was, he still wasn't one hundred percent sure.

On the surface the Masons was a bit of a boys' club. A chance for the nobs to get together and get pissed while swapping favours by exerting influence where required should it benefit the members, but Bryson thought there to be a deeper, darker operation at work.

He had seen it happen. A toff was hauled in after committing an offence, more serious than the kind of antics Crowley got up to, and had walked. The individual, the son of a wealthy financier, had been found at the scene of a nasty murder. He should have been questioned, his knowledge of the incident examined. Bryson would have been prepared to have considered his innocence if that was his declaration, but after making one phone call he was released without charge or caution.

True enough no guilt had been established at that point but it would be difficult to ascertain anything when the prime suspect saunters out of the building and is allowed to decamp to his Exeter home. Equally hard was determine what had happened when the scene of the crime had somehow caught ablaze soon after.

No charges, no press coverage and anyone who questions the matter suddenly finds themselves under severe scrutiny from above.

Bryson didn't like this yet he found himself willing to play the game to a certain extent. Ninety-nine percent of his job was information, and information was a product that was moved around the city just like the apples, the fish, the spices and textiles that landed at the docks. It was exchanged for money or favours, sometimes it was taken by force but the fact was that every time it changed hands it became easier to obtain.

When he needed information concerning a robbery Bryson would head to the public houses, the race track or the knocking shops because this was where the rogues and the desperate enjoyed the fruits of their labour, but for the wealthy and the famous he went to the Freemasons.

He knocked on the door and waited as a heavy lock moved inside it. Slowly the door was pulled back and a pale, aged face appeared in the gap it created.

'Good afternoon Inspector, how may we be of service today?' The man at the door was Eric Tuttle and Bryson knew him well. He had guarded this door for twenty or so years and it was his duty to know every name to every face that appeared before it. If he did not, they had no chance of getting past it.

'I've come to see Lord Pevensy, I understand he's here today,' Bryson said

'I see,' Tuttle replied. 'Could I ask if Lord Pevensy is expecting you Inspector?'

'You may ask Mr Tuttle and the answer is no, he is not expecting me, but if you would be so kind as to inform him that I am here I am very sure that he will be delighted to see me. You might wish to advise him that I only wish to take up a few minutes of his time.'

Tuttle considered his options for a moment and then pulled the door a little wider.

'Please do come inside and take a seat. I shall enquire whether Lord Pevensy is within.'

Bryson knew full well that Tuttle knew who was inside the lodge and probably what they were up to and it was probable that Tuttle knew he knew.

It was simply part of the process of obtaining information, you played the game. Nothing closed doors on a policeman in high society like being impolite.

He took his seat. The entrance to the lodge was large and beautifully panelled with dark wood throughout. On the walls were portraits of former lodge masters, expensive cabinets displayed various certificates, awards and trophies that shouted out the good deeds of its members. There were no other people in the entrance but Bryson knew that there were cunningly hidden doors and behind them were men employed to act should anyone enter without permission. He thought of the secret door at the museum.

Tuttle left the room by a more obvious door. There was a large staircase directly behind where Bryson sat and he wondered at what would be found up there. He had never had good cause to investigate the lodge and it was doubtful that he would still have his job if he tried it but he was curious. He wondered if Crowley had even been in here.

A couple of minutes ticked by until the door that Tuttle had exited by opened up again. Emerging from the doorway was the familiar face of Lord Pevensy, who Bryson was genuinely pleased to see. Pevensy was tall, taller than both Bryson and Tuttle, and his whole bearing announced that he was a military man. Long, solid strides, a ramrod straight back and a jaw that could crack walnuts.

'Ronnie…Ronnie, how good it is to see you old man,' Pevensy said as he marched to Bryson with his hand outstretched.

Bryson stood and met the handshake, 'It's good to see you too Sir.'

'Oh please Ronnie, less of the Sir, I'm sure you aren't here to size me up for a suit,' he gave Bryson a warm smile. For a man of sixty-eight Pevensy was charismatic and a damned handsome bugger to boot, Bryson thought. His hair was still thick and dark, cropped tidily at the sides but a little wild at the top. His beard was the only thing that betrayed his age with its engaging streaks of grey that flashed through it.

Pevensy turned to Tuttle, 'Eric, could we use the Apollo room?'

'Of course Sir,' Eric replied. 'I'll go and prepare it now.'

'You will stay for a bite to eat and a small drink won't you?' Pevensy asked in the way he had that suggested he would be deeply offended if you didn't comply.

Bryson swept a hand though his hair, 'well I do have a lot on Michael but I'm sure I can manage a sandwich while we talk.'

'Nonsense dear boy, membership here costs me a bloody fortune, I'll be damned if my guests will be eating sandwiches.' He turned back to Eric who waited patiently.

'Eric, could you have some of that splendid duck sent through, the trimmings to go with it and if I remember correctly a splash of Remy Martin would be the perfect accompaniment for the Inspector.'

Bryson smiled again, 'that would be a very good accompaniment Michael, thank you.'

At this Eric left the foyer and Lord Pevensy indicated that they should sit. Bryson returned to his seat and Pevensy made himself comfortable next to him.

'Well I suppose I should ask first off whether you are visiting in an official capacity?'

'Sort of,' Bryson replied, 'but I'm really looking for some background information concerning a case I'm working on.'

'I see, and you think I might be able to help old boy?'

'I hope so, there's a couple of things really. First I need to know about a person, I'm sure you'll know of him, and the second is what you can tell me about a place that I know you have spent some time, Burma.'

'Burma eh? My word, going back a bit there, Ron, but yes I was stationed in Burma for three years. What would you like to know?'

'Did you ever come into contact or hear any word, any stories perhaps concerning a tribe called the Tcho-Tcho?'

Pevensy's complexion visibly paled before Bryson. The charming smile that always seemed to play across his mouth faltered and Pevensy licked at his lips as though they were dry. To complement the loss of colour his eyes appeared to fix on something beyond Bryson shoulder. They stared out to memories that he didn't wish to observe.

'Lord Pevensy?' Bryson said after a moment. 'Michael?'

Pevensy blinked and he returned to now.

'Oh, I'm…I'm sorry dear boy… um… look we should wait until Eric comes back, lets get settled into the Apollo room before we talk.'

'Of course, that's fine,' Bryson replied.

A chill crept over him. None of the information he was about to hear was going to be good, of that he was certain.

Part 7

'Shit, shit, shit, shit,' Crowley cursed profusely as he worked his way through the rows of dusty books on his shelf. He had no particular system of organisation; rather whatever he had most recently read would perhaps stick out a little more than others. When pulling books out to check the contents and then finishing with them done he would often just leave them flat on top of the others. At the time this all seemed very well, he rarely had to refer to the same text more than once in a year or two, more often longer, but of course when he did actually require the damned thing he was forced to examine every single spine.

The urgency with which he scoured the bookshelves made his bald dome glisten with sweat and he could feel dust clinging to his brow. He hoped he had appeared casual enough to the Inspector. It had been fine until he had spotted a symbol that lay half covered by a cost of drying blood. The ritual had been, all things been equal, a fairly straight-forward rite of worship. It was the Tcho-Tcho's penchant for carving each other up with the normalcy of changing socks that made any scene they were involved in instantly become a nightmare. A wedding for the Tcho-Tcho wasn't a wedding unless the bride had dined on the best-man's brain.

The book he was looking for was large and deep with yellowed pages and should have been easier to find than the others. Easier to find, that is, if he hadn't performed a ritual upon it that made it difficult to perceive from other books around it. It wasn't invisible, Crowley didn't have the time or patience to commit five or six years of his life to such a spell, rather the rite made it bloody awkward to find.

'Got to be one of these fuckers,' he huffed as he continued along a line of titles that ranged from treatises on palaeontology to Thirteenth Century verse. He tapped the spine of each book five times and whispered 'apparere' close to each. Occasionally he accidently sucked in dust that had become unsettled from the books by his rapid percussion upon them and began to cough and wheeze.

Finally, after a short bout of dust-provoked choking he found it. It had of course been plainly sitting there, between Wittgenstein and Woolf.

Its gold letters and deep red leather binding obvious but only if your mind was alerted to its presence. The spell ensured that unless the key word and specific physical action were performed the observers' eyes would simply see just another ordinary book in a row of titles that were not being sought. Now *Unaussprechlichen Kulten* was plain to see Crowley pulled it from the shelf and tucked it under his arm.

He wanted a cup of tea. He had still not managed to acquire a maid or man for the house, such was his reputation that it was hard to get staff despite him offering a reasonable salary. The other difficulty was that he often found himself on the point of being totally broke and couldn't pay them. Since his fortune had been redressed he had sought out Hannah, his previous maid, but was informed that she had moved to Anglesey and was looking after the family home of a wealthy industrialist. He had liked Hannah, she had the ability to completely ignore him and go about her duties and that made for a healthy working relationship.

Having the boy Lafferty around had been interesting too. He was, Crowley thought, incredibly bright, far more than he appeared to be upon first meeting him. It was as though he were a receptacle for knowledge that had just not been filled yet. His deductive skill was sound, he had a very good memory for dates, figures and excerpts from books that they had gone over in the lessons that Crowley provided. He was awkward in other ways though; he could barely look in the direction of anything that depicted people in states of undress. Illustrations, paintings or photographs of native ladies of Africa whose dress code was limited strictly to a band of straw about their waist, they all discomfited him.

More importantly the lad had talent where magic was concerned. He had allowed Crowley to test him on his aptitude for manipulation of the Essence, only the most basic of implementations though, Crowley knew full well that Lafferty wasn't ready for the heavy stuff. But observing auras, minor sensory perception and other mild forms of magical expression had proven that he had potential. More importantly he was happy to clear Crowley's growing backlog of dishes and washing and made a respectable cup of tea.

He set the book down onto his reading table, large oak rectangle of fine carpentry that was particular for the carved symbols that lined its edges. *Unaussprechlichen Kulten* was not a book that presented any inherent danger in simply opening it, rather it was filled with information that might prove unsettling to minds less worldly than his, but some books were better read with the equivalent of a sealed room around them. The table was capable of handling problems that might occur should the reader stumble across something he shouldn't.

He opened the book towards the last quarter as he knew that the topic he was looking for lay within that region. After flicking over a few of the pages, surprisingly strong given their age, for this was a first print issued in 1839, he found his entry. Pulling up a chair he sat and read through the author's introduction to the pages that followed.

Of all of the more primitive races that I have observed and studied the Tcho-Tcho strike me as the most singularly dangerous. While their practices are abhorrent to our senses and they originate from a quite inhospitable region their intellect is extremely well formed, and this means that it is possible that they could extend their influence to other regions.

It has been suggested to me that it is their devotion to only one God (which is unusual amongst the other tribes of the region) that has produced this extraordinary intelligence in such base creatures. That they do not use this gift to better their own lives and position is alien to me. Rather, they appear to have but one purpose, one goal, and this is to establish a bridge to our world that will allow their God to traverse from its current plane to ours whereupon it may establish its dominance. Of course we see this is almost all cults associated with the Old Ones, this overarching desire to enable the ruin of the world at the hands of these entities.

What drives them to this? Why are they so willing to offer both themselves and others to the hideous and evil practices required that will ultimately bring about the downfall of mankind? I can only offer conjecture here as the Tcho-Tcho are impossible to communicate with in any manner approaching civilised. Every attempt we made ended in tragedy, violence and death at their hands.

Hopefully the information that follows will offer some insight but I will advise you now that reading on is more likely to furnish more questions than there are answers.

Friedrich Wilhelm Von Junzt, 1834

Crowley flicked through the pages searching out a specific section. He had not had any reason to consider the Tcho-Tcho for a good while and his memory of their rites had faded a little, but there was something, something he had seen in the warehouse that had roused the portion of his brain that warned him of possible danger to his person.

He drew his finger down a page, his eyes flicked from side to side looking for key words or phrases that resonated with the warning.

'Where are you,' he whispered as he scanned the text. He flipped over the page and repeated his fingertip search.

'Come on you little fuckers, tell me what you're up to.' He flipped another page. This one contained a sketch that showed a man, at least he assumed it was a man as the genitals were cut away and the chest region entirely hacked off to the spine, suspended by hooks from a tree. Intestines curled up from the gut area and were wound around the spinal column and neck and ended inside the poor fellows' mouth.

Underneath the ghastly image was a single sentence by Von Junzt, *Rite of the Snake*, victim pictured had undergone the Ritual of the Cycle of Lhoigor.

'Lhoigor.' Crowley said. He tapped the page twice. This was their God, the rite depicted the requirement of followers of Lhoigor to feed upon men. Crowley recalled that it was only men, no women or children could be consumed. But this was not what he was seeking. He flipped the page and continued his trawl of information.

He had a measure of the symbols at the warehouse, they were fairly standard representations of fidelity, sacrifice and worship and there had been no intention of summoning anything. In fact despite the horror of the scene to the eyes of outsides it was to all intents and purposes a mundane devotion to their God. What was worrying was that it was not hidden, at least the aftermath appeared to have been left to be found, and that it was here, in London and not in some deep cave in depths of another continent. Revealing themselves in such a way was sheer madness and the Tcho-Tcho, while entirely ruthless, were not insane.

His finger halted in the middle of the page. 'Madness,' he said quietly, 'yes.'

He pulled his finger away and looked down at the open pages, his mind worked calmly through the thought that had just occurred to him. He needed another book. Von Junzt's writing focused on the tribes and their practices but gave scant information on the Gods and Lhoigor was one that Crowley was not entirely sure of. He knew of its reputation. It was up there with the big boys as far as its interest in Earth went, Cthulhu, Nyarlathotep, Shub-Niggurath and that total bastard Hastur were all firmly ensconced in their plans to bring the planet under their control. Just a handful of the Gods that wanted to usurp Yahweh's grip on Earth and its people. The cosmic entities that wanted to bathe in the power it provided to their kind. *Wankers*, Crowley thought.

He had, after much experience of the politics of earthly cults and their activities against each other, long since decided that what stopped them succeeding was that they hated each so much that as soon as one started to get a strong position, the others turned on them. While it certainly meant that there was a little more horror in the world this status-quo was a far better scenario than one of them actually getting ahead. Even Yahweh was kept in check.

But the symbol that lay under the blood suggested something that Crowley hoped was far less ominous than it appeared. He needed another book. His library was good but it had been better, most of his particularly nasty books had been stolen by Brathwaite and his chums and despite his best efforts Crowley had been unable to retrieve them. He recalled the slanderous spouting of the Professor as he stood by Bryson and the lads. Accused of trying to steal books that actually belonged to him!

He let the consideration that there may have been some question, of whether his initial acquisition of them could be called stealing, slide away to the part of the mind where awkward questions were kept busy with light duties.

Most of the truly dangerous books contained rituals of summoning. These were the so called 'Blood Books.' Chief among them the dread *Necronomicon.* There were scant few copies of that awful tome still at large at the world.

If there were a mother-lode of bad ideas, then the *Necronomicon* was it. A Pandora's Box in a handy hardback version, ideal for long trips, but when the authors' foreword opens with 'To read this tome is to welcome a wish for death, but thy wish will be only the beginning of thy suffering', you knew it was never going to be on the bestseller list.

Thanks to the dedicated efforts of a few mind-bogglingly brave souls Crowley knew that the number of copies left was diminishing as they were destroyed, but there were still a few. Some in the hands of private collectors who kept them secret, some buried, waiting to be found and some, hopefully very, very few, were owned by those who had a desire to use the knowledge to be found within. He didn't need the *Necronomicon*, or any other book of summons, he needed a book of Gods.

He closed Von Junzt's great work and tapped the cover five times whispering 'ire' as he did so. He blinked and had to re-focus his vision. Although the book and its cover were familiar to him he could not quite make it out, it was whatever title came to mind that seemed to be right to be on his table. He picked it up and avoided looking at it while he returned it to the shelf. He made a mental note to remember which section of the library it was in, and then threw the mental note in the bin thinking it was a receipt for something. The spell was good.

Part 8

Lord Pevensy had promised to get back to him as soon as he had more to offer and for this Bryson as grateful. Right now he wanted all of the information he could get on the Tcho-Tcho that were at large in London, in the UK for that matter. What Pevensy had told him had been uncomfortable for both of them, for his Lordship it had been the horrific memories brought back to torture his mind, for Bryson the fear of what this tribe or group might be up to in the Capital.

They had murdered their own, and as awful as that was Bryson would be more relaxed if he thought that it would be the case for any further incidence's involving them. Gangs about the city regularly clipped each other's wings through violence, arms and legs were broken, establishments razed to the ground and occasionally, but rarely, someone might get his head caved in or be found in the murky waters of the Thames.

Such crimes were investigated, but not too thoroughly, no one really cared. Only when injuries were dealt to the public, the civilians, did the Met get serious. The message was simple, keep it to your own and it's natural selection, harm the public and we're coming for you.

The afternoon was disappearing fast, the museum and Lord Pevensy had both eaten into the hours Bryson had available and he had the meeting with Crowley later. He hoped it would be useful but he had no real wish to be in his company, Crowley had been his usual arsehole self today.

Bryson wasn't sure what to make of the relationship that had been struck with Lafferty either. It appeared to be harmless, but with Crowley you just didn't know. *God he gives me fucking ulcers*, he thought.

A cab was parked nearby and he decided to get a ride back to the station. Clouds had gathered overhead and threatened to add wet clothes to a growing list of concerns.

No more than a couple of minutes into the journey the inevitable conversation began. The Cabbie, a London institution, switched into opinionated gossip mode and began to inform Bryson of the events of the day which of course included the rumours of plague and horrible murders at the docks.

Bryson rolled his eyes. Only Crowley could make a terrible occurrence improve in its awfulness. If there was a good side to the Cabbies inane chatter it was that it was 'common knowledge' that the ''orrible murders' were a gang war that was going on.

'Yes, it could be,' Bryson said

'I'm tellin ya, guv, it's them wogs what's the problem. Got 'em coming in from God knows where, uncivilised places like. They don't do fings like wot normal people do. You mark my words there'll be more and more trouble unless they has a real eye kept on 'em.'

'Right,' Bryson replied, disinterested.

'Barnabas Street ain't the same these days, I tell ya. Was a time you could pick up a fare any time o' night on Barnabas street but I wouldn't stop my wheels rollin' there for all the tea in China.'

'Shame,' Bryson said, his attention had drifted out into the city. As the cab rolled by grand houses, small shops, great municipal buildings and people of all persuasions he wondered if times were actually changing or if really it was just the same chaos of human existence wrapped up in a comfortable cloak of what the cabbie called 'being civilised.' They approached the station.

'Oh, beg pardon sir, you an officer then?' he cabbie asked Bryson cautiously, as people often did when they discovered his occupation. Then added, 'Or are you helpin' 'em wiv enquiries?' The cabbie gave a wink in his mirror.

'Both I suppose,' Bryson said and handed over a note for the fare. The cabbie began to search through a dark blue cotton bag for change.

'It's okay, keep it,' he said.

'Oh bless ya guv. Very decent.' The cabbie touched his cap and made to open his door with the intention of doing the same for the Inspector.

'No, its fine,' Bryson said and made to exit. He stopped as he pushed the door open and turned back to the cabbie.

'What's wrong with Barnabas Street?' he asked. For some reason it had been fished out of the pool of his unguided thoughts.

'Sorry Guv?' the cabbie asked.

'You said that Barnabas Street used to be good for fares, any time of day, but now it's not. Why is that?' Bryson said with the calm, merely curious tone he used when dealing with people who were like little living radio transmitters.

'Oh, well it's the wogs innit? Always coming and going at night they are, scaring folk off the street, y'know, some of them have things up with their faces, they got scars and they even have things sticking in 'em. Fuckin' 'ell, it's like a freak show sometimes.'

'Indeed?' Bryson said. 'Well, thank you, have a good day.'

'Right you are chief, you keep clear of Barnabas Street eh?' The cabbie smiled and let out a good-humoured laugh.

Bryson painted a smile onto his face, nodded thanks and finally exited the cab.

He strode up the short run of steps to the head office of the London Metropolitan Police Service and entered the building. Inside it was busy, officers came and went and seated around the foyer were various peoples, victims and offenders mingled together here. Some waiting to complain and others waiting to have the complaints against them sorted.

Reed and Lafferty would be here somewhere, his section was across the other side of the building but his two officers might be in the archives, the cells or the detention area. He approached the desk sergeant.

'Afternoon Barry,' he said and Barry looked up from making marks in a large book on the desk in front of him.

'Afternoon Inspector,' Sergeant Barry Allen replied. Bryson wondered if Sergeants were cast from the same mould and then little bits added to make them discernible from each other. Allen was tall, broad and had huge, tough-skinned hands that looked as though the fists they made could drive nails into wood. He was older than Reed by a good twenty years but there any difference ended except perhaps that Sergeant Allen's moustache was not the muscular thing that Reed carried under his nose, and it was almost white like his severely cropped hair.

'Do you know the whereabouts of Constable Lafferty and Sergeant Reed?'

'Your lads left about thirty minutes ago, Inspector. Left a note for you in fact.' Allen reached over to a small black book which he opened and handed to Bryson.

Bryson read the note and a queasy, cold feeling crept up from his balls to his neck. *Gone to check out a lead at 34 Barnabas Street, taking the lad. Reed*, it read in the Sergeant's blocky text.

'Thirty minutes you say?' Bryson asked pensively.

Allen looked at his watch, 'Almost to the minute Sir.'

'Thank you,' Reed said.

'There a problem, Sir?' Allen asked. The man had been thirty years on the job, interrupted only by a world war, he could see apprehension in a person like others saw hair colour.

'I'm not entirely sure,' Reed replied truthfully. 'Did they say why they were going, what the lead was at Barnabas Street?'

'No Sir,' Allen cast his thoughts back and searched for anything pertinent. 'It struck me that it was the lad's idea Sir, young Lafferty, can't say why but I get the feeling that he was the instigator.'

Bryson nodded, you didn't dismiss the gut instinct of a copper like Allen. 'Thanks.'

A connection rose up from the pool of unguided thoughts to join with the mention of Barnabas Street, the wogs, the foreigners. All foreigners were wogs to Cabbies. Dark skinned, strange markings and facial ornamentation? That was tribal. Then exploding from the pool like some grinning leviathan came Crowley and the unguided thoughts came together to form a single, terrible premonition of everything going tits up.

'Sergeant, I have absolutely nothing to back this up but I'm fairly certain our boys are in danger, will you get a few lads together and have them meet me at that address.' Bryson pointed at the book.

'Right away Sir,' said Allen, who also knew not to dismiss the gut instinct of a time-served copper.

Bryson turned and walked quickly out of the station, barely hearing Sergeant Allen bark a series of orders across the foyer.

His car was not out front which meant that it was either at the rear of the station or Reed and Lafferty had used it. This was not unusual, it was a police vehicle first and as Bryson was meant to meet them at the station it wouldn't have crossed their minds that he might need it to get to them.

'Fuck,' he said and ran back into the station.

'Sergeant!' he called to Allen who had three officers in front of him. 'I need transport.'

Allen who had now come to the front of his desk reached into a draw behind him and withdrew a set of keys which he handed to one of the men. The constable with the keys walked quickly towards Bryson.

'Cars at the front Sir, would you like me to drive?'

'Yes, do that. Are you armed?'

'Yes sir.' The constable replied nervously, the question catching him by surprise.

'Good, let's go.' Bryson said.

'The other lads will follow on Inspector.' Sergeant Allen shouted as Bryson and the constable started to leave.

As he got into the car the first thing that came to Bryson's mind was Crowley. He had said that they would meet at eight. It was only six now and he couldn't be sure that occultist would be at home. His instinct told him that Crowley was needed, it raged at his senses *It's connected, it's connected, this is all part of it, get Crowley.*

Was there time? Enough to check out Crowley's home which might or might not contain the occultist, and then get to Barnabas Street? Time for what? The lads had gone to check a lead, it might be nothing, just routine. Bryson knew, he absolutely *knew*, that this wasn't the case. Barnabas Street was a danger.

'Barnabas Street, Constable.'

'Yes Sir,' the Constable replied and started the engine.

'What's your name son?' Bryson asked.

'Timpson, Sir. Stanley Timpson.'

'Okay, Stanley, Barnabas Street is a fifteen-minute drive from here, if you can swing by the Savoy Hotel on the way, and still make it in that time without taking down a civilian, I'll make sure there's a bonus in your pay packet.'

'Right you are Sir.' Timpson replied and hit the accelerator.

They reached the Savoy quickly and with only a small amount of panic caused to the population *en route*. Timpson was an excellent driver. As soon as the sedan pulled up onto the pavement outside the main doors Bryson leapt out and rushed to the lobby.

The commissionaire, seeing Bryson's rush towards the hotel, had attempted to politely block his entrance but was unceremoniously pushed aside, 'POLICE BUSINESS' he bawled at the man, making a mental note to apologise at a more convenient time. On entering the foyer a concierge looked up dispassionately from whatever had held his attention on his desk.

'Can I help you at all Sir?'

'I need to know if Aleister Crowley is here, or has been here recently. Do you know who I mean?'

'Yes Sir, we are familiar with Mr Crowley,' the concierge gave nothing away as far as his opinion of Crowley, 'but I believe that he has not graced us with his presence of late. Would you like me to check if he is in the bar?'

'No,' Bryson replied. 'If he was here, you'd know it.'

'Indeed Sir,' the concierge replied with the confidence of someone who had experienced being in the presence of Crowley for longer than was welcome.

'Alright, look, my name is Inspector Bryson and it's important that as soon as Mr Crowley arrives that he's given a message, could you make that happens?'

'Of course Sir,' the concierge took a sheet of paper monogrammed with 'The Savoy Hotel' at the top of it and handed it to Bryson along with a fine pen.

Bryson quickly scribbled a message.

34 Barnabas Street. Cho people? Come and meet us immediately
Bryson

He handed the pen and paper back.

'I'll see that Mr Crowley receives it as soon as he appears Sir,' said the concierge who folded the page without looking at it. Bryson thanked him and left, rushing past the commissionaire once again but this time not requiring to push the man.

As he climbed back into the sedan he patted Timpson on the shoulder. 'OK son, let's go, and earn you that bonus.'

'Right Sir,' Timpson replied and was screeching away from the hotel before Bryson had time to close his door.

Crowley arrived at the Savoy a little after eight.

He could have made it in good time but didn't want to appear too keen to meet up with Bryson lest he give away his current state of anxiety. When he was presented with the folded note from the concierge he already knew that his anxiousness was about to be elevated. He opened it up. Read it, then handed it back to the concierge.

'What time did the Inspector leave this?' He asked

'I was handed the note at approximately six twenty five Sir.'

'Fucking hell,' Crowley said, gloomily. The concierge was about to ask Crowley to refrain from such language but was cut short. 'I need a cab, right now could you sort one?'

The concierge nodded, 'Of course sir.' He raised his hand and clicked his fingers, the snap produced was loud and distinct and a bell boy came quickly to the desk.

'The gentleman requires a cab,' he indicated Crowley with flourish of his hand. The lad, who looked awkward in his blue and green uniform, looked up at Crowley. Crowley gave him an uncertain grin.

'Chop chop David.' The concierge said giving two short claps to underline his command. The Bell Boy ran to the commissionaire and passed on the request.

'Anything else I can do for you, Sir?' he asked.

'Yes, I don't suppose you have a gun handy do you?' Crowley asked.

Part 9

By the time Crowley reached Barnabas Street the light had faded. Grey skies had given way to a black canopy littered with feeble stars. The cabbie had dropped him off where Barnabas Street began, refusing to park in the middle of it where number 34 would be situated,

'In case those fucking thieves 'ave it away with my takings,' the cabbie had complained.

Crowley growled a thank you, paid the exact amount and got out of the cab.

There were people on the street, standing by lamp posts and doorways. Here at the entrance to it a pair of swarthy-looking men were talking quietly and stopped their conversation to eye up the occultist. Crowley was well aware that he was dressed in his best Saville Row suit and looked every bit the toff. He was wearing a black Homburg hat which he lifted as he gave the men a polite nod of greeting. The two men observed him for another moment and then returned to their conversation.

The houses on Barnabas Street were large and all detached. Once they would have been expensive homes in the reach of only the most affluent buyers but now they were mostly at the point of dereliction. The street was situated on the edge of a slum area since a railway line had been built on what had once been common land. This had acted as a barrier to the more desirable area across the tracks. It was debatable who actually owned the properties now, it was unlikely to be the current tenants no matter how far into disrepair the homes had fallen. Rather, they would be rented out or simply ignored and squatters would move in and fight others for their right to inhabit the shacks.

Crowley didn't particularly want to walk down this street. He would rather face demons and spectres than men with knives and guns. His body was able to withstand powerful psychic and spiritual attacks, but bullets and blades just tended to go straight through tattoos, no matter how nicely inked they were. The positive side was that there should be at least one policeman, an inspector no less, half way down.

There was a wide curve that obfuscated the rest of the road and its houses and of course number 34 was on the wrong side of this arc for him to see it. He started to walk.

To his great relief no one appeared to be interested in him. He strolled past a man leaning against a lamp post but the chap made no motion to look up. Instead he rested against the post, head down and with hands in pockets. A young woman walked by holding a child wrapped in a blanket, she did cast Crowley a suspicious glance but carried on passed him. His mind was almost at ease when he began to take the curve in the road that would bring him to number 34, but as he cleared the bend and the house was in sight he stopped.

There were three sedans parked against the pavement, clearly police vehicles, but there was not a copper in sight or a visible light in any of the houses here. The street lights worked but there was some distance between them and they illuminated little other than the pavement beneath. Many of the houses were shuttered or boarded up, some a combination of both. If he had counted correctly, and the location of the vehicles indicated that he had, number 34 was no exception.

The house was large, three storeys, and with a roof that no doubt held as much space as a standard floor. Its condition was deplorable. Crowley knew that the dark patches blooming over the faded paintwork were rot. Even in the twilight the desiccated brickwork and dislodged timbers were obvious. The house was being consumed by neglect.

Of course it was all quite obviously bollocks. The whole scene. Crowley's sense of self-preservation screamed at him to turn around and leave. Dodgy street, dodgy house, police cars lined up and yet not a soul or even a light to be seen. No noise other than the rumble of some factory in the distance. The whole thing was a huge warning to anyone with a modicum of intelligence and a decent respect for his or her own skin, to just leave, go home and have a cuppa.

The right thing to do, he thought, *is to head back to the main road, hail a cab, go home and call the police from there. They were the professionals. They are the ones to deal with this kind of thing.*

It was a good argument. Crowley's self-preservation delivered it calmly and with sincerity.

It arrived dressed in a smart suit, with tidy presentable hair and a briefcase that he knew contained many more statements that would back up its sage advice. There was no shame in it, no guilt and in fact, the smartly suited explanation suggested that it was more than likely something to be proud of.

Crowley was about to turn on his heels and retrace his steps to the main road, but he had got no further than the thought of it when his ego stepped in to counter the case put forward by self-preservation.

Bryson himself had told him that he, Crowley, was the best at this sort of thing. Outside of Ravensblack Hall he had stated it, he recalled the moment perfectly. In matters of the occult he was the professional, he was the man for the job. He was *needed.*

His ego was large and loud and didn't need a case of arguments to back up its claims. Instead it made expansive hand gestures and smiled a lot. It hugged his shoulders like a best friend and pointed to an island paradise in the distance that was Crowley's, if only he could just rise above the riff raff and the hoi polloi that stopped him reaching his goals. Dancing girls kicked their legs high as they joined arms, moving in time with the grand statements issued from his ego. He pressed on to number 34.

He didn't pause as he walked through the gateway. There was no gate.; if his eyes didn't deceive him that item lying rusting on what was once a lawn and was now a tangle of weeds, briars and refuse. Striding purposefully to the door revealed that it too was no longer a door. It was a solid rectangle of some kind of timber, heavily nailed into place.

'Hmm.' He uttered quietly.

He cast his eyes around the frontage. The windows had planks across them on all floors save for the very top but the panes were missing, long since smashed by the pin-point accuracy of children with time on their hands and an ample supply of stones. He looked back to the empty sedans and then once again scrutinised the house. He could see nothing untoward, there were no sigils, runes, strange patterns or shapes.

He could go around to the back. Check the doors and windows there, but the problem with that was it would remove him from the view of the street. It would be dark. The only light available came from the piss-poor street lamps

'Fuck that,' he said to himself.

Something caught his eye behind him, across the street. Finally some illumination from one of the houses. A curtain had been pulled back slightly on an upper floor. Crowley turned. The curtain didn't suddenly close, as would be the case if it was some nosey neighbour noting suspicious goings on.

Someone was staring at him through that window, but there was no way to tell who it might be. The figure was only a shadow to him. Finally the small triangle of light vanished as the curtains edge dropped back into place. Crowley continued watching and his vigilance paid off as a light appeared to glow faintly around what must be the doorway of the house. It opened and a figure stood within it.

Crowley's furrowed his brow. He was achieving nothing stood here at the front of what genuinely appeared to be an abandoned house and of which there was no fucking chance in Hell he was going to investigate the rear of. Not alone anyway.

Across the road was a person who was…waiting? Perhaps the person had information of use, perhaps the person would be prepared to take look for him? A dangerous activity always mathematically slightly reduced for you if someone else does the dangerous bit.

Crowley strolled away from number 34 and crossed over to the odd numbered side of the street. The figure remained in the doorway, unmoving.

As he neared the house, number 31, he could tell the person was old and probably a man. He was never certain with old people at a distance and had been caught out many times when addressing an unfortunate-looking older lady. If it was a man his stature was slim, bony almost. His clothes hung loosely about him but his shoulders hooked the tatty cardigan he wore like a coat hanger.

Crowley stopped at wall to the man's garden, only a short distance to the doorway unlike number 34, and raised his hat.

'Good evening, Sir or Madam, how are you this fine evening?'

The figure didn't respond. It remained still and Crowley could now see that its arms were folded and it leaned against the frame. Something moved behind him but Crowley couldn't make out what, the shadows pooled to heavily into the house.

He stepped onto the narrow paved path that led to the door and approached the person in the doorway.

'I wonder if I might ask you about number 34,' Crowley indicated the house with the hand holding his hat.

'Madam?' the figure replied.

'*Aha*,' Crowley thought. 'Do forgive me sir, the light, these old eyes y'know?'

He flashed his grin, which he always hoped would come over as warm and friendly but was almost universally considered to be a physical manifestation of insanity by those who witnessed it.

If the old man had really taken any offence he didn't show it and as Crowley towered over him rheumy eyes, like sky blue oysters, looked up and into the occultist.

'What yer lookin' fer over there?' he asked in a voice that belied his age, it was strong and clear although heavily accented with the east London drawl.

'Well, from the looks of it half of the metropolitan police force,' Crowley replied.

'Hm,' the man said. He shrugged his bony shoulders.

'Have you seen... anyone... over there?' Crowley asked.

'When?'

'Recently, tonight, in the last couple of hours, or are there usually a line of police cars outside that house?' Crowley asked. He had hoped the codger had come down his stairs to give him some vital information, now he thought he had only come down to waste his time.

'I seen folks,' the codger replied, then shrugged 'I see all kinds of folks come and go.'

Crowley narrowed his eyes, the penny dropped. He reached inside his jacket and withdrew his purse. He fiddled inside, withdrew a few shillings and rattled them in his fist. The old man didn't alter his expression at all.

'Alright how much are we talking?' Crowley asked.

'Five pounds.' The codger replied.

'FIVE POUNDS!' Crowley almost exploded. 'Five pounds for a bit of information, are you out of your fucking mind?'

'Reckon you'll want a hand if you're thinking of visiting number 34. Five pounds'll get you a bit o' support. Bit o' back-up.'

Crowley's heart rate dropped a little. He would much rather investigate anywhere with someone else. Someone else meant at least one other person to take whatever was coming while he did something else, up to and including running very quickly in the opposite direction.

'I'm listening,' Crowley said.

The codger didn't move from his relaxed position against the doorframe, but indicated with his fluid eyes that someone was in the house behind him.

'I'll send Benny right out if ya want, he'll go with yer. You'll need to go round the back, and given that the coppers you're after did that earlier, and haven't come back since, you might appreciate 'avin' a big fella around.'

Crowley considered this. In truth he really didn't want to go anywhere that half a dozen policemen had not managed to return from, but having a 'big fella' with him went some way to helping him build up the courage to at least take a peek.'

'Alright, five pounds,' Crowley said and delved into his purse again. He pulled out the note and reluctantly handed it over.

The codger now animated. He took the fiver with a gnarled hand and his watery eyes examined it. Satisfied, he called over his shoulder.

'BENNY! Get here lad.'

Crowley heard a muffled thud and then a light patter grew louder as something approached the door. In a moment a head, the size of a bread bin peered out from just below the codger's knee.

'What the fuck is that?' Crowley exclaimed.

'That's Benny.'

The head belonged to a bulldog. It was sizeable, easily weighing over a hundred pounds and its face was a mess of folds and creases. Its great jowls had drool gently dripping down on each side but what most freaked Crowley was that while one of its eyes stared at directly at him with canine curiosity the other appeared to be looking to other side, somewhere in the garden.

'Give me my fucking fiver back you duplicitous twat.' Crowley snarled

'Deals a deal Mr Crowley.' The codger replied unfazed.

'I paid for a fellow to assist me over there not some bos-eyed, slavering shite hound that...' Crowley paused, the uni-cyclist of suspicion had just rolled past his window. 'Wait a minute, how do you...'

'You didn't pay for a fella you paid for Benny, and that's Benny.' The codger looked down at the dog and Crowley couldn't help but follow suit. Benny looked up at his master in return, one eye rolled up while the other seemed to rotate a little and then stare out to fuck knows where.

Crowley straightened. 'First and foremost, this is outrageous. I have paid for assistance in an important police matter and rest assured I'll be advising the constabulary of what is tantamount to misrepresentation. Secondly, how do you know my name?'

Crowley put his wallet away as he spoke, he was already of the impression that his fiver was not going to come his way again, not unless he had something about his person that the codger wanted to buy off him there and then.

'First and foremost, Mr Crowley,' the old coot replied calmly and casually, much to Crowley's irritation, 'I din't misrepresent anyfin, what you 'ave in your head wiv regards to what folks tell you ain't none of my concern. I offered you assistance, which you accepted. 'ow do I know your name? The legendary Aleister Crowley? Well, let's just say that our circle of friends overlaps here and there.'

Crowley gave him a hard and critical stare. He was, as his first impression had suggested, a slim man, but perhaps not bony, or scrawny. The sloppy attire he wore went some way to creating the impression of frailty, his eyes were old and seemed to float like lilies on a pond but they were large and surprisingly bright. If he was less than eighty years old Crowley would happily eat the Homburg he wore but there was a look about him, if you turned your eyes a little there was revealed someone lithe, agile, and capable.

The overworked librarian of Crowley's mind ran through aisle after aisle of his memories seeking for a reference. Somewhere in there was a slim notebook that shivered, trying to make itself known amongst the vast repository of eldritch lore. A story or little known fact that had been acquired many, many years ago.

He looked at the wood that framed the doorway the old codger leaned upon and noticed small symbols that had been carved into it. They were difficult to spot as layers of paint and the coarse effects of the weather had taken their toll. But there they were.

Neither man said anything. Benny dropped down onto his haunches and began to noisily slurp at his magnificent balls and the two took watched in detached admiration for a moment, until Crowley returned his attention to the codger.

'So, behind the house.'

'Be'ind the house,' the codger nodded 'saw about five or six go round there, not all at once mind, but none came back to this side.'

'Was there anyone here earlier? Another Policeman?'

'There was two what came, before the others, a big fella and a skinny one.'

'Same thing?' Crowley asked, he already had no doubt as to who the two policemen were.

'Same thing.'

Crowley looked towards number 34. It still looked like a rundown house and no more than that, but the darkness beyond it, down the gap at its side which led to the rear of the property, had taken on a more sinister hue.

'What's behind there? Crowley asked, 'do you know?'

'No,' the codger replied, 'there's no signs or other indications of what's about there, but there is something. There's fellas that come and go, mostly at night, dark-skinned lads. Benny doesn't like them. That's good enough for me.'

Crowley chewed at the inside of his cheek. The codger's accent had eased a little, his words were rounded out, his deception no longer needed. The memory he had been searching for had been located and brought to his attention. He turned back to face the old man. And decided on a direct approach.

'Aren't there supposed to be three of you?' He asked.

'There are,' the codger replied without surprise at the question.

Crowley couldn't help but stretch his neck a little to gain a look further into the hall.

'Do all those policemen live in the same house?' the old man asked.

Crowley wound in his neck. 'Alright, no need to be arsey,' he said, feeling a little sheepish.

'You know, if you applied yourself a bit more, stopped being such a selfish, self-indulgent ponce, you could make a difference to what's going on,' the codger said.

Crowley scoffed, 'really? Well, I have no interest in any of that thank you.'

'So what are you doing here then?'

Crowley was caught off balance for a second and rushed out an answer.

'Because... I... get paid,' he lifted his chin, 'I get paid for my services, and my interests and pursuits are supported by the information I gain from assisting the Met.'

'Seems like you just paid out five pounds to help the Met rather than them paying you,' the codger replied in his annoyingly reasonable manner.

'I'll claim it back,' Crowley snapped. 'Look, I haven't time for this, wonderful though it's been,' he looked down at Benny who was still heavily invested in his gonads. 'Come on, dog, let's go see if you're worth a fucking fiver.'

'Wait,' the codger said, 'you'll need his leash, he wanders.'

Crowley's jaw dropped, 'he *wanders*?'

'Yeah,' the codger replied and then disappeared back into the house.

Crowley looked down at the great beast and it postponed its activity to take in the occultist. Crowley found himself switching between the points to which its diverse eyes pointed. Was it looking at him or had it seen a squirrel in the corner of the yard? A huge tongue worked its way from one side of its jowls to the other, sliding across its twitching nose as it went. It whined a little.

'Jesus,' Crowley whispered harshly.

The codger returned with a large beige leather collar upon which little bones had been printed, and a long, robust leash.

He fixed the collar around the animal's neck, which was as thick as the old fellow's waist, and then attached the leash to it.

He handed it to Crowley, who took it as though he were being handed a summons.

'Good luck,' the codger said.

'Fuck you very much,' Crowley replied and tried to stride out of the garden in an angry fashion but was hampered by Benny not being in a hurry. No amount of pulling on its leash could make the animal improve on its leisurely gait.

Part 10

The sight that greeted Bryson as he came too would never leave his memory. Directly across from him, with hands tied and stretched up to an iron peg that had been driven deep into the wall was the naked body of one of the constables. His head had been shaved, his eyes and lips removed and possibly his teeth, it was hard to say as the mouth was clogged with the man's intestine. The organ coiled from his ruined mouth around his neck and torso.

His skin had been pared away from his chest and hung about his waist like an apron. Some sort of apparatus had been inserted into his ribs, forcing them open. Bryson could only guess what precious organs had been removed from within the cavity.

Below the ribcage was a space where the man's guts had once been. Only the spinal column remained and the lower intestine was wound up and around it, climbing up to the mouth. Bryson closed his eyes tightly in hope that when he opened them again the scene would be gone. He opened them and the terrible sight remained.

He turned his vision as best he could, his own arms were tightly pressed against his head as he was strung up in a similar fashion to the body opposite him. He could see, amongst others, Reed. The man was without his helmet and his dark hair, longer at the front than Bryson had thought, draped over the Sergeants face, almost reaching his impressive moustache. He appeared to be unconscious, they all did, but only one of their number had been butchered or at least that seemed to be the case.

Bryson looked up to see what the situation was with his secured hands. He could just about make out the thick loops of rope that bit into his wrists. He had been hoisted up in the same manner as the man opposite and to the side of him were other officers, all who most likely arrived shortly after he and Timpson had got there.

He tried to recall what had happened, hoping that it might in some way improve his situation. They had pulled up to the house and seen the boarded door and windows but no sign of Reed or Lafferty. Their first decision from there had been to check the rear of the house which they had done.

Bryson was not a reckless man and Timpson to his credit had been alert and suitably wary. After walking past the side of the house the back garden was revealed to be a large open plot with a single structure, a sizeable greenhouse that didn't have a single intact window situated off to the far side.

The two had looked about carefully, they had not gone barrelling in to the garden leaving themselves open to a possible ambush, and that must have been what happened because all that followed from there was darkness.

He strained forward to get a count of the bodies in the room. He could see five in all, including the dead officer and the unconscious Sergeant Reed. It was possible there were others he couldn't see due to his limited angle of vision. He closed his eyes again as his head throbbed a little and waited until the pulsing ache passed before opening them. This time he examined his prison.

The walls were brick, a dark brown with a touch of red to them. They looked damp. The light came from two large oil lamps that hung upon a nail at either end of the room, which Bryson thought must be about fifteen feet in length, the man opposite him was around seven feet away. The most striking thing was the shape of it.

The wall arched overhead and formed a kind of tube. Bryson knew of only a few constructions that were shaped like this, the Underground, canal tunnels and sewers. He tried to recall if Barnabas Street lay anywhere near the lines that made up the underground network and was fairly certain that the District line would be the closest and that it wouldn't be anywhere near. The lines to the rear of the house ran directly from Euston and there was no tube station or other access point that he was aware in this part of the city.

Canals weren't up for consideration so this left the sewers. The brickwork did have that darkened look that damp applied to stone. He strained forward to get a good look at the floor. It was concrete, spattered with mud and a good deal of the blood that obviously cascaded from the poor soul opposite him.

He sniffed, taking in the air and as he had suspected it was damp and an unpleasant odour had insinuated the atmosphere.

He was in a sewer, he had no doubt, but this new certainty didn't help. This meant he was underground and that meant out of sight.

Was he under the house or the garden? He listened out for the sound of trains crossing the tracks but heard nothing. Surely there would be something if he was within a few hundred yards of a locomotive moving by.

One of the men groaned. Bryson flicked his eyes to Reed and hoped that it was him but there was still no movement from the Sergeant. A gasp now sounded, someone taking in a lungful of air, someone just waking. This person must be at the end of the line at the side of him. Bryson tried to talk but found it difficult. His tongue lolled inside his mouth as though drunk.

'Drugged,' he thought, 'bastards drugged me.'

Sounds came from down the line again possibly in response to his own mumbled attempt at communication. Bryson strained forward and saw finally that it was Lafferty. A small sense of relief washed over him. The lad wasn't dead at least. Reed still wasn't moving. Perhaps more of the drug had been used on him, he was a big man so it stood to reason.

He tried to call out again, 'Lafferty!', although what was produced was 'Larrty.' His throat was dry and swollen, reducing his volume but it appeared that Lafferty heard.

'Guth?' Lafferty replied. Bryson saw the lad stretch his head forward. Bryson rested for a moment and took deep breaths, 'Get the blood flowing son, work this shit out of your system.' He managed to produce saliva, moistening his mouth and lubricating his throat.

'It's me lad. You alright?' He said and although his voice was still quiet and raspy his tongue shaped the words much better.

Lafferty said nothing for a moment then croaked, 'Alright Guv,' and a second later, 'Oh my god!'

Bryson understood that Lafferty had seen the terrible remains opposite him. 'Alright Lafferty, keep your head son, I need you focused.'

Bryson spoke with as strong a voice as he could muster to get the lads attention away from the butchery. 'You can see Reed from there, does he look OK?'

Lafferty kept his view from the far side of the room and concentrated on Reed. Just as Bryson had hoped.

'Out cold Guv.'

'Shit,' Bryson shook his head. Even if Reed was awake what could he do? From the looks of the bindings they were well secured. Reed was stronger than most men but could he pull that iron peg from the wall? Doubtful. This room, this sewer antechamber? It was sturdily built and he had no doubt that the iron pegs were both strong and buried deep into the wall.

'Do you remember anything, from when you arrived at the house?' he asked

Lafferty paused to think, trying to see the moment in his mind's eye as Crowley had been teaching him. He recalled the last few words of his conversation with Reed as they had pulled up at the house on Barnabas Street and then viewed the scene as though he were standing just behind himself.

It was still strange to him that he could actually do this, that he could see himself as though he were an observer to his own actions. In the scene Reed was being very cautious; he had his baton gripped tightly and resting against his shoulder. If anything tried to suddenly appear from around that corner it was going to be on the receiving end of his majesty's pleasure for certain.

Lafferty didn't have a baton, or gun or knife. While he had no problem with employing weapons in a time of extreme threat or danger he didn't like to carry them generally, certainly not amongst the public. He was sure that Reed carried all three and probably more, the sergeant practically bristled with weapons. He knew that the Inspector always had a revolver on his hip but wasn't sure where Mr Crowley stood on such things, although he suspected that the occultist would be happy to watch someone who had crossed him in some way cop for a good kicking, but you just couldn't tell with him.

He saw nothing untoward as he visualised the scene before him other than the old, broken greenhouse but there was a sensation, he focused again on the last few seconds before the darkness had come. They had taken the corner where the rear of the house came into view, the scene, the greenhouse, the wild garden was the same but his vision-self reached up to the side of his neck, and so did Reed.

Again he turned back the scene, Reed had brought his hand to his neck first, as though bitten. Had something stung him? Then Lafferty saw his own hand reach to the side of his neck, he could feel something, his fingers tingled as his brain replayed the moment for him. Something in his neck. Then the lights went out.

'I think someone shot us Sir.'

'Shot?' Bryson asked warily.

'Yessir, not with bullets, but with a needle or something, I think we were drugged by whatever was fired at us.'

Bryson thought about this. A memory of something swam in dark waters but he couldn't be sure. It was possible though. It made sense. A needle or dart of some kind, silent, fired from someone hiding in the long grass.

'Why did you go to the house?' Bryson asked

'The Tcho-Tcho Sir, Reed found a report about a lad who had gone missing, I mean there's lots of 'em, hard to imagine how many until you see all the boxes, but this lad, he had a friend with him an' he was foolin' around on his mate. He had hidden behind some empty crates and was goin' to jump out to scare the lad. But these fellas turned up he says, took his mate and carried him off. Well the lad follows 'em and sees 'em go behind the house on Barnabas Street but when he gets there they's gone. No one in sight. He tells the police and they check it out but they don't see anything either.'

'I don't see the connection, it could have been a kidnapping or some sort of gang action,' Bryson said

'Yeah but this had happened before or at least similar, we began to find other reports of people disappearing around there, an the blokes involved were all described as dark-skinned and they had 'strange markings' on their skin, some on their faces boss.'

'Tribal markings?'

'Could be Guv. Reed said we should at least check out the house and that's how we ended up here.'

'Alright, well… ' Bryson looked to Reed again, he was desperate to see his friend move or give some indication that he was coming to. 'I don't suppose you can get out of that rope?'

Lafferty grunted and Bryson could see his legs flail as he attempted to push, pull and swing his way off the peg.

'No joy Guv, I'm fastened tight.'

'Ok, if it was a drug then the others should be waking soon, Timpson, he came with me, he's not here. Either he escaped, which is good or they have him somewhere else which is probably not good. Reed still being out is probably because they gave him an extra dose, big fella and all that.'

'Aye,' Lafferty replied. 'I think that…' He paused.

'You OK son? Bryson asked.

'I think I heard something Guv… I think someone's coming…'

'You sure?'

'Splashes… getting louder, yeah…' Lafferty dropped his volume, 'someone's coming.'

'Ok, listen up. Play dead, and just…don't do anything. If they think we're all still out cold we might have more time to think our way out of this.'

'Right Guv,' Lafferty replied and immediately dropped his head down, feigning sleep.

Bryson looked over to Reed one more time. *Please don't wake up now,* He thought.

Lafferty was right. As the person approached, the sound of footsteps plodding through shallow water became more apparent until they stopped outside the door. The sound of a latch being lifted, or perhaps a bolt drawn, reached Bryson and he listened out for the jangle of keys or the thud of a lock turning. There was no such sound, no locks, just a bolt or latch, perhaps that would help.

The door creaked as it swung open and Bryson thought he could hear laboured breathing, was his captor old, overweight? He kept his head down but was desperate to look up and face the man, or men who had done this to him.

Footsteps, now on the damp floor. Walking along the row of sleeping men, walking towards him. They stopped, in front of him he was sure. The sound of the harsh breathing was more distinct now.

Bryson decided to risk opening his eyes just a little, enough to see at least the feet of his captor. He allowed the lids to part slightly and could not help but to gasp as he saw what stared back at him.

'Oh, you're awake eh? Playing dead I presume? Good show,' Crowley said.

Bryson barely registered that Crowley had spoken, he was too shaken from seeing the thing sat by his side. The animal, a huge bulldog, was staring up at him, only one eye was fixed on him though, the other seemed to be looking elsewhere. It yawned and Bryson was lost in its massive maw.

'Dear Lord!'

'Oh, don't worry about him, this is Benny. He's my guard dog I suppose,' Crowley said casually.

Bryson lifted his head sharply and stared in disbelief at the occultist.

'Get me out of these fucking ropes!' he shouted.

'Mr Crowley!' Lafferty shouted with joy.

From within his coat Crowley produced a wicked looking blade of about six inches to absolutely no one's surprise.

'No need to get all shouty Inspector, soon have you out.' He reached forward and began to saw at the bindings.

Benny stood and wandered down the line to Lafferty, sat, and looked up at him.

'Allo... er... good doggie,' he said.

Benny observed him and licked his tongue over his nose, which made Lafferty desperate to scratch his own.

As Crowley cut through the rope some of the other policemen began to rouse from their sleep. Bryson could see over Crowley's shoulder that Reed was starting to come too.

'Hurry man,' he said and Crowley fixed him with a scowl.

Finally, he felt the rope separate and he was released from the peg. He stumbled a little, barging onto Crowley who grasped his shoulders and straightened him.

'There, all done,' Crowley said.

'Get Lafferty done, get 'em all done.' Bryson shook his hands and then rubbed at his wrists to bring his blood back into circulation.

Crowley said nothing and made for Lafferty.

'Good to see you Nigel,' he said with a genuine smile.

'You too Mr C. I thought we were done for.'

'Well, there's still time for that constable,' Crowley replied as he carefully cut the ropes.

'Where's the dog appeared from?' Lafferty asked.

'I got conned by some old bastard across the road from the house.'

'He looks nice,' Lafferty said, looking down at Benny and smiling.

'Well don't get too attached. He's going straight back once we're out of this place,' Crowley said while Bryson walked behind him to Reed.

'Sergeant...sergeant are you with us?' Bryson asked and lifted Reed's head so that their eyes could meet. The sergeant blinked. He slowly opened his eyes and Bryson came into focus from the blurred scene.

'Guv...' he said.

'Alright Reed, you're tied at the wrists but Crowley is here, he's going to get you free.'

'Crowley...' Reed whispered, his throat moved as he tried to moisten his throat. 'Fucker...'

'Indeed Sergeant, but right now he's in the process of possibly saving our lives so let's save that until we get back to the station, right?

Reed nodded weakly. 'Right Guv.'

'Give me the knife Crowley and see that the others are alright, warn them about... the lad in the corner, or we might have a lot screaming going on.'

'Right you are Inspector,' Crowley replied.

'You might want to keep that thing out of sight too.' He pointed at Benny. 'This'll be weird enough without that adding to it.'

'I'll take him outside Guv, check what's out there,' Lafferty said. He had crouched down and begun to tickle behind the animal's ears which it appeared to approve of.

'It's a sewer,' Crowley said, 'we're somewhere under the city, towards Holborn I think. I walked a good distance.'

'How did you get here, how did you find us?' Bryson asked as he cut the thick loops from Reed's wrists.

'The Greenhouse,' Crowley said. 'Did you see it?'

'At the back of the house? Yeah.'

'There was a trap door inside. Cunningly hidden I must say. It was Benny that led me to it...I suppose he does deserve some merit in this venture.

Anyway, upon removing a slab from the floor I found a doorway. It was locked, but I have a knack with locks and managed to get it open. There were steps that led down to what was obviously a man-made passage, although it was course and simple, not like the sewers that it ultimately led me to. Again, it was Benny that did the leading.'

'What's down here?' Bryson asked.

'This far? Just sewers, until I reached this place that is.' Crowley busied himself with the other officers as best he could. He warned each of them of the horrible state of their colleague, doing his best to keep their sluggish minds on helping each other.

As Bryson assisted Reed, rubbing at his wrists to help get feeling into them he observed the occultist in action with some small level of admiration. He had no idea how he had found them, the man had entered a place of danger to come to their rescue and was now comforting his officers, trying to protect them from the awful situation they were in. It was hard to like Crowley but sometimes…

'Guv!' Lafferty's head popped around the door. 'I think someone's coming and this time I don't think it's anyone friendly, Benny's been growling.'

'That's good enough for me,' Bryson replied. 'Sergeant, are you ready.'

'Yeah Guv, feeling better.'

'Alright, Crowley, are all the lads free?'

'All sorted Inspector,' he looked around at the constables, all clearly in shock. 'Lads?' he said. The constables, their eyes sore from tears, nodded.

'Right, whoever…or whatever is coming here, we take him down. I want to talk to someone about all this.'

'Right Guv,' Lafferty and Reed replied. The constables with Crowley nodded.

'Ok, here's what we do. Crowley I want you to lock us in again…' One of the constables groaned nervously, 'It's alright lad, we can't let this fella know that we're up and about, Crowley will wait further back in the sewer until this bastard lets himself in. I want us lined up as though we were still trapped. As soon as he steps in we have him. Reed, I'm counting on you for that.'

'My pleasure Guv.' Reed replied, wishing he had his baton.

'Right, positions.' Bryson said and each man dutifully took his place.

As Crowley began to close the door behind him Bryson whispered 'Crowley, don't you go too far.'

'Inspector, I have a drinks cabinet that moves faster than this fucking dog, the chances of me going far are remote.'

'You know what I mean,' Bryson glowered.

Crowley smiled and closed the door.

Part 11

Bryson listened carefully, and it was just as he was ready to think that Lafferty was mistaken that he heard the faint but definite splash of footsteps. *That mutt has really good ears,* he thought. He took a look at each of the officers who were gripping the pegs that they were supposed to be secured to, each had rope coiled about their wrists but what whoever was coming wouldn't know was the loops did not fasten their wrists together. As the splashes grew nearer Bryson reckoned that it was more like two people, not one.

'Reed!' he called in a whisper.

The sergeant looked up at him, Bryson mouthed TWO and Reed nodded. He took a final look at the other constables. Lafferty was fine and the lad next to him seemed steady, across the room, either side of Reed the constables wobbled a little. One was almost certainly trying to stifle sobs. But it was okay. The door opened against them so they wouldn't be seen straight away and Reed could strike before they got a chance to notice, he hoped.

The footsteps stopped as they had done when Crowley had approached and the sound of what he now knew was a latch being lifted ground through him. Reed let his head fall and did the only thing he could, he waited.

For someone who had been hanging by his wrists and drugged to the eyeballs Reed moved with startling strength and agility. Two men entered the room, short by most standards but especially to over six feet of Sergeant Reed. The sergeant listened as they entered and once he was satisfied that both were in reach he struck. He opened his eyes and saw that both were unaware him, they were slowly working their way along the row of officers opposite. One of them, the one to his far right carried a long blade, easily fifteen inches in length which he held down at his side.

Reed didn't waste any time; his target was the knife. Slowly he lowered his hands from the peg and bent his knees slightly, he held his attack until the knife wielder was between Bryson and the constable next to him, then charged.

He presented his shoulder to his target's back and although he had only managed two steps to generate his charge it was sufficient to slam the little man into the wall. Bryson flinched as teeth flew at his face and a sickening CRACK sounded as Reed snapped the man's arm with one deft, brutal pull at his hand and push at his elbow. A scream filled the room.

Reed's manoeuvre had pushed the other man aside, into the path of Lafferty. The constable kicked out and caught him in the ribs, sending him flying against the open door, as he struck its edge he stumbled and fell to the floor. Lafferty marvelled at the man's clothes, they were bright and loose, he looked like a clown and as if to support this opinion Lafferty saw that his face was painted with red, white and yellow daubs.

He didn't give the clown man a chance to stand, he had seen what happened when you let people get back up at Ravensblack Hall, he stepped forward to deliver another kick but the clown man was agile and rolled to the side. Lafferty lost his balance and fell to the floor heavily. Clown man took a quick look to assess the situation with his colleague and was in no doubt that the big policeman had him, he dived out of the door and into the sewer to make his escape.

The knife had dropped from the little man's grip the moment that Reed had broken his bones. Bryson, seeing it. stooped to pick it up and saw Lafferty fall to the floor. The other policemen remained in position, as Bryson had ordered them to do. The last thing he had wanted was bodies tussling all over the place. He moved to Lafferty, as Reed delivered a flurry of punches to the head of his victim. He wondered if there would be anything left of him when he checked again but wasn't too concerned. Lafferty had fallen badly and was struggling to rise, Bryson gripped his arm and helped him up.

'You alright son?' He asked.

'Fine Guv, he got out, ran into the sewer.'

'Don't worry, I'll get him. Stay here with Reed,' Bryson said and stepped out into the sewer before Lafferty could argue.

He saw Crowley. The occultist was stood drinking from a silver canteen.

'Thirsty work, Inspector,' Crowley said with his shark's smile.

At his feet lay the clown man, he appeared to be unconscious and sat atop of him, eyes askew, was Benny.

What happened?' Bryson asked

'Benny didn't like him. It appears that Benny is quite a Lord of the Savannah when it comes to taking down bad men.

'Is he alive?'

Crowley shrugged. 'Who cares?'

'I care Crowley. I need information from these maniacs.'

'Don't you have one in there?'

'Yes, we do, but Sergeant Reed is currently being very angry at him so I'm not entirely sure what's going to be left when I go back in.'

Bryson meant to be furious at Crowley's attitude but couldn't quite convince himself that he did really care whether the bastard was dead or not.

'OK, let's get him inside.' Bryson said and pulled at the man's arm. Benny didn't budge.

'Would you tell your dog to move?'

'Not my dog,' Crowley replied.

Bryson sighed. 'I hate you Crowley.'

'I know,' Crowley said.

'Come on boy, come on.' Bryson tugged at clown man's arm again hoping that Benny would get the message but the great hound stayed put, staring at things Bryson couldn't see.

Bryson gave up. 'I'm going to check on Reed and the others, don't let him escape.'

Crowley looked down at Benny and back to the Inspector 'You think that's likely?'

'I honestly don't know Crowley, that mutt's as awkward as you. You should take him on as an apprentice and leave Lafferty alone.' At this Bryson turned and walked back into the sewer ante-chamber.

Reed was stood over the would-be knife man and clutched the weapon that had been dropped tightly in his fist. Bryson hoped that he hadn't felt compelled to use it.

'Everything OK here Sergeant?'

'Better now,' Reed replied.

'Is he alive?' Bryson asked.

Reed tossed the knife across the room. 'Who cares?' he said, his voice was filled with dark and thundering skies.

Bryson wondered if whatever it was that Crowley brought with him was contagious, but in fairness to Reed one of their lads had been carved up, he had been drugged and the man he had just beaten to a bloody pulp had a knife that probably wasn't going to be used to slice cheese. All being told he decided that he didn't actually care either.

It took a few minutes to get the scene back under control. The constables were a mess and because of this Bryson determined they were a liability and getting them out of the way was as important as getting them to safety.

Neither of the men they had ambushed were dead. Reed had beaten the knife carrier into a coma but the man with the painted face had come to. Bryson had tied him to one of the pegs as Reed held him up. He was so short that his feet didn't touch the floor. He also wouldn't talk.

He looked at them with contempt but refused to make any response to Bryson's questions. Threats of violence did nothing and actual violence from Reed achieved the same.

'We're getting nowhere with this,' Bryson finally admitted to Reed. 'We need to get these lads out, get the Met down here.' Reed nodded.

'I don't think they will make it alone so we'll need Crowley or Lafferty to guide them back,' Bryson said quietly. 'No doubt Crowley will want it to be him.'

'No doubt,' Reed said.

Bryson turned to the group. 'Alright lads, it's time we got you out of here.' The look of relief on the faces of the constables as Bryson said this was obvious. 'We'll get you home and bring the fucking army to scour these sewers if need be.' This elicited a smile from at least one of them and Bryson was thankful for that, they might just get through this with only a few nightmares over the months to come.

'However, we are a man missing. Constable Timpson isn't with us, he arrived with me and I'll be damned if he isn't leaving with me. So Sergeant Reed and I will be continuing on through the sewers, we are going to see where this tunnel takes and us God willing we'll find Timpson.'

'I'll come too Guv,' Lafferty said.

'No constable, not for this. I need you get these officers home, your job is to bring the cavalry,' Bryson said firmly. He walked to Lafferty and put his hand on his shoulder 'It looks like that fall hurt your leg son and I don't think you can move well, that could be a problem.'

Lafferty dropped his head. The boss was right. Something had jarred when he had missed his kick and his leg and knee were very painful.

'Right Guv,' he said.

Bryson turned to Crowley.

'Not a fucking chance,' Crowley said before Bryson could even speak.

'Come on Crowley, we need you, surely you can see that?'

'I can indeed Inspector and the answer is still not a fucking chance.'

Reed stepped forward but Bryson blocked him with a hand. 'No Sergeant, Crowley's done his bit. If it wasn't for him we'd still be strung up to those walls, possibly worse.' He felt Reed relax a little and dropped his hand. 'I was just hoping that the legendary Aleister Crowley might want to lift his reputation in London's elite environment of supernatural appreciation.'

Crowley scoffed. '*Pah*, there's no point trying to appeal to my vanity Inspector. I'm in a sewer. I'm already way above my environment. Once I'm out of this shit hole I'll take stock at what state my reputation is in. Look what I did for you at Ravensblack Hall, what did I get from all that?'

'You got a wedge of money and a free ticket to exit custody, within reason,' Bryson retorted.

'Yes…yes I got money, but what about fame? What about my status? Fuck all, that's what I got. Your lot covered it all up and I was made to look like a proper twat.'

'Yeah but this time we can't do that can we?'

'What do you mean?' Crowley asked as the painted whore of intrigue began to massage his feet.

'Well we can't cover this up can we? I mean I'm going to have these lads bring the Met down here, the army if needed, these fellas, it was you that identified them. It was you that came down and rescued the lads here.' Bryson indicated the shell-shocked Bobbies. 'You think that they aren't going to be eternally grateful, as we all are,' he nudged Reed, who nodded.

'So if I help this time I get all the press, that's what you're saying,' Crowley queried cautiously.

'All the press Crowley. On my honour, I'll even announce it myself,' Bryson added.

'Hmm,' Crowley mused.

'Come on Crowley, these little bastards are up to their nuts in the stuff you like, who knows what we'll find at the end of this?

'We'll find a bunch of fanatic cultists who worship a deity that feeds off the souls of men who have been skinned, carved up and eaten,' Crowley snorted.

'Possibly,' Bryson agreed, 'but we have Reed and myself to take care of them, we just need you to keep an eye out for anything, unusual that we might encounter, you don't need to get involved in the rough stuff. You even have a guard dog!'

'It's not my dog,' Crowley replied forcefully but Bryson detected a weakening in his resolve.

'You should go Mr C. They'll need you.' All heads turned to Lafferty. 'This sort of stuff is beyond us fellas. The Sarge will beat the tar out of anyone who gets in your face and you know that the Inspector is a good bloke. Help 'em Mr Crowley, show 'em what you can do.'

Crowley folded. He was sure that he could have resisted Bryson's entreaties, no matter how much he offered but the lad had no agenda, nothing to gain from putting him in harm's way other than seeing a good outcome for everyone.

Crowley sucked in a deep breath and puffed out his chest. 'Very well. I'll come.'

'Thank you Crowley,' Bryson said. He nudged Reed.

'Yeah. Thanks,' Reed said.

'But rest assured if I get it in the arse on this I'll be your worst fucking nightmare Inspector,' Crowley growled.

'*You already are Crowley, you already are,*' Bryson thought rather than stated as point of fact to the occultist. But he had him now, thanks more to Lafferty than the promise of swag it seemed.

'Okay, good. Now we need to move. We don't know what these pair were supposed to do with us so they may be expected back with their friends.' Bryson pushed at the unspeaking, clown-man, who groaned as his body moved.

'Crowley, any idea about that clobber he's wearing? Some sort of ritual dress perhaps?'

Crowley looked the man over scratching at the bridge of his nose as he did so. 'Not any kind of ritual I know off. I think it's a costume, a fancy costume, something a performer might wear.'

'A performer?' Bryson asked.

'Yes, like a circus clown or a jester. Look at the paint on his face, around his mouth, it's meant to look like a smile.'

Bryson nodded but had nothing to add. 'Fair enough.' He faced Lafferty, 'you ready to get out of here son?'

'Yes sir,' Lafferty replied but there was no heart or desire in his response.

Crowley touched the lads arm. 'It's practically a straight route until you reach the spot where the tunnel that has been dug out reaches the proper sewer channel. I've made markings along the way in chalk, you won't miss them.'

'Right, Mr C.'

Bryson addressed the group of constables. 'Right lads, Lafferty will see you through but his leg's not quite right so you'll need to help him, you need to help each other. When you get out don't fuck about, straight to the nick. Somehow I don't think your vehicles are going to be where you left 'em so just start walking until you get to a road. Once there you obtain yourselves transport by any means necessary short of hurting folks.'

As one they choroused 'Yes Guv.'

'Right, away you go,' Bryson ordered.

The lads shuffled out. Lafferty's limp was pronounced and one of the constables supported him as they went. He looked back at Crowley and Reed, 'No fighting you two,' he said and gave a weak smile.

Reed nodded and his great moustache, which appeared to have regained some of its vitality, twitched at the corners.

Part 12

As they walked deeper into the sewers Bryson was amazed at the sheer size of them. True enough Reed had to dip his head, but both he and Crowley were able to stand upright. Oil lamps lining the wall lit the way. He wasn't sure if these were a normal part of the sewer systems operation or if they had been placed here, by these men, who were using them to move around the city. His domain, where he understood how it all functioned, was above ground and it was where he wished he could be right now.

They had walked a good three hundred yards by Bryson's estimation until they came to a junction that split four ways. Before the inevitable debate with Crowley began over which way they should go, Benny plodded forward and took the tunnel to the left. He pulled Crowley along with ease and none of the men decided to question the animal's decision. There were two more changes in direction taken by the dog within the next ten minutes, and by now the small grasp Crowley had on where they might be was completely gone.

There had been no indication that anyone might be using the tunnels other than the lamps. Crowley had seen no sigils or runes marked on the walls and there was nothing he had seen dropped onto the floor yet Benny continued at his slow but apparently unstoppable pace.

'You think your dog knows where it's going?' Bryson asked.

'It's not my dog,' Crowley replied brusquely.

'How come you've got it then?'

'It's on loan,' Crowley snapped.

'Right,' Bryson said and decided to leave it at that.

They took a final corner and Benny stopped abruptly. The men almost fell over each other as they brought themselves to a sudden halt behind him. The bulldog issued a low growl and stared ahead, mostly.

Reed had taken a lamp from the wall a little further back. He lifted it and walked forwards slowly, past Crowley and Benny. There was a ladder in the middle of the tunnel with a number of ropes dangling next to it. He looked up. Above was darkness and the ladder and ropes reached up into it. The men gathered around and all stared into the blackness above them.

'Looks like this is it,' Reed said.

Bryson carefully gripped one of the ropes and slowly pulled down upon it. As he did so one of the other ropes began to move up at an equal speed.

'A pulley?' he asked.

'I think so,' Reed replied. 'Easier to get bodies to the surface, I reckon.'

The thought hung in the air as the three men contemplated the ramifications of it.

'I'll go up,' Bryson said.

'Nah, I'll go Guv,' Reed said, and before Bryson could argue the sergeant had handed the lamp to Crowley and begun to climb.

Crowley held the lamp aloft but its light couldn't illuminate Reed's progress fully, he vanished into the dark after about eight or nine feet. Save for the gentle trickle of water at their feet and the sound of the sergeant's boots on the ladder it was silent in the tunnel, except for something distant that seemed to emanate from the walls. They had all heard it but had not been able to place the sound other than to assume it was traffic or the general noise of the city. It was Crowley who first began to suspect where they might be, based on that sound.

'There's a trapdoor up here Guv,' Reed called down. 'Want me to try it?'

Bryson called up, 'Hold on Reed.' He faced Crowley. 'What time was it when you entered the tunnel?'

'I'm not completely sure but around a quarter to nine I would think.' Crowley said.

'And how long were you walking until you found us?'

'I don't know, not long I suppose fifteen or twenty minutes at most.'

'And after you found us we were in that room for about half an hour I reckon,' Bryson said.

'Seems reasonable,' Crowley agreed.

'We've been walking through this sewer for about thirty minutes I know it probably feels longer but that's what I estimate, which means it's probably around ten o' clock, maybe a little later.'

Crowley nodded, 'Yes, I think that is about right.'

Bryson rubbed his hand across his chin. Thinking.

'Okay, it's going to be dark, if that door opens up to the outside hopefully no one will see us, if there is anyone up there. If it opens up in some place, like you said it does in the greenhouse, then it could be lit up like Christmas and we'll be spotted.

Crowley nodded again. 'Do we have a choice though? Other than going back to the greenhouse, which incidentally I'm all for if there is a vote.'

'No I don't suppose we do, and we are not going back.'

'We could stay here until the cavalry arrive.' Crowley said and Bryson had to admit that the idea wasn't totally without merit.

'We could, yes we could do that. But how long is that going to take? We had your dog to guide us here and another thing, I'll bet that these guys have eyes and ears all over the city. If a mob of coppers descend on the street, not in dribs and drabs like we did, maybe they'll get wind of it and scoot.'

'I suppose they might.' Crowley agreed. 'It's not my dog.' He added.

'Alright, one last thing Crowley. Tell me what you know, from what you've seen what is going on here. What's going to be up there?'

Crowley lifted his chin and fixed the Inspector with a serious gaze. 'How much are you prepared to believe inspector.'

Bryson didn't hesitate. 'Right now, anything. It's a horrible thing to admit but you have been right about these things so far and I'll be perfectly honest with you, I've begun to question things myself, things I've seen and heard, the explanations I've been given...' He paused as memories of these questions flitted across his thoughts. 'So, just take it for granted that right now you have my attention.'

At the top of the ladder Reed listened intently to the exchange. It grieved him to admit that his thoughts and beliefs had also been troubled since Ravensblack Hall, and since waking in the antechamber he had felt something else embrace him. It was an anger that was dark and terrible and it came from his sense of injustice dealt to the people he wanted to protect.

'This is the Tcho-Tcho, as I stated at the museum. They are a group utterly devoted to their god, Lhoigor. Lafferty said that he and Reed had found evidence of many more disappearances and this is clearly where they bring their victims.

They're using the sewers to go about unnoticed or at least to keep awareness of their presence to a minimum. I would suggest that the poor chap in the chamber was murdered by way of ritual as an offering to Lhoigor in the hope that it would protect them. Kidnapping a bunch of policemen isn't something you can easily keep quiet and this whole street would be torn to pieces by your men this time around.'

Bryson felt the weight of the insinuation. This entrance might have been found if it had been a missing copper instead of a missing youth.

'Who knows, it may have worked too. The Lhoigor has powerful magic, but what the Tcho-Tcho were not aware of is that they were already under scrutiny by other forces.'

'Other forces?' Bryson asked.

'Yes. I wasn't aware of this of course. The group that I am referring to is very difficult to gain any sort of information on, they hide in plain sight and their purpose, whilst not wholly known, is fortunately for us, believed to be benign.'

'Who? Is this the Professor's Order, the... Templarii?'

'What? God no, those twats? No, no. This is older, much older and there are only ever three of them in each region.'

'Three?' Bryson said

'Yes, doesn't matter. The point is that whatever is going on is being watched by some serious people, who only get involved when things are very bad from a… let's say supernatural perspective.'

'Crowley I think we had gathered that this was bad from the moment we found disembowelled corpses swinging from the rafters,' Bryson replied, though not with his usual contempt at Crowley's ravings.

'Of course but what you don't see is how wrong that scene was beyond what we would consider civilised behaviour Inspector.'

Crowley stepped closer and raised his voice a little to ensure that Reed heard him.

'A ritual like that, left to be discovered by us? That goes beyond bold, it tears up the fabric of secrecy that these factions need to keep them undiscovered. The Tcho-Tcho are violent, savage and utterly ruthless, but what they are not is stupid.'

'So what is it then?'

Crowley now looked hard into the eyes of Bryson who felt the sheer conviction of the man bore into him.

'War,' Crowley said.

'War?' Bryson looked both aghast and confused. 'War with who? With us?'

'No,' Crowley shook his head slowly. 'Something's happening in the city. The big guns are coming out. This is related to what happened at Ravensblack Hall. I think that what was occurring there was somehow a part of this. It's possible he, *Ravenstwat*, had taken a side, it wouldn't surprise me, the chance to get on board with the one of the big lads? Roman would have jumped at the chance.'

Crowley paused for a moment and let his penetrating gaze drop from Bryson. 'There is something else. I may not have been entirely accurate in my explanation of the scene we witnessed at the Docks.'

'What do you mean?' Bryson asked

'I told you that the circle was not devised for summoning.'

'You mean it was!' Bryson gasped.

'No, no it definitely wasn't for summoning, but it wasn't purely for worship either. You wouldn't know this but most Gods are happy enough with just total devotion and a few prayers. No, I'm afraid the circle at the docks was for something that is already here.'

'What? What's here? Bryson asked

'I honestly don't know Inspector but I suspect that whatever it is requires certain dietary requirements that are in line with those of the Tcho-Tcho.'

'Dear Lord,' Bryson said. 'So, this is all, Ravensblack, the lads at the docks, it's a fight between rival groups, like gangs? The Tcho-Tcho and who?'

'Not between gangs Inspector. Not even two particular factions. I believe this is a war between Gods.'

Bryson was unable to respond. His credulity, even the greatly expanded and flexible version that he had decided to extend to Crowley had reached its limit. This was a conspiracy of alien ideas that had gone one step too far for him at this time. But he didn't snap.

This was not the time or the place to roast Crowley, the situation at hand was more pressing that questioning the occultists take on matters.

'Look, in answer to your question, what is up there? I don't know. But if these sewers have been used to bring bodies to this spot then the odds are that whatever is up there is what those bodies were for. If it's still there anyway,' Crowley said.

'Will we be able to kill it? We have no guns. All we have is that dagger of yours, which you better have a good reason to be carrying by the way, and that fucking knife, sword whatever, that Reed took off the Tcho-Tcho, that's it.'

'I honestly don't know Inspector, because like I said, I don't know what it is. If it is a creature from the Void and Shadow then just like the Mokoi it is on a clock, it will need to constantly feed on the energy of its victims. How it extracts that in this instance I can't say because again we come back to the fact that I don't know what it is, but you can bet your arse that people being fucking terrified of it is a good place to start. It could be large, small or just like the Mokoi take the form of a host. In that case it could be a man, a woman, one of the Tcho-Tcho perhaps.'

'Well, we could kill that, you killed one of them things from the Shadow place, right? Bryson said

'Of a fashion, yes,' Crowley replied and quickly moved on 'But they are not all the same, you have to understand that these things only obey the laws of our dimension that complement the laws of their own. Bullets and knives…sometimes they are like gusts of wind to these creatures.'

Bryson shook his head. They could wait, it was an option. Lafferty should had to have made it to the station. The entire metropolitan police force will be en-route, they could be in the sewers right now. But it didn't sit well with him, waiting to see what the enemy would do.

'Fuck it,' he said. 'Reed, open that door.'

'Right Guv,' the sergeant replied. He pushed at the panel above him. It lifted with ease.

It was dark outside and they appeared to be indoors. A concrete floor surrounded the trap-door. He listened carefully but couldn't hear anything that revealed where they might be.

Bryson and Crowley stared up at the tube of dark that hid Reed from their view.

'Bring the light,' Reed called down in a whisper. Bryson took it from Crowley and dimmed the flame almost to the point that it would peter out. He had no method of relighting it so he chose to keep the tiny flicker alive. He climbed the ladder until his came to Reed's boots and lifted the lamp up to the sergeant. Reed took it and slowly lifted it above the doorway. He placed it, carefully, down onto the concrete and slowly began to turn the flame up. Gradually a space of about six feet was revealed.

The spot was surrounded by crates.

From the bottom of the ladder Crowley called up to them in a whispered voice 'We're back at the docks aren't we.'

Part 13

Reed climbed out of the sewer entrance, lifted the lamp and took in the scene as the oil lamp revealed it. He had no doubt that it was a warehouse, the crates and boxes mostly stacked like the ones he had seen earlier, and there was a scent on the air that hinted at the nearby quayside. The crates were mostly opened, many with aged wooden panels, and dust had settled everywhere.

He called down quietly to the others, 'Come up.'

Bryson had stayed at his heels and quickly climbed out. Crowley started to mount the ladder but stopped as Benny caught his eye. The dog was sat, staring up at him with an expression that appeared to be critical.

'Erm…' Crowley said to no one.

'Crowley, move it.' Bryson rasped.

'What about Benny?' Crowley called back.

'What about him?'

'Are we just leaving him down here?' Crowley asked, confused as to why he should even care.

'Yes,' Bryson replied. 'The lads will get him when they get here.'

Crowley looked back down at Benny, the animal licked its nose.

'But what if they shoot him?' Crowley replied.

'What? Why would they shoot him?'

'I don't know…but…well its bad light, they are all going to be jumpy and he's…he's a big dog. They might shoot him, y'know, mistaking him for something else.'

'Oh for Christ's sake.' Bryson said.

'Crowley's right,' Reed said. 'They might react badly, not see that it's just a friendly dog Guv.'

Bryson turned to Reed. 'Not you as well.'

Reed looked sheepish. 'Well, I'm just saying that y'know the animal has brought us here and that it's only fair that…'

'Right, yes. Fine,' Bryson said sharply. 'Let's not worry about the life-threatening situation we're in, let's make sure that Crowley's dog doesn't get lonely.'

'It's not my…'

'Shut it Crowley,' Bryson snapped. 'Harness the bloody thing.'

Eight slow and exhausting minutes passed by as Benny was pulled up by the pulley system to be hauled out of the sewer entrance. Crowley pushed at its backside as Reed and Bryson pulled at its massive bulk. Reed took over at the top and strained to get it over the lip of the entrance. Once he had been set down Benny began to lap at his genitals.

Bryson wiped his brow with the cuff of his sleeve. 'Well I suppose we must be fairly safe, because if I wanted to ambush a bunch of blokes I would definitely do it while they were manhandling a giant dog.'

He shook his head and brought his thoughts back to the task at hand. He walked over to a stack of crates in front of him and peered inside. There was nothing to see inside them. These were old boxes, long since emptied of their contents.

Crowley looked about. 'I have to admit, I feel this was a little anticlimactic, this place has been abandoned for years from the looks of it.

'What *were* you expecting Crowley?' Bryson asked.

'Dunno. Something with a lot of teeth I suppose,' Crowley replied casually.

He decided to take a look at the crates too and saw that the shipping stamps, although faded with time, were still legible. Most of them announced that they were from Burma.

'They have been here a long time, this group of Tcho-Tcho,' he said quietly. 'All of this must have taken a while to sort. The tunnel, dug into the sewers, and God knows where else they've burrowed.'

He walked around the circle of light and brushed his hand against the wooden panels.

'And now they are at war with...with who? Who's threatening them, what is it that the Gods are fighting over? There must be something new that's come to light. Something that they desire.'

'Who's going to be able to tell us what's going on Crowley, obviously you can't,' Bryson said, meaning to dig at the occultist, but Crowley seemed pre-occupied with his thoughts.

'There are people who might know. Possibly in London but certainly elsewhere if not. We could ask them. Unfortunately, I'm not very popular with...'

Benny growled.

All eyes looked to the animal. It had stopped the investigation of its nethers and looked, either ahead or to the side, none of the men could be sure, as the rumbling warning issued from its throat.

'Reed, turn down the light man,' Crowley hissed. The sergeant was about to comply but Bryson stopped him.

'No, leave it Reed. Place it over there and leave the trap-door open. These fuckers seem to like the dark so let's keep the balance in our favour. If it's them we can get the jump on 'em from behind the boxes.'

Reed didn't question the order. He placed the lamp high on a crate and looked for a suitable place to lie in wait.

'I suppose I get to mind the fucking dog?' Crowley said.

'You bought, you mind it,' Bryson replied.

Crowley pulled his face at Bryson and tugged at Benny's lead. To his relief the dog stood and followed him to a spot where they could both remain hidden.

'Don't move until I give the word,' Bryson said.

He found a spot that was away from both Crowley and Reed creating a triangle between them. His hope was that there wouldn't be too many, he also hoped that Benny wouldn't start barking at least until they could launch their attack. If the Tcho-Tcho got a heads up they were waiting, they were screwed.

He could hear footsteps now, and voices over them. To his surprise, he had expected some sort of foreign, aboriginal tongue, the language being spoken was English and as the group, he thought he could make out at least four different speakers, came closer, one of them stood out more than the others.

The voice was young and seemed familiar. The connection was made only at the moment when five figures entered the lit space and Bryson could see them through a gap in the crates that hid him away from their view.

It was Timpson.

The young constable had emerged around the corner at the head of the others. None of these looked like the Tcho-Tcho men, they had the kind of white skin that only England's piss poor climate could produce, they spoke with clear London accents although there was a mix of east and west amongst them. Timpson wasn't in uniform.

He wore dark grey trousers and a white flannel shirt that was open to his chest. Against his pale skin was the top half of a tattoo and while Bryson couldn't make out its pattern something about it pinched at his memory.

He almost called out to him but stopped just in time to see Timpson turn to one of the men and deliver a solid slap to his face.

'Who fuck left this open?' Timpson bawled. 'Deakin?'

Bryson figured that Deakin must be the one on the receiving end of the slap. He continued to watch, wide eyed, as Timpson tore a strip off the man.

'Well, your fucking job was to guard this place, what the fuck is this?'

'No one….no one has entered or left my Lord, no one I swear.' Deakin was shaking with fear.

'Anton, O'Leary, get down there, check it out.' Two of the men moved to the open trap-door. Timpson put his hands on his hips and looked around.

'Deakin, Broad, search the place. There's a chance they came back this way instead of to the farm. Little bastards could be hiding somewhere if they saw you morons at the door.'

While two of them were busy at the trapdoor, the others had their attention on Timpson and although Bryson had no idea what was going he knew that this whole scene wasn't right. Timpson wasn't right and now was the time to act.

'Now lads,' he shouted and charged directly at Timpson. Crates exploded as Reed smashed them aside. Timpson was taken completely by surprise, his mouth formed a large 'O' as Bryson stormed into him.

Benny began to snarl aggressively and Crowley decided to let go of the leash. If the animal went at it like Reed and the Inspector had he figured he would be dragged along the floor like a rag doll.

As Bryson crashed into Timpson, he wrapped his arms around the lad's waist and the two of them flew into the crates behind. Deakin and Broad stood, stunned as the ambush commenced. Reed began his assault by placing a foot squarely into the backside of the man who had knelt to climb down the ladder. The punt sent him head first down the hole.

There was a short scream as he fell and then silence as his head connected with the solid floor. Reed followed this attack up with his fist, which was delivered directly into the face of the other man. He felt a satisfying crunch as his target's nose crumpled under the impact.

Timpson wriggled under Bryson, the boy was strong, amazingly strong, and as the Inspector attempted to climb on top of him to hold him down he was thrown aside by a dextrous twist of Timpson's body.

Deakin backed away a little but Broad, coming back to his senses, pulled a pistol out from his belt. No sooner had the gun appeared in his hand than a huge set of jaws clamped down on his wrist. The sheer weight of Benny's head made him bend over as his hand was crushed and the weight of the bulldog dragged him to the floor. Benny shook his head and Broads wrist bones mashed together. The gun went skittering across the floor towards Crowley's hiding place. He emerged from his spot and grabbed it.

Reed delivered a series of punches to the body and face of the man whose nose he had smashed and then grabbed his shoulders. With a mere shrug Reed pulled him over the open trapdoor and let him go.

Crowley saw that Bryson was trying to get back up but Timpson now stood above him, the boy was fast. Reed, seeing the situation had tried to grab him but with startling speed the constable had dodged his attempt and somehow positioned himself to the rear of the sergeant. He kicked at the back of Reeds knees and he went down heavily.

Bryson stood and assumed a pugilistic stance. Timpson sprang forward, he swerved his head to the side as the Inspector tried to land a punch onto him, and then countered Bryson's further attempts with a devastating flurry of blows that sent the inspector crashing back into the ruined crates behind him.

As Bryson went down, Timpson spun on the spot, his leg whirred around and his foot connected with Reeds head as he had attempted to stand. Blood flew from the sergeant's mouth, so great was the impact.

'Fucking hell,' Crowley thought.

He levelled the pistol at Timpson and pulled back the hammer. Timpson looked up at him. Crowley saw that his eyes boiled red. They were orbs of seething crimson matter.

'Oh fuck,' he said and fired twice.

Timpson was a blur, all Crowley could see was the white of his shirt and pale skin as it shimmered in front of him. He had missed with both shots. Timpson was suddenly back. Clear and whole but now more of his face had altered. Along with his disturbing red eyes his mouth had widened, lips became dark and his teeth sharp and ragged.

Bryson tried to get up but again Timpson moved fast, impossibly fast, and brought his knee up into the inspector's chest. Bryson's body lifted from the floor and then he dropped down again, gasping for breath. Timpson lifted a crate and smashed down onto the Inspectors head knocking him out cold.

Crowley fired two more shots but once again Timpson became something vague and without shape. The bullets exploded against crates somewhere behind him.

'Look I don't suppose we can talk about this can we?' Crowley asked.

Despite the apparent futility of the pistol he kept it levelled at Timpson, or whatever Timpson was. Smoke had begun to rise from his body. Tendrils of it slithered and curled into the air. Crowley also noticed the tattoo that Bryson had seen. He thought hard but as he scoured his mental library the Timpson thing began to slowly advance towards him.

'Demon, I'm guessing,' Crowley said to it quickly. 'And not some half-arsed Daemunculi either, the real thing. Impressive.'

He started to back away but found himself blocked by the crates he had first hidden behind. He fired the pistol again but with no real expectation of the bullets landing and wasn't left disappointed. The Timpson thing dodged them with ease and was inches from Crowley before he had released his finger on the trigger.

A hand, leathery and clawed, encircled Crowley's throat and lifted him bodily from the floor. Its strength was incredible, far more powerful than Reed and yet Timpson was half his size. Crowley let the pistol slip from his fingers.

The stench from the creature's mouth was unbearable and despite him being choked, the awful fumes it exhaled found their way into Crowley's throat. His eyes watered and he could feel his head beginning to swell with the pressure of the creature's grip.

The hand around his neck had begun to burn his skin, and through his half-closed eyes he could see that its clothes were beginning to smoulder from the heat of its body.

Fuck me this is a bad one, he thought and reached into his pocket for his knife. *Not big on conversation either.*

The Timpson thing squeezed Crowley's neck slowly, savouring the pain of the occultist, drinking his agony. Crowley knew that it wasn't concerned about Bryson or Reed, it could see everything around it, these things didn't use eyes like people did, not once they consumed their host and Timpson was now almost certainly gone.

In a blink the thing's face was a raw, taut array of purple muscle. Liquid of some sort, perhaps Timpson's blood, dribbled down it bubbling with the heat. It opened its grinning maw, littered with savage teeth and stretched it wide. It would close its mouth around Crowley's face and pull his skin away with one smooth movement.

Crowley jabbed at it with his blade. The Demon could move fast, it dodged firsts, bullets and blades. To Crowley this meant it was nippy, not invulnerable.

The thing stopped and stared hard with its boiling eyes. Then it laughed. It was as horrible a sound as Crowley had ever heard, a sulphurous gurgle that was drawn up from the very depths of the Hell from which it had been spawned. Blades couldn't kill this thing, bullets, rocks, fire couldn't even make it pause in its stride but they could hurt Timpson, or at least while the thing still had Timpson's skin, they could leave a mark.

Crowley knew a few things about Demons, this one especially. It was a Child of Cthugha. The tattoo had been the first indication of where Timpson's loyalties lay and this burning, evil, incarnation of hate left him in no doubt.

Knowing from where the Demon had been spawned meant that Crowley knew which eldritch design needed to be used to keep them at bay. With a practiced hand he swept the blade up, down and across Timpson's skin before it could be replaced by the Demon's own.

The pattern he created wasn't bad considering the angle he was working at and as the last line was carved, completing a complex pattern of lines and swirls the creature stopped its obscene laughter.

Crowley felt its fingers loosen about his neck and abruptly the thing snatched its hand back. Crowley dropped back down to his feet, the lack of oxygen had made him a little dizzy and he couldn't help but fall to his knees.

The Child of Cthugha looked down at its side, in its skin, drawn with the tip of Crowley's blade was a runic inscription. The seal of Atlach'naca. The creature tore at its own flesh to remove the cursed rune. Crowley understood that there was nothing from stopping the monster from defiling its own body to destroy the mark but it gave him time to get his breath back and act.

These things could see everything around them but as it was a true Demon, a creature of Hades there was one thing it couldn't see. For reasons perhaps known only to the Gods, perhaps not even to them, True Demons couldn't see dogs.

'Benny! Crowley shouted. 'Eyeh! Prenah Sheh ah!'

As the creature ripped away the last piece of skin that carried Crowley's handiwork it suddenly leaned backwards and fell to the floor. Benny had leapt onto its back and clamped his massive jaws around the back of the Demons head. His sheer weight brought the thing to the ground. The bulldog gripped the thing with its vice like jaws and shook his head furiously, apparently unaware, possibly unaffected, by the steaming heat of the Demons skin.

The creature screamed, unable to see what was attacking it. All it knew was that something was crushing its skull and whipping its head from side to side with incredible fury.

Crowley could see tiny flames begin to appear on the surface of its body, it was almost fully formed into its True Demon state. If it lived much longer it would become a living thing of fire and even Benny wouldn't be able to resist the inferno it would create. Crowley scrambled over to it and began to carve once again. It was difficult to maintain the pattern as Benny was ragging the thing's head in an attempt to pull it off.

Crowley thought that it was possible that he might actually succeed but he couldn't take the chance.

The flames grew and rippled over its chest as Crowley worked and his hands became raw where they burned at his skin. Its legs kicked at him and clawed hands tried to tear at his face. A boot appeared and stamped down on one of its arms. Then it lifted up and crashed down again. It was Reed.

'Reed! Keep its legs still, I've got to finish this!' Crowley cried out.

Without question Reed dropped his whole body down onto the flaming, naked legs of the thing, they began to burn through his clothes and onto his skin too but he gritted his teeth and remained on top of them. Crowley jabbed and sliced at the thing for a few seconds then stood, casting the knife a side.

'Reed, Benny, let go, get away from it.' His two assistants stopped. Benny released his grip and waddled backwards, Reed rolled off the legs, grimacing as his burned skin sent sheets of pain through him.

'Pyeh etrainis loffh pyeh etiris!' Crowley shouted above the creature's wailing. 'Sont trainis etrainis pyeh sunsha!' As he called out the incantation his arms moved in expansive circles, his hands and fingers dancing to form symbols in the air.

The thing suddenly lifted the upper half of its body from the floor, its blood red eyes fixed Crowley with eternal hate. It began to scream so loud that Benny howled to drown out the sound, Reed and Crowley were forced to cover their ears as the pitch threatened to burst their eardrums.

Suddenly it stopped. The boiling red eyes calmed and turned black, dropping into its skull. It fell back onto the floor and began to boil once again but this time there was no flame.

Instead the demon began to liquefy. Skin and muscle poured from its skeleton rapidly, as though it was being dissolved with acid, until finally its skeletal frame, still mostly that of Timpson, broke down and dissolved in the same manner. After a few minutes there was only a dark patch on the floor and acrid fumes that floated up from the stain.

Benny stopped howling and licked his chops and nose as though to clean away the taste of the thing. Crowley sat on the floor and looked at his burned hands.

'My fucking suit is ruined,' he said.

Reed stood and looked down at him. He shook his head, 'You are a piece of work Crowley.'

He turned to Bryson who lay against smashed crates. The Inspector was showing signs of coming around from the beating the Timpson thing had given him. There was no sound from the men at the bottom of the sewers and the man Broad was out cold. Benny had delivered so much pain that the man had sought relief in unconsciousness. The animal wandered over to Broad and urinated on him.

Good for you dog, Reed thought.

Deakin was gone. Reed wondered if the odds would have turned against them if he hadn't fled the scene. He was also wary that he might still be around and kept a cautious eye on the shadows around them.

Bryson sat up, blood had streamed from his nose and he had a nasty cut above his right eye. He looked around, saw that Reed, Crowley and Benny appeared to be in good shape and moved his jaw around a little, it ached and he was sure a tooth was loose.

'Where's Timpson,' he said.

'Well there's a story in itself Guv,' Reed replied. 'I think you'll need Mr Crowley to answer that one.' Reed checked a couple of crates to find one that would support his weight and sat.

Bryson looked to the occultist who was as unhappy as he had ever seen him. Crowley shrugged. 'It'll have to wait until we get some treatment.' Crowley showed Bryson the palms of his hands, they were severely burned.

'Jesus,' Bryson said.

Reed showed him where the flames had burned through his clothes.

'Was there a fire?' For moment he thought that perhaps the oil lamp had smashed during the melee but then realised that it was what illuminated the area.

'Sort of,' Reed said. Bryson thought he was beginning to sound like Crowley.

Benny looked alright. No burns on him. The big dog had settled down to what Bryson thought must be his favourite pastime.

'So Timpson got away?' Bryson asked, as he had not been adequately answered.

'No, he didn't get away Guv,' Reed replied, 'he's gone but unfortunately we don't have a body. Like I said, that's in Crowley's corner. But there's two at the bottom of the shaft here and that lad, the one they called Broad. No clue if the fellas down there are still with us but that one is.' He pointed at Broad's urine-soaked body. 'Deakin, the one that Timpson was knocking about, he scarpered. Lucky for us I suspect.'

Bryson nodded and got to his feet. He discovered that his ribs hurt too. 'I feel like I've been hit by a fucking express train.'

Crowley snorted. 'Think yourself lucky, I've been flambéed.'

The sound of voices drifted up from the open trapdoor. They were loud and direct. Men giving orders.

'Looks like the cavalry has arrived,' Reed said.

'In the nick of time,' Crowley said rolling his eyes.

'Alright,' Bryson said and took a deep breath. 'Crowley, I know I promised that you would get something out of this and I stand by my word, but I have to speak to those at the top first. This is all...I don't know, this is beyond my wit and my rank.'

To his surprise Crowley nodded solemnly. 'I concur Inspector. I too need to speak to some people. If what I intimated earlier is true then we have a far bigger problem on our hands than I had thought likely, and to be perfectly honest I'm not sure what we need to do about it.'

'This lot, this wasn't Tcho-Tcho was it?' Bryson stated more than asked.

Crowley shook his head. 'No, I believe that these men are followers of another kind. Timpson must have been…well, that we'll talk about later but the fact is that whatever the Tcho-Tcho were up to, this lot weren't involved. It appears to me that they had been following the Tcho-Tcho and intended to let Timpson…well again, this is something for when we're fit and ready to consider such matters.'

'And the thing you thought might be up here?' Bryson asked.

'I was wrong, or at least I think I was. The Tcho-Tcho do have something, somewhere, but it looks like this was a just a part of the network they use to get around unseen.' Crowley pointed at Broad. 'This lot, they're looking for the Tcho-Tcho, or more likely had found them and were watching them.

I do believe we have identified at least two of the factions involved in what is going on, the Tcho-Tcho and a cult that is heavily involved with Cthugha.'

'What's a Cthugha?' Bryson asked.

'WHO'S UP THERE, SHOW YOURSELF, NICE AND SLOW,' a voice bellowed up from the sewer.

'I think that'll have to be talked about later,' Crowley said.

Bryson addressed Reed and Crowley together. 'Alright, keep it tight lads. I need the full story from you two before you say anything to this lot. If anyone has issue with that you direct them to me.'

Crowley and Reed nodded.

'Reed,' Bryson nodded and the sergeant shouted down the hole.

'It's Sergeant Reed, Inspector Bryson and…a civilian.' After this Reed peered over the trap-door so that he could be seen by the men who looked up from below. He saw that the two men he had pushed down there hadn't moved and were being checked over by a uniformed copper and holding the ladder and looking up was a fearsome but familiar face.

'ALRIGHT, WE'RE COMING UP,' the voice boomed again. Reed stepped away from the trapdoor. Seconds later a helmeted head appeared and looked around at the scene. He was instantly recognisable. Captain Brough. Forty years a copper and as tough and grizzled as they came. He looked pale, yet angry.

'Are those chaps down there responsible? Are they a part of what happened to one of my lads?' He asked of anyone in the immediate area.

Bryson wasn't entirely sure about that but he nodded. 'I take it you found the other two as well?'

'Oh yes.' Brough climbed up and exited the shaft. 'Young Lafferty told us about those, told us that there was a gang who had…' The Captain's expression said more than any amount of fury could deliver. What he had seen was boiling inside him. He turned his head and shouted down to his men.

'Alright lads, let's get some of you up here.' He turned back to Bryson. 'What's going on here Bryson?'

Bryson shook his head. 'Right now I don't know Sir, but there is some sort of gang-war happening, or about to happen.'

'Which gangs? The East End Boys, the Barringtons, Lofthouse Crew?' Brough asked.

'No, at least I don't think so, this is…a new lot.'

'Foreigners? The Wops?'

'No Sir, well, possibly foreign but…' Bryson paused to flinch as his ribs sent a burning pain through his chest.

'OK, well, you look like you've been through the mill so let's get you to the hospital. Then I want to hear it all. From each of you,' he turned to Reed and then Crowley.

'Crowley! Is he…'

'He saved our lives,' Reed said. The Captain frowned then pointed at Benny.

'That?'

'Same thing,' Reed replied.

The Captain raised his eyebrows. 'Whose dog is it?'

Crowley closed his eyes and sighed, 'he's mine.' he said.

Part 14

Reed fastened the top button of his uniform jacket, then tugged at the bottom of it to make sure that it was properly fitted across his shoulders. Big men like him were fitted out by a special tailor as there was no tolerance for an incorrectly attired officer in the Metropolitan Police Force.

The downside was that he was only ever granted two uniforms at any one time, because of the cost involved. He spied a fleck of lint on his collar and plucked at it with his large fingers. Concerned that there might be other unwanted bits of fluff or thread about the jacket he examined his appearance in the large mirror that commanded the hallway of his home.

He carefully checked each section, collar, lapels, and pockets but found nothing untoward. He turned and looked over his shoulder to try and spot anything that might be on his vast shoulders or back. All seemed well. Underneath the mirror on a simple table were his keys, a set of handcuffs, and some loose change.

He gathered them up and dropped them into a pocket. A whine sounded, coming from the kitchen. Reed looked into the mirror once more. His straight black hair was slicked back, revealing his eyes, dark brown, easily mistaken for black when he was occasionally seen without his helmet, which was usually worn with its brim low.

He took a deep breath and exhaled slowly. He looked tired, his expression grim. Things had changed. *He* had changed. His moustache, still a large horseshoe of hair, hid much of his face and masked his expression. He liked this, for coppering it was ideal. Criminals respected his size but not being able to tell what Reed was thinking instilled a welcome level of fear in them too. Respect and fear was vital in keeping general crime down in London. But he felt that he was no longer involved in keeping down general crime. What had Crowley got them involved in?

The whine sounded again and was followed by a low growl.

'Alright lad! Bloody hell,' Reed shouted towards the kitchen.

He had agreed to look after Crowley's dog. The animal wasn't too much bother but if it wasn't fed at 7am sharp it began a loud and effective protest campaign.

It was also very picky about its diet. Steaks, chicken with gravy and ham hock were pretty much its list of demands. Anything else was sniffed, dismissed and the noisy protest would begin.

He nodded at himself in the mirror. He was sure that he wasn't a bad person, he could have been with this size and his temper but he had gone another way. He had decided to help people get back what was theirs, he had chosen to fight the bullies and outsmart the confidence men.

But he was no angel. He lowered his head. He had beaten men to a bloody ruin, shot, stabbed and bashed at them with extreme prejudice. His baton, *His Majesty's Pleasure*, had been lost to the Tcho-Tcho and he was glad of it. The weapon had started to become heavy with the blood of the men it had *pacified.*

He turned away from the mirror without looking back and headed to the kitchen. Benny was sitting on his blankets, one eye fixed on Reed as he entered, and the other looking at something on the far wall. Benny gave a small, friendly but also insistent bark.

'You're a pain in the arse dog. It's like having Crowley here,' Reed muttered as he opened up a cupboard and withdrew a parcel of meat and bones. He knelt and dropped the contents into Benny's food bowl, which had been bought for him by Lafferty. Benny lazily rose and began to snaffle them down noisily. As Reed stood a knock sounded at the door.

He didn't get visitors or at least up until recently he had not. After the Tcho-Tcho incident both Lafferty and Inspector Bryson had begun to call over. They rarely talked much, at least not about the cases. Instead they discussed sports, the theatre and books that they were reading.

Ravensblack Hall and the Docks had drawn them together, Reed could see how that might happen of course. He and Bryson had been colleagues for a long time and now he thought that they were friends. Lafferty had become important to them both. The lad had seemed so vulnerable and yet had proved himself to have a line of steel for a spine and a heart as big as horse.

Crowley never came over though. His only visit outside of being dragged away by Bryson, as far as he knew, had been to the Inspector shortly after the Ravensblack affair.

That had been a surprise to say the least but deep down Reed had always suspected that the occultist would get out of the house that night. 'Slippery bastard' seemed to sum him up. No, it didn't really. Reed wasn't sure that Crowley could be 'summed up.' The man twisted and turned, altered his disposition to suit his purpose, one moment he was running for the exit the next he was locking himself in with a psychopath, in a burning building, to save everyone else.

The knock sounded again, not a rapid impatient thumping just a polite indication that there was someone there. Benny didn't appear interested, this was good. Reed thought that the animal had a nose for trouble. '*Probably a handy tool when in close proximity to Crowley,*' he thought. He walked out of his kitchen and headed for the door.

He opened it cautiously. Crowley had advised him to 'be careful for a while,' and other than the pack of lies he had fed the Investigators of the

Barnabas Street Sewer Murders, that headline had run for a while, it was pretty much all he had heard from him until he had asked him to look after Benny for a week or two. It had been four weeks now. All of them, himself, Bryson and Lafferty had been given a month to recover especially as the Guvnor had suffered fractured ribs. The poor lads from the sewer chamber were still in hospital being cared for. Physically sound, mentally shipwrecked.

Opening the door revealed a short, old man in a dark tweed suit. Fascinating blue eyes occupied a slim and time worn face. The man was old but was also timeless. Reed couldn't place his age, he wanted to satisfy himself that the man at the door was perhaps in his seventies but the feeling his got was of someone far more wizened stood before him.

'Sergeant Reed?' the old fellow enquired.

'I am,' Reed answered cautiously.

'Splendid, Sergeant, splendid,' the stranger replied and offered his hand to Reed, a friendly smile on his face.

Reed took the hand, an ancient thing and marvelled at how firm its grip was.

'My name is Penhaligon. Lester Penhaligon,' he said, still smiling.

'Good to meet you Mr Penhaligon, what can I do for you?' Reed said returning the gentleman's politeness.

'Actually Sergeant Reed I'm here to do something for you. I'm here to help you with the problems you and your colleagues are having with…' Penhaligon took a careful look left and right down the street that Reed's house was situated upon and then looked up at Reed with a serious expression. 'The chaps from Burma.'

This took Reed by surprise. He wasn't sure how to react and defaulted to feigning ignorance. 'I'm sorry Sir, I'm not sure what you're talking about.'

The old man nodded and offered an understanding smile. 'Quite right, Sergeant, quite right. This is a matter that requires the utmost discretion, however I can assure you that I am a man who can be trusted.'

Reed couldn't help but feel that this was true. Something told him that this little old fellow at his door was not one of the bad guys, but he couldn't take the chance. Not without speaking to Bryson and Crowley first.

'I'm sorry Sir but I really…' Reed began.

'Ah Benny! How you are old chap?' Penhaligon said, looking past Reed.

To Reed's continuing surprise the Bulldog came lumbering forward at, what was for it, an excited pace. It pushed Reed's legs aside and put its head into the hands of the old fellow who had knelt as the animal had approached. He now stroked and rubbed at its ears with gusto.

'He knows you? You know Benny?' Reed said, shocked.

'Of course dear boy. Benny and I have had many adventures together. I do hope he looked after you and do trust that Crowley has been attentive to him.'

'Er…yes, I suppose so. Crowley's away at the moment…I…' Reed stuttered.

'Yes, yes I sent him on a little fact finding mission,' Penhaligon said, still fussing over Benny.

'You sent him…you *sent* Crowley?' Reed said, his disbelief evident.

Penhaligon looked up from his petting of Benny. 'Well, of course the only way to get Crowley to do anything is to make him think he wanted to do it all along. He's a smart man but a slave to his own sense of self-importance.'

That was enough for Reed. Penhaligon appeared to be well-known to Benny and he certainly had a handle on Crowley.

'I think you had better come in Mr Penhaligon,' he said.

The old man stood, 'Thank you Sergeant that is very kind of you. I see you are dressed for work but I assure you that I will only take up a few minutes of your time.'

Reed stepped aside and allowed his guest to enter. Benny walked at his feet as the old chap walked down the hall.

'Head to the kitchen Mr Penhaligon, straight ahead. I'll make a cuppa, I have time yet,' Reed called to him.

Penhaligon replied 'Splendid.' And continued on.

Reed walked down the hall and paused at the large mirror. He chanced to look into it, to see what the old man might see. To his surprise the Sergeant Reed he had seen only a few minutes ago was gone. He saw in his reflection the steel of his determination, his belief in mankind that existed despite all of the horrors he had seen. Somehow the thought came to him that Penhaligon had seen that too.

He walked into the kitchen and filled the kettle. Penhaligon sat and Benny lay next to him.

'Well Sergeant Reed, what I am about to explain to you is going to sound extremely strange.'

Reed placed the kettle onto a hob and lit it, as he did so he turned to Penhaligon. 'After what I've seen recently, Mr Penhaligon, I find that difficult to believe.'

'Quite,' Penhaligon replied. 'However, I strongly suggest that you take a seat and then we will see if perhaps I can live up to my bold statement.'

Reed took two mugs from a cabinet next to the oven and placed them onto the table in front of him and reclined in his chair.

'Go for it.'

Penhaligon smiled once again, it was friendly and encouraging but his bright blue eyes, which swam in a rheumy film, tinged his expression with a hint of sadness.

'Sergeant Reed, tell me what you know about Demons,' he said.

By Day and by Night

Part One

The Basement of the Cock and Bear, Village of Blackbrook, 1921

'*Fucking, fucking, fucking, fucking,*' Crowley muttered as he worked at the makeshift table Reed had cobbled together.

'Keep it down Crowley for Christ's sake.' Bryson hissed. His temper was badly frayed and holding it in check as Crowley performed his spell was proving difficult. Jut accepting that a spell was being performed would have done it alone, but Crowley rarely failed to exacerbate his impatience.

'Do you want to do this?' the occultist looked up at him with bulging, angry eyes.

Bryson pursed his lips. He often wanted to give Crowley a good kicking and right now he believed he was as close to making the fantasy real as he had ever been, but despite his furious and threatening demeanour towards him Crowley kept his stare fixed for another moment, to ensure that he was being understood, then returned to his task at hand.

Bryson couldn't be sure, but he felt that there was a very good chance that the occultist called him a *cunt* under his breath as he continued to arrange stones and twigs on the table.

Sergeant Reed stood to the side, silent. Watching. The last thing he needed was for the guvnor and Crowley to go at it. Certainly not while all holy hell was looking for them somewhere up above. While a fire, that they had started, raged across the village.

The room was the basement of what had once been the tavern. Reed suspected that this one building once serviced the needs of the whole of Blackbrook village, and while time had eaten away at everything up top down here there was only a film of dust to show its present disuse.

A single set of stairs led up to the trap door by which they had entered. This door was currently the only thing that lay between them and the things that hunted above ground. There was no way to form a barricade it opened upwards. If anyone or anything discovered it, they would be truly cornered.

There was furniture down here with them. It was very old, very tired stuff. Things that were easier to throw into a spare room than to cart off to a dump or even to burn. Crowley had found a use for it though. He had found a narrow sofa chair and sat in it while Bryson and Reed had desperately looked for some way of blocking the trap door. He claimed that he had to *'focus his energy'* and *'tap into the channels of Essence that were strong here'*. It was like being in a fire and the only man who could save you was an arsonist.

'How much longer Crowley?' Bryson asked after a further ten minutes had passed. He was massaging his damaged foot and winced as he spoke. This time Crowley didn't even look up.

'Every time you interrupt you slow me down. Why don't you just do something useful, like shut up until I tell you I'm done?'

Bryson continued to glower but managed to keep his temper in check. His foot ached badly and had swelled to the point that Reed had been required to remove his shoe for him. The truth was that Crowley was probably right, and it stung. He was being impatient, he knew he was trying to pressure Crowley, but he felt he had good reason. Constable Lafferty was God knows where, possibly in a worse predicament than they were.

Reed was certain that the lad was safe and Bryson could sense that the Sergeant was wholly convinced of this. He couldn't explain how he knew this, or how Reed could be as sure as he was, but he accepted it. Just as he accepted that Crowley could help them with his magical words over a selection of sticks, baubles and runes carved into the table. It was madness but these days it was what thought of as 'reasonable madness.'

A further ten minutes passed and during this time Crowley had silently raised his hands into the air, his eyes closed as his face tilted upwards towards the dingy ceiling. He mouthed words but said nothing and his fingers danced in strange patterns. Shortly afterwards he placed his fisted hands on the table and stared down at it.

The man was thinking. Bryson and Reed could see that Crowley was chewing something over in his mind.

The tell-tale signs were how he ground his teeth and frowned as he looked at, or into, nothing at all. The Inspector had begun to know a few of Crowley's ways or at least know as much of the man as was possible. It was like grabbing at mist.

But he had come around to some staggering conclusions about Crowley's abilities. He genuinely believed that there were windows the occultist looked through no one else could see or were even aware existed. Further to this he also hoped that he would never find himself seeing Crowley staring at *him* through one of those windows. He shuddered when he thought of it.

'Ok.' Crowley said, finally. 'There is something we can do.'

Bryson almost leapt from his chair, prevented only by his injury. Reed took a step forward. Both were ready for action, ready to do anything rather than stand or sit around as Crowley played at magic.

'Out with it man. What do we do?' Bryson insisted.

'It's not quite that simple. First off we need to make a promise.' Crowley's eyes flicked across to each man in turn anticipating which one would shout at him, he guessed it would be Bryson. It was Bryson.

'Make a promise? What are you gibbering about Crowley, can we get out of here or not?'

'Well, apparently, we can. However, I can't get the information I need until certain contracts are made and future obligations are understood.'

Bryson narrowed his eyes. It was the kind of language Crowley employed to skip around the truth of things.

'Crowley for God's sake, either just tell us what you know or don't because to be perfectly honest I'm at the point where I would rather face *them* than you for even another moment.'

The insult slid off Crowley like water off a wellington boot. The occultist lifted his hands from the table and clasped them together. He tilted his head slightly and gazed off into the distance.

'I once went through a long and quite arduous process in Nepal to gain access to my spirit guide,' his eyes once again slid back to the officers but his head remained in its classic, rhetoric delivery pose, 'that gentlemen, before you stand gormlessly with your, *'what's a spirit guide'* expression, is an entity, often a human soul, who has chosen to travel across the *Aether.'*

He again focused on some distant memory. 'These benevolent souls can be requested, through the aforementioned process, to become a sort of information bureau pertaining to places beyond our physical plane.'

'Crowley.' Bryson warned, as he did whenever it looked like the occultist was about to indulge in his customary weirdness. He didn't mind Crowley's explanations of what made his world tick but when he was desperate to shoot, or even better punch something that deserved it the man's self-absorbed ramblings became a chore.

'It's *important* Inspector!' Crowley snapped. 'Have some fucking respect for a well worded preamble for pity's sake.'

'They are close,' Reed thought, *'close to allowing the very thin line of grudging, mutual respect they have for each other's abilities to snap.'*

This put him on edge more than the threat from outside the basement. The two of them were masters of their art, Bryson of razor sharp deduction and uncanny instinct, Crowley of everything that couldn't be explained by Bryson. Both were stubborn, wilful and easy to anger. Reed wondered who he would have to knock out first in the event of a brawl.

'It would be Crowley. It would definitely be Crowley.'

'I acquired my spirit guide, an emissary from the God Horus,' Crowley continued as though nothing had been said. 'Who at the time had reason to be pleased with my presentations to him of late, and from then on he directed Aiwass to help me maintain the *The Great Scale*.'

'No. You've lost me,' Bryson said.

'Which bit?'

'All of it really, but let's say 'The Great Scale first and then move on to Aiwass.'

'Hmm. Yes, I can see that you will need some explanation, it might help with the contract,' Crowley stroked his chin as he spoke. 'I have commented previously that our world, the space we and our planet move within and the Galaxy we occupy, are only a fragment of the immensity that we know as the universe.' He looked to each officer with a raised eyebrow. Both nodded. Crowley continued.

'I believe I have intimated that this vast, unimaginable space is in fact but one of... well, I simply don't have a figure to offer so let us say an infinite number of such realms, and that each of these is of a form that can be identical, or utterly alien to us.'

Bryson and Reed nodded again, although with a more pronounced action which indicated that Crowley was approaching the limit of their credulity.

'The God Horus occupies a space, what physicists call a *dimension*, which shares many characteristics with ours. By and large as Gods go Horus is alright, I mean he would like to have control of the Earth and subjugate mankind to his bidding, but what God wouldn't?' Crowley shrugged a little.

'However he had his shot a few thousand years ago and fluffed it. He appears to have gotten over that and like the well-rounded cosmic deity that he is has moved on. *However*, he's not entirely happy with its current overlord and so does his bit to maintain the balance needed to keep said overlord from increasing his power even further. Gentlemen,' Crowley stretched out his arms and pointed the index finger of each had upwards, 'this status quo of position in the heavens is called 'The Great Scale,' and it represents the actions taken by the Gods to ensure the balance of power does not tilt heavily towards any particular faction. Especially while the current dominant entity is dealt with.'

'Current dominant entity? Bryson said. 'Are you talking about God Crowley?

'One of them, yes.' Crowley replied.

'One of them?' Bryson repeated. He shook his head. 'I shudder to think the greeting that awaits you in Hell Crowley I really do.'

'Right.' Crowley said, employing his most patronising tone. 'May I continue?'

Bryson said nothing.

'So. What this all means is basically Aiwass, *my spirit guide*, will help so long as what I'm doing is in some way undermining the big chap upstairs.'

'Like the devil.' Bryson said.

'What?'

'Like the Devil. It's what he does isn't it. He works against God through man,' Bryson said, feeling for a moment that he was actually talking at the same level as Crowley upon the subject. 'God made man and so he, the Devil, messes with us to make God angry.'

'No,' Crowley replied dismissively, 'that's not what the Devil does, not if we are referring to Lucifer anyway. That is a little more…*involved*. You need to forget all that Bible stuff for the moment. Just focus on the fact that we have someone who will help us if we give her a promise and a small offering.'

Bryson felt a little disappointed that what he had thought had been a good contribution had been so readily thrown out.

'Her?' said Reed. 'This Aiwass is a lady?'

'After a fashion, yes. Sort of,' Crowley replied.

'Alright so, Aiwass, this thing from…elsewhere.' Bryson waved his hand in the air indicating, Crowley presumed, worlds beyond his understanding. 'We give it…her, something… and she helps with this mess. Am I right?'

'Spot on Inspector,' Crowley said.

'What do we have to do? What does she want?'

Crowley took a breath. 'Well, the form she has is incorporeal, she wants a human body.'

'What do you mean?' Bryson asked, his suspicions back on full alert.

'These entities cannot contact the physical universe, only through the *Aether*, the *Essence* that I have mentioned before…' Crowley waited to see if any glimmer of recognition flashed across their faces, Bryson displayed nothing but Reed…the Sergeant seemed at ease with this.

He continued, explaining that would take more time than they had to hand. 'Aiwass wants to be able to walk on Earth and for this she will need a willing host, she will have no powers, they have to be left at the door so to speak, but she will be able to move amongst us and observe, which is what she desires.'

'What absolute bollocks.' Bryson said.

'Well, it's that or certain death at the hands of those bastards up there.' Crowley said. 'Your choice.'

Bryson turned to Reed. 'Are you buying any of this?'

To his surprise Reed didn't immediately condemn Crowley and his ravings. Instead the sergeant ran a hand through his hair as he thought, and only after a few moments had passed did he answer.

'I think the bottom line Guv is that we don't really have much of a choice. As Crowley says it's either go with his plan or we try our luck at escaping the village. Right now, given what we've seen, I don't think us getting out without help is on the cards.'

Bryson scrutinised Reed. The man was often solemn, serious and his loyalty to both him and the force unquestioned. If he was prepared to put his trust in the madman Crowley then it was going to be hard to go against it, despite his own misgivings.

'Ok Crowley, it looks like you have centre stage, again. Tell me what happens next.' Bryson said, resigned to more bullshit.

'Right well. Aiwass will contact a person who is about to leave this world...'

'Leave this world?' Bryson interrupted.

'Die Inspector, shuffle of this mortal coil...'

'Murder?' Bryson said, his suspicion firing up once again.

'What? No, well I don't imagine so. I mean it could be but that's not the point.'

'Not the point? Are we to facilitate a murder?'

'Noooo,' Crowley sighed. 'Not like that. Aiwass can't hurt anyone, she's not corporeal you tit. No, she will use her power to speak to someone who is about to pass on...'

'Pass o...' Bryson started but Crowley cut him short.

'Die, she will speak to someone who is about to die, and by whatever method happens to be the cause, murder, suicide a really bad cold, and at the very moment of expiry she will make them a deal. She will guide them to wherever they wish to go and in return will take the body of that person as hers while she remains on the Earth.'

'How? Bryson said. 'How is that even possible?'

'How should I know? I'm not a God' Crowley replied. 'I wish I did, but I don't, its stuff that's beyond my learning.'

Bryson desperately tried to get a grip on what Crowley was proposing. He tapped his head with a finger and then shook it at the occultist. 'Right, so this entity, this Aiwass gets a person to give up her body, I get that I think. Where do we come in?'

'Well, we have to make an offering of blood and life and agree a contract. In a sense, we give Aiwass the earthly fuel she needs to contact this person and perform the transfer of souls.'

'Blood and life? Bryson asked.

'Yes,' Crowley replied

'And what exactly does that entail.' Bryson asked warily and at this Crowley became more animated.

'Well first off we will need a receptacle, a bowl of some kind would be excellent but its form really doesn't matter. We need some matches, which I have about me so no problem there, and then finally we need…' Crowley slowed up at this point, 'a little blood from each of us,' he paused, and then hurried out, 'and a little life essence.'

Bryson held up a hand. 'How much is a little blood'

'Oh. Not much, a few drops from each of us is all that is needed. We just dribble it into the bowl and I set it alight…with the life essence…you see the flame will burn the contents to ash and then the ash is crushed to a powder. The powder is then released into the air with a few important phrases of magical significance, and away we go. Easy peasy.' Crowley beamed.

'What's life essence?' Reed asked. He noticed that Crowley had tumbled over the phrase each time he alluded to it.

'Yeah, life essence. Well, that's probably the tricky bit,' Crowley said.

'Tricky how,' Bryson replied. 'What is it, do we have to lose a limb or something?'

'No of course not. Nothing so drastic Inspector, but…well, it's probably awkward, for you two… I imagine.'

Reed stepped forward again to close the distance between him and the occultist. Crowley was blathering and he felt that he needed to be brought back on course. Just being within touching distance of a man built like Reed usually made other men gain some degree of focus.

'What are you talking about Crowley? Come on man, we don't have the luxury of time to spare here.'

Crowley looked at Reed and Bryson in turn and then once again. 'Well…' he took a breath.

'The Essence of life is semen.' He said.

The silence that followed and filled the room was coated with the frost of chilled judgement.

'Are you out of your fucking mind?' Bryson said slowly and with patent menace.

Crowley spoke quickly. 'I'm sorry Inspector but it is a required constituent of the ritual. Without the offering Aiwass will be unable to do…whatever it is she does to connect to the host body.'

'And how exactly are we supposed to get…*that* for your ritual Crowley.' Bryson snarled.

'Well, you know…the usual way. How we lads do…when we…do that kind of thing.'

Bryson looked to Reed.

'Guv…I have not got a single fucking comment to make.'

'Look,' Crowley came around from the table, 'I know this is a difficult thing to even consider but you have to understand that the universe doesn't give a damn about what we do or what we don't do. The universe is so big that by rights we don't even mathematically matter to it, not at all. If this planet suddenly disappeared into thin air it wouldn't even be noticed. The Moon might shoot off somewhere but that's your lot.' Crowley put his hands together as if in prayer, desperate to emphasize his show of reason.

'What harm can there be in three men, men of the world, sacrificing a little dignity to save not just their own skins but those of a friend and colleague…' Crowley dipped his head a little and looked up from his hooded eyes 'and their poor little dog?'

'You fucker.' Bryson said. Crowley had played the Lafferty card with aplomb and just to ensure that no one could call him on it he had thrown in Benny as well, his Ace in the hole.

'Is he really suggesting what I think he's suggesting?' Reed said.

'I believe he is,' Bryson replied.

'Oh come on, don't be so bloody starch arsed about it. I'll bet you've both been knocking one out since you could tie your own laces.'

Crowley moved away, to the piles of junk that were spaced around the basement.

'Help me look for a bowl and while you are at it try to find some cups or something. Let's get this done.'

Bryson and Reed now chose not to catch each other's eye. Instead, with nothing better to do other than to argue with Crowley they also began to rummage in the mess of dust covered household items and discarded bar supplies.

It wasn't long before Reed found a small box containing little glasses, probably for shots of spirit. He picked out three and brought them to the table.

Crowley noticed him and smiled. 'Excellent Reed, pop them on the table.'

'What about this?' Bryson displayed a wicker basket.

Crowley screwed up his face. 'No not really, we need something solid, no chance of…*anything* running out of the bottom.'

Bryson snorted and continued to search through his pile. After a moment Crowley announced. 'Gentlemen I think I have it.'

Reed and Bryson turned from their search, which they both secretly wished would go on until the end of time, and saw that Crowley was holding a China bowl. Crowley turned it over. 'Wedgewood! Stoke on Trent's finest,' he exclaimed.

He returned to the table and placed the bowl down next to the shot glasses.

'Now, first I will need a little blood from each of you. A little prick should produce all that we need.' He grinned.

Both Reed and Bryson understood Crowley had found something hilarious in mentioning 'prick' but was smart enough to keep his comments to himself at this time.

Reed reached into his jacket and withdrew a small locking knife. He opened it up and without hesitation jabbed the point into his finger. A bubble of thick blood formed on the pad.

'Excellent Sergeant, if you could just smear that onto the base of the bowl.'

Reed did as he was instructed. Crowley turned to Bryson and Reed handed over the knife.

'Inspector,' Crowley said.

Bryson took the knife and copied Reeds action. A quick poke, he squeezed the pad to force a swell of blood to its surface and then moved the tip against the bowl as indicated by Crowley.

'Very good. Now if I may?' Crowley took the knife and rather than jabbing at his finger he curved the blade over his thumb. This produced an instant and more copious amount of blood to be produced

'Better to be safe than sorry,' he said and allowed droplets to fall into the bowl.

Each of them rubbed at the place where they had intentionally wounded themselves to clear away the blood and to pacify the throbbing it produced.

'Now, I'm afraid we need to obtain the remaining ingredient gentlemen.' Crowley lifted the three shot glasses and handed one each to Reed and Bryson, keeping one for himself.

'I suggest that we each make our way to a corner, for the sake of dignity, and get on with it. Do take your time but bear in mind that terrible violent death awaits us if we don't get a move on.'

'Thanks a bunch Crowley, I'm sure that will help a great deal,' Bryson said.

'Do we really have to do this?' Reed said as he stared at the little glass.

'I'm afraid so,' Crowley replied. 'and bear in mind that this is as uncomfortable for me as it is for you.

The two officers gave Crowley a final hard look and then turned to seek out a corner that was bathed in as much darkness as possible.

Crowley felt no need to go to such lengths. He placed his glass on the table before him, undid his trousers and got down to business.

Within a minute he was done.

'Phew... I needed that.' he said.

Part 2

Three weeks earlier. London.

The rain had finally abated. London now basked in unexpectedly warm weather and although Sergeant Reed found it to be somewhat stuffy, due to his thick, heat absorbing uniform, he welcomed it. Brilliant sunlight pushed back shadows that had been suffocating the grim streets and allowed them to breathe.

He had decided to patrol although he wasn't required to do it anymore. All of that had changed with his transfer, along with Bryson and Lafferty, to the new division. He wasn't even expected to wear the uniform but he had absolutely no desire to give that up. To him it was more than what identified him as a copper, it was his armour and a reminder of who he was and what was expected of him. Although even that had changed he supposed.

Unlike officers of the Met Reed was no longer called upon to attend petty crimes. Burglaries, muggings, small matters of breach of the peace weren't placed before him. Even crimes of a more serious nature were passed on to other officers. Rape, arson, riots...he used to love a good riot, these were things that other departments, other Sergeants dealt with.

The only time that a senior officer would appear with a case file would be when he had a 'weird one.' Complaints of strange noises, sudden disappearances of people, only reports in which persons of wealth or of note might be involved of course, those and suspicious deaths. But these came to him and the lads only after every possible *normal* avenue had been explored.

It didn't take long for Reed to become aware that the department that had been created specifically for Bryson. What he and Lafferty had been seconded to was not at all what it seemed. He wasn't sure he liked it either.

To begin with there was too much time available. On the beat with the Met he had been constantly under the cosh of the clock. Chasing down bad people, following leads, controlling situations that could spark into riots, or Friday nights as they were more usually called. Now he sat in a large office with a typewriter, which he was incapable of using, sat in front of him.

He did his duty. He read through the case reports. He examined evidence and followed where it took him. This was usually nowhere. Or at least nowhere interesting or challenging. Mostly he chatted to Lafferty and the Guvnor.

Lafferty appeared to enjoy his role, which to Reed was the only surprising thing about the whole situation. The lad had begun to carry his notepads everywhere and was burning through them with some speed. He had looked at one of them once. In the margins, there were often little sketches, symbols or cryptic words.

He had no doubt that the lad's education under Crowley was continuing, although the occultist was rarely mentioned, but the notepad doodles were like the occultists signature under everything that Lafferty wrote.

'*Crowley...*' Reed removed his helmet and wiped his brow. His thick hair was helping to pump sweat down his neck and forehead. Crowley was still around.

There was an unspoken rule that where possible Mr Aleister Crowley, who was now contracted to the force officially as a consultant, should be omitted from any conversation. Occasionally his name, and sometimes his deeds, would surface but overall he was only background noise to what was at hand.

It wasn't the man's personality, abrasive and infuriating as it was, it was that Crowley represented the very last resort. If they had to turn to him then the odds were that men with burning skin would be involved, or heads lying in driveways or young men with their bellies opened up and their guts spilling onto the floor. It was as though when Crowley was around everyone's second language suddenly became screaming.

No. He was happier for Crowley to be a bad memory if that was at all possible. Happy to let the horror and the pain of his previous encounters with the man fade away, but his new role wouldn't allow that and so, uncaring of what his superiors might say he had decided to patrol his former beat by way of rebellion.

He called in on shopkeepers, artisans and other businesses who were always pleased to see a familiar face that they could trust and who they knew was looking out for them. Along the rows of drab terraces housewives hung out washing or cleaned their steps. Reed welcomed the smiles, the polite '*Mornin officer,*' greetings and more than one lurid look from a lusty spinster or occasional married lady.

He liked it because it was evidence of life, of people who were getting on with living. Up until recently he felt all he had encountered was people who were looking at death, welcoming violence or purposefully seeking to follow a path that would lead them straight to Hell.

He stopped.

If he continued walking, he would need to cross the Thames and in doing so he would move into the more affluent parts of the city. This he thought of as Crowley's domain. Many of the cases he had dealt with had their origins there. There was something about wealth and education that drew many of those lucky enough to have both into a way of thinking that was alien to him. They seemed to get bored with being comfortable and free of care and because of this they sought out adventure, excitement and danger. Was life less interesting if you had the money to live free of concern?

Crowley had explained that the membership of the Golden Dawn, the occult group that had expelled him from their order, was almost entirely populated with wealthy, bored individuals who relied on any number of narcotics to get them through the day.

'This kind of world especially attracts the artistic and creative mind,' Crowley had said. 'They are the most susceptible to suggestion and coercement through the Aether,' he had explained, referring to his strange idea that there was a fabric under all things that transmitted some sort of power. Reed still wasn't sold on this.

'*Never* trust an artist,' Crowley had warned him, 'Spineless, weak willed, debutantes all of them.' He had waved a finger at Reed to underline this opinion. 'Total wankers.' He added.

'What about writers? Reed had asked.

'Those especially.' Crowley snapped. 'They take the lies that are spoken, that would just disperse into the air, and encase them forever with ink onto paper. Can you imagine anything more diabolical?'

'Aren't you are writer? Reed asked.

'Precisely.' Crowley had replied and without any indication that he was trying to be ironic.

Reed had always considered these clubs, clandestine meetings of society's elite, to be nothing more than an excuse to indulge in the kind of activity they collectively forbad to the lower classes. Sexual mostly he supposed, but that wasn't the whole of it. Danger played a part too, some sort of desire to risk their souls or perhaps just the souls of others. He couldn't understand that.

He didn't mind what people did to each other so long as they were both consenting, he didn't even mind that some of the blokes did it with other blokes. Crowley had been brought in more than once for that kind of behaviour. He had to admit that couldn't see the appeal, in fact he couldn't bear the thought of it. Perhaps it was his upbringing, or perhaps it was just that it was something that seemed unnatural to him and so his mind automatically revolted at the idea.

But after all he had witnessed he had come to understand that there were very wide and deep levels of unnatural, and two blokes fancying each other was a long, long way down on the list of threats to mankind.

The stuff with the magic though. The supernatural. Here his comprehension of people broke down. He knew that many of them only played at it. They entertained the strange environment solely to eat the forbidden fruit it offered. They probably only signed up in the first place to engage in the kind of sexual activity they were denied by the civilisation they were supposed to represent. It had crossed his mind a few times that society was all about wearing masks. The higher you climbed in its ranks the more varied masks you wore. How tiring that must be.

Crowley though, he was the real deal. Until Ravensblack he had thought that the man was simply a massive arsehole who liked to prance about in robes and show off how educated and loud he was. Crowley was *still* a massive arsehole, he was still loud and an arrogant braggart, nothing had changed there, but he had proved that his belief in the supernatural, in demons, monsters and maniacs was not something that Reed could deny.

The press called him the 'Great Liar,' amongst other things, and when it came to keeping his own skin free of scratches and tears Reed was quite sure that Crowley was an Olympiad.

But what they failed to consider was that name-calling in articles didn't hurt him. He didn't give a toss about people's opinions of him, so why would he need to lie?

Perhaps it was in his writings, the tremendous volume of work that Crowley had penned, that he was telling the truth? After he had thought about this Reed had begun to collect Crowley's publications and spent his new found free time becoming accommodated with terms that were becoming familiar to him now, the *Aether*, the *Essence*. What was it that Penhaligon had said that day?

'*Crowley is dangerous man, not because of what he does but because of what he knows.*'

Reed did think that Crowley was dangerous. His greed, recklessness and cavalier attitude to how his vitriolic outbursts upset people certainly made him someone to be cautious of, but far more important was that Crowley was considered dangerous by his enemies. That meant that they took him seriously. As did Reed.

He decided not to go over the river. He couldn't bear the thought that he might bump into Crowley no matter how low the odds. Instead he turned and took a circuitous route back to the station and soaked up a little more of the London that he was beginning to miss quite badly. He would go to the East End, because that was where Penhaligon lived.

Part 3

Two weeks earlier. London

The fallout from the Barnabas Street incident hadn't been as far reaching as Bryson had expected. It had run the press for only a few days and the headlines had all sung the same tune, '**Immigrant Gangs Clash,**' or '**Bloody Mayhem in Docklands Turf War.**'

Happy to be back at work he reflected on the series of events as they had unfolded after he had been stretchered out of the warehouse. To begin with he hadn't fully appreciated at the time just how much of a beating he had taken from Timpson. His hospital stay had lasted six days, with three broken ribs and a concussion. The upshot of this was it had kept him out of the loop with what was happening over the case.

He was also without Reed who had been placed on leave for a month to recover from his burns. Lafferty had damaged his leg and so he too had been conveniently sent home with full pay. Convenient because by the time the three of them could get together the whole affair was already old news.

Crowley's lie about the plague descending on London still carried more interest than the death of a police officer and the institutionalisation of four others.

Chief Brady, his new immediate superior, had sat with him and explained at great length why it was important that the matter was not seen to be anything other than a bloody conflict between rival, foreign gangs. The public wouldn't understand anything that strayed too far from their expectations. Murders they were fine with, the public had soaked up Jack the Ripper, they had lived through a World War and the carnage that had delivered, but ritual slayings? No. It had to be this way.

Bryson hadn't revealed that Timpson had thrown all of them about like rag dolls, he certainly hadn't told him of what Crowley claimed happened with Timpson, of his transformation into a burning, superhuman demon. He wasn't entirely sure that he believed that himself. And how had a dog, never mind how big it was, brought down something like that? Crowley had said that the demon couldn't see dogs. It was typical Crowley bollocks.

He had alluded to the eldritch symbolism of the scene to the chief though, the circle, the way the poor constable had been ritually murdered. All of this and more. Bryson had it laid out to Chief Brady as well as he could and yet all that emerged out of that meeting was that it was a gang war, not what he *thought* but what he was *told*.

And to cap it all now Crowley was missing, Reed was acting odd and Lafferty was... well, Lafferty seemed fine. He was still walking with a slight limp but, by and large, the lad was good. Bryson still had his team and for that he was thankful.

The idea that they were a team had become much stronger too. While they had been convalescing, they had visited each other's homes, eaten meals together, they had even spent a day in the countryside as part of their recovery. As the weather had finally turned from the chill and the rain that had dogged the country right through to March, they had taken advantage of it. They had driven out of the city to enjoy rolling green landscapes and the calm that such scenes brought.

Crowley hadn't been a part of this though. Bryson was still at odds with the man and it was possible that Lafferty was the only person on the planet who could tolerate him for more than very short periods of time. Bryson had tried to not let this bother him but Crowley's uncanny ability irritate him both when present and absent had been in full force of late. Every time he was in a room with both Reed and Lafferty it was as though a space existed between them that Crowley should be filling.

He wanted to at least be pleased that he was now back and able to get on with his job, except even that wasn't entirely the situation. His job had altered, his cases were few and far between and it was fairly obvious what was coming his way. Reed had complained about it too. All they got were the reports and complaints brought to them either by rabid freaks, or they were reports about something rabidly freakish.

Some of the incidents they had been asked to cover were months old, the regular investigation having come up with nothing satisfactory, normally these would just be filed away and forgotten. But cases that had some heavyweight in the political or industrial sector involved meant that they couldn't just be buried.

Bryson lifted over a few of the papers that were piled onto his deck. He looked at the heading of each, considered whether to begin investigating them, and then let them drop. He had no interest in this. He wanted a case that involved thieves, thugs or pickpockets. Something normal. Everyday crime for an everyday copper.

He did have one break in the monotony planned for today though. He planned to see Lord Pevensy. The old General had promised to dig deeper into the Tcho-Tcho and although it was a million miles from everyday crime Bryson was pleased that he would at least get to see the old man. Until recently he had thought that the war would be the greatest horror he would ever experience, he had certainly hoped it would be so, but recent events had brought his experience of the conflict into sharp focus.

Very few of the men who had seen the carnage that the likes of he and Reed had witnessed ever talked about it. Once, shortly after they had returned to England and recommenced their duties as police officers, after he and Reed had been newly promoted, they had talked. Reed had been on the front line since war had broken out, he had volunteered, buoyed by the feelings of camaraderie and patriotic zeal that had swept through the country. Bryson had followed a few months later.

The two had a passing knowledge of each other before the war, enough to know each other's first name at least. By the time the conflict was over, after both had endured loss and pain, the like of which they could never have imagined, they were more than just brothers in arms they were friends, who would have no hesitation in stopping a bullet with their own heart to save the other. Reed was very glad that Lafferty had been unable to sign up due to his age. One good strong heart ready to die for him was quite enough.

Meeting Pevensy had been a stroke of luck that Bryson would wonder at for many years. The General had turned up at the forward HQ just a day before the bloody events of the Somme would chew up thousands of young men on each side. Had Pevensy not requested that two men to be assigned a special mission, had he not insisted that it be himself and Reed then Bryson had no doubt that both he and his friend would be another set of fractured bones lying under blood drenched fields.

They were tasked with using a tunnel system that had been dug under no-man's land to the German side, and to deliver a message to a person involved in sabotaging supply convoys to the enemy troops. A straight forward mission with no small amount of risk associated with it, but certainly one that Reed and Bryson were capable of performing. What puzzled him at the time was Pevensy's absolute insistence on it being him and Reed that should go. There were other brave lads who were more than capable of handling themselves in a fight but more than that he was a big bloke and Reed was simply enormous.

Two men of their stature crawling through a tunnel, dug out by blokes whose build was slight and wiry, was never going to be easy. Yet Pevensy wouldn't hear of any other candidates. It was to be Reed and Bryson he had told their commanding officer, and that was that. It had saved their lives.

They had been behind German lines when the battle began. By the time they had completed their mission and found a route back to their own side, as the tunnel had been destroyed behind them, the terrible exchange of lives that would be forever known as The Somme was over. Their unit had been decimated in a terrific artillery strike.

When Bryson finally managed to approach Pevensy, once the world had calmed, he had asked about that mission. Why he and Reed had been selected. Pevensy had answered that 'something told him that it had to be them, a premonition,' he had said and it was all he ever offered on the matter.

They became friends after the war also. Pevensy for all his high status and wealth was a very cordial and down to earth sort. He was very active and had travelled a great deal before the conflict but now stayed very much within the London area.

Curiosity had made Bryson look up a bit of the man's history but he found very little, which seemed odd for a man with a title. Pevensy clearly moved in privileged circles, where the power behind the nation resided, yet he had no apparent ambitions to enter politics or to stamp his name upon any mercantile empire.

He was much older than he looked too, according to the very few people who had anything to say about him.

Pevensy was easily in his nineties and yet the old bird had the apparent agility and stamina of a man half his age, not to mention a considerable degree of charisma.

He had arranged to meet the Lord at a small café near to Piccadilly Circus. Besides a decent afternoon meal the owner's wife produced a sponge cake Bryson thought finer than any he had ever tasted and he was in the mood for something sweet. Upon arrival he found Pevensy already sat at a table, beneath a colourful awning that stretched out from the building in the European style.

Pevensy stood as Bryson approached and gave a small wave. As he neared a chair was pulled out for him by a waiter that appeared from within the café.

'Good to see you Ronnie.' Pevensy said. 'Get yourself sat old boy and I'll get us a pot of the good stuff.'

Bryson obliged and Pevensy instructed the waiter to bring cups and a large pot of Earl Grey. The waiter nodded, turned and disappeared back into building.

'I thought it would be nice to take advantage of the sun before the bloody rain returns,' Pevensy said. The weather had been good for the last few days, before that it had rained so heavily that flooding had occurred along some parts of the Thames.

'Yes, it's good to lose a few layers of woollens.' Bryson replied.

'Ha! Quite so,' Pevensy said jovially. 'Now, you wanted to ask me about the Tcho-Tcho I believe?'

'Yes.' Bryson pulled his chair closer to the table and leaned in so that he could keep his voice low. Pevensy reciprocated. 'Do you know what happened at the Docks?'

Pevensy nodded. 'I've read the papers.'

'Do you know what *really* happened?' Bryson asked.

Pevensy said nothing for a moment and casually turned his head a little to see who might be within earshot.

'Yes.' He finally replied. 'I was made aware of what was found in the warehouse and of course of the tragedy of the young constable in the sewers.'

Bryson wasn't surprised. He couldn't say why, perhaps he was simply used to the fact that information haemorrhaged from the police station. Confidentiality was a joke in there.

The full details of a crime report could be bought for the price of a pie and a pint.

'Then you must know that the Tcho-Tcho were involved. That they killed the officer and held us prisoner with an intent to do only God knows what with us.'

'I do.' Pevensy replied and I'll save you the trouble of wondering how to explain what occurred with you and the others before the lads from the Met arrived.' Pevensy took another look around, this time even more thoroughly observing those sat or stood nearby.

'You and your men stumbled into a situation between the Tcho-Tcho and a group of individuals known as Children of Hastur. You encountered…' Pevensy shook his head and raised his eyebrows '…a True Demon, and somehow survived that meeting intact.'

The skin around Bryson's eyes twitched and his expression became dark. 'You *know* about these things,' he said. The accusation in his tone was clear.

'Yes Ron. I'm afraid I do. But I must tell you that I did not believe that such a creature as you encountered was involved. Fortunately, a colleague of mine had greater insight than I and made sure that you had something to help, should he be right.'

'He did?' Bryson said. Suspicious.

'Yes. He gave you Benny. Via the inimitable Mr Crowley of course.'

'The dog?'

'The dog.' Pevensy agreed.

'I don't understand.' Bryson said suddenly finding himself approaching the haze of confusion he encountered when talking to Crowley.

'True Demons can't see dogs and by and large dogs are not affected by the emanations of such monsters. Such as the fiery aura that no doubt caused the burns to the valiant Sergeant Reed.'

'Wait, before I even start on the dog situation, your colleague?'

'My friend of a long, long time, and a friend to everyone in this city Ronnie.'

'How did *he* know?'

'He has a talent for such things. We all have our little gifts Ronnie. Like you my friend, you with your reason and perception. Penhaligon is his name and like you he can see the things that others overlook, myself included. We have been aware for some time that forces within the city were preparing for something. That they were becoming emboldened, and it was Penhaligon who suggested that the signs we had discovered pointed to certain alliances having been formed. That very powerful rituals were taking place. He saw the handiwork of this Hastur lot and concluded that they were being led by a True Demon.'

Bryson said nothing. He stared at Pevensy trying to see the old General that he knew and respected but there was another man sitting in front of him now. To some extent another Crowley. A man full of mysteries and strange thoughts. Another person who appeared to be somehow involved with all of the death and violence that was occurring.

'Look Ronnie,' Pevensy began, his voice was gentle and sympathetic. 'I know that you have seen and experienced a great deal in a short space of time that must make you question your own sanity and perhaps question your whole understanding of the world you exist within. To be perfectly honest that is no bad thing, but you must understand that you are amongst the most rational and practical men on the damned planet. This is why I chose you.'

Bryson blinked. 'Chose me?'

'Yes dear boy. Do you really think that singling out both you and Reed for that mission was done through pure fancy?'

'I don't know.' Bryson said, uncertain. 'I've never really thought about it.'

'Of course you have.' Pevensy gently retorted. 'The pair of you, excellent front line soldiers, especially Reed who is built like a bloody brick outhouse, do you really think that I would send two men like you through a network of tunnels, that a jockey could just about manage, without good reason?'

'I...' Bryson started. 'It was the war. Your lot made some strange decisions. I don't know, at the time yes I thought it was odd but the mission was dangerous and...'

'You had to leave your unit.' Pevensy said. 'You and Reed. If you stayed all of the signs were that you would be killed and that would render Diggers vision obsolete.'

'What... what do you mean, *Diggers?*' Bryson said. The wave of confusion had now crashed down upon him and he was desperately paddling to stay clear of the current that would drag him down.

'Digby, another friend. His gift is foresight, of a kind that you might call prophecy. He suspected that if you and Reed remained with your unit that you would die with the others, unfortunately I could do nothing for the rest of them. There is only so far we can go with these matters. You could well have died on your mission, that was out of our hands but at least we could give you two a chance and that is what we did.'

'You and your friends sent us into those tunnels because of...'

'A prophecy Ronnie.' Pevensy completed for him. 'Foresight? I'm not sure which is the best term in this instance, sometimes it matters more, but yes, that is why we did it.'

Bryson continued to stare at the man before him. He *was* still the General. His eyes didn't glow, his teeth weren't sharpening and he couldn't detect anything malicious in his manner.

Reed had told him about Timpson. He had been a monster. Had he always been that creature or was he possessed in some way, like Roman Ravensblack had been. None of them had detected anything wrong with the lad, for Christ's sake he had sat next to him in the car on the way to Barnabas Street. Nothing.

Now Pevensy was sat here. Claiming to have engineered his and Reeds survival at the Somme. His friend had supplied an animal to aid them, like one of Crowley's Talismans he supposed. Why? This was now the most pressing thing on his mind.

'Who are you?' Bryson asked.

'If you are prepared to listen and to accept old boy, then I'll tell you. Are you ready to understand more than is safe for most people?'

Bryson nodded.

'Then tell me Ronnie, have you ever been ill? And I do mean *ever.*'

Part 4

Digby Allen could feel the presence of his friend long before he awoke and so, when his eyes opened, his lips were already drawn into a weak smile. He lay upon his large bed, in his large country home, with only a thin sheet covering him to protect against sudden chills. His temperature had been quite high the last two days and to help maintain his comfort his usual layers of blankets had been removed.

'Hello Lester, who have you brought with you I wonder, could it be the young Sergeant at last?' He said.

'It is, Diggers. He insisted on seeing you.' Penhaligon said and indicated that Reed should step forward. He did so. His helmet was tucked under his arm and he wore a decidedly shame-faced expression that even his great moustache couldn't conceal.

'I do beg pardon Sir. Mr Penhaligon said you were ill but I'm afraid I didn't fully appreciate...' Reed started.

'Oh apologies be damned Sergeant. I'm old and haven't the time for them like you young fellows have. This is the first time I've been ill in my living memory, and as it is likely to be the last time I'm sure it's only fair that I carry on regardless.'

'Right Sir.' Reed replied maintaining a respectful tilt to his head. The man on the bed certainly looked old. Was he ninety, a hundred? Reed couldn't say. And he certainly looked ill, his skin was pale and although he spoke with surprising strength his breathing seemed a little shallow. Digby turned his eyes, which Reed realised did not look at all old, towards his friend.

'Lester, I would love a cup of tea. Francine is in the kitchen I believe, could you be so kind?'

'I'll see to it Diggers.' Lester said. He looked at Reed. Put a hand on his shoulder and then left the room.

'Would you sit Sergeant?' Digby's hand lifted from his side and pointed to a chair at the side of the bed. Reed obliged. Placing his helmet at his feet.

'The fact that you are here means that Lester has told you who were are I presume. Who I am?' Digby said.

'Begging your pardon Sir, but Mr Penhaligon spoke about a good many things over the last few weeks and I'm still not certain what's what.'

'Yes, I'm sure.' Digby rolled his head to the side so that he could observe Reed without straining his neck. 'It must be incredibly difficult for you. It was for me you know. As time moves on Sergeant we find that people are becoming more sceptical. The marvel of scientific progress has made them more aware that their age-old beliefs are often ninety nine percent fabrication, the result of thousands of years of mixing myth with tradition. How unsurprising that when someone calls out 'magic' and 'monsters' that we look for the bottle of gin about their person.' Digby's appealing smile widened revealing perfectly white teeth.

'I suppose so.' Reed replied. 'He...Mr Penhaligon, said that you were the...strongest, that you brought them into...all this.'

Digby nodded. 'Yes, that is true. I met them both at the same time of course, they were serving in the same unit. I knew immediately that they were the ones. I had absolutely no doubt.'

'That they would become...what Mr Penhaligon says, they would become Guardians.'

'Yes.' Digby said.

'And it was you that found me and the Boss, Mr Bryson.'

Digby nodded again.

'He says Lafferty is the third man.'

At this Digby frowned and shifted a little on his bed. 'That is possible yes, but I'm afraid I can't see exactly what is going on there. Something is getting in the way of seeing that future.'

'In your visions.' Reed said carefully.

'Yes. Lester told you about that I hope.'

'He said you could see the future, sort of.' Reed said, again with caution.

'Well, it is like seeing into the future but not quite so straight forward. I don't wish to appear rude or evasive Sergeant but it is a subject that requires some explanation that I am unfortunately not fit to give at the moment, however I promise you that it will be covered in as much detail as you require. Once we are able to gather you all and get a measure of your interest in our offer we can talk at length.'

Reed nodded. 'What's the deal with Crowley?' He hadn't meant to be so abrupt but speaking of the occultist seemed to chaff at his politeness.

'Ah...Crowley.' Digby sighed. 'I've been putting out fires that man has started for far too long.' The smile that had been present since he awoke slipped a little.

'Crowley is something of an enigma. At one point I thought he might be actually be a candidate but I have never seen anything in my sightings to suggest that this might be the case. He is knowledgeable and a powerful wielder of the *Essence*...' Digby paused, 'You understand what the *Essence* is I take it?' He said.

'I think I have it yes. Mr Penhaligon has done his best to explain it but I'm not completely sure...'

'Don't you worry, there is time for all of that too. So long as you understand that what Crowley is capable of is nothing to be overlooked. While he doesn't appear to be overtly evil, he is malicious, vindictive, capricious and bloody annoying.'

Reed said nothing. He wanted to add a few more choice descriptions to the list that Digby had rattled off but decided to stay silent.

'But…for all that he has his uses. He has contacts everywhere and I mean *everywhere.*' Digby nodded his head and raised his eyebrows in a 'you get my meaning' fashion and Reed also nodded, but wasn't entirely sure what he meant.

'Be careful of him Sergeant. Use him, don't let him use you. Something happened with Crowley recently. After that Ravensblack thing. I can't put my finger on it but there is something not quite right with the man.' Digby suddenly gave out a long yawn.

'Oh dear, please do forgive me. I'm afraid I'm very drained in the afternoon. In the evening when it is cool I come back to a more alert state.'

'Not at all.' Reed replied. I'm sorry to have disturbed you. It's just that I had to…'

'You had to see whether Lester was full of shit.' Digby's smile returned. 'Perfectly understandable.'

'I'll let you get some rest Mr Allen and if it's alright with you I'll speak to you when you are feeling better.'

'As I said Sergeant it is fine, and of course we will speak again, however I'm afraid that I will not be getting better.'

'Oh.' Reed said. Surprised. 'Mr Penhaligon said that you never got ill, that it was *part of the deal.*' He almost added '*like the big house and unending wealth.*'

'That is correct, he has told you no lie Sergeant. However, all men must die, that is the way of things, and my time is nearing.'

'I'm very sorry to hear that.' Reed said.

'I assure you dear boy that I am not. I have served this city for a long time now and I am looking forward to my next journey. Life is a privilege I am thankful to have experienced. I have loved and laughed and although I have also felt great loss I regret none of it. Go know. Let an old man get some sleep. Go to see your friend. He needs you I think. Tell him nothing though. Michael… Lord Pevensy, is to see him and after that it will be time for you to decide between you what you wish to do.'

'And Lafferty?' Reed said.

'I need to look deeper Sergeant and that will take some effort.'

That was the last that Digby said before slowly closing his eyes. His head turned a little on his pillow and he slept. Almost on cue the door opened quietly behind him. Penhaligon appeared.

'Asleep?' He asked.

'Yes.' Reed replied.

Penhaligon nodded. 'The effort of talking takes a great deal out of him, he doesn't have long.'

The sadness in Penhaligon's voice was clear and Reed found himself feeling very sorry for him. These two had obviously known each other for a long time. He had heard only a few stories so far but they had been sufficient for him to appreciate the bond that they must share.

'Come.' Penhaligon said. 'Francine has prepared us some tea.' He left the room and Reed followed, quietly closing the door behind him.

Part 5

Lafferty understood he was not cut out to be a leader of men. He accepted that his appearance, slim, skinny some said, was not something that made a lasting impression on those who were looking for a man to turn to in a crisis. He was tall. That and his earnest disposition, perhaps coupled with the fact that he was a good reader and knew his numbers had been enough to get him into the police force.

He also knew that this wasn't what had caught the attention of Mr Crowley. It was the talent that he had kept hidden all his life that he was interested in. Somehow Mr Crowley had known that he, Nigel Lafferty could see things that other people, normal people, couldn't.

He read the letter from Crowley once again.

Dearest Nigel,

I will be gone for a few days as something of personal interest has come about in Derby. I've booked transport and will be travelling tomorrow. Would you be so kind as to ensure that Benny is looked after? I should only be a day or two at most. If anyone should require my most immediate attention you can wire a telegram to the station and I'll collect it there. Unfortunately, I have no contact number for the place I am visiting other than the address.

It's some god-awful mining village called Blackbrook so make a note of that. I'm certain I'll not be difficult to find amongst a bunch of farmers and other assorted shit kickers.

One other thing. What I am hoping to acquire is something that those pricks at the Museum would love to get their hands on, so not a word to Braithwaite, and it's probably best to keep Bryson and Reed in the dark too. You know what they are like. Reed will try to hit it and Bryson will try to arrest it.

See you in a few days,

Yours
Crowley

He *had* been gone for two days and no word had come from Blackbrook. His first thought had been to tell the others but in the letter Crowley had specifically instructed him not to. He understood the man's reticence. Despite all of the evidence of a world that existed outside their own both of them resisted any form of discussion about it.

They talked about how the recent events had affected them personally, how they had to implement new ways of investigating the cases. They even began to draw up a list of possible informants generated from records of those who were known to dabble in the arcane arts. But that was where it was left, still firmly in the domain of 'honest coppering.' That was Bryson, he seemed to think that by denying the supernatural aspect of the events they could just carry on as they would with any crime or incident.

'A few days' Crowley had put in his note. Something was wrong. Crowley wouldn't stay away from London without good cause but this thought was second to Lafferty's feeling of danger that burned in his marrow. His last few nights' sleep had been rough. Visions of teeth, of feral eyes and blood had haunted his dreams. Many months ago, he had seen eyes, in his dreams, disembodied orbs that stared at him as he walked through dark corridors. Just a few days later he had been called to a disturbance at Ravensblack Hall and look where he was now.

He had asked about Blackbrook. One of the lads who had recently joined the Met and who Lafferty had become acquainted with was a Derby boy. His folks had moved into the city as his father had found good employment as a carpenter. His name was Alfie Platt, or Platty as he was more regularly known around the station. Platty told him that he had heard of Blackbrook but that he had never visited the place, nor any of the villages around that area. It was near to the South Yorkshire border, whereas his family had lived to the south of Derby.

'Queer lot up there.' He had said. 'My mam had a sister who lived up that end, married a fella who bred sheep, or cows or something.'

Platty wasn't particularly bright. He was amiable, friendly and wasn't the run of the mill thug that usually signed on to walk the beat.

But when it came to intellect Lafferty understood that not Platty wasn't the sharpest knife in the drawer. He had waffled for a while about his mum constantly moaning, about how her sisters had all married well and that she was 'stuck with his dad.' Apparently, this was until his dad had been offered a job working for a very well respected furniture maker and was now earning enough to keep his mum solidly stocked with fine clothes and a decent house. Finally, he came around to the stories of what he called 'the north o' the county.'

Plague had been the first thing that came up. The midlands had caught the tail end of the outbreak back in the fourteenth century and tales of it were still told throughout the region. Some villages had disappeared as the inhabitants were decimated. There were stories of witches burned at the stake, old crones who had been accused of conjuring and spreading the disease. In turn this had led to centuries of ghost stories, of bedtime tales of forgotten places still haunted by the victims of that time.

Platty had said that Blackbrook was once of a collection of villages that hugged the border, he could remember two others that way, Chiverton and Wolstone but was sure they were the only places 'still going.' When Lafferty had asked him what he meant by that Platty has said that 'no one lived in the other villages anymore.'

'Why's that?' Lafferty had pressed.

'Dunno,' Platty had replied with an honest shrug of his shoulders. 'Too many ghosts I suppose.'

Lafferty wasn't shocked or puzzled at the reply. There were places like that here in London, in the heart of the country. There were certain spots, streets, houses, parks, particular corners and even spots just a few feet wide where people didn't dilly dally. They walked through them, but they wouldn't stop, not if they could help it.

There were sites where there had been great tragedy, loss and violence everywhere in London, but some incidents left a more lasting impression than others.

'*Why would Crowley go to a village that had been abandoned?*' Lafferty turned the thought over and over. To begin with what was he after? It was 'something of personal interest' and also, 'something that... the gentlemen at the Museum' would be interested in.

The bits about Bryson and Reed were just his usual condescending put downs. Par for the course from Crowley every day.

Lafferty couldn't explain why but he felt it must be about a book. Crowley was very interested in discovering the whereabouts of ancient texts and positively rabid about obtaining them for his own collection. He had observed the occultist talking to his library on occasion, or at least this is what he appeared to be doing. He would walk along the rows and rows, of dusty, forbidding tomes, clearly unsure as to where the book he was looking for was located, tapping on them and whispering to their spines. Unfortunately, it was one of the least disturbing of about Mr C's habits so Lafferty hadn't given it much thought. But now...

Somehow Crowley had been made aware of something he wanted, no, something he *desired* being available in Derby. Crowley wouldn't get out of his chair unless it was to satisfy his deep and powerful avarice. The item was in Blackbrook and he would have to travel there to acquire it. If he was acting upon a message Crowley would need to have good reason to believe that what he was after was a train journey away. He was no fool, for all his flaws, which probably couldn't be catalogued due to their quantity and variety but Crowley was sharp. Dangerously so.

In the end, it was quite simple. To overcome his feeling of dread about this trip Lafferty was going to have to do exactly the opposite of what Crowley had stated in his letter. He would need to visit Braithwaite at the Museum to see what he knew about Blackbrook, he would need to tell Reed and Bryson about the letter. It was a level of deliberate disobedience Lafferty felt Crowley would almost certainly revel in, but it gave him the jitters.

His first port of call would be to Reed. Reed didn't say much but when he did you listened. When they had visited the Inspectors house, his comfortable terraced home in Bermondsey, Reed had barely said a word. Instead the Sergeant sipped at the cider than Bryson had given them and listened. He listened as the Inspector explained the political struggle that was going on in the East End.

How the Miller Boys, a gang of up and coming thieves was trying to wrest control of the area from Blue Harold's lads. Things had started to get ugly.

Reed nodded throughout. He was aware of the situation on the street but the information that Bryson had about the leaders, the effect it was having on the docks, the racetracks and meat markets was new to him. Whereas Reed was the iron fist of the streets, Bryson was the eye atop the steeple, watching it all and planning his moves. Lafferty hadn't known that Reed and the Sarge had fought side by side in the war and this went some way to explaining the loyalty the two shared, but both were reluctant to tell their stories. Some men would sing songs of their exploits in the taverns but there were far more who only wanted to forget, these men often had a gaze that looked past you as they spoke. As though you were a ghost and they were looking at the wall you stood in front of.

Lafferty liked to hear the war stories though, he never said as much to either of his colleagues. What was of deep interest to him was what Mr Crowley had done during the war. Reed and Bryson said that as far as they knew Crowley had avoided the whole thing. Reed said that he had heard that 'the old bastard went to India,' but Bryson had said he had been told otherwise, that Crowley was in the Americas.

Yet one day, while he had been clearing away the mess that Crowley left whenever he had been searching through his draws for some documents, he had seen several government papers, bearing military symbols, which all bore Crowley's name. So far he hadn't had the courage to ask about them but he intended to do so the next time he saw him.

He hoped that would be soon. It was true that he missed Crowley. While his relaxing chats with Reed and Bryson were nice they paled when listening to Crowley talk about ghosts, demons, dimensions and supernatural powers. The occultist listened intently to everything Lafferty said, it was something the young man had never had happen to him before. Even when he had joined the police force he was still treated by the other officers as an awkward beanpole that hung uselessly around the station.

What Crowley found most interesting was his dreams.

Every Sunday he would have Lafferty lie down upon a large chaise lounge and tell him of any symbols, visions or other unusual aspects he could recall. To him his dreams had always been just confusing and occasionally very scary but Crowley could explain what many of them meant and even pointed out things that had been present in the dreams he had forgotten about.

'What you are seeing are paths to the future Nigel.' Crowley had said one evening. 'It is not *the* future of course, but rather *a* future, one of many.'

Crowley had explained to him that visions like his were called prophecy and that it was a much sought after talent.

'In ancient times a shaman or witch might have the gift and would earn his or her place at the side of a powerful ruler by making prophecy based on their dreams. You might recall that in Le Morte d'Arthur, Mallory wrote that a wizard named Merlin said that whoever drew the sword Excalibur from the stone, in which it seemed to be permanently fixed, would be King of Britain, uniting the regions under his crown. That was prophecy.'

Lafferty had not read Le Morte d'Arthur but was aware of the tale of the ancient King and his knights and listened with relish at Crowley's version of events.

'The thing is Merlin wasn't really telling the whole story. You see while his dreams will have revealed a path, that if followed, would lead the person who drew the sword to be King, there were many other paths that could have been walked. I mean, did Merlin see what would happen once Lancelot slipped Guinevere a length of good old French sausage? No of course not. In his vision, I imagine that Arthur became King and he and Guinevere went at it like bunnies and sired a whole royal dynasty. Rather than the patricidal, fratricidal fuck up that eventually ensued. Merlin was a fucking moron. He saw the route to the outcome he liked the look of and ran with it. He made it happen, and that my boy is how prophecy works. You can see many futures but you can only walk one path at a time.'

'I don't follow, are they seeing the future or not, why does the route matter?' Lafferty asked.

'Because if prophecy states that for a boy to be King he must draw a sword from a stone, first off you find a stone with a sword in it, then you find a lad that can draw it, probably the one you saw in your dream, then when the kid whips it out he's on the road to being King, and you are his trusted advisor. When Jesus found out that to be taken seriously as a Messiah he would have to ride into town on a donkey you can bet your mum's tuppeny bits he went straight to Honest Abdul's and hired himself an ass.'

'I still don't follow,' Lafferty said. 'Are you saying that if the things that the prophecy says to do aren't fulfilled that the dream won't come true?'

'Sort of. You must stop thinking of the future as *the* future and instead that it will be one of many possible futures. For example, let's say that I had a dream that the King will be assassinated'

'Oh my God! When?' Lafferty exclaimed.

'What? Oh, not for real Lafferty you idiot. It's hypothetical. Besides which I've got the precognitive ability of a doorknob.'

'The what?'

'Precognition. It's what it's called when you see...when you do what you do, alright?'

'Alright.' Lafferty replied.

'So, I see in my dream or vision that the King is going to be murdered and I also see that the killer is wearing a blue jacket. That would be a prophecy, understand? King killed, bloke in a blue jacket does it.'

'Right.' Lafferty said.

'Now, that being the prophecy what would happen if I stopped anyone who was wearing a blue jacket from getting near the King? Crowley asked.

'Er...I guess he would have to wear a different jacket.'

'Aha, but if I saw the King killed by a bloke in a blue jacket what happens to my prophecy.'

'I suppose it turns out to be wrong.'

'NO!' Crowley bellowed. 'The prophecy is *never* wrong; it is merely not followed correctly. For the outcome to be realised as I had witnessed it there had to be a killer in a blue jacket, and had there been so then the odds are that *my* prophecy would be the future I had seen.' Crowley paced in front of him now. Animated.

'What happened was that *another* path was taken and this meant that an entirely different future could have come about. Do you see?'

Lafferty shook his head. 'What happens to the bloke in the blue jacket then?'

'Nothing happens to the bloke in the blue jacket! Well, nothing that I've seen in my dream anyway, he could still job the King for all I know. What is important is that if I had ensured that he could wear a blue jacket, the King would almost certainly have been killed. It doesn't mean that the

King wouldn't be dead, that may still yet play out. What is important, what is critical, is that by ensuring the events unfolded as I had seen them, the future I saw would resolve. Do you see know? Sword from a stone. Enter Jerusalem on an ass. Wear a blue jacket if you are planning on offing the head of state.'

'Ok, so my dreams are like a knitting pattern? If I follow the pattern the result will be a scarf but if make a mistake as I'm doing it the result might change, although it could still end up being a scarf? Lafferty asked cautiously.

'Precisely! Crowley beamed. 'I mean, could young Arthur really have become the King of the Britons without that magical sword to help him cut through the opposition? It's possible, but following Merlin's instructions made it almost inevitable.'

'Wow, that's really amazing Mr C. And, my dreams, they are prophecies?

'Not all of them. Most will simply be the usual run of the mill frustrations and desires working themselves out as you sleep, so that you don't go crazy sort of thing. But when a true vision comes along you will know.'

'I saw you once. In a dream. Just before Ravensblack Hall.'

Crowley stopped his pacing and turned to Lafferty more directly.

'Did you now...?' he said.

'Yeah. I saw you give me the spuds and you told me about how to use em.'

'Hmm.' Crowley put his fingers to his chin. 'Anything else? Anything with myself or the other lads, Bryson, Reed?

'No sir. Not then.'

'And more recently? Crowley said, moving a little closer to Lafferty, now watching him like a hawk with his dark recessed eyes.

'Teeth sir.'

'Teeth?' Crowley echoed.

'I had a dream a few nights ago. I saw the moon, clouds were drifting across it, and there was you and the others, the Guv and Sarge.'

'You weren't in your dream?' Crowley asked.

'No. I don't think so anyway. I was sort of watching from someone else's eyes, not mine if you follow. I saw you all running. There was someone else with you too. No, *something* else. I'm not sure, it was strange but this other person or thing I couldn't quite focus on him.'

'Interesting. But vague. I find myself running a good deal when Bryson and Reed are about me, so that's not helpful. That the Moon caught your attention, which may be something, and the stranger with us, also of note. Anything else?

'No sir, sorry.' Lafferty replied.

'Well not to worry. Make sure to make notes when you awaken.'

'Do you have visions Mr C?'

'No. At least none that I can remember. The only way I can obtain insights into future events is through undergoing rituals. You know the model ship over by the fireplace?'

Lafferty didn't look, he knew the ship very well. It was the boat that Bryson had carried from Ravensblack Hall on Crowley's orders. 'Of course.' He said

'It was a dream ritual that brought that boat and the good fortune I am currently enjoying.'

'How did that happen exactly? You've never said.' Lafferty asked.

'Ah, I'm afraid that must remain secret at the moment. While the good fortune was welcome there was something else that came with it. A sort of clause in the contract that I need to fulfil at some point. Until that time, I'll be required to keep mum. Not everything is best shared.' Crowley gave Lafferty a look that indicated that any further conversation regarding the boat was now off limits.

'Regarding the visions however, I suspect that we all have some degree of precognition available to us but some are far more receptive than others due to the...well that is a conversation for another time.' The occultist then shook his head and looked genuinely apologetic.

'I'm terribly sorry to have to give you half answers and only hints of the things that you must learn Nigel. I am constantly seeking answers myself, I am driven by it. This is why my travels have taken me across both the charted and uncharted portions of our world.'

To his surprise Crowley then walked to the large window, which was closed shut by wooden boards and opened them, allowing a brilliant stream of light to fill the room.

'Something is happening.' Crowley said quietly as he looked out and up into the sky outside. 'A change I think. I say I have no visions but I do have sensations that take me occasionally and now I feel a tide coming in. It is mild, as though the sea is gently lapping at my feet but with each surge it is becoming a fraction stronger. I fear that if I do not investigate this feeling I may one day wake to find myself drowning.'

Lafferty said nothing. When Crowley spoke like this it was often to himself. But he wondered at what he meant about the tides and the surges and whether to mention that he had once seen Hell in his dreams.

**

Reed wasn't home when Lafferty had reached his house but he had been given a key, Bryson too. He went inside and found Benny fast asleep in the kitchen. The great hound didn't wake until Lafferty pulled at his ears. Patting him did nothing and now, stood on the platform at Victoria Station these thoughts played through his mind. He had sent a note to both Reed and Bryson explaining that he was going to Derby, to Blackbrook.

With Benny for company he would be fine. He knew that Reed and Bryson would come to the village because he had seen it. He knew that there would be a bright, full moon and that Crowley was in some sort of danger.

There were things with jaws full of sharp teeth and dark feral eyes. He had seen it all in his last dream.

As his train approached, billowing massive clouds of steam before it, Lafferty pulled Benny back a little from the edge of the platform. The animal seemed unmoved by the thunderous approach of the locomotive. He had seen Benny in the dream and that meant that it was prophecy that he should come along. He wondered what would happen if he got on the train without him.

'*Something awful.*' Was all that he could think.

Part 6

The nearest train station to Blackbrook was located in Glossop. This meant that Crowley had to endure a three-hour coach ride mostly along roads that were no more than dirt tracks. What made this even more intolerable was the discussion he had been required to endure with the coachman.

'You're sayin want to go to Blackbrook.' The shabbily dressed and almost entirely dust covered man had said for the third time in as many minutes.

'Yes. That is correct. Nothing has changed since the last time you asked me, nor the time before that. My good man, Blackbrook is my destination, my destination is Blackbrook, and it is Blackbrook that I wish to travel too. Does that help to clarify the matter?' Crowley said as his frustration quickly rose and took up a combative stance.

'Right.' Replied the coachman. As he had done twice previously.

'So. We are good. Yes?'

'Well I suppose so.' The coachman said carefully. 'but...'

'But?' Crowley snapped. 'But what? Dear God what is so difficult?'

'Well, the thing is right. I don't really go to Blackbrook.'

'You don't go to Blackbrook.' Crowley repeated. 'Are you trying to be fucking funny?'

'Well no Sir. Begging pardon but the thing is see, Blackbrook ain't there.'

'Ain't there.' Crowley mimicked the Derby man's bumpkin drawl. 'What's that supposed to mean.'

'Well everyone ere knows that Blackbrook ain't been a village since, oh well, back in them days. Y'know, forty or fifty year gone by.'

Crowley scrutinised the man. He searched his road weary face for any sign that he might be having a laugh at the 'stupid Londoner's' expense as often happened in towns north of pretty much anywhere past Kent. He could see nothing.

'Obviously I'm not from *'ere'* so why don't you explain why when I called ahead from London to book your services I was told that you could take me to Blackbrook.'

Oh well. Marion, at the Post Office, she would have just thought you meant Chiverton. That's the biggest village up by them parts and all the others are quite close. You can walk to each one.'

'I don't want to walk. I don't like walking. That's why I booked a coach.'

'Oh. Well. I can take you to Chiverton.' The coachman said in the same calm and vague tone.

'I don't want to go to Chiverton. I want to go to Blackbrook…'

'But it ain't…'

'Yes, yes. I understand. You are saying that it no longer functions as village *per se* but there must be someone out there as I have an appointment.'

The coachman frowned and then appeared to enter a state of thinking that required various facial tics and raised eyebrows.

'Oh p'raps you are meeting the folks who live in the big hall. That's not far from Blackbrook!'

'Right. And what's the name of these folks.'

'That'll be the Mabbots Sir.'

'No. That's not them. The person I'm seeking is named Fairacre.'

'Oh.' The coachman said looking disappointed.

'Look. I'm getting the feeling that you really don't want to take me to Blackbrook regardless of whether it bloody exists or not, am I right?' Crowley said. He was becoming dangerously annoyed and the coachman and began to believe that the simple rural type demeanour was somewhat staged.

'Oh. No Sir, it's just that Marion probably thought that you meant Chiv…'

'Tell me what's wrong with Blackbrook driver.' Crowley interrupted forcefully. 'Why don't you want to go there? Tell me or I'll have half of London's bored, wealthy idiots up here within a week strolling around the place thinking it's a Spa resort.'

'No Sir!' The coachman exclaimed looking genuinely fearful. 'You don't want your friends up there Sir.'

'Trust me they aren't my friends. So tell me, why I shouldn't be going to Blackbrook. Why are you willing to risk a bloody good fare to keep me away?' Crowley stepped forward. And don't lie to me because I'll know.'

The coachman looked around. He had met Crowley a short walk away from the station and the immediate vicinity was clear of people.

'It's a shunned place Sir. Not somewhere people like to go to or talk about. That whole region, in the past, it's been…it's had a bad history.'

'Explain.' Crowley said.

'It would take some time and I'm really not the man to be telling it all. You want the vicar, Flowers, he's your man.'

'Where can I find him?'

'Oh, he's away Sir.'

'How fucking convenient.'

'He's actually in London Sir, brought him to the station myself just yesterday, you only just missed him. Gods truth.'

Crowley paused to judge whether the coachman was taking the piss or not and decided that he was being honest. About this at least.

'Alright. Tell me then if this place has some kind of history about it, which I get, what's the problem there now?'

The coachman looked at his feet for a moment and then took another look around. Satisfied there was no one near to hear him he lowered his voice and leaned in to Crowley.

'Something's been killing sheep, cattle.' He said.

'Something?'

'An animal. Or if not an animal then it's a maniac because those poor creatures are torn up Sir. Looked to be part eaten.'

'You have seen this? Seen it with your own eyes.'

The coachman cast his eyes down once again.

'No Sir. Not with my own eyes. It's Michael Greyson who lost sheep to the beast, and Mrs Potts Sir, she says she's seen something running through the woods.'

Crowley sighed. '*A fucking beast in the woods. Terrific*' He thought.

'Alright, alright.' Crowley said, resigned to where this was going. 'Take me as near to Blackbrook as your balls will allow you. I'll walk from there.'

'Sir are you sure you…'

'Yes, just…let's just go.' Without allowing time for further discussion Crowley climbed into the coach and began to get comfortable. When he was settled, he turned his head and saw the coachman still standing there looking pensive.

'Well get a fucking move on man. I'd rather not be walking towards a shunned village with a beast in the woods in the middle of the fucking night.'

The coachman started. And then moved to his seat. He cracked his whip and called out a long practiced '*Geeupgal*' to his single horse and the coach began to shudder off towards Blackbrook.

***

It took a little over two hours for the coachman to bring Crowley to an apparent crossroads in the dirt track they had travelled upon since leaving Glossop. During the journey he had thought carefully about his situation. He was by his nature an impulsive man. He had long ago recognised this as a severe character flaw but had chosen to do nothing about it. Because he was also a lazy man, a character flaw that he refused to recognise and this helped to balance it out.

It was the promise of obtaining a book that had made him act upon his rarely beneficial impulses, that had made him drop everything and immediately make for the middle of nowhere. It was his laziness that had prevented him from considering the history of the place or even the credentials of the person who had contacted him with enticing details of an old family heirloom that appeared to him to be suspiciously like one of his sought-after tomes of eldritch lore. And now he was here. At a crossroads. If you wanted symbolism Crowley thought that this was as good as it gets.

He felt the coach stir a little as the coachman got down from his seat. Crowley looked out of the open window and the driver appeared, his dusty cap clutched to his chest.

'Beg pardon Sir but this is as far as I go.'

'Is it.' Crowley said evenly.

'Ain't even me Sir, I'd be happy to go a bit further but my old gal,' he jerked his head back to indicate the horse, 'Polly, she won't go past the crossroads without getting all of a picture Sir.

Crowley sighed. 'I suppose we can't be having Polly in a picture now can we.' He exited the coach and took in his surroundings. It was much as it had been for the last twenty or so miles. Various shades of green grass, undulating hills, drystone walls and many, many sheep.

'Where am I going? Crowley asked as he was handed his paisley patterned travelling case.

The Coachman pointed up the road they had travelled on.

'Just keep following the track Sir and that'll be Blackbrook when you comes around the bend near the Old Man.

'The Old Man?' Crowley asked.

'Rocks Sir, there's some rocks that stick out of the side of a hill, looks like the side of an old fella's head.

'Lovely.' Crowley replied absently.

'This ways an that is Chiverton and Wolstonely Sir.' The coachmen pointed to the other exits of the crossroads. 'If you've a mind to go to either then make it Chiverton.'

'Reason?' Crowley asked.

'That's where the vicar lives Sir.'

'Right.' Crowley nodded. 'Yes, perhaps we can have tea.'

He walked to the centre of the crossroads and as he passed by Polly she snorted and stamped at the dirt road a little.

'My thoughts entirely my dear.' Crowley said.

He stood in the middle of the junction and slowly turned. He could feel something amiss here. There was something close. He closed his eyes and tried to pick up whatever was coursing through the *Essence* but was unable to grasp anything. He was not particularly good at reading the mystical channels that fed magical energy into the world. But there *was* something.

He also didn't have to be a gifted seer or medium to know that someone or something had been following his coach since leaving Glossop. Whoever, or whatever, had been keeping up with its sedentary pace for twenty miles. Crowley had seen the fast-moving shadow blur in and out of trees, beyond walls and hills. Distant enough to be obscure but close enough that it could see if Crowley left the coach. He wondered if the coachman had seen it and decided that he probably had. He doubted much got past the watchful eyes of his polite and nervous driver, who returned to his seat and called upon Polly to '*errupgirl*'.

The obedient horse began to manoeuvre to the centre of the road and turn, very much willing to return to Glossop. Crowley moved so he didn't get in her way and called to the coachman.

'Can I rely on you to collect me this evening? Let's say around seven?'

The coachman halted Polly so he could still face Crowley.

'I'll be here at seven and for one hour after that.' He said. If for some reason you aren't here by then I'll return each evening at the same time for a week.' He said.

Crowley wasn't sure how to reply to this and so instead nodded in agreement and thanks.

The coachman gave another instruction to Polly and she hauled the coach away.

Crowley took a final look around, '*Between Chiverton and Wolstonely,*' he thought. Crossroads were often considered to represent a place where worlds met. In Brazil the *Besta Fera* was meant to emerge from places like this. A Centaur like thing, half horse, half man, which in turn was really the devil. He had never encountered such a thing but had been informed of something similar that had haunted a village on the edge of a coffee plantation.

The story he had been told had not been pleasant. He rarely heard pleasant stories that were told by fearful inhabitants of remote villages no matter which continent he was on.

'Bera Festa,' Crowley said quietly.

Something stirred within him. His self-preservation had been taking time out to enjoy the countryside, mindful only of the thing following the coach, now it was fully awake preparing reasons to walk back to Glossop. But Crowley's avarice was made of sterner stuff.

It was known throughout his field that there had once been a book located in this area with an exceptional history, but of course Crowley was aware that most ancient books have exceptional histories.

This was an old, old tome from the days before Christianity had been accepted by the Romans. It was suggested by a few who studied such things that the book had been used to expel a terrible force that was causing chaos in several settlements. Crowley never could confirm this, although it was certain it reached the hands of the Proconsul directed to rule the region and that he managed to pacify the area. Hard to avoid the obvious conclusion.

The book was said to have come to the Proconsul via an arch-magus of the pagan tribes who was unable to protect his people and sought the aid of the Romans but Crowley knew that the tome was not given with purely altruistic intentions. It was then sent on and received by the Emperor Constantine. Speculation once again would have him believe that the book was used to defeat forces that Constantine's legions could not.

Yet, despite having used the magic of the old world to defeat creatures from hellish dimensions Constantine had turned to Christianity and used that as his foundation of spiritual order. Perhaps it was the origins of the tome that gave him cause for mistrust for the book. Its title, 'Deus Viris Fingat' literally, God Takes the Demon, was said to have been gifted by none other than Nyarlathotep. A cunning bastard of the first order. Crowley had to wonder which God would be taking that Demon, to what ends?

Perhaps therefore Constantine, who was a smart man, had turned away from the promises of Nyarlathotep. Preferring the more vague and contradictory nature of the Bible to the blood drenched, abhorrent demands of the Old Ones.

It didn't matter though. Crowley wanted this badly. Most forbidden tomes were so called because they were instruction manuals on how to bring creatures of the Void and Shadow into the world. There were very few that he was aware of, at least still in existence that sent them packing. This was one of those few and would be priceless to him. It was a forbidden book because of its unholy connection with Nyarlathotep. Because it might be a vehicle to feed the Great Messenger with power that he was unable to get in other ways. 'Perhaps the old bastard had other covert demon gathering methods going on,' Crowley packed that thought away for another time.

It wasn't long before he came upon a large outcrop of rocks and as the coachman had said the outline of an old man's head could be distinguished in their form. As he neared it the scene became nothing more than a rough collection of boulders but Crowley was intrigued at how our minds could find familiar shapes and patterns in the chaos of nature. He remembered that he had once seen the face of a man upon the bark of a tree, then it came to him that it had been the face of a man.

He grimaced and walked on.

Part 7

The journey to Derby and then on to Glossop had been exciting for Lafferty. He had never travelled outside of London. Seeing the small houses with large gardens, acre after acre of grass and trees and fields of crops was like having honey poured onto his thoughts. Everything appeared bright and clean and somehow wholesome.

Occasionally, the reason why he was taking the trip crept up on him and darkened the scene but he did as his friend and mentor would do, he pretended that it wasn't a big deal and ignored it. Benny had slept through most of the journey, until they reached the station and embarked upon a coach. This had been the end of the good feelings he had enjoyed headed to Derby and it had begun with a conversation.

'Why'd yer want to go to Blackbrook?' The coachman had asked. A quite forward question Lafferty had thought, and he had no doubt that had Crowley been asked he would have told him to 'mind his own effing business.' However, he considered it a harmless enquiry and so replied politely and honestly.

'I'm meeting a friend there. A gentleman who would have arrived from London recently.'

'Oh aye.' The coachman said, nodding.

'Yes. He will have reached Derby yesterday and I…'

'Aye, twas me that picked him up.' The coachman said, carefully Lafferty thought.

'Ah well, then I presume you presented him to his destination safely?'

'I did that Sir,' the coachman said and then he looked about the station. There were a few people going about their affairs, paying no attention to him and his fare. 'I also promised to pick him up at seven o' clock and he wasn't there at the spot.'

'How do you mean?' Lafferty asked.

'See. Thing with Blackbrook is, well it ain't there no more.'

'Isn't there!' Lafferty exclaimed.

'Wait. I don't want to go through all that again. What I mean to say is that the village has been empty, abandoned, for a good many years, your friend insisted on going though. So I took him like he asked.'

Lafferty looked down at Benny as the animal might have something to say on the matter. Benny was otherwise engaged. Lafferty returned his attention to the coachman.

'To your knowledge did he meet anyone there?' he asked.

'No Sir. Well, that is to say I don't actually know as we had an arrangement as to where he was to be dropped off. Sort of thing.'

'What do you mean?' Lafferty asked. He had seen this sort of behaviour before. When people were being almost truthful, but not quite.

'Thing is, my Polly, my horse. She don't like to go past the old crossroads so the good Sir agreed to walk a short ways and for my part I promised to return each night at seven for a week, to collect him should he wished.'

'Crowley *walked?*' Lafferty said.

'Yessir,' the coachman said, 'It's a short journey and the gentlemen looked like he was in proper condition.'

'Oh he's as fit as a boxer, don't you worry. But him leaving a perfectly good coach to go on foot...'

'It was on account of my Polly Sir. I think the good gentleman has a kindly disposition to animals.'

Lafferty looked down at Benny again, who was still engaged in a very deep and focused washing of his generously sized balls. 'I suppose he does.'

'I'll be headed there this evening to see if he's waitin for me. Perhaps Sir would like to come along then?'

Lafferty could easily detect the hope in the man's question. The last thing he wanted was to head out to Blackbrook village now and then to return later. Why, he had no idea. But there it was, the coachman was evidently a good man, true to his word, but he was not at all happy with travelling to this abandoned village.

'I'm sorry but I need to get to my friend today. I'm concerned for his well-being.' Lafferty said firmly.

'Of course Sir, right you are.' The coachman replied with no small amount of shame at his attempt to avoid the trip. He opened the door to allow his fare to step in to the coach but Lafferty didn't move.

'What's your name?'

'Oh, Chell Sir, Tom Chell.'

Lafferty held out his hand. 'Lafferty, Nigel.' Lafferty said.

Tom looked unsure as to what to do but then took Lafferty's hand they politely shook.

'Mr Chell, would it be too much to ask if I could sit with you on the ride? I would like to ask you a few questions if I may.'

Tom studied Lafferty carefully and with suspicion.

'Are you a policeman?' Tom asked.

Lafferty almost swelled with pride. He had trouble being taken seriously as a copper when in uniform so to be recognised while in his day clothes filled him with pride.

'I am Sir.' He said.

'Am I in trouble?' Tom asked. 'Leaving the gentlemen like that?'

'Not at all Mr Chell.' Lafferty said. 'It speaks well of your character that you agreed to return each evening to collect him.'

Tom appeared relieved.

'So. Would you entertain my questions at your side?'

Tom nodded. 'Aye Sir. I will.' He stepped aside to allow Lafferty to move to the front of the coach.

Tom advised that it would take a couple of hours to reach the crossroads where he had left Crowley and so Lafferty decided to ease into his questions. He asked Tom about his home town of Glossop, about his family. He was a single man with no children, having lost his young wife four years ago. She had died of Tuberculosis and he had never sought to re-marry.

He told Lafferty that the rail connection at Derby kept him busy, that he was hoping to save enough to buy a small place in the Dales and live out his life there. Tom struck Lafferty as a good and honest man but when he began to ask about the villages Tom's demeanour changed. He had chatted freely about Glossop and honestly about his wife's passing and his continued mourning for her, but whenever the history of the villages that made up the parish of Wolstonely, those being Blackbrook, Wolstone, Chiverton, and Cawdwick were the topic Tom became careful and evasive.

'What made people abandon the village?' Lafferty finally asked, deciding to go for a more direct approach.

Tom, as he had done whenever the questions moved that way was silent for a moment as he thought what to say, but this time Lafferty pushed him.

'The man who you brought here Mr Chell, his name is Aleister Crowley and he's...he knows a lot about what I think you are afraid of.'

Tom looked briefly at Lafferty and then back to the road. He stayed silent.

'Mr Chell... Tom, if there is something I should know about Blackbrook it's your duty to tell me. If something happens to me or Mr Crowley that could have been prevented with your help, well...'

'Bad stuff.' Tom said. He looked again at Lafferty, his eyes danced around looking for signs of mocking or derision in his passengers face.

'There's stories, y'know, from the old days. They've been carried on through the tales we tell's kids and in superstitions they ave round here. I'm Glossop born and bred but we know some of it down there. My folks always said to keep clear of Wolstonely, but specially Cawdwick and Blackbrook.

'Why those?' Lafferty asked.

'Cawdwick had the plague once. There's stories, like I said. Blackbrook's always been a bad un. Old religions Mr Lafferty, they die hard round these parts.'

'The others?'

'Not so bad. Chiverton's a nice enough place. It's where the vicar lives, Flowers. He's a solid bloke. Seems they managed to move on. If I make a fare this way it's usually Chiverton that I'm headed too and I don't mind it.'

'And Wolstonely?'

'It's Wolstone,' Tom corrected him. 'They calls the Parish Wolstonely but the village is Wolstone. One of those historical things I suppose.'

Lafferty nodded. 'And how's that?

Tom shrugged. 'Wolstone's alright I suppose, problem is that it's the closest to Blackbrook so it kind of sits in its shade if you get my meaning?'

Lafferty nodded again.

'So is it superstition that stops you from going all the way to the village?'

'P'raps. A little. But in all honesty, my Polly she won't step a hoof past that crossroads, not a whisker. I've tried to get her to on occasion, when I been in a mind to test my own fears I suppose, but she won't ave it.'

'So, is it haunted? Is that why people stay away?' Lafferty asked.

'Haunted? Ghosts?' No Sir. There's no ghosts. At least none as I know of. Whatever is around that village, in the woods around it, it ain't ghosts. Sprites and spirits don't snatch people away or gut livestock. They don't follow my coach, watching to see where I'm goin, seeing if I'm headed to that damned place.'

'Something follows you?' Lafferty asked.

'Aye, something follows me. Nothing's ever come too close.' He patted a length of cloth next to him that Lafferty had failed to notice due to its shabby colour camouflaging it against the dirty wood. 'I reckon they know I got a piece o' work here filled with silver shot.'

'Silver?' Lafferty said. Thoughts of Crowley's tuition came to him. There were many instances where Silver thought to be a defence against creatures of all manner of existences.

'I melted down my wife's necklace Sir. The only thing close to as pretty as her, I had it melted and turned to shot. Truth is there were times that I thought I might be best just joining her and it seemed a good way to go.'

Lafferty wasn't sure what to say. He could hear the man's grief in his voice, he was clearly still very much in love with his wife and had only the memory of her to see him through life.

'You told Mr Crowley that you would come each evening at seven, why?'

Now Tom shrugged. 'I dunno. I just thought that he was the kind of man that would be able to come out of the village.'

'Why seven?'

'If I'm away by eight I can be back in Glossop before half nine if I puts the whip to Polly, and in truth she probably wouldn't need it. Means I'm home before the sky is black and the Moon is high.' He kept his face forward but turned his eyes to Lafferty.

'You don't want to be out here when the Moon is high Mr Lafferty.'

Part 8

Tom deposited the young policeman at the same spot as he delivered the previous gentlemen, Mr Crowley. Once again he turned Polly, who was as ever happy to be travelling away from Blackbrook, and hastened back to Glossop. He had made the same promise to Lafferty too. He would return at seven each tonight and again for the next five nights if he and Mr Crowley failed to show.

Had the vicar been at his residence in Chiverton he would have gone to see him but he driven the Reverend Flowers to the station just a day before he had collected Mr Crowley. He supposed he could have returned by now, he wasn't the only coach for hire in the area and the Reverend was not a man who publicised his comings and goings. It was as though everyone around here kept secrets.

Still, it would have been good to see him. The Reverend was a bit of a toff but he never talked down to anyone. He was always keen to listen to anything you had to say and was especially interested in the local gossip. Tom had told him of the feeling he experienced whenever he took the crossroads to Chiverton, of someone watching or even following him.

The Reverend hadn't dismissed his concerns out of hand, rather he had advised him that while it was probably nothing, perhaps a curious buck, or even children at play it was wise to be cautious. Remote roads could also be the haunt of less than savoury men who might take a lone coachman as easy pickings for his fares.

Tom very much doubted that it was children frolicking or up to high jinks in the woods. Not even the bravest or most soft-headed wandered through the tall, dense firs, spruce and broad Oaks. Things hid behind trees, sometimes inside them. He shuddered and Polly whinnied as if reading his thoughts. The idea that it might be thieves was sound. He had never fallen victim to robbery but more than a couple of his fellow coachmen had.

Thankfully none had been killed but they had been given a proper roughing up. No coachman would give up his hard earned coins lightly. And so he brought along his shotgun and its special ammunition. For while the threat on the road might well be a robber, it might also be something else.

He reached Glossop station at five thirty and was immediately greeted by the station master. This wasn't unusual, he had a good reputation for punctuality and a fair price despite not using two horses and thereby not being quite as fast on the road.

'Aft'noon Tom.' The station master called as he waved him over.

'Aft'noon Master.' Tom replied respectfully using the station masters title.

'I've had a call from London.' The station master said with obvious excitement. 'From the Metropolitan Police no less.'

'Oh aye?' Tom said, trying to display only passing interest.

'Aye. They says they want to book a coach and asked specifically if I could get the coachman what took some fella named Crowley,' he pulled a piece a paper from his pocket and took a quick look at it, 'or another by the name o' Lafferty.'

Tom said nothing but gave a slight nod.

'So I says well, you're in luck cos it's the same fella what took both un. That's right ain't it Tom?' He looked up with expectant eyes.

'Aye, I took em both.' Tom replied.

'Well, that's grand then. They've asked if they could book you for this evenin. Want you to take em to wherever it is you took the other fellas. Was to the same place?'

'Twas.' Tom replied.

'Chiverton?' The station master asked.

'Blackbrook' Tom replied. The station masters expression dropped in an instant.

'Blackbrook! Why in God's name would they want to go there?'

'I don't know Master. My job is to take folk where they want to go, not to ask em why.'

'Well, did you take em in, did you take em all the way?'

Tom dipped his head a little. He felt a little ashamed, as he had done when he told Lafferty that he had dropped Crowley off at the Crossroads.

'No. I took em as far as the Crossroads.'

'Right.' The station master also became uncomfortable with the conversation and looked at his feet.

'What do these fellas want?' Tom asked

'Oh…well as I said they's lookin for you to take em to…where the other fellas went…*tonight.*'

'Tonight!' Tom exclaimed

'Aye, they's on a train right now headed up from London.'

Both men knew full well that to get to Glossop from London via Derby would take a good five hours. To get them to Blackbrook after that would mean getting to Blackbrook, or near to Blackbrook by nine at the earliest.

'I could tell em I couldn't get a hold of ya Tom.' The Master said. 'Tell em I ain't seen you since you took the last fella.'

Tom shook his head. 'No, that would just mean that someone else would have to take them.

'But they might go in the morning if no one's around. I could send em over to Patty Brides place to stay for the night.'

Tom continued to shake his head. 'No Harry, these men are policemen, London policemen. If they are coming all this way then they are on serious business and men like that like to get things done. They'll make sure that some poor sod gets them there. Might even be you.'

With the civilities of position dropped Tom the Coachman and Harry the Station master spoke man to man.

'I'll take em.' It's my job after all and they's officers of the law and have asked for me in particular.'

Harry couldn't hide the look of relief on his face when Tom said this. Now he nodded.

'Will you be waitin on em?'

'No. I'll head home. I'll get some rest and make sure Polly looks good for the city bobbies. Can't have em thinkin we're just some bumpkins out here now can I?' He tried to conjure up a smile but it was no more than a slight rise in the corners of his mouth.

'Ha. No we wouldn't that Tom.' Harry said with as much humour as he could muster.

Tom tugged at Polly's rein to turn her and as he did Harry shuffled up to her and took her head gently in both hands as though to fuss the creature. Stopping the turn.

'Tom, you know how my Agnes is, with her tea leaves an tarot.'

'Aye.' Tom replied. Everyone knew that Agnes liked to dabble in such things. She was never involved in anything too controversial, she told fortunes for the ladies of the town over a cup of tea and helped to pick out names for the new babies that came along and which were meant to bring luck. As the names were usually just some combination of parent and grandparent no one objected.

'Of late, that is to say the last year or so, she's been gettin pretty good at it. I mean, y'know, it's always just been a bit o' nonsense in my opinion but recently she's told me things that...well, she's been uncanny accurate like.'

Polly whinnied a little. She was hungry. Harry stroked her head gently.

'How so?' Tom asked. He rarely had cause to enquire of Agnes's predictions. They were usually that someone would be getting married. Usually some young man or woman who the villagers had already determined via the infamous Glossop knitting circle were 'at it.'

'You know how Bert Haney lost his thumb in the spring when that damn cutting machine of his broke for the hundredth time.'

Tom nodded. Predicting that Bert would suffer an injury from a contraption that consisted mostly of spinning blades and cogs, especially as he was usually half-pissed was hardly a feat of supernatural gymnastics.

'Well, Agnes, she said it would be his left thumb that he would lose and that Bert would never use that machine again. This was a few days fore it happened Tom and you know, Bert scrapped that thing as soon as he came back from the hospital.'

Tom shrugged. On the surface it sounded a little eerie but he also believed that the power of coincidence was stronger than any supposed prediction. Bert hurt himself frequently, the machine wasn't maintained properly and the man probably saw double for the better part of the day. And finally scrapping it? The man was in his seventies.

'I know, I know, 'one o' those things.' Harry said. 'But Tom, just the other night she said that she had a vision of the road, the road to the crossway. She said it had run with blood. That the whole road was a torrent of dark red blood. It proper put the wind up her it did. I was up in the night having to bring her strong Brandy.'

The station master was a simple man. Efficient, polite and practical, all you needed to live in a small town and earn the respect of others. Tom knew that like almost everyone here he liked to partake of a little gossip, but wasn't irresponsible and he was not a man whose humour would lead him to performing japes or practical jokes.

Tom said nothing for a moment. He thought of his Angela, the woman he loved, quite possibly more than life, and he could feel her lips press to his ear and whisper '*be careful my love.*'

'I'll be careful.' Tom said. 'I'll be here at nine, if they ain't here by ten I'm away and they can be indignant and important in the morning.'

Tom called '*geeupgirl,*' and Polly left the soft strokes of the station master and heaved the carriage away.

Part 9

A small bridge, made from local rock Crowley presumed, was the first indication that he had arrived at the village. Beneath it a weak, trickle of water flowed and he supposed that it might be the actual brook of the title. It didn't look black.

Ahead he could see a few wooden structures, sheds, coops and the usual paraphernalia of a farming village. He narrowed his eyes and looked a little deeper, further than the obvious. Everything he saw was in a state of decay. The wood was warped or rotten or both. He felt in his jacket pocket. Inside he carried a Colt pistol. A recent acquisition. Crowley lost guns like other people lost bits of paper. Satisfied that the fully loaded pistol was suitably angled should anything suddenly appear he pressed on.

That this was a trap or set-up of some sort was not in any doubt. Crowley knew it and whoever had arranged all of this knew that he knew it. The expectation was that Crowley's curiosity would get the better of him and this was met in full. He cursed himself as he walked past dilapidated homes, some no more than bramble covered piles of stone and wood. The contact had revealed many details about the book. Only someone with great first-hand knowledge could have such insights. It had to be someone like himself. That was a concern.

Blackbrook village was bigger than he had expected. There were far more houses, albeit ruins, and streets that ran between them at varied angles. He wondered if this place had once vied for the position of the main hub, the place most likely to grow into a town, which was apparently the case with Chiverton these days. It clearly dropped out of the running some time ago.

He was to meet at an address. 17 Pleasant Avenue. At the time he had naturally though that this would be the home of some retired professor or perhaps a book dealer who had stumbled upon an item he wasn't comfortable in holding. The communique had been professional and polite, enough so that Crowley had thrown his usual caution to the wind and not investigated the place.

The name on the telegram had read A. R Tanneman. German, almost certainly. It was still tough having a German name in England. Memories of the war were fresh and attitudes hostile. Crowley briefly wondered how it might be for a German living in a village, how he might be treated, now he realised that it was probably fairly easy as if A. R Tanneman actually lived here he had no fucking neighbours.

He had been given directions. To continue straight from the bridge, to take the third right and to continue until a small green appeared. Mr

Tanneman's house would be directly across from that patch of grass. Crowley followed them diligently. All the while taking in his surroundings.

It was remarkable that the place was so untouched other than by the slow, pernicious assault by nature. Almost all of the buildings that were standing still had their windows. No children played here. The panes of empty houses were a delicacy to kids and it was an unwritten law 'that thou lobbest a brick' into them.

With three other villages within walking distance it was almost incomprehensible to Crowley that Blackbrook was untouched by juvenile pranksters. Unless they feared this place so much that even their childish curiosity for the unknown kept them away. He sighed, stopped and looked around for a suitable candidate. It didn't take long to find a good sized piece of masonry that had crumbled away from the side of a house.

He threw the brick straight and hard at the top floor window of the house to his right. The glass fractured, then exploded to the floor in a satisfying cacophony of tinkles and smashes. Crowley looked around. No dusty curtains twitched, there were no shadows slinking back into corners. A completest, he finished off the remaining three panes.

When he had finished his short round of therapeutic vandalism he looked once again at the house across the green. Number 17, he guessed given the numbers of the houses nearer to him, was the cottage that sat between two almost identical homes, the chief observable difference being that each door was a different colour.

Since climbing aboard the coach his instinct of self-preservation had been working ceaselessly at him, entreating him to go home. It had reminded him of the dangers of walking into anywhere alone, without anyone to run faster than. But his curiosity had been the better player. If he had been lured here to be killed, why wasn't he dead already? They could have murdered him the moment the coach pulled away.

And why so elaborate a ruse. Why the book, the train journey, this forgotten village? No, he told his self-preservation, while he did not dismiss that there was danger here, he didn't believe that he was in immediate peril. He walked over to the cottage.

He stopped when he reached the gate and called out.

'Hello?'

There was silence. Nothing stirred.

'Hello?' he called again.

Still nothing.

'My name is Aleister Crowley. I believe I'm here to be made to look a tit.' He shouted. A light wind picked up but Crowley didn't think it was anything supernatural, put on purely to give him the willies.

He opened the gate. It swung awkwardly, the ancient hinges hampered by rust. As he approached the door, the paintwork of which had no doubt once been a bright blue and was now faded almost to grey, it slowly swung open although Crowley could see no one near it.

'Oh I see. *Going to be like that is it?*' He lost a little confidence in the fact that he had bought a gun rather than Benny.

He stepped inside the open door and into a gloomy hall. A single candle was lit towards the rear end, there was an open doorway immediately to his left which lead to the front room. He walked in and found that it too was lit with candles although the window let daylight stream through also.

Sat to the side of a small unlit fire, in a dusty sofa chair was a lean looking man in a suit. The light from the window cast a across his chest but his face remained in shadow.

'Mr Crowley. Please do take a seat.' A voice with an indistinguishable accent said. The man in the armchair casually indicated the chair opposite him.

Crowley sat, as he did so a small puff of dust emerged from the tired cloth of the upholstery. He tutted. His jacket had been cleaned at the weekend.

'You must be wondering what all this is about.' The voice said in a placid tone designed to hide a simmering hostility which Crowley easily detected.

'I understand that you have a book that I am interested in purchasing for my collection.' Crowley said as though everything was perfectly normal.

'Oh…ha…yes, my little ruse. I do hope that you will forgive me but I needed to ensure your attendance here today.' The voice said, almost gleeful.

'I see, so no book. What a shame. I would dearly love to have it in my collection.' Crowley said. '*God I do hate to be taken for a twat,*' he thought.

'No Mr Crowley. I knew that a damsel in distress or promise of some financial gain wouldn't drag you away from London with any haste, but a book like that? Well, let's just say I'm well aware of your tastes and proclivities.'

'Well. That's super.' Crowley replied. Already bored.

'So, to the reason you are here. Have you guessed yet, as you entered this remote and unvisited place? Have you determined why you would be called here?'

'Could I ask you something before I answer that?' Crowley asked in a serious manner. As though the two were discussing a difficult physics question.

'By all means. I believe we have a few hours to spare.' The suited man said, now he was curious.

'That chair...' Crowley pointed to where the man sat.

'Yes?'

'Did you have to move it into position so that it covered your face like that or did you just get lucky? I can never pull that stuff off without a lot of pissing about. Furniture moving, lights angled, that sort of thing.'

'Ah...' the man said. You clearly haven't changed as much as I had anticipated, the Crowley rudeness must be very much a part of you from birth.'

Crowley blinked. Something froze his mind for just a brief moment. What the man had said resonated. It ping-ponged off his memories causing dust to rise and loose papers to flutter from the writing desk of his thoughts. A second blink shook him free.

'What do you mean changed?' Crowley asked.

'Naturally Mr Crowley you think the reason you are here is because of you, because you are in some way special, however that is not the case, and while it will no doubt come as a great shock to your overinflated ego the only thing *special* about you is the people around you.'

Crowley heard none this. He couldn't. His mind was filled with a montage of images and sounds. Memories many of which made no sense whatsoever. He saw people he had never met, situations he had never been in, he saw himself engaged in them all and yet it was impossible to him.

Lafferty appeared, they were in the library. He had just given Nigel instruction regarding the manner in which ghosts, spirits of the deceased could be trapped in a particular place such as a house or other location and be unable to escape. The boy had quoted a line of poetry to him, he could remember each line with absolute clarity.

'*Without being or form or abode, without motion or matter, the fold*
Where the shepherded Universe sleeps, with nor sense
nor delusion nor dream,'

And had then asked if that was what *he* had meant in *his* verse.

Crowley recalled being confused. What was the boy blabbering about? Lafferty liked poetry but surely realised that *he* had absolutely no truck with it. It was pretentious, poncey garbage. He hated poetry and poets with equal measure. He had ranted this to Lafferty, who by this point was quite used to, and comfortable with, him delivering vitriolic and profanity laden libels against any one, any group or concept that he felt like at the time.

'*His verse*' It refused to be beaten away by Crowley's mental manservant, who darted around shooing away the irreverent thoughts that sometimes clogged his thinking when he needed to focus. Like now.

'What do you mean the *people around me*?' Crowley said carefully, now that his sudden mental flux had stabilised.

'You see Mr Crowley, while you no doubt think that this was all done to entrap you, in fact you are merely the bait. A reason for people who are far more caring of others, certainly than you are of them, or than you are of anyone for that matter, to come out here to this village in the middle of nowhere without taking too much time to find out what they are actually running in to.'

The man's face was still hidden by the convenient, or well positioned band, of shadow and Crowley desperately wanted to see who, or what he was being threatened by. He had been fairly relaxed up until now. He had a gun. He had a few powders about him, and some spells that he was confident he could pull off in combination with them that would ward off most choice creatures of the Shadow and Void, at least for a short while. Now he was nervous.

Whoever this was before him was no imbecile but there was a feeling that the man, just like his fool's errand to Blackbrook, was stage managed. Crowley could certainly feel the man's confidence in his words, in his demeanour but men like this, and Crowley was sure that he *was* a man, only had balls this big when they had back-up.

'Who are you?' Crowley asked.

'Oh Mr Crowley...*who* am I? Surely you realise that I am...'

Crowley suddenly stood and pointed the pistol directly at the man's chest. He fired three accurate shots into his heart. The man in the chair shook a little and then slumped, his chin falling onto his bloody chest.

'I was being rhetorical mate.' Crowley said.

His eyes darted about the room, the only way out was back to the hall or the front window. Whoever or whatever this bloke had as muscle, looking at the spindly frame of the suited man in the chair Crowley doubted that he was expected to handle him in the event of a set-to, they had to be in another room or outside, or both.

'Fuck.' Crowley muttered and ran towards the window.

Part 10

Reed didn't speak for the whole of the journey from London to Derby. Instead he sat, looking out of the window, his face a canvas for dark looks. Opposite him Bryson had not felt inclined to prompt discussion. When he had received the message from Lafferty, stating that he had gone to find Crowley in some godforsaken midlands backwater, he had immediately known that things had suddenly taken a bad turn.

'The mad bastard could take care of himself. Why had he gone?'

Bryson turned variations of this over in his thoughts, that ad and whether Lafferty had armed himself. He knew that Reed had given him a pistol to keep at home, *just in case*. Bryson hoped it wasn't needed, that there was nothing to be concerned about, but he also hoped that Lafferty had taken the gun with him. He looked over at Reed again but the Sergeant didn't take his eyes from the unfolding scenery outside the carriage.

'We are all being tested,' he thought. *'Our wits, our strength, our integrity and our sanity. All are being pushed to the limits.'*

His conversation with Pevensy had almost brought him to the point of punching the old chap in the mouth. It was ridiculous, stupid, unbelievable, what he had suggested,

'No! He had stated it as fact.'

As the train beat down upon the track he thought back to the conversation.

'You have never had a day's illness in your life Ron, no measles, no colic, no flu or even a cold.' Pevensy had said.

Bryson had felt his temperature rise. He recalled how his mother had trailed him from aunt to aunt, neighbour to neighbour, hoping he would catch the measles, the best way to prevent it happening when he was older. He didn't catch it, just as he had never experienced a sore throat or a rash of any kind.

He had broken his nose once, in a fist fight he had lost. This was also unusual as he was an excellent fighter generally, more so after his wartime training. But he had been exceptionally drunk and only sixteen, fighting against a beefy and experienced man with ten years on him.

'While you will have suffered as anyone does from mishaps, slipping on ice, cutting yourself on a sheet of paper, although I'm sure you are more agile and more dextrous than many, natural illness has never struck you has it?' Pevensy had continued.

He was right. Other than the odd bruise and scrape from generally being a child and then a boy and then a solider and copper there had been nothing.

'You will find that Sergeant Reed is a man with a similar story of unusually robust health.' Pevensy said.

'How would you know that?' Bryson asked, his attitude hostile.

'Oh, I don't know for certain.' Pevensy said casually. 'I haven't inquired into his past nor have I investigated yours. All I needed was for Digby to advise me of what might be.'

'Digby?' Bryson asked.

'A colleague.' Pevensy replied. 'I hope you will get to meet him.'

'And what might be?' Bryson pressed.

'Digby has a talent for it. A little like a meteorologist, he sees patterns and can predict, to some extent, the outcome.'

'What...' Bryson scoffed, 'he can see the future?'

'My dear boy, no one can see the future, at least not to my knowledge. What Digby can do is see...outcomes, possible futures if a particular set of circumstances are met.'

'I don't understand.' Bryson said.

'Let me put it in more practical terms. Have you ever seen a knitting pattern?

'Yes, of course.'

Good, then you will know from the image on the front that the instructions inside, if they are followed, will produce an item identical or certainly extremely similar to it. Yes?

'Yes.' Bryson said.

'Now, if you were to skip say the middle section of the pattern it is still possible that you may get something like the image but the odds are that it would be different, perhaps even wholly unalike.'

'I suppose so. Yes.' Bryson agreed.

'However, if you were to miss just the odd knit or pearl instruction, here and there, you could still arrive at the same product, the bits you missed would make very little difference overall.'

Pevensy placed his fingers on the table as though he were about to play a piano. A knitting pattern, or a sheet of music, whatever suits your understanding, follow them to the letter and when the final chord of the composition has been struck you will have arrived at the conclusion of the piece, producing the same collection of sounds that the composer has envisioned.

This is what we call *prophecy*, the observing of a set of particular instances that will lead to a predicted outcome. There can be many, many different outcomes of course, but by following as strictly as possible the pattern that has been seen it is possible to make the future that is only a possibility one that is most likely.'

Bryson was surprised that the concept came to him so easily now. When examining a crime scene he worked in a similar way, only in reverse. He would look for the set of circumstances that up to the situation that was in front of him. With hindsight he could follow the trail, the jealous wife, the husband leaves his wallet behind, inside a note, an address, that of his lover, to send her flowers. The bullet riddled corpse of a young woman, flowers shoved into her throat. If the husband had managed a glimpse of what Bryson saw that day, could he have hidden the note better or chosen not to send the flowers? Would that have destroyed the pattern and led to another future?

'You think that I am a part of some prophecy?' Bryson asked, barely believing the words that came out of his mouth.

'Yes and no my boy. We are all part of what is possibly an infinite number of futures and so whatever is seen, you are a part of it in some way, as is everyone on the planet, what is important is if something that you will do will make a *difference*.'

'Whether I am a part of the pattern or I destroy it.' Bryson said.

'Precisely.' Pevensy said with satisfaction.

'Is this Crowley's doing?' Bryson asked. It was the first thing that came into his mind. Something utterly bat shit was happening so surely it was Crowley.

'Oh Lord no.' Pevensy quickly replied. 'The man is not a seer of any sort. True, he knows way around rituals and spells better than almost any other person I've had the misfortune to meet, and he is certainly aware of the nature of such things, but no he's not gifted in that way. Very few are and those that are particularly adept are very, very special.'

He had sat back in his chair and considered this. He had thought that it was Ravensblack Hall that had brought them all together, Reed, Lafferty and of course Crowley. But now he realised that this pattern of Pevensy and his colleague must have been there during the war, possibly before, because he and Reed had been sought out specifically.

Was the Ravensblack affair seen by this Digby fellow? And if so why didn't he stop it? What could he have seen, what could have been worth allowing the death of all those people to the Mokoi? Crowley clearly had no forewarning of it all despite him knowing that there were people who could theoretically him of such a future.

Pevensy sat patiently waiting for questions but to his surprise Bryson stood and checked his watch.

'I have to go, but before I do I need to know something.' Bryson said.

Pevensy leaned forward. 'Of course dear boy.'

'Crowley. What is he, really? Is he good, bad? Should I trust him?'

Pevensy looked as though here was about to answer but caught himself. He reclined once again, looking uncomfortable.

'Ron, would you sit again? For just a short while, this is not something I can say to a man about to dash off.'

Bryson instinctively checked his watch again despite knowing that only a few seconds had passed since the last time. He sat.

'Had you asked me that question a year ago I would had told you that he was no more than the press make him out to be. A man of varied and occasionally extreme sexual desires, a rogue, a hellraiser and a danger to decency. But recently his actions and attitude appear to have altered. Something about him has changed but I cannot, nor can my colleagues say what it is exactly.'

'Yes,' Bryson said. 'There *is* something. Since Ravensblack he's been, strange, stranger that is. He has also taken one of our lads under his wing, the boy who was with us in the house, Lafferty. It concerns me.'

'Yes, I'm aware of his new apprentice. It seems that Crowley has cast aside all of his former followers and disciples, it has caused a good deal of upset and animosity in that corner of society.'

'I suppose Satanists are as petty and political as every other religious group.' Bryson said.

'My dear Crowley is no Satanist.' Pevensy replied.

'Oh?' Bryson said, surprised.

'No. Crowley has his Gods alright, but he does not so much worship them, as is usually their demand, he bargains with them in the way a market buyer might attempt to haggle over the price of a rug.'

'But the papers…there are photographs, he is a member of groups like the Golden Dawn…' Bryson said, but sounded uncertain.

'Newspapers are a refuse heap of conjecture, estimation and lies, I wouldn't trust the date printed on the front of them without checking with at least two other sources. What you see there is sensationalism and gossip, borne of the kind of scandal that only exists in the closed and repressed minds of the masses. Half the time Crowley has engineered it himself. I tell you Bryson, he could give the Devil a run for his money in manipulation and deceit.' Pevensy chided.

'But…to answer your question I am afraid I don't know. We have been unable to fathom Crowley's part in what is going on, and in truth he appears to have been useful, especially where you are concerned, in ensuring that…the pattern we have been following remains intact.'

'Is he dangerous?'

'Yes. He is as dangerous as any man alive. He is smart, he has tremendous knowledge and he is deceptively physically capable.'

'Has he killed people?' Bryson said.

'We have all killed people my boy and Crowley was as involved in the war as much as you and I. That is something that he hasn't chosen to leak into the papers.' Pevensy said.

Bryson nodded. He supposed that was true but was surprised that Pevensy was hinting at wartime action for Crowley. It went against what he had been led to believe.

'Look, everything that is happening, all of this I know is difficult for you. Try to take some time to get your head around and then come and see me. Rest assured I'll be trying to gather as much information as I can regarding the Tcho-Tcho and our friend Crowley.'

'Actually, what is strange and worrying to me is that it all seems to make some kind of sense. When we were at Ravensblack Hall with Crowley he had us walking around with potatoes inscribed with runes. Even at the time, before I saw what could be achieved with such a bizarre item, for some reason I accepted it. I overcame my initial sense of ridicule and disbelief almost immediately.' Bryson shook his head. 'I think that I've always known that something like this was going on.'

Bryson had placed his hands on the table and Pevensy leaned forward and took one them in a fatherly show of tenderness. Patting it twice.

'Everyone will be affected by what is happening here Ron, everyone, one day. What myself and my colleagues are trying to do is ensure that the best possible outcome for us all is achieved, and you are a part of that.'

'I believe you.' Bryson replied. 'Christ knows how I'm going to explain all of this to Reed.'

'Ah, I wouldn't worry about that too much. Sergeant Reed is more informed than you might think. A similar conversation will have taken place with my colleague by now.'

'Oh?'

'Yes, it was important that he be brought into the light at the same time as you.'

'And Lafferty?'

'Young Lafferty is in the care of Mr Crowley. I would think that it's likely that the lad is already a street or two ahead of you. What particular bias has been placed on Crowley's version I cannot say but again, I feel that he is an ally rather than an enemy, although he tends to lean towards a more self-serving approach.'

Pevensy patted Bryson's hand twice more. 'Go, do what you have to do and we will meet soon.'

Bryson stood once more. Bowed his head a little and then walked away from the café.

The train shook a little as lines were crossed. He looked over to Reed again. His friend was still lost in his own thoughts, looking out at the rapidly approaching signs that they were approaching the city of Derby, the roads, houses and lines of warehouses. Their next stop should be Glossop.

***

Tom pulled up to the waiting area at the station and jumped down from his seat. Harry came out to greet him. He had seen the lights on Tom's carriage from the window in his little office.

'Evenin Tom,' he said. He looked pale.

'Evenin Master,' Tom replied. 'Is she on time?'

'Aye, she is. Won't be more un a few minutes now,' Harry said. He walked over to Polly and fussed her. 'Have you been over to the Crossway?'

'I have.' Tom replied. He wasn't going to go with him making an additional journey later but couldn't bring himself to break a promise for the sake of his own convenience.

'I see.' Harry said, Tom didn't need to elaborate on the outcome, clearly the two men had not appeared to meet him.

They said nothing more. Tom walked to the platform and Harry returned to his office.

Tom felt the arrival of the locomotive through his feet before he heard it. Then the horn was blown as it approached the station, he had heard it a thousand times before but tonight it sounded like no other. It was deep and menacing and made his stomach turn. The nose of the engine appeared from around the mild bend that led into the last stretch of track to the station, the trees that lined its side hiding the hulking machines arrival until the last minute. It looked like an angry, violent beast that billowed smoke from its head, and fire at its feet as the brakes were engaged to haul to monster out of its charge towards him.

As it came to a halt steam filled the station and swirled around Tom and from within it two figures, one a giant of a man came towards him.

'Excuse me.' The shorter, but by no means less impressively sized of the two said. 'Is this Glossop station?'

Tom took a breath. 'I'm Tom, you must be the gentlemen officers from London. The blokes you want have gone to a village called Blackbrook, it's an empty place, no one lives there anymore. I've been back there the last two nights to collect them and neither has showed up. If you'll bring any luggage you have with you my coach is over yonder.' Tom tilted his head to the side and looked back. 'I'll take you as far as my horse will allow and then we are on foot.' He said.

Bryson looked at Reed. Reed shrugged.

'Lead on.' Bryson said.

They followed the coachman to his vehicle. He took their cases silently and secured them to the rear of it. Reed climbed in, it was awkward, the small doorway was not designed for a big man like him. Bryson waited for Tom to come around from the back of the carriage and lightly took his arm as he made to pass.

'Tom, could I ask you a few questions before we go?' He said.

Tom fixed him with an uncompromising gaze.

'No. I'm afraid not, we don't have the time.' He looked up to the bright, full moon that was already high and washed the land with pale light. 'We need to be there as soon as possible.' He said, backed away from Bryson and climbed into his seat.

Bryson stood for a moment, considering challenging the man but decided to let it go. He climbed into the cab and heard Tom call out, '*geeupgirl.*' The coach began to move

Part 10

As he drew near to a small stone bridge Lafferty was almost pulled over as Benny abruptly sat on his haunches and refused to move.

'Come on boy.' Lafferty said. 'Come on, not far now.'

Benny wouldn't budge. He looked straight ahead towards the bridge as though expecting something to climb from underneath it.

Lafferty continued trying to coax movement out of him but the Bulldog refused to budge.

'Bloomin Nora.' Lafferty said.

He looked around but couldn't see anything untoward. He looked at Benny. The big dog looked back. They were at an impasse.

'Benny, Mr C is in there somewhere. Don't you want to see Mr Crowley?'

Benny lifted up one of his paws to almost behind his head and begin to slurp at his bollocks.

Lafferty sighed. He knew full well that if Benny had decided he wasn't going somewhere then it would take a traction engine to move him.

He didn't like the idea of leaving Benny alone on the road. As big an animal as he was and despite having seen him try to tear the head off the most terrifying thing he had ever encountered he felt that it wasn't safe to leave him to his own devices.

After a minute of trying to come up with some alternative method of getting Benny moving again and failing he decided to walk along the road a little. He would check out what lay beyond the bridge and still have Benny in his sights. As he walked towards it he looked back a couple of times to see if the dog had given up and begun to follow but Benny was still otherwise engaged.

Lafferty realised that the road must have climbed a little. Not drastically but enough for the bridge and the small rise to hide the far side of it until he was very close. He saw what Crowley had seen previously. The run down, former home to just over two hundred souls. He looked back once again to Benny. There was no significant change other than that he had adjust his position to get better access to his genitals.

He decided to try something. He had experimented with a procedure Crowley had called *Channeling*. The aim was to focus and produce a sort of external version of himself made entirely of the Essence that Crowley claimed was the foundation of all matter in the universe. An infinite see of energy that all things seen and unseen moved within. Crowley said that humans were the best conductors of this mysterious energy, that it was how all things considered supernatural or magical were produced.

He had encountered little success with it. Besides the dreams and visions he had Lafferty had never been able to produce any other form of paranormal or supernatural manifestation. Crowley had been very disappointed. He had confided in him that he personally had no magical talent at all, everything he achieved was through the spells and rituals he performed. For him to utilise the Essence he had to call on the power of others and the most powerful wielders of it, after the Gods, were demons.

But what he lacked in magical power he more than made up for in his knowledge of the arcane and skill at drawing out creatures and entity's through ritual. Crowley knew every God, every Demon and every sprite or spirit type.

Lafferty remembered the look on Crowley's face when he realised that Roman Ravensblack, for all of his slander concerning the man's ability, had been able to produce a Gate inside the house. His jealousy had been almost tangible. No wonder he hoped that his protégé would have some latent talent.

He focused his thoughts, drew on the weak energy of the Essence around him, he had expected it to the slight, weak thing he encountered in London, but it was stronger here. He tried to push his consciousness out of his mind and travel through the invisible sea all around.

He couldn't do it. Although he did feel as though he was close, as though he were a Russian Doll and a second, smaller version of him was about to step out of his skin, he failed to get any further. But something did become apparent. While he couldn't move his 'second self' out from its shell for a brief moment the extension he had created, made as it was from the very fabric of existence, was receptive to greater manifestations of the same energy nearby.

Lafferty detected a presence. Close by, perhaps in the trees to the right of him. He felt emotions, he felt smells and *touched* sounds. He felt the sexuality of this being, knew instinctively that it was female and suddenly dropped his intense concentration as the powerful, radiating energy of this creature came into touch with his own weak and poorly constructed conjuration. His skin became electric and a charge ran through his body and into his balls. He felt a flush of sexual desire flood through him, ignited by the connection as though he had been dosed with a pure draught of whatever intoxicating chemical it was that made men lose their minds at the touch of a woman.

'Oh my gosh.' He said out loud as his senses returned to inside his head.

He backed away from the bridge then turned and hurried back to Benny who to his surprise was now standing. He wondered if the dog could see the incredible redness of his skin as a mix of sexual adrenalin and embarrassment illuminated him. He thought that he probably could.

He found that he was breathing heavily as he tried to once again talk to Benny.

'Come... on... boy, we... need to... get going,' he panted despite not having exerted himself.

Benny began to amble forwards.

'Unbelievable,' Lafferty gasped. He walked after the dog and picked up the trailing leash.

It was then that he saw the girl. She was of average height.

Her hair was long and loose, it fell about her shoulders in an untidy fashion. Although he was surprised at her sudden appearance Lafferty didn't break his stride, not that he could have without Benny pulling him over if he stopped as the hound plodded on towards her. As he drew nearer Lafferty decided the polite thing to do would be to say hello but before he could the girl, who thought must be about eighteen, beat him to the punch.

'Hello,' she said.

'Hello.' Lafferty replied.

'Where are you going?' She asked but without suspicion.

'Uhm...to the village.' Lafferty pointed past the bridge. Over there, he wondered if he was ever going to cross over the blasted thing.

'Why?' the girl asked as though Lafferty had said he was going to jump off a cliff.

'Well... erm... I have a friend there. I need to see him.' Lying didn't come easily to him.

She looked at Benny and smiled. Benny licked his nose.

'Nice dog.'

'Yes.... but he's not mine, he belongs to my friend.'

'Your friend in the village?' the girl asked.

'Yes.' Lafferty said. He felt uncomfortable. The girl was beautiful. The long, untidy hair was auburn, her face was exquisitely curved and skin looked soft, a few freckles were dotted about her nose and under her eyes, her lips were slim but shapely.

'You should be careful around here.'

'Oh?' Lafferty said as though he were not already of full alert for any possible danger. Even from an attractive young woman. 'Why's that?'

'People go missing.'

'Do they?' Lafferty said, even more wary now. Having heard her few short phrases he thought he detected a welsh accent in her words.

'People, sheep, cows all sorts,' she said.

'Not young ladies though?'

'I can look after myself,' she replied.

'Of course you can,' Lafferty said, and blushed as he realised that he was being patronising.

'Whys your friend in there?'

'I'm sorry?'

'You are here for your friend but why is he here?'

At this she walked forward and got on one knee to fuss Benny, she looked up at Lafferty as she rubbed at the big dogs folds of skin.

Lafferty was almost dizzy at the sight of her. He was sure he had never seen such *life* radiate from a person like it did this girl. He felt a similar heat to the one he had experienced when attempting to channel rise inside him.

'Erm... he's on a business trip, I think.' Lafferty almost stuttered each word.

'That's strange,' she said in a manner that suggested she didn't really think it was. 'that someone would take a business trip to an empty village don't you think?

'I... yes, I suppose it is.'

She scuffed at Benny's large head which seemed agreeable to him, then stood. As Benny had been at his side she was now very close to Lafferty.

'Don't suppose you know your way around there do you?'

Lafferty was hypnotised by the movement of her mouth, he didn't dare look her in the eye in case he fell to his knees and pledged his eternal soul to her.

'I don't. No. I've never been here before.'

'Well, don't worry, if you should find yourself getting lost, or in a bit of spot, there's always the church to the west of the village, as though you were headed to the tall trees. You can always find help in a church I bet.' She said.

'Erm...yes, I suppose that could be the case.'

The girl smiled at him and Lafferty felt as though she might swallow him whole as she revealed her beautifully white teeth.

'Well, I hope you find your friend....' She raised her eyebrows, two dark arches that directed his attention to the eyes he had tried to avoid. Two perfect chestnut centred orbs set alluringly above freckled cheeks.

'Uhm, Lafferty. *Nigel* I mean. Nigel Lafferty.'

'Alright Nigel Lafferty, I hope you find him.' She grinned and turned away, walking back along the road towards the crossway. Lafferty saw that the light cotton top and modestly patterned skirt she wore had a few dry leaves and small pieces of twig caught in the fibres, as though she had being lying on them in the woods.

'What's your name?' Lafferty called after but she didn't reply. He thought about hurrying after her but remembered why he was here and that he had more pressing business to attend to than flirting with the locals. Not that he had any clue how to go about flirting.

'Country girls eh Benny?' He said.

Benny offered no opinion. It was only as he began to cross the bridge that he thought about the sensation he had almost been overwhelmed by as something had touched the projection he was trying to push out from his body. That had been distinctly female in its character, sensuous and filled with a kind of wild energy. Was it pure coincidence that a girl who had all but taken his breath away had appeared only seconds later?

'*History is driven by coincidence*' Crowley had insisted, but that meeting did not feel at all like chance.

After crossing the bridge he saw the houses that lined the first street were in a terrible state of decay. As he moved further in they did appear to be a little more sound and those that still stood had windows that were intact. Except for one. All of the panes were smashed, no doubt the work of youngsters from the other villages in the area.

'*Vandals.*' He thought.

He carried on but gradually became aware that he didn't actually know where he was going. All he knew was that Crowley was coming to this village, he didn't know where in the village he was supposed to have been meeting the alleged book vendor. He had assumed that there would be at least someone who could point him in the right direction.

The girl had sort of given him directions though. She had been oddly specific about how to find the church while being generally vague about why he would wish too. *West of the village, which is where the tall trees are.* He looked about the tops of the houses and sure enough ahead and to the right he could see that there was a line of individual treetops behind them.

He recommenced walking. Benny barked furiously. Everything went dark.

Part 11

Nothing was said by the policemen as Tom's carriage thundered along the dirt track. Bryson wanted to talk to Reed about the lad, about Crowley and the whole mess they had suddenly found themselves in. But he couldn't. Reed appeared to be entirely lost in his own thoughts. It was hard to tell what might be going on with him, even out of uniform, even without his helmet dipped low over his eyes, revealing only the enormous moustache. He was a man who used silence like an iron wall.

He was also concerned about the speed of the carriage. It shook dreadfully as its wooden wheels, sturdy as they had looked, bounced and slammed on the uneven track. But still Bryson said nothing to the coachman either. He was another who seemed unapproachable at this moment. Occasionally he heard the crack of a whip and *'gerrupgirl'* shouted at the single horse.

'Christ I'm going to die before I get there.' He muttered.

Reed appeared not to have heard, understandable given the volume of the rumble created by their journey Bryson thought but he had hoped that the Sergeant might have at least nodded or made a light quip. Instead, as he had done on the train journey Reed stared out of the window. This time into a darkening countryside.

It seemed like an age before Tom called from above *'eeeasygirl'* and the carriage began to slow from its break neck-speed. As soon as it came to a halt Bryson climbed out, quite done with being shook like a rattle.

He looked about. There were fields around him and ahead he could see the road carried on, broken by a crossroad, towards land that rose a little either side of it.

'Is this it?' Bryson asked Tom as the coachman climbed down.

'Aye Sir, this is the Crossway. Chiverton and Wolstone lie at either end, ahead is Blackbrook.' At that Tom walked to Sally and patted her tenderly.

Reed disembarked and as Bryson had done he took in the surroundings. Night was falling fast and the moon, suspended in a clear sky was the only light they would have as neither had thought to bring a torch.

'We'll need some light.' He said to Bryson.

'Don't worry about that,' Tom called to him from Sally's side. 'I got torches for us all.

Bryson turned to Tom, surprised. 'For us all? Are you joining us Mr Chell?'

'I am Sir, if that would be alright with you.' Tom replied. He walked to Bryson and the Sergeant.

'I've left two gentlemen out here and to be honest it don't sit right with me.' He said.

Bryson looked at Reed who shrugged. 'He's got the torches.' He said.

'Alright, I don't see why not Mr Chell. As I have no idea what bloody hell we are doing out here anyway I'm fairly certain that your good company will be an asset.' Bryson said.

'Thank you Sir, and its Tom if you will. Just plain old Tom.'

'Right, Tom. Of course as you wish.' Bryson smiled amiably. 'And I take it that we are following the path ahead to Blackbrook?'

'Yes Sir, excuse me.' Tom said and walked to the rear of the carriage. The sound of a lock being turned and dusty hinges grinding together sounded in the still air. A moment later he reappeared with a lantern for each of them.

'Oil lanterns.' He said as he handed each out. 'Good for a few hours apiece. I reckon we light up two and keep the third in reserve.'

Both policemen nodded. The suggestion was sound. Tom placed his lantern on the floor and moved back to his seat, he reached up and slid from it a long cloth covered object. When he removed the cloth from it his shotgun was revealed. He looked up at the officers.

'I take it you gentlemen have firearms?' He asked.

Bryson and Reed nodded. Bryson lifted the corner of his jacket to show his holstered revolver.

'Good.' Tom said, but didn't advise them of the special ammunition contained within his cartridges.

'Well then officers, let's go and find your boys.' He said.

When Penhaligon stepped into his living room he was surprised to see Benny sat in the middle of the carpet, looking up at him.

'Benny!' He said. Benny stood and pattered over to him, his tongue was hanging out and his breathing heavy.

'One moment son,' Penhaligon said and rushed into his kitchen. He returned with a large bowl which he carried carefully as it was filled with fresh water. He placed it down in front of Benny and stepped back to allow the animal to drink.

This situation could mean only one thing. Wherever the dog had been there was great danger. Something that was beyond the animal's ability to defend against. Penhaligon got to one knee and stroked Benny's head as it lapped at the bowl. He was very warm to the touch. Hot and thirsty? Benny had travelled a good distance through the *Aether*.

He stood, walked to his telephone and dialled.

Pevensy answered immediately.

'What's the matter?' He had sensed the call was coming.

'Benny's here.'

'At your house?' Pevensy replied, shocked.

'Large as life. He's very warm and very thirsty,' Penhaligon said as he watched Benny continue lapping up the water.

'Good lord, he's crossed the Aether!' Pevensy replied.

'Aye, looks like it. And that means…'

Trouble wherever he was,' Pevensy said completing the sentence. 'Do you have any clue where he's come from?'

'I've no idea. Reed didn't say anything about taking him anywhere. He did mention that Crowley was away from the city however, could be something in that d'yer think?'

There was silence down the line for a moment, until Pevensy sighed. 'Yes, it seems likely that if Benny was in danger enough for his ward to activate then most likely Crowley is somehow involved.'

'We need a plan,' Penhaligon said, always the one to push the group forward.

'Yes, yes we do. I'll head over to Digby now. See if he's able to help.' Pevensy said

'Have you had any contact from him?'

'No, nothing today. I think it would be fair to say that it's likely he hasn't seen anything of this.'

'Aye.' Penhaligon replied.

'As soon as I've seen Digby and I'll come to you in my car.'

'No, I'll head to the station, get me from there. They should have some knowledge as to where Reed and Bryson are, Lafferty too. If Benny isn't with them it means they are somewhere they shouldn't be.' Penhaligon said.

Silence again.

'Yes. Do that. Give me an hour. I'll get some things together. We may need too…' Pevensy stopped, remembering that he was on a telephone, '…travel urgently.' He said.

'Christ I hope not.' Penhaligon replied.

'An hour,' Pevensy said.

'An hour,' Penhaligon agreed. He returned the receiver. Benny had finished drinking from the bowl and looked up at him expectantly.

'I'll get you another bowl old boy,' he said to Benny as the animal licked the last drops from it.

'*God I hope we don't have to travel,*' he thought

***

As they walked along the path Reed held up his lantern to light up the rocks ahead.

'See something?' Bryson asked.

Tom stopped and brought his shotgun up.

'I'm not sure guv. Those rocks look like a geezer to you?'

Bryson peered into the darkness as the shape the light revealed. The outline of the outcrop and surrounding boulders did actually look like the face of a tired old man.

Tom relaxed a little and lowered his gun.

'It's alright, that's one of the few things around here that's natural, it's...' He paused and looked back to the officers. They could see his expression, worry that he had said something he shouldn't.

'Don't worry Tom. Not natural is something we have become accustomed to of late.' Bryson said. At his side Reed nodded.

'Right,' Tom said.

They carried on a further two hundred yards until the stone bridge came into view.

'Beyond that bridge is where Blackbrook begins.' Tom said pointing the way.

'There's lights in the village. I thought it was abandoned?' Bryson now indicated the faint orange glow that seemed to radiate from distant rooftops.

Tom observed the glow carefully. 'Aye looks like someone lit up some lanterns or torches about the place, but trust me, that place ain't had folks living there for gone fifty years.'

Bryson stepped a little closer to him and spoke in a whisper.

'We're being followed, I assume you know this.'

'Since Glossop,' Tom said.

'Who could follow us for over two hours on foot, at the speed you were going?'

'Who indeed Sir?' Tom replied, 'we better go and find out.' He hefted his shotgun a little, making it more comfortable in the crook of his elbow.

'Alright.' Bryson said. He pulled his pistol free of its holster and Reed did the same.

Reed stepped forward 'Guv, I'm telling you now, if a Troll comes out from under that fucking bridge, that's it for me. I'm done.'

Bryson looked at him with mild incomprehension, until the great moustache twitched at each end. A smile.

He laughed, quietly at first but then could not help himself from letting the volume increase as the thought tickled at his mind. Reed joined in, a booming *hur hur hur*, his lantern shook in his meaty hand.

At first Tom stared at the two officers in horror, but as they laughed, as they broke the still air and the tight grip of tension, he too felt his mouth widen. He laughed, loudly. Daring the night to find fault with this sudden escape from his melancholy. The three men laughed until tears formed at the corner of their eyes and finally, when the fit subsided they each shook hands and wished each other good luck, because they each knew that something waited for them beyond the bridge and in the village that shouldn't be lit.

Part 12

'Fucking hell, fucking hell, fucking hell.' Crowley gasped as he ran from the house, across the green and into the streets. He had smashed through the window with considerable grace and rolled perfectly out of the dive. His long strides took him to the small fence at the end of it which he leapt over with ease and landed on the other side already prepared to run as fast as he could.

His mind worked furiously to offer him some way of escape. He didn't know the village but he was sure he could find his way back to where he entered. The problem was that he would then have to get back to…where? Glossop? He had no chance.

He ducked into a street, looking for somewhere to either hide or to present a defence. He had his pistol. The fellow at the house had been human, he didn't know who or what was chasing him but they seemed human by their shouts to each other. No, defence wasn't an option, not yet. He had only a dozen or so bullets in the little cloth bag he kept tucked away in his jacket. He had to hide.

Another intersection quickly came up, the village streets weren't particularly long. If his pursuers knew the place they would soon figure out how to cut him off. He had to make them think he had escaped beyond it. Make them head into the woods or onto the road to Glossop. He took the turning. By his estimation if he went right again he would be headed around the village towards the east, if he could take a left, it should lead towards the outskirts. He ran until the correct turning presented itself, then went in the opposite direction.

The gamble, whether they would assume he would try to exit the village relied on them thinking he was smart, but not smart enough to try and bluff them. It also meant that he would have to stop, to hide and stay quiet so his footsteps couldn't be heard running off back into the village.

The first house on the street, immediately to his left, had a sprawling mess of bramble that had taken over its lawn and spilled onto the path. Crowley dodged ably around to the rear of the mass, got to his knees and crawled into it as best he could. Keen thorns pricked at his scalp, face and hands but he kept silent and as still as he could. He could hear the thud of boots on the road, they had been very close behind him. He watched the junction ahead and held his breath. A man appeared and stopped. He looked around, taking in each route, looking for signs of his prey. Two more men joined him and each mimicked his search for Crowley.

'Where'd he go?' One of the new arrivals said. He was bald, thin and had a tattoo that Crowley couldn't make out that snaked down his neck and disappeared into the collar of a grey, dirty vest.

The man who had appeared first. He had short cropped black hair and wore a similar vest that had no sleeves. He was muscular, very strongly built, his vest rippled with his physique.

'Fuck knows,' Muscles replied, 'he's gotta be headed out the village.'

'*Good, good,*' Crowley thought.

'What do we do?' Sleeveless said, a little panicked.

'We go back. Tell him. He can send something out there to get him.'

'*Something?*' Crowley didn't like the sound of that.

'Those fuckers should be here anyway, why the fuck are we running around chasing people.' Sleeveless said.

'They're already chasing somefin.' This was the third man, his Cockney accent was instantly apparent to Crowley. 'Boss sent em out to find that fucking girl din't he.'

Muscles but his hands on his hips. 'Fuck me. He could run.' He shook his head, gathering his wits.

Sleeveless and Cockney nodded.

'Aye, and who'd have thought he'd have straight up murdered Peasley?' Sleeveless said.

'Come on. Let's get back before he gets too far to track.' Muscles said and started back around the corner.

Crowley heard Cockney reply. 'Heh, I ain't never seen anyfin those fuckers can't track, they sees you from up there an that's it innit?'

Crowley waited until he was as sure as he could be that they had moved out of earshot of any movement he might make. Once satisfied he scrawled out from his hiding place ignoring the little bites of the brambles. They were going to get something to chase him, to track him down. Dogs most likely and they would be almost impossible to shake.

He needed somewhere his scent would be masked. He looked around as he thought what options there might be in a village. He looked at the houses, the gardens. Most had their windows, some had doors open, some closed. Curtains. No carriages or carts, no cars. He turned to the house behind him, the one the garden belonged to and walked towards the door. He pushed at it and it swung open.

Walking through he saw pictures on the wall. The first room, like the one he had dived out of, was the living room. A table was set for a meal, chairs were pushed aside but other than that, other than a few signs of a rapid exit there was nothing to say that the owners hadn't left and were expecting to come back in an hour or so. He checked the kitchen. On the counter was the skeletal remains of a chicken that had been prepared for some meal. No doubt for the table he had just seen laid out.

'They *left in a hurry.*' Crowley thought. '*Whatever happened here, all that time ago, everyone left quickly, no time to take family pictures or to eat a meal.*'

He exited the house, still careful to make little sound. If they were going to set dogs to find him he had to make himself invisible. Spells didn't work on dogs. They saw straight though them, even the mangiest mutt in London could spot him even if he had spent ten years covering his presence in glamours and rituals of obfuscation. It was quite irritating at times. No wonder they were first animal man chose to befriend.

'*Something strong, something potent.*' As he though what he could use to achieve this he took time to reload his pistol. He snapped the chamber shut once the gun was fully loaded and as he did so a sound issued from further down the street. A light crash or thud. Crowley raised his pistol and stepped into the road. He couldn't see anything moving, the upside to this was that nothing was moving towards him. Hopefully.

'*Fuck off right now,*' his self-preservation advised him. '*Just run, if they send dogs you can shoot them.*'

Crowley couldn't shoot a dog. He was fooling himself he knew. He could shoot a man without skipping a heartbeat. He just had. But a dog? No.

'*Then you are a dead man. You will die here in this shit hole and no one will come to your funeral,*' his self-preservation said, goading him. '*Your wake will be the saddest event on the planet. The only people who will drink to your absence will be all the landlords in London and the police.*'

It was probably true. He had no family, he had no real friends and he certainly didn't have… '*Landlords.*' The word fixed in his mind.

Every village had a pub, sometimes two. But they could be anywhere. He looked for rooftops to see if any peeked above others, pubs were usually large as they often offered accommodation too. The only building taller than a pub was a church. He saw a broken spire reaching up like a smashed molar.

'*If I owned a pub I'd want it as far away from the local church as possible.*'

Keeping his pistol handy he made for the street that lay in the opposite direction of the broken church.

Part 13

The street they stood in was quiet aside than the sound of flaming torches that lined it, they crackled and wavered in the mild breeze. The road under their feet was more solid than the dirt track beyond the bridge, back towards the crossroads, but it was overgrown with weeds and grass and was soft underfoot.

Tom extinguished his lantern and placed it on the floor at his feet. Reed lowered his also, but left it lit.

'Someone must be home.' Bryson said. 'Looks like these have been placed all around the village.' He nodded towards a torch nearby. It was fixed onto a stake that had been driven into the soft soil of a garden.

'Aye.' Tom said. 'Doesn't feel none too welcoming though.'

'No.' Bryson said. It didn't feel at all welcoming. He took a few steps forward, half expecting someone or something to burst from a doorway of one of the shabby homes, or perhaps all of them. A horde of screaming Tcho-Tcho or some re-animated versions of Lafferty and Crowley, with forks for teeth and knives for fingers. Nothing stirred.

'Do we have a plan Guv?' Reed asked.

'Find Lafferty. Find Crowley. We will have to deal with the rest as it comes.'

Reeds moustache twitched in agreement.

Bryson looked back to Tom. 'What happened here? You said it was fifty years ago, what was it that killed this village?'

'Truth is I don't know.' He said apologetically. 'I wasn't born around here, I'm a Glossop lad so all I know are rumours of rumours.' He thought for a moment. Giving his response as much thought as the situation would allow.

'If there is one thing that all the stories share it's that whatever it was it came from the mines.' He lifted his arm, pointed a finger, and drew an arc directed ahead of them. 'There's tin mines towards the north east of the village, Wolstone and Blackbrook are the closest to em. I can't even begin to tell you all the tales but I reckon that everyone I've ever heard started with those mines, or at least that area.'

'Right. Fair enough.' Bryson took a breath. 'I can only suggest we move through the village. Look for signs of Lafferty and Crowley or whoever went to the trouble of lighting our way for us.'

Tom and Reed nodded.

'I'm leaving my lantern.' Tom said as he lifted his shotgun to a more ready position.

Reed decided to keep his for the time being. He didn't need both hands to keep his pistol prepared as Tom did with his weapon. Without further discussion they moved together, keeping the formation of Bryson leading as they followed either side.

The group had walked only a few yards when Bryson stopped. 'Is there a church here?' He asked.

'Of course, aye.' Tom replied.

'Might be somewhere to take a look at. Big place, sanctuary and all that.'

'Fair enough.' Tom replied and stepped ahead to take the lead. 'Follow me,' he said and in his head a voice whispered to him, distant, barely audible as though struggling to make herself heard, *'be careful my love.'*

They had walked a further hundred yards or so and turned into a couple of streets until the old church appeared. It was a complete ruin. Fire had, at some point long past, done tremendous damage to it. The blackened masonry evidenced how far soot had covered both the remaining structure and tombstones that lay flat or stood at irregular angles. The bricks looked as though they might crumble before their eyes. The steeple, still a good twenty feet high, was a broken cylinder of precariously balanced stones at its peak. They could see it so well because torches had been festooned about it. It was lit up like a shrine.

'Do you get the feeling we were expected to come this way?' Reed said, the suspicion in his voice evident.

'Yes I do.' Bryson replied gravely.

Tom lifted his shotgun to his chin. He began to turn on the spot. Scanning homes near to the churchyard. Looking for a potential ambush. There were too many places to consider. Thick trees, sepulchres, doorways, windows, walls and thick clumps of uncontrolled brambles.

Reed lowered his lantern to the floor once more and pulled back the hammer on his pistol. Bryson's eyes darted across the churchyard, looking into shadows. Expectation heightened their senses. They were primed to react to any movement, any attack. Except from the skies.

***

Crowley almost cheered when he saw the three story building ahead of him. Attached to a length of wood above its large door was a sign of which he had no doubt would bear the name of the public house. As he drew nearer he could just about make out the faded writing, 'The Cock and Bear.'

He ran up to the door and tried the handle. To his delight the thick old door swung open. It was gloomy inside but the uncovered windows provided at least some light. He stepped in. Nothing attacked him, which was a good start. He quickly navigated his way to the bar but was disappointed to find that the shelves were empty.

'Fuck,' he said bitterly.

He looked around the room, at dusty tables for bottles that might be unopened. Only empty glasses remained their contents if they had once been left unfinished had long since evaporated. Crowley thought hard.

'Cellar,' he said.

He listened first, checking to see if anything might be moving outside or even inside the building, but there was nothing. Satisfied he moved around to the back of the bar and immediately saw the trap door in the floor. It was hard to lift even with the iron loop recessed in the wood but he managed to pull it up. It was pitch black inside. He could only see the first couple of steps leading down.

He fished into his pocket and pulled out a box of matches. Lighting one he dropped it down. A little orange sphere of light fell no more than twelve feet. It burned for a moment having remained alight for the journey then was extinguished as its little wooden stick was exhausted.

Crowley looked about the immediate area. There had to be some sort of light available nearby. He was correct. On the lower shelf just to the right of him was an oil lamp. There were also packs of candles, some balls of string and a long knife. He took the candles and lamp but left the string and knife. The blade looked crooked and blunt.

He lit a candle and then used it to try and fire up the oil lamp. To his disappointment it wouldn't take. The wick was useless and the can that held the oil felt light. He decided to take it down the ladder with him in case there was fuel to be found in the cellar. Gripping the candle tightly he climbed steadily down the ladder, thankful that his feet soon hit a solid floor.

He held the candle aloft and was surprised to see that there were many tables and chairs down here. They had not been stacked particularly well and Crowley guessed that they must be spares or broken pieces. What he was hoping to find was directly ahead of him. A wall of spirits.

There was at least a dozen bottles of whiskey and numerous other wonderful beverages. Rum, wine, sherry, brandy and vodka bottles, all full, all sealed, lay in rows along the deep shelving.

'Perfect.' Crowley said. He took a couple of whiskey bottles from the shelf and stuck them into his pockets. He then took a bottle of Brandy, opened it and took a long draught. It felt like sweet fire swirling down his throat. As he took the bottle away from his lips he let out a satisfied '*ahhhh*' and then drank a little more.

Next he set up candles strategically about the cellar. There was a lot of junk about, lots of wood, so he was careful to avoid anywhere the little wax columns might fall and cause the immediate complication of burning him to death. He then quickly climbed back to the first floor of the pub. He made his way to a window at the side of the door and peered outside, the street looked empty.

He opened the door and stepped outside, looked about once more and then took out the whiskey bottles. Once he had opened them both he began to splash the content of a bottle over the door and the immediate entrance. The remaining bottle he used to try and cover up where he had walked into the building. He walked as far as he thought the alcohol could manage, where there was a couple of directions a person could walk, and splashed the strong smelling whiskey around as he crept backwards towards the pub.

It wasn't much of a ruse he knew, but dogs had an incredibly keen sense of smell and in this instance it might work in his favour, the alcohol would have far stronger scent, probably overwhelming his own and might lead the animals away. He went back inside the pub and returned to the cellar.

From the stacks of chairs, the found one that seemed to be solid and sat down on it. He needed a plan.

He had been incredibly foolish. He couldn't deny it. The only person who knew where he had gone too was the lad. He had given instructions for him to keep it a secret.

'What a cock,' he thought, 'what an absolute prize winning twot you are.'

He shook his head at his own stupidity but his self-preservation kicked in to keep him focused.

'You have to get out of here, you can't just lay low. Eventually they will find you.'

'I need to know who they are.' Crowley said to the empty room. 'This was a trap, but what could they hope to gain?'

He considered this. He had his fortune back, thanks to Ravensblack Hall, but how could they obtain that by luring him here. His home was a repository of some powerful items but no one could gain access to them, they would destroy themselves first with the rituals he had placed in their defence.

They could just want him dead, maybe the Children of Hastur or Tcho-Tcho, but even that made no sense, besides the queue of others who would like to see him swinging from a yard arm why drag him to the middle of nowhere when they could just job him in London? No. They wanted something from him. Whoever it was wanted something so badly that they had prepared this whole charade to entice him to a remote and shunned place.

'They must be expecting a hell of a fight from one man to prepare a whole ...' he stopped. They were expecting a *fight*. Not just from him, he was one man, what could he do alone? But if he had friends that came to look for him. Friends with guns say. *That* might lead to something a little more explosive. What better than to ambush them here in the village that time forgot?

Crowley stood. He felt he was on the right track but there was something else that worried at his thoughts. *Why* did they also want the others if that was the case?

'*Lafferty, Bryson, Reed, their only connection was Ravensblack Hall and the events since then. Was it part of the war between the Hastur mob and those in-bred Tcho-Tcho?*' His mind was working fast now trying to form connections from the pathways he was finding.

He was missing something. There was information he had yet to discover. This was a gathering of some sort, there was a plan to bring them all here and eliminate them in one fell swoop, that at least seemed logical. But why? With the exception of himself and to some degree Lafferty the others had no real knowledge of the forces at work, not knowledge that could be used effectively. They were men of laws and guns and big sticks. Not magic, not talismans and rituals.

Benny came to his mind. For a moment he thought of the dog as part of their little team. He had been surreptitiously given that dog by one of the three Guardians. Now *there* was a group that *could* cause problems for these factions. Men with power, with abilities and with knowledge. Three people charged with protecting their region from supernatural threats. *Three people.*

Something small and dark and desperate began to form in Crowley's mind. *Three good men.* There were always three weren't there. Perhaps this wasn't about him, perhaps it wasn't even about Bryson and his lads.

He heard a dog bark. It was faint down here in the cellar but he heard it nonetheless and he recognised it immediately.

It was Benny.

Part 14

Lafferty regained his consciousness slowly and all the while the back of his head throbbed causing a pulsing, deep pain. He breathed deeply and found that he couldn't move his arms. He was sat and his hands had been tied behind his back. He licked at his lips. His mouth felt dry. It took him a while to open his eyes but when he did he struggled to believe what he saw.

A creature, because it could be nothing else. Stood with its back to him at the far side of the empty room he was being held prisoner inside. As tall as an average man, there the similarity to a human ended. Its body was that of some sort of insect, it didn't appear to have skin, rather a carapace that was light brown in hue and chitinous. Great translucent wings hung down its back.

It stood upon two slight but sturdy crab-like legs and further up its torso Lafferty could see four similar appendages, two either side, working like arms and hands, the extremities being claws. The head of the creature, if it could be called that, was a mass of pinkish tissue that so closely resembled a large human brain that Lafferty could only assume that it must be just that. A brain without benefit of a protective skull and skin or in this case the carapace that the rest of the creature was clothed in.

Lafferty saw that the thing was about to turn and closed his eyes, pretending that he was still unconscious. He heard as the creature took strides towards him. Its crab-like appendages clicked upon the floor as it came closer. He thought he might scream, he thought he might go mad as the image whirred through his mind. He felt a touch. A claw from one of its four arms was gently resting upon his temple. Lafferty used all of his willpower to remain inert, as though oblivious to the thing, but his stomach crawled as the claw traced a line down his cheek. Next he heard the click-click of its feet as the thing moved away once again, back to its table.

Lafferty slowly opened one eye and saw that it was once again busy with whatever occupied it at the far side of the room. He risked a more detailed look around. There was one door and it was beyond the thing, to its right. There appeared to be nothing else in the room except the table and upon that Lafferty could see various items that he couldn't place. Tubes, coils of some strange material and various containers. He couldn't see Benny and this made his stomach turn over. He remembered that the dog had begun to bark savagely, looking up to the sky, then it had gone dark.

He tested his bindings. They were tight, the rope was cutting into his wrists. He wondered if the creature had tied them. From what he could see of the claws they would only be capable of simple procedures, but then it did have four of them.

He heard more footsteps. This time more like the *thud thud* of *normal* feet. Beyond the door. He closed his eyes once again and listened. The door opened.

'They're here.' A voice said. Deep, course. A local accent perhaps. 'We're ready to go.'

What came in response was a kind of heavy vibration, interspersed with clicks and grunts.

'No, still no sign. It looks like he headed out the village, into the woods maybe. He won't last long in there.'

More clicks and grunts responded. The vibration under it all was of a slightly higher pitch.

'He doesn't matter. We have the three, the others will come for them. We are still in control.'

The vibration dropped now. Lafferty couldn't be sure but as alien as the sound was it carried threat upon it, a warning. There was no reply from the person who had entered the room. He heard the shuffle of feet and the door closing.

'*They had the three?*' If the person in the woods was Crowley did that mean that Inspector Bryson and Sergeant Reed had come for him? It was the only sense he could make of it. '*If so, who are the others?*'

He heard the clicking of the creature's feet again. The door opened and then closed. '*Has it gone?*' Lafferty listened. No sound around him but possibly something above? Another floor.

He parted his eyes a little. The thing couldn't be seen. He lifted his head properly and now took a full look around. Nothing more to be seen other than he could now see all that was on the table. There were tools. Strange things, certainly not fashioned for human hands. The creature had been working on something. There were objects on the table seemingly opened up as the creature had been working upon a transistor radio and its wires and electronic components had been pulled from within it. It did not look metallic though, it was more like a duller version of the things own skin.

Lafferty fidgeted in the chair as he tried to use his fingers to loosen the rope that bound him. It was too tightly wound. He considered the chair he was sat in. His arms had been pulled back and then his wrists tied. He couldn't stand to free his arms but the chair *was* wooden. Probably something from the village. Probably very old.

He put his feet forward and dragged forward. It was difficult with his weight but it did move. So, only he was secured, the chair wasn't. He leaned forward and bowed so that it lifted from the ground and stuck out behind him. He couldn't be sure how long the thing would be gone but he felt that it was now or never. He was alone, no matter the noise it had to be better to try this now than later, he may not get another chance.

He used all his strength to jump, lifting his feet forward and forcing the chair to come back to the floor at an awkward angle. The tired wood and joints of the legs couldn't handle the force with which it landed and went flying across the room with a crunching, crashing sound.

The fall hurt Lafferty's hands as he landed on his back but he gritted his teeth and began to straighten his legs. He forced himself to lie flat. As he had hoped, the chair couldn't take it. The backrest snapped at the base where it joined the seat. Lafferty quickly rolled to the side and slipped his arms free.

He listened for a moment. No click-clicks of alien feet or the thud of boots came from beyond the door. He struggled to bring his bound wrists under his backside, rolling about the floor as he contorted with the effort. Finally, he managed it. He drew them forward, from under his legs so that he now had his secured hands in front of him.

He chewed at the knot with his teeth but it was far too tough and tightly compressed to make any impact. Lafferty walked to the table and looked for a knife or anything with a keen edge. The array of strange items was bewildering to him. Nothing appeared to have a hard, straight edge, the creature's tools were all weirdly organic in form.

He closed outstretched fingers around one of the pieces and picked it up and as he did so he felt a slight tingle on his skin as it began to lightly hum. It was thin and shaped like the outline of a frying pan, a long stem, like a handle, then a dip that lifted back after about four inches. There were no sharp or even rough edges, it was made from something strong, but light and smooth to the touch, despite being bumpy. He turned it over as best he could with his restrained hands. If a blade had been present on the implement it could have been a small hacksaw.

As he tightened his grip the hum became a high pitched, though not uncomfortable whine and the tingling sensation increased slightly. He dropped it to the table and looked for anything else that might be useful. The object the creature had been working on was a cube of sorts, each of its walls had been collapsed revealing its strange interior. It was a complex mess of threads and bubbles. A viscous liquid covered much of it and Lafferty was sure it was the source of a heavy marzipan smell at the table.

There were parts lying around that he thought must have come from inside the opened cube, bundles of tubes that at once looked like wires but were more akin brightly coloured blood vessels. They had been sliced perfectly. Where was the knife that had been used to do this? Lafferty couldn't see anything like a blade amongst the strange tools.

He began to feel something very much like panic rising up inside him. How long had he stood here dithering, how long since he smashed the chair? The thing could return at any moment. The man who spoke could be right outside the door. He ran his fingers over the mess of the cube, closed his eyes and tried to see what the creature saw, immediately he became dizzy. He could feel himself swaying, he saw the table, saw the thing.

He looked over its shoulder, witnessed the four appendages at work, seemingly independent of each other but working in perfect harmony. The creature was altering the configuration of its device. Adjustments were being made to accommodate the sensitivity of it. Lafferty knew this as surely as if he were the creature himself. The thing picked up the object he had handled and its claw applied a gentle pressure. It swept the seemingly empty gap, where a hacksaw blade might have been, and the bundle of vessel-wire things it held with another claw separated instantly as though cut with an impossibly sharp, invisible blade.

He opened his eyes. He found the strange object he had just handled once again and pressed a finger against what he thought of as the grip. It hummed once again. Carefully he angled the thick binding against the apparently empty space. His jaw dropped as the rope began to part instantly, as though a razor blade was slicing through it.

He didn't allow the invisible blade to cut right through in case he caught his skin. Once a sufficient slice had been made he lifted his hands and with minimum effort forced the rope apart. It dropped to the floor and Lafferty shook his hands to get blood flowing through them.

He took a moment to compose himself then ran to the door, listening for signs of anyone or anything approaching. There was nothing, but as he walked away a distinct sound of gunshots rand out. First a series of cracks, small arms firing a rapid volley, then a *boom* something bigger, a shotgun most likely.

He ran to the table and grabbed the cutting device. It hummed as he picked it up and Lafferty determined that however it worked it was activated by touch. He tore his sleeve off and wrapped it completely around the alien knife. There was no hum. Lafferty was satisfied that this stopped it from becoming live.

'*Please don't cut my balls off.*' He thought as he pushed it into his trouser pocket.

He ran to the door and this time slowly turned the knob, it wasn't locked and he was able to pull it open. There were stairs going up to the next floor immediately to his left. A single flickering torch lit the way. Lafferty began to ascend as another round of gunfire punctuated the air.

***

Reed had seen the attack coming first. A shadow, cast by the moonlight as the thing that fell upon them opened its bat-like wings, slowing its descent as it prepared to strike. He looked up just in time to see the horror of the shadow spread over them. Its awful reptilian maw opened wide. Bryson raised his pistol without hesitation and fired three shots into it.

The Byakhee screamed and twisted away from the assault, leaving room for another of its kind to force the attack. Tom and Bryson were caught entirely unaware and were too shocked to react quickly enough to dodge the second creature.

It gripped Bryson's shoulder with a tremendously powerful claw and lifted him bodily from the floor. He clutched at the thing, trying to pull the wickedly serrated barb away but it was far too strong. Its wings flapped with amazing strength and Bryson felt more distance come between his dangling legs and the floor.

A third monster swooped down, it let out a *'crawwwww'* ululation as it went for Tom, hoping to grasp the coachmen as its fellow hunter had done. But luck was with Tom. As he stepped back in shock he tripped upon his one of the lanterns and fell to the floor. This placed him directly under the creature with his shotgun pointing at its belly as its claws snatched at thin air. He let both barrels go at the centre of the monster.

As buckshot ripped in to it at such a close range its skin was vaporised its guts flew out in a cloud of blood and gore around it. It's *'crawwww'* cut short and it dropped in heap at Tom's feet.

'Jesus fucking Christ.' He gasped.

Reed pointed his pistol at the thing that was making its escape with Bryson hanging underneath it. He could barely make them out as they rose out of the light the torches offered. Doubt iced his blood as he realised that if he shot may well hit the guvnor.

Suddenly there was a flash of fire above and crack of gunfire sounded. Bryson landed heavily a few feet away. A few seconds later the thing that had grabbed him also dropped to the floor and began to crawl away. Reed ran to Bryson keeping his pistol pointed at the Byakhee as it struggled to retreat into the shadows. Reed emptied his pistol at it, two shots missed but a third found its mark and punched a hole through its skull. It collapsed and was still.

'You alright guv?' Reed asked.

'Yes, I think so. Might have sprained my ankle.' Bryson grimaced as he said this and Reed suspected the injury might be worse than he was making out.

Tom had gathered his wits and came over to them, reloading his shotgun as he walked.

'Reload Sir.' He said to Reed who looked confused at first but then understood.

'Yes.' He said and pulled bullets from his pocket.

Tom helped Bryson to his feet. The inspector leaned heavily on him as he rose.

'We have to get out of the open.' Tom said. 'Need to find a place to hide.' A chorus of 'crawwww' noises sounded as he finished his statement, it came from above the rooftops.

'Jesus, there's more of them.' Reed said.

'Aye, sounds like it. Where'd the one you shot go to?' Tom asked Reed.

'It crawled away, over that way. He pointed his pistol, now reloaded to a darkened street corner.

'Alright, fuck him then.' Tom said. 'Can you walk?'

Bryson nodded, 'Yes, I think so, with help.'

Reed immediately came around and wrapped his arm around the inspector's waist, almost hauling him off the floor.

'Steady Reed, no need to carry me.' Bryson said.

'Sorry guv.' Reed replied. He turned to Tom, 'Right where to?'

'You know where we have to go Sergeant.' He nodded towards the church. 'Where we are expected to go.'

'No!' Bryson said. He hopped a little and straightened up to offer some authority, some control.

'There are more of those fucking things up there, Lord knows how many but more than three I'm guessing, even with our firearms they could have us I'm sure, yet they haven't come at us again while they had the element of surprise.' He pointed to the church with his free hand, which Reed and Tom saw still held his pistol.

'We have been led here, Tom is right, that's where they want us. So that's where we definitely aren't going.'

'Fair enough,' Said Reed. 'So what now?'

'They can see us but we can't see them. They have the skies on their side and…' Bryson looked about and the shadowed houses, 'who knows who or what else they have in this place.'

Tom nodded.

'So let's burn the place. This wood is old, everything in the houses is dry. We can turn this village into a funeral pyre for us *and* them if that's how they want to play it.' Bryson looked up to Reed. 'You on board Sergeant?'

'Aye guv.' He said.

Bryson turned again to Tom.

'Mr Chell, I'm really sorry about all this, but I'd rather die before I'll leave my friends here. If you think you can get away then by all means do so, you have no obligation to stay.'

To Bryson's surprise a broad smile appeared on Tom's face. 'Miss watching this wretched place burn to the floor? Mr Bryson, it would be my genuine pleasure to assist.'

Bryson nodded. 'Good. Thank you.'

'We should make a move, wherever we are going now is the time.' Reed said.

'Agreed.' Bryson replied. 'Grab the lights, let's starting warming things up.'

Tom went to the lanterns and scooped them up.

'Where do we start?' He said.

'Right here.' Bryson replied. Tom nodded and turned up the flame on a lantern, he then tossed it at the door of the nearest house. Orange and blue flames immediately leapt across the surface and burned brightly. He walked across the street and fancied that he saw wide, illuminated eyes staring at him from the rooftops. He threw the second lantern into the house as this had its door missing. The dark hole instantly brightened as oil spread across the floor and became a fiery slick.

Tom returned. 'Do we go now?'

'No.' Bryson said. 'Make sure it catches. If anyone or anything tries to stop this we shoot them.'

'Fair enough.' Tom said and scanned the rooftops again looking for watching eyes.

After only a few minutes flames had begun to lick at the windows of the houses. Flames could be seen on the wooden walls and a great plume of black smoke was billowing up into the night sky. Nothing else had come near to them in this time. Tom hadn't seen the glowing eyes since he had commenced his arson.

'Ok' Bryson said. 'Let's get moving. As we go we toss the torches from the streets into the houses.'

The men moved into position. Bryson tried to walk but couldn't put any weight on his right foot and so hopped along. Reed stayed close by him. Tom walked ahead his shotgun barrel held to his chest.

'Those things.' Bryson said as they moved. 'They can be killed easily enough. I don't think they are...'

'The Shadow and the Void?' Reed said.

'Yes.' Bryson replied. 'I can't believe that I wish Crowley was here right now.'

'I'm sure that will pass.' Reed said.

'The thing is, why? Why are we here?' Bryson asked.

'Well, it's Crowley isn't it. The usual reason for everything being truly fucked. The same reason Ravensblack was a nightmare hole of undead monsters, the same reason a murder enquiry became a fist fight with a fire demon.' Reed replied bitterly.

'No.' Bryson shook his head. 'I don't think it is. There's more to this. Crowley came here because he thought there was something he wanted, Lafferty came for Crowley and we came for Lafferty, this has all been planned to get us here. But why? What do we have that they want?'

Bryson could feel that he almost had the answer. Crowley had tried to keep his trip a secret, he was keen to keep anyone else away. Clearly someone knew that it would pan out like this, it was like a *prophecy*. The word bounced around his head and it was Tom who fished out the answer. He stopped and turned to Reed and Bryson.

'Beg pardon but listening to all that is...well for a start I'm a little concerned to be hearing London's finest discussing demons and the undead, but in light of what just happened I'm prepared to let that go for the moment.'

Unsure of what to say in response to this Reed and Bryson remained tight lipped.

'However, it seems you have something there. That each of you has been drawn to this place because you felt that another was in danger, am I right?'

'Yes, that's the gist of it Tom.' Bryson said. Reed nodded.

'Well, could I ask you, who might be concerned that you fellows were here, I mean, is there anyone who might come to rescue you lads?'

The thought struck Bryson like a lightning bolt. 'Prophecy!' He said out loud.

'Excuse me?' Tom said.

'Oh Christ, this isn't about us, or Crowley.' Bryson said excitedly.

Reed became aware of what Bryson was saying. 'Oh shit. Penhaligon.'

'And Pevensy. They want to bring the Guardians here!' Bryson said.

'Guardians?' Tom said.

'Some men, a group.' Bryson said. 'Good Lord yes, that has to be it.'

'No one else is coming here tonight Sir's. Not by rail at least, there's no more trains. By car, it would take until tomorrow if they travelled all night and it's not exactly easy to find this place if you don't know where it is.'

'That might be why we haven't been attacked again, they want to keep us here so that they come to find us. Lock us up perhaps.'

'Why don't they just kill us?' Tom asked.

'I'm not sure Tom but these men we are talking about are…special, they have abilities and ways of knowing things, maybe they would know if we were dead and wouldn't come.'

Tom decided not to pursue this any further. It had already gone beyond his degree of learning and knowledge of the world at large by a good distance.

'Right. So what happens when these gentlemen arrive?'

'I imagine that's when it's ok to kill us.' Bryson replied realising he sounded a little like Crowley.

'Well, let's hope your chaps aren't good with a road map.' Tom said. With that he walked over to another torch and threw it into a doorway.

Part 15

Digby wasn't in a good state when Pevensy reached him. He looked very pale, almost ashen and was in a deep sleep. Francine also looked extremely worried. She had cared for Digby long before he had begun to fade and was as close to a wife as a woman could be in their circumstances.

'Francine, has he said anything at all concerning the gentleman that visited him, or anything that seems odd, well more odd than usual.' Pevensy asked.

Francine brought a fingertip to her mouth as she thought. She was fully aware that what the man under her care, and whom she loved very much, was not like other men and that his words carried far more weight than others.

'I can't say he has, he's been restless but hasn't said anything I could understand.' She said quietly.

'What about things you might not understand Francine, you know that Digby speaks many languages, perhaps a word or two that seemed foreign?'

Francine shook her head. 'I'm sorry but I don't think so.'

'Blast.' Pevensy said.

'Is there trouble. Are you in some sort of danger?'

Pevensy knew that by 'you' she meant Digby. He couldn't bring himself to lie to her. The truth was that he wasn't sure Digby would around alive each time he came to visit.

'There is always danger for us Francine but yes, this is very serious we think.'

'Oh my.' She said. Tears rolled down her cheeks. Pevensy took her hands and held them together in his own. 'Dear, dear Frannie, don't you worry, you know that we can look after ourselves. I just hoped that Diggers might have said something to help us with a trip we need to make.'

'A trip? Out of London?' Francine looked at him with questioning eyes, they never left London, not in all the years she had known them had any one of the three stepped foot outside of the city.

'I know. We are always so busy here but this…this is important.' Pevensy said.

Francine shook her head and tried to regain her composure.

'Well, I know what must be done if you…if you are away for a long time.' She said.

'Good.' Pevensy smiled and gripped her hands a little more tightly. 'You will be looked after, you know that, but don't worry, we will be coming back.'

Francine nodded and tried to smile but her eyes were already reddening from her tears and Pevensy could feel her shaking a little.

'Benny is over at Lester's house, could you check on him later?'

'Oh, he's back, I thought those gentlemen were looking after him.' Francine said.

Pevensy said nothing and Francine understood.

'I see.' She said. She gently pulled her hands from Pevensy's and stepped to the side. 'You had better go, it seems like you have a busy evening ahead.'

'Yes, I think I do.' He began to walk away and stopped. He turned to Francine. 'If he wakes, don't tell him I was here, not until tomorrow at least.'

Francine nodded. 'As you wish. Anything else? When he wakes?'

'Yes, tell him one way or another I'll see him soon.' Pevensy didn't wait for a reply, he turned away and exited the house.

***

After the gunshots had sounded Lafferty had heard movement above him. Feet running across a wooden floor. But no one came to the stairs. He waited for the sounds to fade and then continued up and walked through a few rooms. Another short set of stairs appeared, he went up and found himself inside what could only be the remains of a church.

There were two men at the far end and they were stood upon a table, peering out through a through a stained glass window. He wasn't sure what time it was, there was light at the windows, but not strong, more like an orange glow as though the sun might be setting.

The church interior was a shambles. There had once been a fire here. The floor was covered in burned shards of wood, most of which had once been the pews. There was no roof, a few beams, charcoaled and withered remained above but after that was only a clear sky. He could see the thing. It hovered, impossibly, he thought with its size, its wings beat so fast that they were only a blur at its back.

In two of its claws it held something like a book or tablet while a third tapped at it. Lafferty was sure that it was overseeing whatever was happening.

'*They are here…we have the three.*' The man's voice whirled around his thoughts. Crowley was out there, causing trouble no doubt, Bryson and Reed? It didn't sound as though they had them, they '*still had control,*' but that implied that they were in control *despite* the circumstances. And where was Benny? He had heard him bark and then…nothing.

He brought his attention to the problem at hand. The two men looking through the window at the far side. Lafferty carefully stepped back into the shadow offered by the doorway. Walking or running across the church would be noisy there wasn't much hope of sneaking past them. He couldn't fight two of them, Reed had been instructing him in the finer arts of martial combat but it mostly revolved around hitting people very hard, and with an object if possible. Which was fine for someone who had the size and muscle to back it up.

As he tried to think his way out of his predicament the solution was made for him. The men suddenly scrambled down from the table, the thing in the air abruptly surged forwards, away from the church. Something had happened in the village. They were going to it. Lafferty moved.

***

The Mi-Go had not been surprised that the simple task entrusted to the humans had failed. They were stupid, craven and ridiculous beings. Their minds were entangled with hopes, fears, love, hate, jealousy and greed. They rarely had one focus or purpose and so swayed and bent in the face of what they perceived as options.

They had not predicted the ruthlessness of the one called Crowley. That when faced with only one way to escape he would actually take that option whereas other humans would submit themselves to restraint rather than cause harm. The others had come and fought, as was expected, but had not come to the church. Why had they not sought out their symbol of safety, of sanctuary? Instead they had begun to destroy everything around them. They were truly built in the image of their creator.

The Byakhee needed clear skies to attack, they were all but useless on the ground and now they feared what the humans might do to them with the cover of flames and smoke on their side. Its great brain considered all of the possibilities. As the High Priest had said they were in control. The humans were alive and still served their purpose. When the *others* came they could all be destroyed in one great moment of annihilation.

Once this was achieved the great city would be less well defended. What matter a few witches and warlocks about the place when its Guardians were destroyed. It tapped upon a series of icons that flashed up onto its transceiver. The message was simple, simple so that the full truth need not be relayed.

'*All is well, soon we have them.*'

The Mi-Go was satisfied to let the men burn the village. As much as it stopped the Byakhee from striking from above it also kept the humans at the very edge of the inferno, they daren't run from its protective cover. Unfortunately, the High Priest of the Children of Hastur had other plans.

Alan Benton had been a High Priest for only a few months. The position had become his after the debacle in the London docks. He was an ambitious man which had been proven in his rise to such high status in only a decade. His cruelty and obedience were the key factors. The proper implementation of both had earned him great favour with those far higher than him. He had ensured that the great wealth that was being generated from his region of the country, the Midlands, was not causing suspicion.

He had maintained a steady supply of sacrifices to their Lord without bringing down the forces of law upon their religion, he had brought new believers into the fold and had ensured that the children they stole were trained to be unflinching servants of the King in Yellow.

But he did not trust the Mi-Go. True the creature had bought with it the Byakhee, strange vicious creatures with a mind no more complex than that of a dog, but *it* was an alien of another kind. It had its own plans, own agendas and it did not embrace the rule of his Lord and master. The Mi-Go were mercenaries, worse than that they were rivals. They had at their disposal technology beyond the ken of The King in Yellow. On dark nights when his mood was low and his fear bubbled under the surface of his sanity Benton wondered if his King actually feared the power of these creatures.

The thing had ordered them to hold back. Benton didn't like this. The policemen were burning the place to the ground. By the time it was all done it would be morning and who knew what they might have prepared should they not return to London. The army could be on their way up here by now. Unlike the *others* these men were not sworn to uphold the secrets of the war in the shadows. They had no obligation to sacrifice themselves to prevent the knowledge of what happened under the noses of the ordinary people, the sheep and cattle of the world, every day.

He decided to make sure that this whole issue would be resolved by this evening. The dog had vanished, Crowley was gone, most likely to his doom in the woods. All they had so far was the young policeman. No, it wasn't good enough, their position was precarious at best.

Benton moved amongst his people and advised them of their new orders. Now was the time to take the advantage.

***

Reed saw them first. As usual his keen eyesight picking up the slightest movement or flicker that shouldn't be. They were coming from the direction of the church, moving through the thick smoke and heat of the fire either side of them.

'Must have been hiding inside the church or its grounds' He thought.

As a group they had been moving steadily back through the village. Staying at the edge of the fire which appeared to keep the flying creatures at bay. A couple had tried to swoop in from the beyond the smoke cloud but had been quickly taken down by accurate shots from Bryson and himself. But their ammunition was limited and what he saw caused him to feel the cold night at the back of him on his spine.

'Guv, we have company.' Reed said.

Bryson and Tom looked towards the oncoming crowd. There were easily a dozen to be made out in the heat blur.

'Fuck.' Bryson shouted. His foot felt like a ball of pure pain when any pressure was applied and even when held off the floor as he hopped along it caused him to grit his teeth as severe ache burned at his ankle.

He looked back to where they were headed, the street diverted four ways.

'We could split, try to lose them.' He said.

To his surprise Tom laughed a little. 'With all respect Sir, are you out of your fucking mind? How far are you going to get with a gammy foot?'

'He's right' Reed said. You wouldn't get more than a few yards before they were on you.

'Alright, if you can help me,' he said to Reed, 'Tom could probably get out of the village,' he turned to the coachman, 'you will be much faster. Reed and I can pull a few away, keep them busy. We might be able to kill or wound enough to make them scared.'

Tom shook his head slowly. 'You ain't thinking straight Inspector. They only need to chase us away from the fire, after that those flying bastards can get at us.'

Bryson's look was of total resignation. 'Damn, you are right.'

He sighed. 'I'm so sorry Reed. Tom.'

'No need to be sorry Inspector. I didn't come here in chains and cuffs. I'm here because I want to be.' He took off his cap and wiped sweat from his brow. 'Now, if you will listen to my plan?'

'Of course, please.' Bryson said.

'You need the big lad to get you moving. I know he ain't going to leave you because well, that's how it is. So what I reckon is that I stay here and hold the fort, I can get into one of the houses an anyone who tries to get past cops for it. I'll need both your pistols though. Anything that flaps over your way I can have a shot at. Keep them in the air busy too.'

'You'll be surrounded Tom.' Reed said. You've no chance.'

'Nope. I reckon not, but you just have to take it on good faith that there is nothing I'd rather do. Today is just one more day that I've not decided to slip a rope around my neck and kick away the stool. I'm done with this world gentlemen, after today I don't think I want to see any more of it, ever. This for me is a fine way to say goodbye and to perhaps make my Angela proud.'

The two officers said nothing. Tom's expression was carved in stone and neither doubted that his resolution was any less firm.

Reed stepped forward and handed Tom his pistol. He placed his huge hand on the coachman's shoulder. 'It's fully loaded.' He said.

Tom nodded and put the pistol into his pocket.

Bryson limped towards him awkwardly and handed his pistol over too.

'You'll not be forgotten Tom, if you can get out this, if we can all get out of this I promise we will make a difference.'

'I have no intention of walking away from Blackbrook Inspector.' Tom said solemnly, 'but I'm going to make sure that I have a lot company with me when I go, just make sure you pair aren't part of the party.'

Tom put Bryson's pistol into his other pocket. Bryson shook his hand, Reed did the same.

'You better go. I think they are only walking slow for effect. 'T'give us the willies,' Tom said with a slight grin.

Bryson looked at Reed. Reed nodded and gripped his guvnor under his shoulder.

'So long fellas,' Tom said as he walked to a house two doors away from where the fire raged.

Reed and Bryson began their flight.

Part 16

With the men gone and the thing no longer flying above the church Lafferty took his chance. He ran across the burned wood and detritus of the ruined church until he reached the double doors at the end. They had been left partially open when the men had vacated. He peered out and was stunned to see that the orange glow at the windows, that he had assumed was a setting sun, was in fact the whole street in front of the church afire. The heat was so intense here, where blaze was firmly in control, that he could feel it's heat upon his skin.

He looked about but could see no one, although there were plenty of places to hide in the church yard. He stepped out.

'*They have to be after the Sarge and the Inspector,*' Lafferty thought as he walked cautiously amongst the tombstones. '*That fire has to be them, they are fighting this lot.*'

The thought made him bold. Reed and Bryson were incredible to him, strong, dedicated men, everything his father had never been, the one man who should have had his respect.

'*They came for me.*' He thought, and smiled.

A Byakhee dropped down in front of him and hissed loudly. Its long, beak like mouth was wide open showing off an array of serrated teeth top and bottom.

He heard another light thud behind, then another to the side, and another. Clearly the thing in the sky had left guards, he just hadn't been able to seem them.

The first creature he saw, the one directly ahead, took a couple of rapid steps forward. Lafferty instinctively took two steps back but then twisted his neck, realising that he had merely moved closer to the creature behind him.

He could barely believe what he was seeing, they were large, almost man sized, their wings were leathery, bat-like, not the translucent delicate things the creature in the basement had down its back.

The creature in front snapped its jaws open and shut and he heard the ones either side of him slide over the fallen stones, closing in.

'*Either they are herding me back to the church or they are closing in for the kill in their own time.*' Lafferty thought, '*but it doesn't matter because I'm screwed whatever the case.*'

He slipped his hand into his pocket and withdrew the shrouded device he had taken from the table. He unwrapped it as the thing in front took another step and threatened him with its open maw again. This time Lafferty stood his ground. He let the shirt sleeve fall from the device and gripped the handle tightly, it began to whine although it was barely audible with the sound of the huge fire to the right of him.

The first Byakhee lunged, unhappy that the human had not moved back towards the church as it was supposed to. It didn't realise that its lower jaw had been cut from its face until blood began to spurt from it and the pain of severed nerves were recognised by its brain.

As the thing had lunged again Lafferty had flicked out with his hand and the device and cut through the bottom of its beak with incredible precision. Half of its beak dropped to the floor and the creature didn't appear to have noticed, at least for a few moments. Suddenly it began to squeal and then roll about on the floor, its mind was torn with agony.

Lafferty quickly turned to see how immediate the threat was from the other creatures. It was very immediate; they were practically on top of him. He lashed out with the device hoping he could catch them as he had the first but the Byakhee had realised the human was now armed and dodged his flailing arm.

One of them leapt into the air, back to where it was more dangerous and more agile. The others sidestepped around Lafferty, snapping with their eager maws. He could see they were preparing to strike, he could perhaps hurt one of them, but three or four attacking at once would overwhelm him. He was done for. He heard the beating of the wings above him stop as the flying Byakhee prepared to dive.

Lafferty was ready to die. He knew this, he had wondered how he might be when faced with death and he had come close more than once now. This time he had no friends to help him, no runic spuds from Crowley, he was alone but he was not afraid. He would take at least one of these of these flying twat bags with him. He wasn't at all embarrassed to find himself thinking like Crowley.

But the attack from the diving Byakhee didn't come.

He had expected it any second and was ready to twist and sweep the knife device above him to try and catch it. Each of the other creatures looked up. They had seen their brother prepare his assault and were ready to follow up and execute their attack at the same time. But he was gone. Something had happened as he had dropped, something had contacted with him, had impacted and sent him flying beyond the tombstones around them.

A single 'craw!' sounded above the ambient din of the blazing houses. Then nothing more. The Byakhee became unsettled, rather than striking at the human as they had planned they shuffled backwards, looking around for any sign of movement.

Suddenly something rushed past Lafferty, something big, brown and very fast. He twisted and saw something leap onto the creature to his left. The Byakhee lifted its great membranous wings as its attacker took it by the throat which was then savagely ripped away. The force was so great that its blood sprayed across Lafferty.

The thing then leapt again, an agile manoeuvre that allowed it clear the few gravestones still standing. It landed on the back of another Byakhee and claws like scythes shredded the creature with rapid strikes.

Garbled sqawks and *crawwwwws* filled the air as the thing was eviscerated by the new monster, for it was a monster, a beast Lafferty saw, a thing of brown fur, razor sharp claws and a bestial face.

The last Byakhee tried to break away from the scene of the carnage being wrought upon its brothers, it leapt up and managed two strong flaps of its wings only, in the next instant the beast was on its back, it bit into the Byakhee's neck and worried at it like a dog at a rabbit. Both crashed to the floor.

'Oh my,' Lafferty said. He couldn't be sure that he wasn't going to be next. Just because the thing had killed the other creatures didn't mean it was going to be his friend. He turned and ran through the graveyard, deftly weaving through the stones. The thing he had seen had been fast, strong, could he outrun it? Could he get enough distance before it had finished with the flying creatures?

He couldn't. It was already waiting for him as he leapt over the crumbing wall of the church yard.

***

Reed and Bryson moved as fast as they could. Bryson tried to use his foot but the pain was too much, he suspected that it wasn't just sprained, it may well be broken. Shots began to ring out behind them, Tom was picking off anything he could see flying towards them, they heard a *thump* as a Byakhee fell to the floor.

Once they were out of sight of the street he was in Tom wouldn't be able to target the creatures, it would be down to Reed to fight them off if they came near.

As they struggled on Bryson looked back, they had covered a good distance but in a straight line, to allow Tom a line of sight, the blaze was very strong and the broken steeple was illuminated at the back of it all, but now they would have to turn.

'This way guv.' Reed swung Bryson around as he turned into the new street. The Inspector was slowing him down so he lifted him bodily off the ground and carried him on his hip. Bryson never ceased to be amazed at the strength of his Sergeant, he was a goliath.

Two Byakhee's had managed to keep sight of the fleeing policemen, while two other of their number had been taken down by Tom's withering fire from below. Now that they were out of sight of the man in the house they could attack. They swooped hoping to knock over the big man and to grab the injured one. The big one was far too heavy to carry but if they could separate them they might at least take the other.

One of the creatures dived down and then swooped up just above the heads of the two, causing a distraction, meanwhile the other dropped to the floor and charged in as best it could to snap at Reed, hoping to catch is arm or leg and disable him. It almost had him, but the big man had turned just in time to dodge its lunge. The Byakhee backed up and leapt into the air again, not wanting to risk being alone with the two of them still able. These humans didn't threaten and were very resourceful.

Reed continued to press on up the street but as he approached the top of it the Byakhee attacked again. This time one of them managed to push at Reed with its strong legs and force him to the floor. He dropped Bryson who also crashed down, grimacing as his foot twisted. Had the Byakhee pressed its attack it might have been able to catch Reed while he was exposed but it had chosen to err on the side of caution, gliding over him to land a few feet away. From there it would leap in and strike with its hardened beak and snap the big man's arm. The other dropped down by its side ready to aid its brother once it took the advantage.

Reed pushed himself up from the floor, on his hands and knees he looked first to Bryson to make sure he was alright, then to the creatures and saw that they were going to take him.

The head of the lead Byakhee exploded as bullets tore through it. The second, stunned, only had time to turn its own head and then it too received shots to its face from Crowley's pistol.

It collapsed in a heap on the floor. Crowley marched towards it, his pistol still pointing at its head and delivered the final shot. He looked over to Reed and Bryson.

'Well, you pair took your fucking time.' He said angrily.

Tom took a few shots at the figures walking up the street first of all, to keep them back, despite the heat from the fire they were not in any real danger there so he thought they might hold back a little and was proven right.

He then looked out for the creatures above. He had only seen four in total and watched carefully as Bryson and Reed moved away. Not long after, great wings reflected the red and orange hue of the fires and Tom blasted away at them. Two fell, it had cost the rounds from both guns to take them but that left only two others for the policemen to contend with. He wished them all the luck in the world.

Now he had to keep the human pursuers off their backs for a little longer. All he had left was his shotgun. In his pockets were eight more cartridges, he would save one and one only.

The first few men came into sight from the heat haze, they looked about nervously but Tom saw that they didn't carry guns but each had a long, vicious looking knife. As he had fired at them from within the house they weren't aware that Tom was right at their side, he let them pass a few feet, so that others would be confident to follow.

As the procession moved forward he counted eight people, two he thought were women. He lined up the shotgun. He didn't like the idea of shooting anyone in the back but he had to cause the most disarray and panic that he could. If there was any chance that he could kill or disable all eight it might go well for Bryson and Reed.

He was just about to fire when he caught sight of the thing that hovered above the last of the men. It looked like a giant ant to him, at least how its body was segmented and its head a bulbous thing on top of it. Two legs hung down while four similar appendages acted like arms at its chest and worked at something it gripped within claws.

It was a demon. A creature spawned from the gates around this cursed place. He took aim at it, ignoring the men and women that walked past looking for the policemen.

Tom couldn't know that bullets couldn't penetrate the barrier, invisible to him, that surrounded the thing. That it floated in the air in plain sight because it felt secure and safe with its protective shield, free from the dangers of mankind's pitiful weapons. Yet nor could the Mi-Go have known that Tom's cartridges were not just powder and buckshot. It wasn't to know that he was a man wrought by grief, who had melted down the necklace his wife had treasured and turned it into a device that one day he knew he would use to send him to her. The Mi-Go would only understand that something had gone awry as silver shot, that the shield couldn't deflect, bypassed the energy shield and ripped into its body.

As the two barrels boomed the Children of Hastur scattered, unaware that the blasts had come from behind them, they started to retreat. The Mi-Go performed almost acrobatic contortions in the air as the effects of the blasts from Tom's gun were felt by its sensitive nerves. Its wings, peppered, began to tear as they beat against the air and finally it fell to the floor writhing in agony.

Tom wasted no time watching what was happening. He broke the barrel, reloaded two more cartridges and snapped it shot once again. In only seconds he had the shotgun ready to fire and looked for his next target. Two men ran towards the Mi-Go as it lay sprawled upon the road. Without remorse Tom fired one barrel into each. The impact twisted one of them around a full three hundred and sixty degrees, the knife he had held flew from his grasp. The other took a blast directly to the side of his face. It disintegrated in a mist of red.

Tom reloaded.

He repeated the procedure, taking out any of the people who moved towards the dying monster until there was only one shell remaining.

He hoped that Polly would be looked after. He had made provision for her care in his will. If the policemen made it out, if his sacrifice had meant something he was sure that good men like them would see him right.

He lifted his chin and placed the end of the warm barrel to it. He had no regrets.

Angela came to him with her hand held out. She wore the white lace dress he had always liked, they had danced at a Summers Eve festival one evening and she had worn it then. He had said she looked like no less than an angel.

He took her hand, he could feel the softness of her skin as they touched and it filled him with a soft energy that coursed around his being. He had no body now, this was clear to him yet he saw both himself and Angela as whole, living creatures.

'We can go now my love, we can go together.' She said and smiled as he closed towards her.

'Am I dead now?' He said, although he didn't mind if he was.

'In some ways Tom,' Angela replied, 'but we are also very much alive. Will you come with me, we can travel if we wish it.'

Tom pulled gently at her hand and drew his wife into him. 'I wish for nothing more in the world.' Tom said as tears spilled from eyes that didn't exist.

Their energies entwined as they kissed and together they began their journey.

Part 17

Basement of the Cock and Bear

Crowley was murmuring strange words once again. He performed more weird gestures over the bowl into which they had all offered their blood and semen. To Bryson and Reed it seemed to take forever. Their patience was at its absolute end.

'He's insane.' Reed whispered to Bryson, who was trying to locate where his foot had been damaged.

'He's all we have.' Bryson replied.

'They are going to find us. They won't even have to shoot us, they can just burn down the building.'

'No. They want us alive.' Bryson replied. 'They want Pevensy and the others to come.'

'Penhaligon and Digby?' Reed replied, surprised.

'I'm sure of it.'

'Why?' Reed asked although he had the inkling of reason forming in his mind.

'This is all to do with London. Ravensblack, the docks, us…they want us all in the same place, they mean to remove as many threats as possible in one shot.'

Reed said nothing. It confirmed what he had begun to think himself. This was an elaborate trap.

'Pevensy told me about how a prophecy could result in the future that you want to happen. I have to wonder if one of their lot has seen something that allowed them to make this happen. Have then seen that us trapped here would lead to the others coming to save us?'

'Their man, Digby, he can see into the future!' Reed exclaimed.

'No, Pevensy explained that too, what he must see is a *possible* future, nothing in set in stone. He clearly didn't foretell this but maybe *they* have.'

Reed thought for a moment. 'Or maybe he has and they won't come?'

'Maybe. I think it might be better for everyone if that's the case.'

Crowley coughed.

'I'll tell you what, the next time you are performing one of your *delicate* interrogations I'll stand in a corner and talk all the way through it shall I?'

Reed and Bryson looked at the occultist. He stood defiantly with his knuckles resting on his hips.

'Are you done?' Bryson asked

'There's no need to be brusque Inspector but yes I am done.'

'Thank fuck for that. Can we get out?' Bryson said.

'I don't know.' Crowley replied.

'What!' Reed boomed.

'I don't know.' Crowley repeated. 'Aiwass said that the means of our escape was already at hand.'

'Already at hand, what does that mean?' Bryson asked with a bitter tone.

'I don't know.' Crowley said once again.

'I knew it.' Bryson raged. 'I knew it.' He stood as best he could and hopped towards the table that Crowley stood behind.

'You're a madman Crowley, a fucking crazy, weird, perverted madman.'

Crowley appeared unmoved. 'Are you done?'

'NO, I'm not done.' Bryson shouted. 'I'm not at all done. I had to let a man die out there tonight, alone, so that he could save my worthless skin. Lafferty is out here, he came because he was worried about *YOU*, a maniac who can somehow get himself off while the whole world is falling apart.'

'Guv.' Reed called to him.

'No Reed. I'm sick of it. I'm sick of him. You just waltz through it don't you Crowley, through the death and the madness. All those people dead at Ravensblack Hall, the poor copper in the sewers, *TOM*, a real fucking *hero* Crowley. A man who came into this hellhole to help us. God knows what became of him and yet *you*, the first on the scene, the first in the chain, you're still alive, still pissing about with spells and rituals and fucking *prophecies*.'

'What do you mean prophecies?' Crowley asked as though he had only caught the last word of Bryson's rant.

'*What?*' Bryson shouted.

'You said prophecies, what made you say that, have you spoken to Lafferty about them?'

Bryson calmed a little but only due to confusion. What? No, not Lafferty, Pevensy. He explained how it's all supposed to work.'

'And you Reed, have you been instructed in any way, on matters like this?'

Reed looked a little taken aback. He wasn't sure what to say to Crowley. It always felt like you were giving the occultist ammunition that he could fire back at you, even if it was just your name.

'Well Sergeant? This is important?'

Reed nodded. 'Yes, I've met a man named Digby, he's a friend of both Mr Pevensy and Mr Penhaligon.

'Three of them then?' Crowley said

'Yes. I suppose so.'

Bryson was surprised to hear that Reed had seen another of the Guardians and had not told him but said nothing. Crowley appeared to be in deep thought, he stared at the Wedgewood bowl and repeated 'Three good men.'

'Look, Crowley.' Bryson adopted a more reasonable tone. 'We need to get out. Out of here at least, the longer we stay the more likely they are to find us.'

'I concur Inspector.' Crowley replied. 'And while you may be dismissive of what Aiwass has said you must understand that she is under contract, her words will be truthful.'

'And what does that mean exactly? Bryson asked.

'She said that our means of escape was at hand. That it is already within our grasp, we just have to see it, to understand what it is.'

'Why doesn't she just tell you what it is?' asked Reed.

'She doesn't like me.' Crowley said. He shrugged, 'Women eh?'

'Not just women Crowley.' Bryson snarled.

'I take it we are leaving then?' Reed said.

'Yes. We should get out. The Inspector is correct, the longer we stay here the more the danger of being discovered rises. Further to that I believe that Aiwass meant for us to find our salvation in the village.'

'Why?' Reed asked bluntly.

'Because with spirits it is as much about what one feels as one is told Sergeant.'

Reed sighed. 'Fair enough.'

***

They assembled at the bottom of the ladder with Reed at the front. He climbed up and listened carefully. He looked down to Bryson and Crowley.

'Nothing.' He mouthed.

Bryson nodded and began to climb, pulling himself up so that his right foot could hand free. Reed pushed open the trap door and exited to the bar. On hands and news her crawled around and examined the empty room, the door was still shut and through the window he could see that in the distance the fire still burned but it hadn't spread this way.

Bryson and Crowley emerged from the cellar. Bryson found it impossible to crawl and so had to stand. Crowley stayed down until he was sure nothing was going to spring out at them.

They gathered at the door to the pub, once again Reed took point. Bryson reluctantly used Crowley's shoulder for support. Reed silently indicated that they should stay back while he opened the door and checked the immediate area. Crowley and Bryson shuffled back. Reed slowly opened the door and peered outside. As he turned to view each end of the street they saw him suddenly freeze. He pulled his head back.

'What's out there?' Bryson whispered.

'Er…' Reed said.

Bryson waited. Reed looked confused.

'Well Sergeant what do you see?' Crowley insisted.

'It's Lafferty…and a young lady.' Reed said almost as though dreaming.

'What! Bryson said abandoning his whisper. 'Good Lord man! Get them in here.'

Reed put his head around the door and sharply whispered, 'Lafferty! Lafferty! Over here son.'

Lafferty just about made out the sound of his name being called and looked down the street they had just walked through.

'It's the Sarge!' He said to his acquaintance.

'The big one,' she said and smiled. Her eyes saw Reeds head poking out of the door far more clearly than Lafferty's.

Reed took in the girl as she walked towards him. Lafferty was shirtless and this was because she was wearing it. The lad's white cotton shirt, missing an arm, was caked in blood and soot and because she was a good six inches shorter than its owner it hung down to the middle of her thighs. She was barefoot and barelegged.

Her hair was long, looked to be dark and it hung down over her shoulders, ending just above where her bosom began. Only Lafferty's garment maintained a degree of modesty about her and as the two drew closer Reed could see that she was pretty too.

He stepped back into the bar.

'…they are coming.' He said.

'They?' Crowley asked.

'Is Tom with him? Bryson said with undisguised hope.

'No…not Tom.' Reed replied.

When Lafferty entered both Crowley and Bryson smiled broadly.

'Lad!' Bryson shouted, but all eyes immediately switched to the girl as she stepped into the room. Bryson spluttered his words as he asked Lafferty, '…and…who is your…friend?'

'This is Marga,' Lafferty said as though introducing a cousin. 'She saved my life.'

Bryson smiled even more broadly 'Well I'll be damned. It's a pleasure Miss Marga, my name is Bryson, Inspector Bryson and the gentleman is my Sergeant, Reed.'

'Ma'am.' Reed said, touching the brim of the imaginary helmet that all police officers kept for these occasions.

'Inspector...Sergeant.' Marga said acknowledging each of them.

'My dear.' Crowley stepped forward, took her hand and kissed the back of it. 'Aleister Crowley, it seems I owe you a debt of thanks for protecting my protégé.'

'Thank you Mr Crowley, you are very kind but it was a pleasure.' There was no mistaking an accent from the deepest valleys of Wales.

Something had happened in the few seconds that had heralded the arrival of Marga. Bryson couldn't quite place it but it was sufficient for the moment to say that the presence of a young girl, a practically naked young girl, had upset the dynamic in the room.

He had a hundred questions for Marga and Lafferty but they would have to wait. What he had come to Blackbrook to do, was done. They now had the lad and they also had Crowley. It was time to get out, the mystery of Lafferty's surprising companion would have to be put on hold until their safety was assured.

'Alright, we need to get out of this place, while we are together and at our strongest.' Bryson said. Keen to keep the group focused. 'Lafferty, which way did you use to get here?'

'We came from the church Sir. Pretty much a straight road, then took a couple of turns. Half the village is on fire. There's people everywhere, dead and wounded. Looked like they've been shot. I figured it must have been you and the Sarge.'

Bryson lowered his eyes a little and shook his head. 'No. That wasn't us.'

'Did you see the things? The bat things?' Lafferty asked with no small amount of excitement.

'Byakhee.' Crowley said.

All heads turned to him. Crowley shrugged his shoulders a little. 'They're called Byakhee. I actually do this for a living you know.'

Bryson turned back to Lafferty. 'You saw them then? How many?'

Lafferty looked a little pale.

'Y...yes Sir. Saw a few.' His eyes slid to Marga who said nothing and appeared relaxed.

'One of the fucking things tried to carry me off. I think I've broken my bloody foot.' Bryson spat. Then paused. 'Beg pardon ma'am.' He added.

Marga smiled sweetly. 'It's alright Inspector, I've heard a lot worse.'

'Are you hurt miss?' Reed said, Lafferty's shirt was splattered with gore.

'No I'm fine thank you Sergeant. This isn't my blood.' Marga said, still apparently unfazed by what was going on around her.

'Marga, are you are local to the area, do you know your way around here?' Bryson asked.

'I've only been here for a couple of years but I know my way about the village.'

'Could you lead us out? To the woods perhaps?'

'Oh…you'll not be wanting to go into the woods right now.' Marga replied.

'Why?' Bryson asked.

'I'm sure Mr Crowley can explain that.' She said, and all eyes turned to him.

'Crowley?' Bryson said expectantly.

Crowley stared at the girl quizzically. 'What?'

'Ich bin eine der wolf menschen.' Marga said, her deep welsh accent suddenly taken away by perfectly accented Bavarian, which Crowley knew well.

'Oh for fucks sake,' he said resignedly.

'What? What's the matter? Bryson said. 'Why's she speaking like that?'

Crowley didn't respond. Instead he turned away and rubbed a hand across his forehead. Reed and Bryson watched him, waiting expectantly for his word. Lafferty in turn watched them. And waited.

Pevensy struck a match and lit each of the eight candles placed about the circle that Penhaligon had drawn onto the floor.

'When was the last time we did this I wonder?' He said absently.

Penhaligon grimaced as he etched intricate signs into the stone floor. His knees ached as he worked. 'It was four years ago. It was April fifteenth and it was a Thursday.'

'Ah, yes, of course it was.' Pevensy replied. What a day of adventure that turned out to be.

'Somehow I think our experiences of that trip are remembered somewhat differently.' Penhaligon said as he scratched the last of his alignment of symbols into the floor.

Pevensy smiled a little, recalling the events. 'You didn't have the best of times did you old boy.' He said, and stepped to the middle, offering his hand to his friend.

Penhaligon took it and got to his feet. 'I can't abide this. Of all of the things we put ourselves through *this* has to be the worst.'

'You really do think that don't? I've never found it to be more than a little uncomfortable.' Pevensy took a folded page from his pocket. He opened it but didn't look at the words written there, not yet.

'At the end, when we arrive, that's when it's the worst. My god, it takes me days to get over it.'

He went to the far corner of the basement in which they worked upon the ritual. The unremarkable plastered walls and solid stone floor had seen many rituals performed here, had seen the three men embark upon perilous journey's through space and time. It was situated in the basement of Penhaligon's home. Although each man had a similar place prepared in their homes this was where they travelled from due to its situation along a Ley Line. It ran from central London and across to Epping Forest. It was by far the strongest line in the area and made casting spells here less taxing.

From a small non-descript wooden table in the corner Penhaligon retrieved two satchels. Two pistols lay upon it also.

'Are we taking the guns?' He asked

'Absolutely. Not everything can be scared off by a few choice phrases old boy.'

'I suppose not.' Penhaligon replied and picked both up.

He re-entered the circle and offered a satchel and pistol to Pevensy.

'I've always been a bloody awful shot you know.' Penhaligon said.

'Trust me Lester. I know.' Pevensy replied.

Penhaligon smiled and held a hand up, fingers wide.

'Ready?' He asked.

'As I'll ever be.' Pevensy said. 'But I have to admit, this will be tough. Just two of us, it will be a huge drain.'

'I know.' Penhaligon looked ahead, steeling himself.

He grasped a hold of Penhaligon's other hand and held it tightly. Both men closed their eyes. To get from where they were to where they were required to be would mean passing through places when some of the things you might see could follow. Opening your eyes to creatures of such worlds invited them into yours. This was to be avoided at all costs.

Penhaligon began to say the words. Pevensy pushed his piece of paper back into his pocket, it would come in handy later. It would take an hour or so for the ritual to be completed. One couldn't just step from one reality to another without taking some time to prepare the journey. Crossing time and space was never without danger, never without cost. They had memorised the ritual over the last few years. It had to be re-learned each time it was used and it took a human, even though they were a little more than the average man, a great deal of energy to perform.

Sometimes it wouldn't work. They could be interesting times.

Crowley turned and looked directly at Marga. Accusation and suspicion in his glare.

'She's a Werewolf.'

Marga's expression did not alter one fraction. She only looked back at Crowley in the same neutral manner with which she had delivered her statement.

'What's a Werewolf?' Bryson asked.

'Why don't you explain it to them yourself my dear?' Crowley said. 'Or are we going to be dead before then?'

Marga smiled. 'Mr Crowley, you do appear to have a very low opinion of my people.' She replied, back in her sensual valleys accent.

'Not without good reason, believe me.' Crowley replied.

Marga looked to Bryson and Reed. 'I'm afraid that Mr Crowley has obviously had some unfortunate experience of Wolf Menschen or as he calls us, *Werewolf*. But I assure you that we are not all the same, we are not all the things of dark legend that you may have heard of.'

'What are you talking about?' Bryson said, confused.

'I've heard of em.' Reed said. 'Werewolves that is, stories about men what turn into wolves.'

'Men that turn into w...' Bryson said, still struggling with the information.

'She can do it guv.' Lafferty said. But she ain't a bad un. She saved me from those bat things.'

'Byakhee.' Crowley said.

'Yeah. She killed em all...while she was a...wolf thing.'

Bryson looked hard at Marga. She was pretty, attractive in fact, disturbingly so. Her hair, her eyes, her mouth, her body was crafted in such a way as to be almost impossible for a man to move his gaze away from it. Even the way she spoke, with the sing-song lilt of her welsh accent was an enticement. A thought came to him, of mermaids, singing their siren song and luring poor souls down into a murky sea.

'Crowley?' Bryson said.

'I'm afraid so Inspector. Wolf Menschen, Lycanthrope, Varúlfur, call them what you will.'

'Men that turn into wolves...'Bryson said slowly. All the while staring at the beautiful, nearly naked thing in front of him.

'Not just men.' Marga said with a little irritation.

'She saved my life.' Lafferty said again, more firmly this time. He knew that Bryson and Reed were lost at the moment. They hadn't seen what he had seen, hadn't witnessed the ferocity with which Marga, no...not Marga, had torn apart the creatures that had attacked him, but they had seen other things from the shadows and those things had all tried to kill them.

'Look. This is probably difficult for you gentlemen but you have to, for the moment, accept that I'm here to help, to get you out of the way if nothing else.' Marga said.

'Out of the way? Out of the way of what?' Bryson asked.

'This has all been about bringing you into this place, the Children of Hastur have grand plans and they don't want your friends in the big city to get in the way of them. They want...'

'Friends in the big city? What are you talking about? Bryson said, still not fully prepared to believe what had already been said.

'She means your confidante the Genera, and the fellow who has been guiding Mr Reed.' Crowley said, he turned back to Marga, 'Don't worry, he interrupts like that all the time, do carry on.'

'It's safe to go into the village now. They have all moved into the woods, the followers and their pets. 'The coachman, he killed one of the Mi-Go... Silver... in his shotgun, we didn't anticipate that.' Marga actually shuddered a little. 'Your friends will be coming soon. They are waiting for them.'

'Pevensy, Penhaligon, Digby? It will take hours for them to get here, and how would they even know where to find us?' Reed said.

Marga looked to Crowley, it was now his turn.

'Benny.' He said. 'He's not around and if he was near or dead I would know. You will just have to take my word for it for now. I suspect that the dog is back in London and that the city gents are going to be here shortly. They will use Benny to figure out where to come to and then appear at some spot in this area that is able to allow an exit from the *Aether.*'

'I don't know what you are talking about Crowley.' Bryson rounded on him. 'You are literally saying words that mean nothing.'

Crowley sighed. 'I know.'

He looked back to Marga 'So, why are you here Marga, are you alone?'

'No. Of course I'm not alone, my pack his here. Those maniacs in the woods are calling something from the Void, to take care of you, your friends, that's why they made this happen. We are here to stop them succeeding.'

Crowley stepped towards her. 'This has been quite an elaborate ruse, how do we know that you are aren't here to ensure we all die?'

Marga stepped away from Lafferty, closer to Crowley, almost close enough to reach out and touch him.

'Do you think that if I wanted to kill you, to kill all of you...I would still be talking to you?'

Crowley lifted his chin a little as he thought about this. 'Hmm,' he said. 'S'pose.'

'You suppose?' Bryson said. 'You think this girl could kill us all?'

'In a heartbeat Inspector,' Crowley replied, 'well, a few heartbeats perhaps.'

'How long do we have before they come Marga?' Lafferty asked as he stepped back to her side.

'Not long. Can you feel it Mr Crowley?'

'Yes,' he nodded. 'The air is thickening.'

Both Reed and Bryson had felt this too, a sensation as though all the oxygen in the room had slowly become heavier in some way. They had put it down to the inferno that raged only a few streets away but deep inside they knew that it was something deeper, more fundamental even than fire.

'So what now?' Bryson asked.

'You need to leave the village,' Marga said, 'head back, go to Chiverton along the road from the Crossroads.'

'But you said that Pevensy and the others were coming,' Bryson said.

'Yes they are, and I am here to help. It's best if you and your colleagues get away from here. We will take care of this.' Marga turned away indicating that no more was to be said. She moved past Lafferty and towards the door.

'Wait!' Lafferty called out. 'Surely we can help.'

Marga turned her head and looked back at him with sympathetic eyes.

'I'm afraid what's coming is probably best left to us.' She opened the door and stepped outside. Immediately, the heat of the fire could be felt inside the pub.

'We really should get out of here gentlemen,' Crowley said with some urgency.

Bryson shook his head, 'I don't know. I feel like I did that first night, back in Ravensblack Hall, it's as though I've taken another step into insanity.'

'You know what? I don't think you can go insane Inspector,' Crowley said, he looked to each of them, 'any of you in fact.'

He took in their confused but entirely unafraid expressions. 'I think it's a part of it all, that you can handle this…mess. I think you have all been chosen.'

'Chosen?' Reed said.

'Yes, exactly that.' Crowley looked out of the open door, at Marga's back as she stood looking up at the smoke clouded moon hanging over the burning village.

'You are *three good men*,' he continued, 'I did some reading recently, since my own little encounter with your friend Penhaligon.' He turned to Reed. 'This is all starting to make some sense to me.'

'Well I'm glad someone is catching on because I'm fucking lost.' Bryson snapped. 'What do we do?'

'We do as the lady suggests. We leave. She and her kind will be able to take care of this,' Crowley replied.

Lafferty stepped up, 'We *leave*?'

'Yes.' Crowley said, 'like we were told too,' he made for the door.

Lafferty grabbed the thick cloth of Crowley's coat sleeve. 'Mr Crowley, we *can't just leave*, we have to help.'

All in the room were taken aback at this. They had never witnessed such a forceful reaction from Lafferty. So often he had been the cause of concern and fear for his safety, even now they had come all this way to protect him and yet here he was, prepared to question their concern for others.

He looked out of the door. Marga was gone, or at least not within view.

'I saw what she can do Mr Crowley, saw it with my own eyes, and she says she needs *more* like her to take on whatever these crazies are summoning. Do you really think we aren't needed here?'

'Careful lad,' Crowley warned, he brushed away Lafferty's grip upon him, 'don't step above your ability. This is beyond any of us. We *are* leaving.'

'Wait a minute,' Reed said, 'you don't speak for us Crowley.'

Now the big man stepped up to Crowley, glowering.

'I'm a copper. First and foremost, no matter what you and your weird friends seem to think about me. I protect the public and I help to serve justice to those what disturb His Majesty's Peace. What's happening here, it's disturbin the peace. Plain as. It's my duty to restore order in such circumstances and that's exactly what I'm going to do.'

Crowley looked singularly unimpressed.

'You just set fire to a fucking village, officer. You call that keeping the peace?'

Reed narrowed his eyes. His moustache raged in bristled silence.

'He's right Crowley,' it was Bryson. He could see that the next word to come out of Crowley's mouth would be punctuated by Reeds fist and so was compelled to speak. 'We have to help. It's what we do.'

Crowley looked beyond the hulk in front of him, having to tilt his head to see past Reeds shoulders.

'You Inspector, *not* me. This isn't what I do. I came here to purchase a fucking book. You came here for him,' Crowley pointed his thumb back at Lafferty, 'and the others are coming here for you. At no point was any of this caused by or at the request of myself. So, with that clear, I hope, I'm fucking off. To Chiverton or whatever the hell it's called.'

'It's *prophecy* Crowley,' Bryson retorted. Crowley stopped but didn't turn around. Instead he fixed questioning eyes on Lafferty, who raised his eyebrows and shrugged his innocence.

'Someone has seen how this plays out. How do you know that you running off isn't a part of that prophecy eh?' Bryson stepped around Reed. 'That the great and knowledgeable Aleister Crowley would toddle off as soon as the going was good.'

Bryson looked at his colleagues. 'They probably know that we will stay, but without him,' he cast his thumb back towards Crowley, 'there really isn't anything we can do to stop them. So their prophecy will be fulfilled.'

Crowley now slowly turned.

'Well, well. Someone has been doing their homework.' He said, seemingly non-plussed by the backhanded compliment, but curious.

'But tell me this Inspector, if it is prophecy as you suggest, then what if me *staying* is what this seer of yours observed. What if your demand for me to hang around and most likely have my head handed to me is what was seen?'

Bryson said nothing. It had been his only gambit and hadn't really thought it through. He just hoped that talking Crowley's language would get through to him.

Crowley looked at each of the officers. His considerable intellect worked at speed. '*Three good men.*' He thought. He had no doubt now, none at all. These were to be Guardians. Was this situation some prophecy being acted upon, or like most things, something he hadn't explained to Lafferty, just men doing what they do, which is whatever they feel like doing.

They had seen things, an actual demon for starters, and the werewolf which was a fell or earthly creature, although it was in its prettiest form at the time. They had experienced an honest to God entity from the Shadow and Void, the Mokoi would have driven most mortal men into the very deepest corners of their own mind, yet here they were, fighting Byakhee's as though they were no more than just big dogs.

Perhaps there was something at work after all, something bigger than he could see in its entirety. But what? After Ravensblack he thought he had seen what was to come, it was impressive, and it was exciting yet it was also in its own right terrifying, but it wasn't monsters, or dimensional entities that had made his mind reel, it had been mankind.

'*What a species we are.*' He thought, and then shook it from his head. He had no time for reminiscing on the past, or the future. He had made a vow to Aiwass. He knew that she was out there now, she would be a human and going about her little reconnaissance. He would return to Ravensblack Hall and meet her there. She had told him that the way to escape the village was to simply wait.

'*Guardians are coming,*' she had said. '*Stay hidden. You are not alone in your fight.*'

Clearly the girl was the aid she had promised and the Guardians were indeed coming, he could feel the charge in the air increasing. What the Guardians were doing caused all manner of upset in the *Aether* as they moved through it. Tremendous energy would gather at the spot they would arrive, ready to bring them back into the world.

'Alright Inspector. Let's do it your way.' Crowley said. 'Much to the surprise of everyone, including himself.

'Really?' Bryson said, stunned.

'Yes, really.' Crowley looked at each man again. 'But remember that I was against this, each of you are responsible for what happens to the other. Not me.'

'Fine.' Bryson said.

'Mr C I didn't m…' Lafferty made to speak.

'You too Nigel. This is a course action you have chosen. I think it is folly. I'm going because you insist, not because I think this is the right thing to do.

'Alright Crowley, Bryson said. 'We get it. Let's get going, we have a fire coming this way and the air feels like it's about suffocate me.'

Crowley nodded. 'Yes, it won't be long now.'

Lafferty walked out of the pub and the others followed behind him. They all stood in the road.

'How will we know where to go?' Reed asked.

'Look up.' Crowley said.

All of them did, and they saw. Slivers of luminescence streaked through the smoke oiled air. From all corners of their view the little lines of line sped towards the woods at the far side of the village.

'That gentlemen is a very rare sight. Those fleeting lights you see are magical energy condensed, being drawn to a channel that your friends are creating somewhere in London. Such is the power required to travel as they intend.

'How are they travelling?' Lafferty asked as he gazed in wonder at the marvellous light show.

'Through the *Aether.*' Crowley watched with some degree of awe himself, seeing the essence manifest never failed to impress. 'It's hardly surprising that a region like this has some gateway or portal nearby. The whole region reeks of some eldritch horror. I'll bet every shaman and witch in the country has this place on speed dial.'

'What?' Lafferty said.

'Oh…nothing.' Crowley shrugged. 'It's just, y'know…one of those creepy places.'

'Oh…' Lafferty said. He had noticed that sometimes, when Crowley uttered strange things and was questioned on them he would suddenly either change the subject or gloss over what he had mentioned.

'*Speed dial.*' Was that what he had said? Lafferty wasn't sure, his attention had been mostly of the rivulets of mystical light. He decided to let it go. If they came out of this alive it would wait for a more relaxing evening.

'Are we going? Bryson asked.

'Lay on MacDuff.' Crowley said.

They began to walk towards the place wherever the magical lights were converging. Behind them Blackbrook continued to burn fiercely. The glow from flames that crackled high above the rooftops could be seen from every village in the area. But no one came to investigate. No one was coming to save Blackbrook.

Crowley hoped that the fire would burn long into the morning. If he had to run this is the way he would come. If a pack of Werewolves were concerned enough about what was happening here to aid humans then burning in a fire might be preferable to what might be found in those dark and forbidding trees.

Epilogue – Ravensblack Hall

The deal was struck and just in time. The Mokoi was struggling, the last vestiges of its energy were being sucked into the gate. Crowley felt more secure now, the creature was far too weak to even attempt to assault him with Roman's body. He no longer needed the protection of his symbols and snatched up his dressing gown. It was by the door and as he pulled it on he could hear the creaking of timbers above as they turned to charcoal. The whole house would come down soon.

'Crowleeee.' The thing hissed, no longer threatening though, no longer filled with menace. There was only fear and a sense of malignant hope.

'Yes my dear?' Crowley replied as he tightened the belt around his middle.

'We mussst go, it takesss me.'

'I'll bet it does.' Crowley replied. Utterly unimpressed by its whimpering.

'Pleasssssss Crowleee.'

'How's Roman?' Crowley asked as he walked towards what looked like him, but wasn't. Despite its fear and weakness the Mokoi managed a chuckle

'Heh heh heh… Romansss lost. Roman roamsssss. Heh heh heh.

'Ah. Very droll, I see what you did there. Well done, you really have picked up the lingo haven't you?'

'Heh heh heh….'

'Alright, remember now you ridiculous little psychopath, a contract has been made, if you attempt to break it…'

'Yesss.' The Mokoi spat as best it could. 'Contract. Crowleee, Mokoi, Romannn.'

Crowley grasped Roman's hand. The Mokoi took the ceremonial knife and cut a deep line across Romans forehead. Deeper than was really necessary Crowley thought. Blood began to pour down Romans face and Crowley pressed his finger against the wound.

He recited the required lines. Words and phrases he had never thought he would ever get the opportunity to use. Roman suddenly stiffened and his eyes closed. Arms locked at his side, his fingers stretched out. The knife clattered to the floor. Crowley was half tempted to snatch it up. He could get a tidy sum for a piece of kit like that. But he resisted. Roman began to shudder, his body almost vibrated but Crowley kept his finger pressed against the wound as blood continued to flow from it.

Suddenly the eyes opened and Crowley could see it was the Mokoi behind them, for the last time. It couldn't speak now, it was almost at its end here yet the eyes shone bright with violence. Should Crowley attempt to cross it, to cheat it of their accord somehow it would return and it would exact its revenge. Crowley didn't doubt that it would at least try.

'Toodlepip.' Crowley said.

The eyes went blank. The gate gave the slightest quiver. The Mokoi was gone. Romans body fell to the floor.

This was it. He had only seconds to prepare himself. His jaw worked as he silently intoned the ritual. If he got it wrong he could only guess at the hell that awaited him within the Shadow and the Void, but if he got it right...what treasures, what knowledge.

There was a terrific crash from above him. The raw earth of the chamber began to rain down as the great hall began to collapse upon itself.

Roman stirred, his eyes opened slowly. He looked up and saw Crowley, who looked down at him and smiled his sharks smile.

'Rough night?' Crowley said.

'Crowley...what the fuck...' Roman said. Crowley vanished before his eyes.

The door to the chamber began to swell and buckle. Roman looked about the room, he saw blood. His blood. He felt heat from the door, soil dropped onto his head.

'Oh fuck...oh fuck...' He croaked. The chamber door refused to burn but it couldn't hold off the sheer weight of the collapsing house, instead its magical locks broke under sheer pressure. It exploded inwards and the raging fire, hungry for oxygen, consumed everything inside in a few painful seconds.

Crowley didn't dare open his eyes. He knew he was moving and yet staying perfectly still at the same time. He had thought he might be cold, instead a balmy warmth surrounded him. Deep inside he held a small fear that it might be the fire, the inferno that was Ravensblack Hall, trying to embrace him. He concentrated on not seeing and continued to mouth words of power and protection. He had to travel to the marker. He had to hope that there would be a marker.

'There's always a marker.' He told himself. Anywhere a gate had opened was marked. He had no idea who did it. Whether it was an actual job, perhaps handed down generation to generation, he didn't know and he didn't particularly care. Someone placed a marker. Stonehenge was a marker. The Rollright Stones was a marker. But they were old, old examples.

They were far more subtle these days. A house might be a marker, until it fell to the ground, or a chair, or a road even. There was always something to show where a gate had been.

It was believed that gates, once opened left a trail to where they had opened. Making it easier for anyone or anything who was trying to get to the plane of Earth to attempt to re-open a previously sealed gate. This is why they were watched. This is why they were marked.

Crowley felt a sudden change in temperature. It was cool. The cloying heat of the house and the strangely comfortable warmth of the *Aether* were now definitely gone. The hairs on his legs stiffened as a light breeze pushed the new cool air around him. He slowly opened his eyes. It was morning he thought. A grey sky was overhead.

He was stood in an area enclosed on three sides by fir trees cut down to about seven or eight feet. On the other side was a small fence, no bigger than two feet in height and painted bright blue. A little gate was in the middle. He looked about him. Erections of wood and metal were around him and many were covered in what appeared to be pastel coloured Bakelite. Regardless of the strangeness of the construction it was clear to Crowley what they were. They were swings, a slide, a roundabout and a see-saw. He was in a fantastical park of some kind.

He took a step forward. The grass should be moist with dew but he saw that instead it was practically dry. He knelt and ran his hand over it. Whatever it was it was certainly not grass at least not any he had ever encountered before.

Beyond the little fend a small path curved to the right. There was a sign. It stood at head height but faced away from him. He walked carefully towards it, stepping over the small fence. When he reached the sign he saw that if he followed the little path there was a large building that had bunting hanging from its windows. Round wooden tables with uncomfortable looking chairs placed under them were situated around its walls.

He looked at the sign. It was made of the Bakelite substance and was painted with greens, browns and blues. It read

Little Monkey's Play Area

Children must be supervised at all times.
No drinks or food to be taken into the play area

Crowley frowned. '*A play area for Monkeys?*' He looked about but couldn't see anything more than the side of the building and its tables and chairs. '*Is this a zoo?*'

He plodded on along the path until he reached the front of the building. There was a large area tidily gravelled in front of it and what could only be cars parked in neat rows. They weren't cars like Crowley had ever seen before. He began to get a warm tickling sensation in his stomach. He began to think that his plan might have actually worked.

He walked up to the large doorway. Crowley knew a pub when he saw one and he was looking at one right now. He banged his fist onto it. He waited a few seconds and then banged again. A light came on upstairs and shortly afterwards the window to the room with the light opened. A large shouldered man, bare-chested leaned out.

Can I help you mate?' A rough voice with a crystal cut east end accent asked.

'I rather hope so,' Crowley called up to him. 'I'm afraid I'm probably lost and possibly a little bit mental. Could you tell me where I am and what year it is please?'

'You what?' the man said and as he looked a little harder saw that the man he was talking to was apparently only wearing a dressing gown and slippers. 'Are you alright mate?'

'I'm not sure to be perfectly honest. I've only just got here you see. Could you tell me where I am?'

'You're in Kensington mate. Just off Bridge Street.'

'Bridge Street?' Crowley said, 'Is that near to Springland Avenue at all?

'It *is* Springland Avenue, the name was changed in the Seventies.

'The Seventies you say? I'm sorry to continue to be a little strange but could you tell me what year it is please.'

'What year it is?'

'If you would be so kind.'

'It's twenty twelve mate. Look I'm coming down. Stay there ok?'

Crowley didn't respond. The man withdrew from the window and closed it. As he waited Crowley ran the number and its ramifications through his mind. Twenty twelve, two thousand and twelve anno domini.

'*Fucking hell,*' he thought.

The door opened. The man, who was as large as he had seemed in his window, now had on a vest of some sort. There was a faded image upon it, printed Crowley thought. His hair was short and straight. His jaw looked like it could take a swing from a sledgehammer. This was definitely a London landlord.

'Hello,' Crowley said.

The man took him in from slippers to shining dome.

'Where've you come from? Are you from a home?' he asked.

'Actually I'm quite aways from home at the moment,' Crowley replied, 'I don't suppose I could chance a cup of tea?'

The landlord blinked. He was sailing in uncharted waters here. The geezer was a big bloke, but nothing he felt he couldn't handle, plus he was in a dressing gown and slippers.

'You'd better come in mate.'

'Most kind, my name is Aleister, but everyone calls me Crowley,' he waited to see if anything registered with the landlord upon mentioning his name.

'I'm Terry, Mr Crowley. Come through to the lounge bar and take a seat.'

Crowley did as he was requested; all the while smiling his sharks smile.

CROWLEY'S LAST STAND

Blackbrook Village, 1921

Benton approached the centre of the circle slowly, reverently. The forest had been cleared for over a hundred feet around the single, large tree that sprawled at its centre.

It was an Oak, old and magnificent. Its muscular bough's reached out from a trunk which was as wide as a carriage, but upon the branches that stretched like crooked fingers, scratching at the air around it, not a single leaf grew.

He walked around it, all the time looking for any indication that a gate was opening, but saw nothing. He, however certainly feel the power that was being absorbed by the great Oak. He could also see it being drawn in from the surrounding area by the sheer strength of the ritual being performed.

He had never witnessed such a thing before. A call upon the Essence so strong that it condensed the substance that made it into the flashing slivers of light, which came like little spears towards the tree.

When *they* arrived they would be drained, they would be weak. No matter what preparations had been made previously, and they must have been substantial, the Guardians could not be unaffected by such a manipulation of the Essence. Travelling through a gate was one thing, but opening one? It was a sobering thought to him, the magic that these men could wield.

The only way to obtain even greater force was to dip into the Shadow and Void and allow the two realities to combine. Benton couldn't imagine any circumstance under which the Guardians would do such a thing. That was a sure fire way of inviting things into their world that would eat their very souls. Every one of them.

He turned his attention to his assembled troops. Their number had been diminished by the assault in the street and he had been barely able to believe the scene when he came to it. All about his people lay upon the road, dead or dying. Further to this not only had a number of Byakhee been shot from the sky one of the Mi-Go, unbelievably, had dissolved into the floor in front of him, as whatever technology it used to allow it to exist in Earth's atmosphere failed.

He had actually felt his knees buckle a little, at this last incredible realisation, and needed to sit upon a small wall that enclosed one of the abandoned cottages.

He had expected a fight from the *Three*, this whole plan, forcing them to use a gate to travel had been designed to make them weak enough to engage, but he had not envisioned a massacre at the hands of the occultist and the ridiculous, untrained and inexperienced would-be Guardians.

This is why he had ensured that a large area had been cleared around the gate. While his troops were fanatical, loyal and eager to please their God's, they were for the most part untrained in firearms and their correct operation. Even those recruited from the military were inadequately trained. The War had produced many lambs among the lions.

Positioning his people in a tight ring around the Gate when it opened would almost certainly result in them shooting each other as an inevitable crossfire ensued. He had thought it better to open up the circle and increase the range at a further cost of accuracy, but there were almost thirty of them, the volume of gunfire should do the job, he hoped.

He couldn't afford to lose any more people though. Peasley had been his right hand man and he was gone due to an error of judgement. According to his lieutenants Crowley had murdered him in cold blood. Just straight out shot him. Naturally the plan had been to do a similar thing to the occultist but he had not for one moment considered Crowley to have such a ruthless streak in him.

He had clearly, *severely* underestimated the Great Beast. Sold on the lurid lies of the press, Benton realised that he had dismissed Crowley as nothing more than a panderer to the rich and a slave to his desires. He knew now, he had been foolish, cavalier perhaps, and was paying the price.

They were out there now, none of them chained to the walls as they should be, none to be offered to Lord Hastur at the end of all of this, as a gift beyond the heads of the Guardians. He could only hope that all worked out well for him from here and that he might not have to take their place.

He had spread his followers out as best he could to cover both the perimeter and the tree. They wouldn't see the gate appear, he knew that, one minute there would be empty space, the next there would be the Guardians. Everyone was armed, some with a pistol, some with rifles.

Their connections to the Children had kept them out of the pointless debacle in France, but it meant that they were not at all battle hardened. Their kills had all been tied to a chair or stake, or nailed to a wall. There was very little resistance when your target had been disembowelled first.

With any luck the policemen would just run. They would head to Chiverton or Wolstone. They wouldn't find any help there of course, although maybe the Vicar, Flowers, he could be a problem, but the word was that he had travelled to London and so was out of the way. Besides, he was still only one man, and even if they reached Glossop they would be far too late to affect the outcome.

No, his chief worry now was the woods. Something was in there that was not to be trifled with. Benton thought it ironic that he had spent the last few months slaughtering livestock around the area to keep the locals away only to have something turn up and kill his own people in the same manner.

The girl was involved; of that he was certain. She had been spotted at various incidents. Whether she was some local witch conjuring a spirit or a particularly nasty familiar he couldn't be sure, but he had set the Byakhee to hunt her down only to have that had end badly too. Just one more thing added to his catalogue of mishaps.

He shook his head and took a deep breath as the beautiful light show continued around him. He had no doubt that there would be blood on the ground where he stood soon enough. He just hoped that it wouldn't be his.

***

The Oak had long since forgotten how to interact with this world in any normal way. It didn't need to absorb sunlight to generate energy, instead it tapped into the Aether. The flow of the Essence was its source of life now. After centuries of being used by humans as a conduit between worlds it had become more than it once was. It could no longer be used as though it were just some convenient icon or ingredient, no more than an egg in a baking recipe where any egg would do. Now, to seek to use its power as a gateway required both its permission and an offering.

But it was not evil, at least not in the sense of those who steered clear of the ancient Oak understood it. It, like most things that existed, wanted only to survive and to grow, but as its desires might be at a cost to others it was also not truly good. The Oak was a neutral force, up to now it had taken no side and maintained only its own integrity.

A Gate had been requested and granted. The Essence was being channelled towards it by a powerful ritual, which was being cast from a great distance. The price for this was a simple tithe. Energy must be offered to it from the flood that was being drawn. Those wishing to open the Gate would be required to work that little bit harder, to consume their own stores of the mystical energy that all humans, most of them unknowingly, conserved and conducted. The tree would take its offering and it would allow the portal to form.

The Oak understood that the group of humans around it, and the creatures alien to the Earth that had floated in the sky, waited for these travellers and that they waited with ill intent. This was of no concern to it. So long as the price was paid and its own safety was not threatened it would not act. It would allow the Gate to open and its interest in the matter would end.

Yet, these humans had destroyed all of the trees, plants, nests and lairs that had formerly surrounded it. Although this offered no direct threat to the Oak, for it was certain that the plants and trees would return, that the animals would soon re-home themselves, it was suspicious of such an upheaval to its domain. It had learned much of human nature and had embraced some of their principles as it had seen fit. One of these was respect.

The Oak wondered whether those who had trampled into its kingdom had shown proper deference to its strength and power. Humans demanded this, why should it be any different?

As powerful energy flowed through it the Gate began to form the Oak channelled Essence into its own manipulations of the fabric of reality, and as it did so it watched for any further sign of discourtesy. It would allow their Gate but it would suffer no more impudence.

***

They walked in a line across the street, away from the blazing village towards the dark and forbidding forest. They had no need of directions now, as the fantastic light show around them guided the way.

'Werewolves Crowley.' Bryson said, 'Start talking.'

Although he didn't care for Bryson's tone Crowley didn't feel like retorting, his mind was busy with other weightier concerns, so he told the Inspector what he knew to give him time to consider other implications of what was happening.

'They have been around for a long, long time. It is suggested by those who study such matters that they might have once been in contention as the dominant species on Earth. Of course as history has proved, anything that gets in the way of Homo-sapiens tends to go the way of the Dodo, but for all of their strength and agility and let's not forget, ferocity, Werewolves are slow to breed, their children are not guaranteed to be Lupus and they have a mortal weakness to Silver.'

'Do you think that too Mr C? That they could have been...in charge?' Lafferty asked.

'No.' Crowley replied confidently. 'While they are Earth born, and therefore not reliant on the Essence to exist here, the fact that even a child conceived of two Were-creatures may only have a small chance of producing a similar offspring leads me to the conclusion that they are an aberration. They would never have the numbers to threaten us as a whole.'

'What about a human and a Werewolf, could they produce…*them*.' Lafferty asked carefully.

'Yes.' Crowley replied, intrigued by the line of questioning, 'While my observation was that two Werewolves might not produce Werewolf young it is quite possible for a mix of human and Lycanthrope to do so at pretty much the same chance.'

'Lycan….'

'It means Werewolf.' Crowley said.

'Oh.' Lafferty said, embarrassed.

'There was an incidence not too long ago,' Crowley continued, 'a man by the name of Talbot found himself succumbing to bouts of frenzy and violence. Apparently he was especially agitated when the Moon was full. As far as he was aware he had never exhibited any signs of Lycanthropy as a child but confessed to 'strange dreams' as he grew older. He was in his forties before he finally became able to shift.'

'Shift?'

'Switch forms. To become a Werewolf, or whatever the duality of your nature allows. Poor Mr Talbot had a rough time of it I'll tell you.'

'Gosh.' Lafferty said.

'Gosh in-fucking deed young man. Little more is known about Mr Talbot other than that he was of Welsh origin and had at least two children.' He looked sideways to Lafferty, 'I'll leave that thought with you.'

Lafferty's questions dried up as he considered what Crowley had just intimated.

'These things, are they on our side?' Reed asked.

'I do hope you just heard all of that because I'll be damned if I'm going through it again.' Crowley replied.

'I heard.'

'Good. Well, yes and no. As a civilisation we've been clearing out creatures like this since we first picked up sharp sticks. It's hard for our primitive mind to discern what is wholly different from the Fell and Fey creatures and what originates from such pits as the Shadow and Void

'Fell and Fey?' Reed asked.

Crowley tutted, realising that he was now creating a forum for more questions.

'Fell and Fey are…let's say fantastic creatures, but that are home-grown so to speak. Not of the Shadow and Void. Although to be honest the terms are misleading. Fell is supposed to cover the bad things and Fey the good. This is poppycock however, I've known some pretty nasty things that supposedly reside under the 'Fey' epithet, and what do you think Werewolves come under? They are almost always thought of as Fell, monsters of the shadows, and yet they are as diverse in their natures as any creature.'

Reed nodded. To Crowley's surprise the big man appeared to grasp the issue.

'Makes you wonder what humans would be listed as.' Reed said.

Crowley raised his eyebrows. 'Yes indeed Sergeant. Yes indeed.'

They soon came to the edge of the village, where gently rolling land met the large forest ahead. To their far right, barely visible, was the bridge they had all crossed to enter Blackbrook.

'What's going to be in that wood Crowley?' Bryson asked.

Crowley shook his head a little. 'I don't know Inspector. More of them, the followers, you can be certain of that.'

'Those flying things?'

'Byakhee? No. I shouldn't think so. They like towns and cities, where they can perch and swoop. Trees make life difficult for them.'

This made some sense to Bryson. He nodded. 'What's going to come through the Gate?'

'Just your friends, at least that's what *should* happen.'

'And these arseholes are waiting for them.' Bryson said.

'Yes. I can only think that this whole scenario was played out to force their hand. Opening a Gate…it takes a lot of energy, a lot of focus, when they arrive they will most likely be tired, disorientated.'

'An ambush.' Reed said

'Precisely.' Crowley said grimly. 'We have been used gentlemen. Done up like kippers.'

'Can we stop the Gate being opened?' Lafferty asked, returning his attention to the group after scanning the area for signs of Marga.

Crowley replied with a degree of admonishment. 'Good God no! If we even tried we could end up sending these men to places I do not want to even think about. No, the Gate will open. What we have to do is stop what happens afterwards.'

'*We*, Crowley? Can we rely on you in this?' Bryson said, his tone abrupt. His foot was causing him great pain and his temper was rough.

Crowley stared at Bryson with piercing eyes. 'Inspector, I know that your opinion of me is quite low but trust me I do not like to be made a fool of. I'll be damned if I'm going to let this mob of cum juggling fuckwits fist me like some slack fannied whore.'

At this Crowley raised his nose and marched on with imperious silence.

The assembled men remained quiet too, as they walked on they tried to erase the vision conjured by Crowley's statement from their minds.

When they reached the edge of the forest and started into the strange half-light caused by the fleeting shards of Essence and the radiant moon they stopped.

'Do we split?' Reed said. 'Try to get around them?'

Bryson nodded and pointed to Crowley. 'Myself and Crowley, you and Lafferty.'

'No.' Reed countered. 'I'll go with Crowley.'

The occultist twitched his eyebrows with surprise.

Bryson too seemed a little taken aback but nodded again. 'Fair enough.'

'We should wait when we reach the spot, stay hidden.' Crowley said. 'When the gate is about to open it will be the first and only time you will see it, after that it will be all but invisible, just like it was at Ravensblack Hall. That is when we should strike.'

'Any plan in mind Crowley? Bryson asked

'Shoot them, as many as possible.' Crowley replied.

'Right, to be honest that's my plan too.' Bryson said. 'What about *other* things?'

'I can't know for sure but it's likely they have some kind of back up, something weird.'

'I assume you mean *more* weird, but I suppose we can only do what we can do.' Bryson pulled out a pistol and handed it to Lafferty.

'Thanks guv.' Lafferty said as he took the gun.

'It's loaded but there's no spare bullets. Reed, how are you for ammunition?

'One spare load guv.'

'Crowley?'

The occultist produced his pistol. 'Loaded and a few to spare.'

'Right.' Bryson offered his hand to Reed who immediately took it and shook. 'Good luck.'

'Good luck guv.' Reed replied.

Bryson offered his hand to Crowley and looked him directly in the eye. 'This could be where you make a real difference Crowley.'

Crowley took the inspectors hand and Bryson was surprised at how strong and firm the grip was. 'Don't worry Inspector, it'll be fun.' He grinned his shark's smile, winked at Lafferty and turned away.

'Come on fatso, let's get to it.' He said to Reed as he walked into the tree line.

***

If Reed took any offence at Crowley's jibe he didn't show it and this annoyed the occultist. He didn't know why he found such delight in his prods at people who were, on a civil and moral level, probably performing cartwheels around him. He just did.

They pressed on through the trees, which as they were not too closely spaced gave ample room for them to walk side by side although Reed appeared to be prepared to allow Crowley to lead the way. In truth the occultist was only following the flow of the dashes of light about them, had he been wrong about the direction of their flow being the destination he would have been utterly lost, however, as they moved on it was clear that the convergence point was getting closer.

'Can you hear anything?' Reed asked as they worked their way around a large clump of brambles that blocked their way.

'What? What like?' Crowley asked.

'That's what I mean. I can't hear any voices, chanting and stuff. Won't they be doing all that?'

'Oh. No. Probably not. These people aren't performing the ritual, that's being done at the other end. All the cultists have to do is wait for it to finish and the Gate to open.'

'Then Penhaligon and the others will…appear?' Reed said cautiously as though he had been singled out to answer a geography question in school.

'Yes. Then the arseholes will shoot them or something equally subtle.' Crowley replied.

'Can we stop it?'

Crowley stopped. Reeds questions were interrupting his train of thought and he wanted him to shut up. Reed also immediately drew to a halt.

'I assume you mean the gate opening, which I've already explained could lead to other things taking advantage of the ritual.' Crowley said evenly. 'You also have to appreciate that is something that is happening elsewhere, probably in London. They are dialling a number and the phone will be picked up in this forest. All we can do is try to cause some kind of distraction before they arrive. If we can keep attention away from the gate long enough for the old timers to gather their wits they will have a chance.'

'*Can* they be shot?' Reed asked.

'What?' Crowley snapped.

'They asked me if I'd ever been ill, which I never have, I don't think they can be hurt these…Guardians.'

Crowley sighed. 'No Sergeant, no. Not being ill is not the same as not being hurt. As far as I'm aware they are just like us, they grow old, albeit much more slowly, they bleed and they feel pain, all they have is a resistance to the kind of bullshit that kills your average bloke for no good reason, like diseases or dodgy hearts or boredom.'

'So what makes them…?'

'Guardians?'

'Yes.'

'They can manipulate the Essence far better than most humans. They have abilities that are potent, usually a different thing for each one of them. One might have the gift of prophecy for example, another might…'

'What's that!' Reed said with a gasp and pointed to the sky.

Crowley frowned at being interrupted but looked up in the direction Reed was indicating. There was no mistaking a humanoid shape seemingly floating across the forest.

'Fuck me.' Crowley said.

The thing didn't appear to notice them. In its hands, such as they were, as it had four insect-like appendages that ended in claws, it held a glowing tablet before it. It was only visible in the night's gloom as a shimmering, translucent bubble surrounded it.

'That's not one of those things.' Reed stated.

'A Byakhee? No it's not.' Crowley said darkly.

'Do you know what it is?'

'It's a Mi-Go.' Crowley replied staring as the thing vanished from view. 'Oh my, oh my, this just gets worse.'

'What is it? Is it from the Void?'

'No.' Crowley said flatly. 'And it's no Fell creature either. These things are from a long way away.'

Crowley chewed at his lip for a moment. Then put his hand on Reeds arm, taking the big man by surprise.

'I don't know enough about these things to give us any real advantage. I've only seen them once before and that was from a distance, but they are very dangerous. They have…devices, weapons that are beyond our current understanding, but I do know this, that bubble, did you see it? Around the creature?'

'Yes, it was hard to see, the colours around it…like oil on water.' Reed replied.

'Indeed, and nicely put Sergeant. That bubble protects them in different ways. They need it at all times to keep them safe from our atmosphere but it can also be used to…deflect bullets somehow. I understand that it takes a lot of energy to do that so they will only activate it if they believe there is a threat. If they do, you can shoot at it all day and your bullets will just bounce off. It's some kind of physics thing, I don't know. Tesla tried to explain it all to me, but I got bored. The main thing is if you don't catch it by surprise, don't waste your ammunition.'

'Right.'

'Also, and I could be wrong on this mind, these creatures don't usually get involved in the rough stuff. They aren't cut out for it. They are like…supervisors in a way, whatever they are up to it mostly involves watching, examining. Scare it enough and it might just fuck off.' Crowley gave Reeds arm a comradely pat. 'With me?'

'Yes, I think so.'

'One other thing.'

'Yes?'

'Don't go near the gate.'

'Right.' Reed said.

Had Crowley tried to offer him advice on how to handle a fight, dealing with armed men, or any kind of attempt at rousing his courage he would have dismissed it out of hand but when it came to the weird stuff, monsters and magic, he was prepared to listen.

Crowley looked about him. 'It's slowing. Can you see?'

Reed could see. The slivers of light were still moving towards the general area they were heading in but were definitely slowing, thinning out.

'Yes, it's almost time. I think I can feel it.'

Crowley nodded. Reed definitely had some kind of grasp of what was occurring, the big man could *feel* the energy that was being drawn and manipulated, gathering somewhere in the woods.

'We should hurry.' Reed said and took the lead, which was fine with Crowley.

***

Bryson and Lafferty moved slowly through the trees. Bryson was finding it almost impossible to manage the uneven ground, his foot was aflame with pain at every tap and twist. Finally he had to rest. He leaned his back against a tree, meaning only to catch his breath but found himself sliding down it until he was sat upon the damp, forest floor.

'Sir!' Lafferty came to him and knelt at his side.

'I'm sorry Nigel. Give me a moment and I'll be fine.' Bryson said with a strained and entirely unconvincing voice.

Lafferty looked around. The flow of the Essence had slowed, weakened and he could feel the gathering of energy as a great pressure against his chest. It was almost time.

'We have to move Sir, got to get going.' Lafferty said, hoping he could cajole some spirit into his boss.

Bryson breathed heavily and the sound of a man defeated was obvious to both of them.

'I'm not going to make it son,' he shook his head. 'It's taken all I have not to cry out every step and right now my foot feels like it's on fire.'

To his surprise Lafferty saw tears begin to roll down Bryson's cheeks and he felt compelled to turn away. He couldn't bear the thought of the guvnor not being the man in charge, the rock upon which they could all cling when things became strange or out of hand.

'Don't worry guv, take a breather an catch up if ya can.' Lafferty said through a half-hearted smile.

Bryson nodded. 'I'm going to catch up. I will, but you need to get to Crowley and Reed. Go to them.'

Lafferty shook his head 'I dunno guv. If we are supposed to get one up on these people, with there being just four of us...' Lafferty paused as he realised that there would now only be three to deal with the cultists, 'it's probably best if we stick with the plan, get around em like.'

Bryson's thoughts had started to become muddled, the pain he knew, he wanted to just lie back and sleep for a while. Perhaps the pain would fade, his foot would calm and reduce from the swollen thing it was right now.

'Could you remove my shoe for me, please.' he said, thinking about the swelling had focused his thoughts back to the pain.

As carefully as he could Lafferty pulled off the Inspectors shoe, which thankfully didn't seem to cause any further discomfort to him, and as he did so he could see that it was terribly puffed out. There was no chance that the Inspector was going to be walking properly for a good while. He looked about again. He could feel the pressure of the energy as it condensed somewhere in the trees.

'It's going to be soon Sir.' Lafferty said.

'Take this.' Bryson lifted his pistol from its holster and handed it to Lafferty. He then took spare bullets from his pockets and passed them over too.

'What about you?'

'I'll be fine. I'll hide, camouflage myself or something.' Bryson said, wishing that Lafferty would go so that he could just give in.

'Right Sir.' Lafferty said. He stood. He checked the pistol. It was loaded.

'Lafferty,' Bryson said, looking at his constable with obvious concern ironed into his face.

'Yes guv?'

'Don't trust Crowley.'

Lafferty blinked, his jaw dropped a little. He wanted to say something in Crowley's defence. The occultist had been good to him, he had taught him all manner of things, not just of the dark world that he walked but of science, biology, maths and English. Crowley even ran through the correct application of social etiquette, which had surprised Lafferty as the occultist rarely deployed any of it himself. But he said nothing, because despite understanding his own flawed nature, to try and see the best in all people, Lafferty knew that Crowley only had an interest in one person.

'Right guv.' Lafferty said, his complexion, had the light been better, would have revealed a reddening of his cheeks as shame fought with his conscience. 'I'll be back with the Sarge shortly.'

'Good lad.' Bryson waved him away. 'Get going, you're falling behind.'

Lafferty nodded, turned and started off. He looked back after he had walked a hundred feet or so but couldn't see the Inspector due to the intervening trees. He was sorely tempted to run back to him but knew that the guvnor would bawl him out. Reluctantly he continued as ordered.

The glow of the lights streaming past him illuminated his path and he was further aided by the radiance of the full Moon glaring down where the canopy of the trees thinned.

It was, he thought, quite beautiful but there was a feeling of ice-cold dread in the pit of his stomach. As he progressed into the forest after every few steps he would see eyes, they were everywhere, in the trees, in the shrubs and brambles. They watched him without blinking. He shook his head and they would vanish only to reappear shortly after.

They weren't real, he knew that, there was nothing in the trees or shadowed clumps of flora observing him. This was his mind, what Crowley called his ability at work. He was being warned of what might be, and had he had Crowley's instinct and powerful sense of self-preservation he might have been able to gain a better idea of what the warning was, because unlike Crowley his only thoughts were of others and not the threat to himself.

Bryson watched Lafferty quickly disappear, swallowed up by trees and deceptive shadows. He sighed, a heavy mournful escape of air and emotion that was the precursor to his eyes beginning to water again. He had never felt so helpless and useless at the same time. His lads were in grave danger, all brought on by the man whose services he had enlisted.

He often directed his anger towards Crowley but deep inside he knew that it was his own ridiculous initiative that had started the ball rolling. Had he not considered trying to fight fire with fire, in bringing along a madman to placate another madman at Ravensblack Hall none of this need have happened.

Yet, something told him that this was not entirely true. He had been forced to endure many run-ins with Crowley in the past, wasn't this inevitable, was it fate? Was it all actually out of his hands and he was only a part of some prophecy, foreseen by manipulative forces beyond the shadows? He shook his head, the ache which throbbed from his foot caused his thoughts to scatter like marbles falling from a bag.

'*Think Ron, think!*' he demanded of his own conscience. '*You have to be able to help. Don't just lie here again.*'

He had failed them at the warehouse, when the Demon had struck, a Demon that had sat at his side, fooling him completely. Was this to be the same thing all over again? Would he sit on the side-lines as the men under his command, his friends fought against unspeakable evils?

'*I'll be damned!*' he cursed and tried to stand.

He got no further than pushing his hands down onto the damp forest floor. His foot sent a spasm of pain through his entire body forcing him to slump back down.

'Oh my God.' he called in a weak voice. He bowed his head, 'God help me.'

Tears began to roll down his cheeks and he muttered words of hopelessness and failure. When he lifted his head and looked out at the forest he could see that the light show was coming to its end, the little zipping shafts of light were intermittent now, his vision was only aided by the intense radiance of the full moon hanging over the forest.

He didn't sense the movement and could not have heard the stealthy tread of clawed feet upon wet leaves and soil. He only knew he was being surrounded when figures appeared from the gloom, outlined in the silver lunar light. Something hard and razor sharp touched the side of his throat and Bryson knew he was a dead man.

***

'It's done!' Crowley said, as he came to a sudden halt.

Reed knew this was true. He could feel it, the pressure that had built up, pregnant, was now ready to give birth to the gate. The streaks of light were gone and there was only a cold, empty silence about the forest until a terrific volume of gunfire punctuated the air.

'We're too late!' Crowley gasped.

***

Benton watched as the last slivers of light disappeared into the tree and braced as if expecting the thing to explode into a storm of splinters. It didn't. A haze appeared a few feet from the Oak, blurring it at first and then strange colours, as if out of space, danced in the air about it. This lasted only seconds, the impossible shades then moved out from the chaotic haze and towards the edge of something almost circular. The Gate was forming, it was being created from the Essence and somehow connecting to a portal very similar hundreds of miles away

He didn't dare move, as though even sudden drawing of breath might break the weird performance he was witnessing. The colours were gathering at the edge of the gate and appeared to be solidifying, creating a frame. In front of his eyes a portal that cut through space was being fashioned and Benton was filled with awe. This was why he failed to react quickly enough.

For all of his planning for the moment that the Guardians would step out of the gate, despite the commitment and discipline instilled by years of devotion and training he was caught off guard. It was a simple thing, he had expected the men to walk out of the portal as they would any door or other earthly entrance. Instead they had materialised, they had faded in to existence.

His people had looked for his command, many didn't even have their guns raised, they only stood and waited to be told when to act. By the time Benton managed to martial his attention fully the Guardians were wholly present, they were through the gate and were quick to see that they had been led into a trap.

It was their sudden movement that gave him the push he needed. The two men, something else that caused his thoughts to stall, only two of them were present, dived for cover. The ancient Oak had large sprawling roots that grew about its base providing a good deal of cover.

'Fire! Fire!' Benton shouted, almost screamed.

He raised his own pistol and began to pump the trigger. The clearance was immediately filled with the reports of rifles, shotguns and pistols. As he had expected dozens of the shots went horribly wide, he even saw a man fall to his back a few feet away from him, the victim of one of his own colleagues being unable to handle the recoil of his rifle, but he didn't order a cease-fire.

Pieces of the Oak flew into the air and showered the ground. At least some of the shots were reaching their mark and Benton hoped that enough had reached the Guardians because after his next shot he would need to re-load and so would most of his followers.

He raised his hand and shouted. 'Cease fire!'

He was required to do it twice more until the volley finally dissipated.

'Reload!' He called out.

Without taking his eyes off the roots of the Oak he took out more bullets from his pocket and began to chamber them. There was no movement to be seen from the base of the tree and the Gate was no longer visible but he knew it would still be there, it would last for hours.

The instant the last bullet was chambered Benton snapped the revolver shut and pointed it at the roots. There was still no movement.

'*We got them,*' he thought, allowing himself a moment of elation, '*they couldn't have survived that, no one could have survived that.*'

He stepped forward a little, as though being an extra few inches closer would allow him greater insight as to the condition of the men hiding amongst the roots. There was still no movement and now all eyes were upon him, waiting for a new order.

'Slowly,' Benton shouted, 'move toward the centre.'

His followers immediately began to shuffle forwards.

'Keep your guns low, keep them *LOW!*'

There was a ripple around the circle as barrels were dropped an inch or two from their current position. Benton pushed his gun into his belt and from the sheath at his side withdrew his sword.

He and seven others carried these blades. For all intents and purposes they looked like a short sword or long bladed dagger, but closer inspection revealed that their hilts were fashioned from a strange material, like some light absorbing ceramic. The blade was metal but like no other, it had about it a faint glow and its edge, were it to be tested against a block of granite would slice right through it. They were a gift from the Mi-Go and had only one purpose today.

Benton gently ran the pad of his thumb against a section of the pommel and a light vibration coursed through the knife, there was sharp enough to cut through granite then there was *sharp*.

***

'Penny!' Pevensy twisted his body so that he could face his friend at his side. The gunshots had finally abated. 'Penhaligon old boy, are you still with me?'

As he turned Penhaligon groaned.

'I think so,' he gasped as he spoke, 'I took one.'

'Where?' Pevensy said, but as he faced Penhaligon could see blood spreading from a hole in his jacket just to the right of one of the lower buttons.

'Side I think, not stomach.' He looked down at his gut as he gingerly plucked at the buttons.

'Let me do that.' Pevensy said but Penhaligon shooed him away with his other hand.

'No. Keep your attention on those bastards out there, I imagine they have a lot more bullets.'

As if in response to this they heard a call to 'Reload!' from one of their assassins.

'Well. This is super.' Pevensy said.

Penhaligon unfastened the last button and pulled his jacket aside revealing his wound. As he had suspected a bullet had entered his side and fortunately not his stomach.

'Side,' he said.

'Thank God, that's something at least.' Pevensy replied. 'Although I'm not really sure what we can do about the current situation. What about you?'

'No clue old chap. Right now I'm thinking about how to not bleed to death.'

'I think they have us surrounded.' Pevensy looked at the bullet holes and gouges in the tree bark.

They were in a natural trough formed where rain had taken soil away from the huge expanse of the Oaks foundation. The roots cradled them within, offering a natural but limited defensive position.

'Good job this old chap has splendid roots.' He patted one of the twisting but solid arms of wood at his side and as he did so he felt a sudden surge of energy through his palm.

'I say!' Pevensy exclaimed and looked at his palm.

'What is it?' Penhaligon asked, he looked over to Pevensy.

'The tree. There...' He placed his hand down upon the root once again and lightly gripped it. 'There is an awfully large amount of power flowing through it.'

'Still?' Despite his wound Penhaligon lifted himself up a little.

'And when I say awfully large I mean bloody enormous. I think that…'

Shots rang out again and more splinters showered down onto their heads as a second crashing volley filled the air. Both men dropped flat to the soil.

'*Christ!*' Penhaligon said as his wound delivered its own volley of agony.

'The Gate is open,' Pevensy said, 'I could summon something?'

'What?' Penhaligon gasped. 'A demon? I think I'd rather be shot again than be turned inside out.'

'Fair comment I suppose.' Pevensy replied.

The gunfire thinned a little for moment but as Pevensy started to rise from the floor it quickly resumed. As he dropped down again he gripped the same root he had patted for support, and heard a voice.

'Impudence!' it said.

'Did you hear that?' Pevensy asked.

'What? I can't hear a bloody thing, my ears are ringing.'

Pevensy listened carefully. He squeezed the root a little more firmly and felt the familiar energy of the Essence flowing through it.

'Despoilers!' The voice said as though through gritted teeth. It wasn't human, nor demon or ghost, Pevensy was certain, and it was in his head not his ears.

The gunshots died once more. 'Who are you?' Pevensy asked, 'are you near?'

'I am the way.' The voice shouted now, so loud in Pevensy's head he screwed his eyes shut.

'I am the path. I am the gate! I am the journey and the destination. I will not be ignored. Ia! Ia! I have the words. I have the words!'

'Pevensy! Pevensy for Christ's sake. What's happening?' Penhaligon rolled over despite the screaming pain in his side. He reached out to Pevensy, seeing his knuckles turn white as he gripped a root of the great Oak and shuddered with obvious pain. He gripped his friend's free hand and heard the voice.

'Ia! Cthulhu ftghn, Ia! Chtulhu…'

'NO!' Pevensy screamed. 'YOU MUST *NOT* DO IT.' The gunshots suddenly stopped. Pevensy opened his eyes and turned to Penhaligon.

'The Tree Penn, it's the Tree, it's sentient.'

Penhaligon quickly took in the information. This, as strange as it was, wasn't new. It had happened many times before where the Essence was strong and where humans manipulated it through sacred effigies or natural formations given form purely through their own desires. The tree was perfect of course, it was organic, it was old, and it lay directly above a convergence of Ley lines. Penhaligon could imagine the rites, which had been performed before it in a place like this.

He grasped at a root and allowed his mind to look into the aura of the Oak and immediately saw its fury.

'Let go, I'll take it from here.' Penhaligon said.

Pevensy didn't question his friend. Surviving encounters like this depended on their absolute trust in each other and he lifted his hand from the root he had been gripping tightly.

He watched as Penhaligon relaxed to the floor and began to move his lips silently. He was talking to the tree. There were still no shots being fired, either their attackers were reloading or moving in towards them. He suspected the latter and took out his own pistol despite what little protection it would offer against an army.

Slowly he lifted his head above a root to see what was happening. Shots rang out again, almost all of them way off target.

'Bloody awful shooting,' he muttered as he ducked down just in case someone got lucky as they had with Penhaligon. His observation proved him correct, they were close and they were all around the tree.

He looked again to his friend. He couldn't be sure what he was doing, trying to talk the Oak into not summoning something from one of the darkest hells probably. It had no doubt learned of such places from one of the many religions that had offered up their sacrifices and energies to it, but to incite the rituals of *Cthulhu?* The thing had no sense of proportion.

'Blimey, we really are in a pickle,' he thought.

He pulled back the hammer on his pistol and prepared to shoot whoever stuck their head over their natural foxhole.

***

Benton wasn't prepared to take any chances with the Guardians. They were human, but they were smart and could act with a strength that belied their age. Trapped as they were, nestled in the roots of the great Oak he wasn't sure that they would be able to perform their magic. Rituals needed space, concentration and time.

After the first volley he ordered his people to reload and prepare to fire again. He would keep them pinned down, make sure they couldn't slither off or step back into the gate. After a couple of minutes had passed, and no movement could be seen at the tree, he gave the signal to fire.

Above him the Mi-Go hovered, still tapping at its little tablet. Why didn't it *do* something? It just floated up there, watching, observing, while he did all the fucking work. One of its friends had been done in. Benton smiled at the thought of that. He had been shocked to see the creature dissolving into vapours on the road, but he had enjoyed watching it.

He couldn't question his orders, he would never do such a thing, and this is why he had risen so quickly in the ranks, why he was here today eliminating such a powerful threat, but he didn't like the Mi-Go, not at all.

Pride swelled inside him at the thought of his elevation to High Priest though, after he had come up with this plan to take down the Guardians. He took his attention away from the alien creature, he had never wished to involve them but his masters had other ideas.

He lifted a hand and looked to his right and caught the attention of Brisley, one of his lieutenants. Brisley was a big man with a bald head and a knotted face, he had a shotgun pointed towards the bowl of the tree.

Benton signalled him. Brisley nodded and began to move towards the Oak. All other eyes were on Benton, waiting for their own orders, but he only watched as his man stepped closer to their prey.

Brisley was no fool and only inched closer. His shotgun had been sawn down to ensure the maximum blast at close range. He wouldn't risk peering over the roots, he would simply level the twelve gauge at them and let both barrels go. Anything beneath the Oak would be torn to shreds. He pulled the barrel up and stepped closer. He could see a hand, it held on to a root, the hand was covered in blood.

'One of em must have been tapped,' he thought. 'Close enough now.'

As he presented the barrel forwards, careful not to lean over and become a target he felt the soil vibrate beneath his feet. Instinctively he looked down. The last thing he saw was a blur of movement near his boots and then...darkness.

Benton's mouth opened wide and he staggered back. Something had shot up from the ground and spiked Brisley's head like a stick through an Olive. His lieutenant hung limply, his arms loose by his sides, his head had been speared and blood poured from his mouth.

Suddenly the shaft of what Benton could only think was some kind of spear disappeared back into the soil and Brisley dropped onto his face.

'What the fuck?' Benton's thoughts went into free fall.

He heard a scream. The pitch was that of a woman, one of the acolytes he thought, as it came from the far side of the circle where the lesser ranked followers had been placed, as far away from him as possible. He looked and could see.

She gripped at what looked like a spear, the same thing that had pierced Brisley's head except this time it had come from the floor at an angle and punctured her stomach. He heard more shouts of pain around him. Before he could look to see where they had come from the spear retracted with lightning speed from the woman and she too dropped onto the ground.

'*Sorcery!*' he said quietly.

Somehow they had managed to perform a ritual of some kind. They had been too slow and now the Guardians had cast some spell.

'Fire! Fire!' he shouted as loud as he could and as he lifted his head to shout to the Mi-Go a spike of wood erupted from the soil and scraped his cheek as it jabbed the empty space where his face had been only a second before.

'Argh! He shouted and stumbled, almost tripping.

All about him the spears of wood were shooting from the ground and those who hadn't the wit to move were staked where they stood.

'*MOVE! MOVE AND FIRE,*' he ordered and made sure to zigzag as he backed away.

'DO SOMETHING YOU FUCK!' he called up to the Mi-Go.

It remained stationary but Benton could see that its protective bubble had darkened a little. It had taken the precaution of hardening the energy against any possible attack.

'YOU FUCK!' he screamed.

Shots were still being shot towards the tree but now that the followers were moving they were even more erratic. Benton saw two of his own people struck by wayward bullets.

'CLOSE IN' he waved them forwards while he continued to back away. 'GET CLOSER, SHOOT *THEM* NOT EACH OTHER YOU FUCKING MORONS.'

Bullets continued to splinter the Oak and its roots but none were finding their way to the men who hid within the tangle. Benton looked up to the Mi-Go again but couldn't see it. He snapped his head around, scanning the sky, there was no sign of it.

'Where'd you go? Where'd you go you fucking insect.' Benton said.

A moment later it appeared in front of him. Benton froze, despite his fear of the deadly spears from the soil. The surface of the energy bubble was inches from his face and the Mi-Go floated within it about six inches of the ground. The eyeless brain-like mass that he assumed was its head seemed to stare at him with indifference.

Letters began to appear on the surface of the bubble forming words. 'WE WILL FINISH THIS,' they read.

Benton blinked. The Mi-Go continued to tap upon its tablet. 'WE WILL REQUIRE FOUR OFFERINGS,' appeared across the surface replacing the other letters, which seemed to fade into the swirling colours of the energy shield.

Benton wasn't sure what the thing meant at first but then realisation dawned on him.

'Anyone, take anyone,' he said keen to increase his speed.

The Mi-Go stopped tapping and lifted back into the air.

Benton turned his attention back to the Oak and at that moment saw a hand finally appear over the roots. In it was grasped a pistol. Shots began to fire out at his followers and they paused in their move towards the tree.

'Damn it! Keep moving. He can't see a fucking thing and if you stop you'll…' before he could finish a root shot out from the ground and took another of his men in the chest.

'*MOOOOVE!*' Benton bawled and made sure to follow his own advice.

There was a cry from above him but this time it wasn't one of pain. Byakhee circled above, four of them. He watched as they swooped down as one and plucked four of his followers up like hawks snatching mice. He kept moving, as randomly as possible around the tree and followed their progress away from the clearing and away over the trees. The Mi-Go trailed behind.

He was back on his own. Whatever the alien thing was doing he was still in control here. So long as his people moved whatever magic the Guardians were using to make the spears was ineffective. The shots from the tree were just to warn his people away, as useless as the ones being fired towards shooter. Benton began to relax a little. If this was the best the Guardians could do he would have them.

He felt embarrassed now. He had shown his arse to the Mi-Go in a moment of panic and he knew he would pay for that unless he could redeem himself. He had to take them alive. His orders had been to kill them and only if absolutely without risk to take any one of them alive, but not all, that had been firmly stated, no more than one was to live.

'HOLD YOUR FIRE. KEEP MOVING' he shouted.

Shots continued to ring out across the clearing.

'HOLD YOUR FIRE I SAID.' As he shouted this he saw the top of the skull of a bearded man, Carpenter he thought his name might be, lift a little and a spray of blood burst into the air.

Benton realised that it wasn't his people, or the Guardians that were firing.

***

Once the shooting began Crowley and Reed no longer required the streaking lights to guide them. They ran as fast as the thick foliage and twilight would allow them too.

'Ahead!' Reed called back to Crowley who was struggling to get through Ferns that the Sergeant had somehow cleared with ease.

'Yes, thank you Sergeant. I'm quite aware of where the enormous volume of gunfire is coming from.' Crowley growled.

'Hurry man.' Reed insisted.

Crowley broke through the ferns and continued after Reed who had already resumed his journey. When he caught up the Sergeant was stood at the treeline.

Crowley could see that the whole of the clearing was manned, there were easily twenty or more of the cultists, possibly more than thirty. All were armed and all pointing their weapons towards an enormous Oak tree at the centre of a well-cleared area.

'Do you see them? Crowley asked quietly.

'No. They must be behind the tree.'

Crowley observed the Oak closely and then shook his head. 'Not behind it. There's people all around, they are *in* it.' He took a hold of Reeds arm and pointed with his free hand. 'Look at the roots. There's a kind of drop at its base, they must be hiding amongst them, using them for cover.'

Reed nodded. 'What do we do? We can't take them all.'

Crowley chewed his lip as he thought. He peered across the clearing to see if Lafferty or Bryson was visible but he could only just about make out the line of trees and vegetation.

'There'll be a leader, a High Priest. For something like this they wouldn't just send some clown.' Crowley scanned the circle of followers, looking for the one who was running the show.

'Crowley, look.' Reed pointed into the sky over the clearing. The Mi-Go floated there again, the Moon over its shoulder.

Suddenly the firing recommenced and Crowley and Reed took a step back. There were men a mere six feet in front of them but for the moment they could only watch as shots were unloaded into the centre of the clearing.

After what seemed like a minute or so to Crowley but he understood was more likely seconds the men in front ceased firing and took a few steps forward. Both he and Reed stepped back to their position, keeping trees and foliage in front of them in case keen eyes looked their way.

'They are closing in.' Reed said. 'We need to do *something*.'

'Getting ourselves murdered isn't *something* Sergeant, it's nothing. Doing nothing right now? That's something. Just keep it calm and let me think OK?'

Reed puffed but acquiesced.

It was practically silent for a while, certainly compared to the violent racket of the gunfire, and from the still air came a shout.

'YOU MUST *NOT* DO IT!'

Reed looked at Crowley, his eyes asked the question.

'Yes, I think it's one of them.' Crowley said, 'alright we…wait and see.'

He could see one of the men walking forward, towards the tree. He held a shotgun, shortened at the barrel in his hands.

'Fuck.' Crowley said.

Reed pulled out his pistol and raised it. He gripped it with both hands.

'Can you hit him from here?' Crowley asked.

'I don't know.' Reed replied.

'If you miss they will know we are here.' Crowley said nervously.

'I have to try.' Reed said sharply.

'I'm not sure you do.'

'Shut it Crowley.' Reed hissed.

'Even if you hit him we're fucked.' Crowley continued. 'It will be like a bullet festival over here when those pricks catch on.'

Reed tuned Crowley out and focused on his aim. It would be a difficult shot in daylight, in the twilight of the clearing he knew it was almost impossible, but he could see the man's bald head reflecting the moons silver light and hoped that it would help him to guide the shot.

He took a breath and then slowly exhaled out as the man approached the Oak. Crowley, in sympathy, held his breath and stared.

Their jaws dropped as something shot from the earth and staked the man's head where he stood.

'Well…' Crowley said in a whisper. 'I didn't see that coming.'

Suddenly all hell broke loose in the clearing.

A mans voice shouted above screams of pain 'FIRE! FIRE!'

Reed and Crowley watched as the lightning fast stakes shot up at the cultists, spiking any that were standing still.

'What's happening?' Reed said in bewilderment and horror.

'I don't know.' Crowley said. He looked towards the Oak to see if the Guardians had emerged from their foxhole but the voice in the clearing ordered the panicked followers to 'MOVE AND FIRE.'

As more shots splintered the Oak something tugged at Crowley's thoughts. He fancied that the branches of the tree moved and not in any natural way. It was as though the branches were flexing, pointing and waving…in anger. His intellect began to perform cartwheels of conjecture across the lawn of his reason. He looked at the spears of wood that were shooting up from the ground.

'I think it's the tree.' he said, cautiously.

'What?' Reed exclaimed. 'The tree?'

'Yeah. Its uhm...' He thought for a moment. His intellect was taking a bow and was therefore too busy to retrieve this salient piece of information at the moment. 'There's a word for it...I don't recall, but yeah, I think it's the tree. It's pissed off.'

Reed lowered his gun. Only just realising that he was pointing at a man who was already on the floor and quite dead.

'A killer tree Crowley?

Crowley shrugged. 'I've seen worse.'

Reed said nothing. For once he had no doubt that Crowley was telling the truth.

A few shots came from the area of the tree. Crowley and Reed looked towards it but whoever had fired couldn't be seen.

'Warning shots.' Reed said. 'The Guardians are trying to keep them scared.'

'Yes,' Crowley agreed. 'One of those chaps running around is the man you want to shoot, the one giving the orders. Can you see him?'

Reed shook his head. 'No. It's like a merry go round of madmen in there.'

'*A carousel of cunts more like,*' Crowley thought.

A shot whizzed over their heads and cracked as it impacted into a tree.

'You know what, I'm going to get a little lower. These fellows aren't exactly Buffalo Bill.' Crowley said as he began to crouch.

Reed followed suit when he saw one of the followers fall to his knees, apparently shot in the chest by one of his colleagues across the clearing.

***

The Oak could see that its punishment for the disrespectful abuse laid upon had not been sufficient. It had been prepared to unleash something mighty upon the humans but had been stayed by one of them. One of the creatures that nestled in its roots had called to it, begged it not to use the powerful summons, but it had not demanded it be done, it had not disregarded the mighty Oak's presence and power. This was good, this was proper.

There was a conflict at hand here, those in its protective roots were sought after by those who used their fire weapons to splinter the Oak's physical form. For centuries it had remained silent, passive to those who came to it and performed their rites without acknowledging its being. Now they would pay for this indignity.

It withdrew its roots, many slick with the blood of the ones it had pierced. It began to push them out, over the two humans, crossing, meshing them, to form a wall of natural wood, it then infused them with essence, as it did its whole form. The bullets began to bounce off it.

'Penny! The roots!' Pevensy gasped.

'It's protecting us.' Penhaligon shrank back as the lattice of twisting roots rose over them.

Fewer shots than before made their way at them but this time those that did whizzed away with a *twannnnng* as they ricocheted.

'Incredible.' Pevensy said.

'Indeed.' Penhaligon replied. He gripped a root near his side and said clearly, 'Thank you Great Tree, you honour us with your mercy.'

'What do we do now?' Pevensy whispered. They were still surrounded and he couldn't be sure how long the Oak would keep them safe. It had hardened itself against bullets but fire would still burn it, he was sure of this.

'I can reach out.' Penhaligon said.

Pevensy suspected that his friends voice was getting a little shaky. '*Blood loss,*' he thought. '*Got to get him out of here.*'

'If Crowley or the others are still around I may be able to contact them, get them to leave.' Penhaligon said, wincing as he pressed at his side. 'I think that Reed or Lafferty… one of those might be able to receive me. I think the boy?'

Pevensy nodded. 'Yes, young Lafferty. Crowley has been instructing him and he certainly has some ability. If Reed is here it's unlikely he is going to be open to any kind of psychic contact, his willpower is considerable.'

He took Penhaligon's free hand. 'Do it Penny,' he said, 'our combined energy should be enough.'

Penhaligon closed his hand and tightened his grip upon Pevensy. Essence flowed strongly through them both and for a moment they could each feel the ancient Oak observing them as their thoughts slipped into the Essence.

They found Lafferty with ease. He was close, very close. This worried Pevensy, if it was so easy for them to locate the boy then….

'Lafferty!' Penhaligon called to him, 'Lafferty, I am a friend. I am Penhaligon, you must leave now, if the others are with you make them leave. You have to get away from here while you can.'

There was no response but Penhaligon was sure that Lafferty had heard him.

'*I don't think he's accepting it, he doesn't trust his thoughts.*' He communicated to Pevensy.

Pevensy concurred. '*Tell him something he knows that only a friend could know...tell him about Benny.*'

Penhaligon focused again, this time he presented an image to Lafferty. The Bulldog sat looking up at him with its indecipherable expression but one that was usually interpreted as hungry.

'*Lafferty, Benny was my dog originally. I gave him to Crowley to help with the True Demon you fought. He gets terrible wind if you let him eat bacon.*'

It was true. Benny loved Bacon and would howl all morning if he caught a whiff of it being cooked. Placating him by feeding him a few rashers would result in an entire morning of noxious vapours permeating the house and was now avoided.

Penhaligon sensed that this had got through to the lad. Lafferty's thoughts coalesced in the Essence and came through to Penhaligon strong and loud as though Lafferty were talking while deaf.

He was inexperienced and unsure with his talent and so expended more energy than he needed too.

'WE WILL SAVE YOU!' he said.

'NO!' Penhaligon shouted back. '*RUN!*'

'WE WILL SAVE YOU!' Lafferty replied.

The link collapsed. Penhaligon could feel the lad's aura step away from the Essence.

At that point Lafferty stepped out from the trees and into the clearing, and began to fire.

'There they are!' Crowley shouted into Reeds ear.

'I just see Lafferty.' Reed rose and cocked his pistol.

Crowley could see that he was right. Lafferty had emerged from the tree and begun to fire at the circling followers. His first couple of shots had been deadly accurate.

'Perhaps Bryson is following. He hurt his foot so...,' Crowley said unconvincingly.

'Perhaps.' Reed replied.

His face was dark, his eyes hard as steel as they stared through the clearing. Crowley could almost feel the violence emanating from the Sergeants thoughts. Reed raised his pistol to eye level, arm outstretched, he stepped into the clearing like Lafferty had done and began to fire into the mob.

'Oh fucking hell.' Crowley said as he watched the huge man stride into the maelstrom. He readied his own revolver and stepped out behind him but held on to his shots.

He looked about for the person in charge. Rather than trying to reduce the numbers of their enemy and win through attrition, and they had a lot more to lose then his own little group, Crowley sought out the High Priest.

'*Pop the leader and they will crumble*' the idea had been delivered adroitly by Crowley's frantic instinct for self-preservation.

But it was difficult here. Usually the big nobs had fancy cloaks or ridiculous looking hats. You could spot them from a mile off. He had once had a nasty encounter with a cult whose High Priest wore ceremonial headgear which looked like a foot tall vagina. He had suffered from nightmares in which giant lady parts had chased him for days afterwards.

He scanned the cultists as they ran, fearful of the spears that shot from the floor but still firing as best they could at the men beneath the tree. It was chaos. Reeds pistol boomed ahead of him as he kept a slow but determined pace towards the Oak.

Cultists fell to Reed and Lafferty's expert shooting while others tripped over their fallen comrades in their panic and went sprawling into the dirt. Those that didn't get up quickly were staked where they lay.

Crowley also saw some of the Oak's roots had given the Guardians cover which now wholly enclosed them.

'*Interesting*' he thought, '*the Oak is protecting them?*'

As he looked away from the tree he finally saw his man. As the others ran, this one walked, quickly but not with a sense of panic. This particular fellow was *moving* not running. He barked out orders, pointed with his pistol at the base of the tree. He berated the men and women as they ran past him.

Crowley raised his gun. He had his man and this one wasn't sporting a huge vagina.

ButJust as he was about to fire something caught his eye. It was the Mi-Go. It had returned and was floating up above the clearing. Its energy bubble was clearly visible, no doubt engaged to protect it from the wild shots of the cultists. Its eyeless, brain-tissue head looked down as precise claw tips tapped at its strange little tablet.

Crowley's spine tingled and his neck twitched, a reflex he couldn't control and it moved his arm a fraction just as he fired. His shot had been close, so close in fact that it caught Benton's ear and took a piece of it with it to the far side of the clearing. Benton shook his head, as though bothered by some insect, and then bent his knees as the pain registered and his hands clutched at his wounded and bloody skin.

'Tits!' Crowley cursed.

Then he heard the noise. The sound, above the boom of guns and the screams of men and women, of trees as they cracked in the forest and thumped onto the floor, forced aside by something huge and unstoppable.

Crowley allowed his eyes to slip to the side and he saw as the thing burst into the clearing.

The battleground almost became silent. Gunfire from all parties ceased, the screams and moans stopped as every eye did as Crowley's had done and looked at the creature.

It was as vast as it was incomprehensible. It stood upon three legs each as wide as the trunk of the ancient Oak, thick hair, black and course covered them and its feet were cloven, akin to those of a goat. Its torso bulged above the legs and was pale in hue, the colour of rotting flesh and from it, appearing randomly across its bulk, insane glistening eyes and awful mouths filled with jagged teeth opened and snatched at the air. As the vile mouths appeared and disappeared, opened and closed on its body, fat worm-like tentacles lashed and writhed above it.

'Oh for fucks sake.' Crowley said with weary resignation.

As they came to their senses the cultists, those whose minds had not snapped at the sight of the cyclopean beast before them dropped to their knees, their fear of the murderous spikes forgotten.

'Ia! Ia!' they shouted in reverence and adulation.

Reed stared in horror at the thing as it stood, still and quiet after its dramatic entrance, as though taking in the scene before it. The tentacles moved sensuously about it and the mouths and eyes continued to appear upon its loathsome body.

'Ungodly.' Reed said quietly.

Crowley carefully stepped to his side.

'Actually it's very Godly,' he said, 'just not yours.'

A cultist rose from his knees. Crowley saw that it was his man, the High Priest, he could see blood spattered across the side of his face from his wounded ear

'*Almost had you, you lucky fucker,*' he thought.

He looked again to the thing, it was a Dark Young, a beast spawned from the vile God Shub-Niggurath. No doubt the floating, buzzing space-arsehole above them had summoned it somehow. How it could have done it so quickly was beyond Crowley's knowledge and he trembled a little at the thought of such power in the hands of something so completely alien.

'*This is why they exist,*' he looked towards the Oak, '*they are supposed to prevent this kind of thing.*'

Crowley wondered if this all proved that the Guardians were incapable of preventing the doom of mankind, they had all been played, but he had to admit, none had been suckered more than him.

As the cultists chanted 'Ia! Ia!' and as the Dark Young stood, threatening, yet unmoving Crowley realised that the men, defended but also trapped in the roots of the tree were actually doing something. The monster wasn't moving because *they* weren't letting it move.

Inside the woven cage Pevensy and Penhaligon had sensed the thing approaching as the connection with Lafferty had been lost, they conspired with the Oak to bar the Dark Young entry to the Trees appealing to its vanity.

'How dare these ingrates bring in this foul thing without your leave!' they had chided. 'Such disrespect!'

The Oak had agreed wholeheartedly and could see no other reason for the spawn of Shub-Niggurath, Black Goat of the Woods with a Thousand Young, to be here other than to tear at its bark and roots, to destroy it, that the humans may take the courteous ones it harboured. As one they used their energy to force it back against the treeline.

Benton came back to his senses fully. His temporary awe of the Dark Young had passed and he turned to face the man who had almost shot him in the face. He pointed towards Crowley and Reed.

'Kill them!' he screamed and began to move among the kneeling and supplicated cultists, pulling them to their feet.

'Enemies are among us! Kill them all!' He caught sight of Lafferty and pushed some of his people towards him.

'Take them down. Their blood will be nectar for our Lord!' Benton screamed.

Lafferty didn't run as the cultists began to move towards him. He coolly raised his pistol once more and began to fire at those closest and who posed the biggest threat. He couldn't shoot them all so any who were not carrying firearms he dodged or swung at with the butt of his gun knocking them senseless. His goal was to reach Crowley and Reed before the thing at the far side of the clearing attacked.

Reed, seeing Lafferty move, also started into the centre. The tree held the Guardians, it was the focus of all of this carnage so it was there they would meet. It would be where they made their last stand.

The cultists were moving again, following orders from Benton not to stand still in case the earth sent up fresh spikes to kill them where they stood. Gunshots were less frequent from them now, most had used up all of their rounds or otherwise lost their ammunition to the floor in the initial confusion.

Reed fired his own final shell into the stomach of a portly man whose face was flush with fanatical zeal as he ran awkwardly at him. The man clutched at his immense gut and fell to his knees, blood poured over his hands as he looked down at them. A second later he fell face down into the soil.

Reed continued on. As cultists came at him he struck them with his fists and feet, he towered above them and threw them about him like rag dolls.

Crowley deftly sidestepped those that came past Reed and delivered a few well-timed jabs of his own. He hadn't the sheer stopping power of the Sergeant but he was fast and accurate. The problem wasn't the martial skill of the attackers, there were simply too many and the cultists began to encircle them.

As their guns had run out of ammunition some had picked up stones and lengths of wood, which they used to bash at Reed seeing him as the biggest threat.

Crowley held his breath as one of the mob charged forward with a long, nasty looking length of wood, possibly a bough blown away from the Oak. The cultist crashed it down across Reeds neck. The big man staggered under the blow.

'Fuck.' Crowley thought. '*Reeds down.*'

But Reed shook his head and lunged forwards, dislodging two other cultists who were trying to hold his arms. He threw a punch forwards with incredible force striking the man square in the face. Crowley was convinced that he heard the CRACK of the cultists skull as it fractured from the impact. He dropped dead at Reeds feet.

The Sergeant was frenzied now. He spun and his arms flailed out knocking aside two others who had come towards him. He lifted one of them bodily from the floor and threw him onto the other. As they tried to rise Reeds boot connected with both of their heads in a sweeping roundhouse and they immediately sank back to the floor.

'REED! Get a grip man.' Crowley shouted as he pushed away a screaming woman who tried to rake her nails across his eyes, but Reed paid him no attention. He continued to press towards the Oak taking down every cultist that attempted to block his way. Crowley followed him, stepping over unconscious and bloodied bodies whilst lashing out at any that found their way around the Sergeant.

Finally they were there. The Oak loomed over them and Crowley could just about make out Penhaligon and Pevensy inside the cradle of roots. Lafferty came to them. He had left his own trail of injured cultists behind him and both he and Reed were spattered with blood from wounds of their own and their attackers.

'Nigel.' Reed said, as though he didn't quite believe it was him.

'Sergeant.' Lafferty replied breathlessly.

'Where's the guv?' Reed asked urgently. 'Is he alright?'

'Yes,' Lafferty nodded, 'but he couldn't walk, had to stay behind.'

Reed breathed a sigh of relief and Crowley watched as the big mans shoulders visibly sagged. He was spent, he was sure. He had exhausted all of his energy to get them to this place.

'I'm fucking fine. Thanks for asking.' Crowley said bitterly. He could scarcely believe the smile that lit up Lafferty's face amongst the blood and reddening swelling.

'I knew you would be alright Mr C.' Lafferty laughed a little. 'You've got the devil on your side.'

Crowley was speechless at first, his mouth hung open at this slanderous comment, but then a smile began to form, and from the very deep and hidden depths of Crowley's soul a laugh travelled over seldom seen territory and out and he chuckled at himself and his outrageous fortune.

'Yes lad...I sometimes think that might be the case.' he said.

It was then that the thing from the woods emitted a triumphant ululation. It had broken the barrier. The Guardians and the Oak could no longer hold it and it began to thunder forwards.

Reed straightened and stepped forward. Crowley gripped his arm, his hand barely holding the Sergeants building bicep.

'No Reed.' Crowley said, 'there's nothing you can do. Even you can't fight that thing.'

The tension in Reed's arm didn't drop. He didn't care if he couldn't beat it, he would still fight it.

As the Dark Young took enormous strides towards them it crushed under its cloven hooves any cultist too struck with terror to move, it's tentacles lashed out as though of their own mind and gripped and squeezed the life out the ones it plucked from where they stood. Mouths opened up on its torso to accept the limbs of its victims as they were torn apart by the terrible arms.

Benton understood that the creature had no care for him or his followers, it had been summoned to perform a task and that was the limit of its obligations. He stepped away from the monsters path, making sure that there were dumbstruck followers in front of him which would make more convenient targets.

From here he continued to direct those who still had their wits about them.

'Take the enemies down! Our Lord has provided!'

The cultists once again turned to Crowley, Reed and Lafferty. They were blood-crazed now, insane with the violence and the presence of the Dark Young. They would fight until the last man and woman.

'We are so fucked.' Crowley said and wondered where this devil that Lafferty had claimed watched out for him was right now.

Then something, that wasn't quite a devil but was also no angel, spoke to him. She called to him through the Essence, across time and space.

'*Perdurabo, prepare yourself. Bryson is coming. Hold fast,*' the voice of Aiwass said from a distance which Crowley could only imagine at.

He quickly looked around, *everyone* was coming. The cultists, the Dark Young, above Byakhee circled the clearing as the Mi-Go ceaselessly tapped at its pad, they were all coming towards him...where the fuck *was* Bryson?

They came from trees like streaks of grey and brown lightning. They leapt upon Benton's people and the Dark Young and tore at them. The cultists, only human after all were ripped apart with just few quick slashes of their claws. The Dark Young was made of stronger stuff, yet they hurt it.

The Werewolves leapt away as its lithe arms tried to grasp them, they sprang back and continued to rend its flesh. The Dark Young screamed in pain and fury as its myriad eyes were torn away when they popped up from its skin.

The new creatures darted around the clearing, Crowley couldn't count them but he was sure there were at least a dozen, and one of them...he screwed up his eyes and leaned forward as though it would telescope his vision...one of them was wearing what was left of a suit.

'Bryson?' Crowley said.

'WHERE?' Reed demanded and spun to face Crowley. The occultist said nothing, he could only point at the creature in the torn suit that ripped and tore at the Dark Young's frantically waving arms.

'Guv?' Reed said.

'It's Marga!' Lafferty said. 'It has to be.'

'But...the chief...' Reed said, unsure how to feel about what he was seeing.

'Lads. Right now this is our chance to get out of here...this is it. Those things are taking care of that thing, the Guardians are being baby-sat in a bullet proof tree and...'

'We're going nowhere Crowley.' Reed snarled. 'We stay here until it's done.'

'Fuck that.' Crowley snapped. He turned to walk away. He had partaken of his fill of this adventure now. The clearing had gone to hell in a hand basket and no one was paying attention to him. It was time to get back to London and spend a week off his tits. Minimum.

He felt Reeds colossal hand grab his shoulder and pull him back.

'You stay right *here* Crowley. We are all in this mess because of you.'

'Not a fucking chance.' Crowley bawled back at him. 'I didn't ask you to come and find me, in fact I explicitly forbade it,' he glanced at Lafferty. 'If you and your merry band of brothers hadn't decided to come waltzing into town in your size twelves none of this would have happened.'

'We saved your life!' Lafferty exclaimed.

'No you fucking didn't,' Crowley retorted. 'I'd saved my own bloody life hours before you lot even got off your train.' Crowley put his hands on his hips. 'In fact if I remember rightly I was the one who rescued you lot from blindly wandering around a burning fucking village. A fire, which incidentally, *YOU DOCILE BASTARDS STARTED.*'

Reed stepped up to Crowley, so close that their puffed out chests almost touched.

'I could beat you to a pulp Crowley.' Reed snarled.

'So what.' Crowley replied.

Reed blinked. Crowley wasn't even remotely scared of him or any beating he might receive. Reed could spot fear and intimidation in a man from a dozen yards. He couldn't understand it. If there was a man more likely to run from a fight on the planet, it was Crowley, he was about to do that right now in fact, yet...it wasn't through fear.

'Are we done?' Crowley said.

'We're done.' Reed said. 'Fuck you Crowley.'

'Yeah, yeah.' Crowley replied dismissively. He peered around Reed to Lafferty, 'I know you won't but it feels wrong not to ask, are you coming with me?'

'I can't Mr C. I'm a...'

'Copper first. Yes, I thought as much. Fair enough, don't say I didn't try.'

Crowley turned away and began to walk towards the treeline. As he neared it a figure darted past him, a werewolf charging after a cultist who was running for dear life. Crowley looked away when he saw the beast catch up with its helpless prey. He didn't need to see any more bones and blood today, but as he turned his attention back to his destination, he was barged to the ground as Benton slammed into him. They both tumbled onto the floor.

Benton stood slowly, his chest hurt but he quickly recovered his wits. One of the things, the snarling, wolf things had almost got to him. Fortunately one of his men had managed to intervene, it had cost the man his head as the thing tore it from his neck but rather a devotee than a High Priest.

The facts were now that their creature had been brought to its knees, the other wolf monsters swarmed over it. The Mi-Go was gone. It seemed that it knew when the game was up but Benton didn't agree with this at all. The Dark Young had managed to break free of whatever magic the Guardians were using to hold it back and that meant they had been defeated, that meant that they were still weak, quite possibly dead.

He had begun to run towards the Oak. He would use his Mi-Go gifted sword, blessed with over a hundred rituals to carve away the Oaks protective roots. He would gut the Guardians where they lay, alive or dead. All he had to do was get past the policemen and the occultist. His remaining men would keep them busy, the wolf-things wouldn't dare leave the Dark Young until it dissolved into the floor.

He hadn't noticed Crowley break away from the group and as his attention had been taken away by a wolf-thing speeding past him as had Crowley, the collision had occurred. It had been a hard impact. Crowley seemed to have the constitution of a brick wall and Benton was convinced that he had fractured a rib when his chest hit the occultist's shoulder which would explain the pain he felt as he rose.

Crowley rolled back with surprising agility and was up and on his feet quickly. He stared with malevolence at the man who had brought him down.

'You.' Crowley grunted.

'Ha. The infamous Aleister Crowley.' Benton replied.

The Dark Young screamed once again, this time its cry was almost deafening and both Benton and Crowley winced. Crowley risked a look towards it. He could see Reed striding towards it. In his hand he held a long sword not unlike the one that Benton was wielding. He had no doubt that Reed was going to stick it straight into the Dark Young's repulsive torso and try to carve out anything that might resemble a heart.

'You think you have won don't you Crowley?' Benton said.

'Yes, and that's because I *have* won.' Crowley replied with an air of smugness that burned at Benton.

'Your big bad monster is going to be a puddle of black ooze when that fellow guts it, your large brained friend that was floating about in his fart bubble has fucked off, and all of your friends are probably going to be dog food shortly. So, yes I'm thinking I've won.'

'Hah! Pitiful.' Benton scowled. 'You have no idea of what is coming Crowley. You cannot even imagine the power the Great Old ones will bring to this war. You think you saved the Guardians? They are dead or at least two of them are which means they are broken. London is ours.'

Crowley didn't allow his surprise to show but realised how the creature had broken through the barrier, the Guardians must have died and the ritual ended.

It was a shame. He had no problem with them. He knew that they were good, selfless people who only wanted to protect humanity. He knew that they had high hopes for Bryson, Reed and Lafferty, he had no problem with that either, but they shouldn't have come after him. He could look after himself. None of this was his fault.

'I don't give a fuck.' Crowley replied. 'I really don't.'

Benton nodded. 'Well, that may be so Crowley but I am certain that when my masters return, when the power that was once theirs comes back to this world, then you will have something to think about. Although of course, you won't actually be around for that.'

Benton raised his sword and swept it in front of him with a certain deftness that told Crowley that the man knew how to hand a blade like that. This was not so good. He wasn't bad in a fight, a strong and agile man for his age and with a fast and unexpected left jab, but when faced with a man who knew how to handle a blade he liked to be armed with a shotgun, or pistol or a policeman armed with both. As Benton took a step forward Crowley eased back a little.

Crowley had no doubt that Reed was busy getting his anger out of his system against the Dark Young so he could only hope that Lafferty had watched him, with eyes full of sorrow, as he had stormed off, but Crowley knew, deep in the heart of him that the lad would have immediately sprung to the aid of the Guardians. Fat chance he was being observed as he kept this prick waffling.

And what the *hell* had happened to Bryson. He was a Werewolf? Since when had that been a thing? Life was certainly full of surprises. Crowley shuffled back as Benton took another step nearer.

The High Priests life was over anyway, both men knew this. A catastrophe of this magnitude wouldn't be tolerated by his peers, but taking Crowley down might just save him from something worse than death.

Another step. Crowley backed away again. Any moment now Benton was going to perform some bullshit oriental move on him and that blade was going to cause him some real pain and he was struggling to think his way out of this. If he turned to run he would get it in the back, if he tried to move to the side Benton would slice his front.

'The Great Beast.' Benton mocked. 'Crowley, the wickedest man alive.' The High Priest laughed and drew his sword up, preparing to strike. 'Pathetic.'

Something inside Crowley snapped. He had been about to try and edge back just a little more. To anticipate the fall or sweep of the blade and to counter the attack. Instead he stood rigid and fixed Benton with a hateful stare.

'Why you pretentious little shit beetle.' Crowley growled. Benton stopped.

'You think you can talk to me as if I'm some tenth rate illusionist? A parlour magician with doves and playing cards?' Crowley stepped forwards, he jutted his chin out.

'I've crapped out things more evil than you after a midnight curry. You think you scare me? You half soaked sack of shit?'

At this Crowley reached up and tore at his shirt revealing his heavily tattooed chest. He pointed to a design that appeared to be half serpent, half eagle.

'See this you twat? I had go through a ritual cleansing that lasted five fucking months to have this burned into my skin. I spent a week with five pounds of assorted fruit stuffed up my arse just to pass through the first fucking week.'

He pulled up his right sleeve. 'See this?' he indicated another design, this one a star around which a pale blue band seemed to shimmer.

'Cut into me with the claw of a Hound of Tindalos. Know what one of those is? I'll bet you don't you craven fuckstick. It's a thing so fucking evil that if it sees you it will chase you across space and time until it gets you and rips you into pieces so small you could be buried in a chamber pot.'

Crowley took another step forward. He spat his words out at Benton who began to lean back a little. 'Can you guess which poor cunt they used as bait to get that particular trinket?' Crowley raised his eyebrows, daring Benton to answer.

'That's *right*.' he sneered. Perdurabo, The Great Beast, The Wickedest Man Alive, CROWLEY! And my name will go down in history you fucker, while you,' Crowley jabbed a finger sharply at Benton,' you will disappear into nothing, along with all the pathetic non-entities that we turned into worm food today. So you can take your fucking sword and stuff it up your arse, because that's how much I fucking care about you, about the Old Ones and about your floating brain on a stick friends. *Christ almighty*, you don't even have a giant vagina on your head.'

Benton's bottom lip quivered with outrage. His eyes were wide and the pupils shrunk to pencil dots. He raised the sword in both hands and prepared to cut the hateful, grinning bastard before him in two.

His body shivered slightly as the root shot from the earth beneath him, up through his groin and out of his neck, its tip slick with blood and with a length of his intestine caught upon it.

Crowley stepped back when he saw the spike appear out of Benton. The sword fell from the High Priests grip. He tried to utter words but was hampered as dark blood flowed out of his mouth. Slowly he began to slide down the spike created by the Essence infused root of the Oak.

As he slid down to the floor his eyes remained fixed on Crowley, staring with incredible surprise.

Crowley's gaze followed him, and as the angle of his body prevented Benton from dropping any further the occultist winked and tapped his chest.

'Aleister fucking Crowley mate,' he said, not questioning his miraculous good fortune.

It all came to Crowley as he stood over the impaled High Priest. The Mi-Go had fled, the Dark Young and cultists were dead, or fleeing into the woods pursued by Werewolves. Perhaps a Guardian or two had bought the farm but they could be replaced, Bryson, Lafferty, Reed? It was a safe bet. What it all came down to was that, as he had boldly stated to Benton, he had indeed won, he had done it once again and his future as the greatest living occultist was assured.

He smiled and would have laughed, heartily and happily were it not for hearing his name being called from behind him.

'Crowleeeeeeeeeee,' the sound was a harsh, course whisper forced past unwilling lips.

Slowly, Crowley turned and saw Lafferty stood a few yards away, in his hand a revolver no doubt snatched up from one of the bodies that lay about his feet.

'Lafferty?' Crowley said.

A grin stretched across Lafferty's face, obscene and awful, as though his skin were being pushed into place by invisible fingers.

'Crowleeeeee,' Lafferty repeated in that same awful voice.

'Shit.' Crowley said. 'Mokoi.'

'Yessss Crowleeee,' came the dreadful reply and the Mokoi laughed a rasping, dry hoot of delight.

Crowley looked at the gate, he could just about make out its presence. Somehow the thing had found him, used some link to him or one of the others and then crawled through, finding Lafferty. They had all been so busy, so distracted, how could they have noticed? He could see that the roots had retracted from the cocoon keeping the Guardians safe, one of them, he recognised him as the General, Pevensy, stood with some difficulty. So at least one was still on this mortal coil.

Crowley held out his hand as though trying to stop traffic.

'Right, first off, before you do anything hasty let's talk.'

'*No talk Crowleee, only dieeee, die Crowley dieeeeeee.*' the Mokoi replied, then choked and jerked a little.

Crowley feared that its spasmodic twitches might make it accidentally pull the trigger, but it gave him hope. Clearly Lafferty hadn't been spirited away to some nightmare realm within his own mind just yet, he was fighting the thing.

'I can appreciate that, I really can.' Crowley said hurriedly, 'but just wait, we had a deal remember.'

'*No deal!*' the thing barked, '*Crowley broke deal, Mokoi take Crowleee, Take his soul!*'

Crowley dropped his hand and gave the Mokoi a conciliatory look.

'Yes well, there may be a bit of a queue for that I'm afraid.'

***

Reed took a step back from the Dark Young. He had carved into it almost with a butcher's expertise and the thing's innards seeped around his heels, smoking with putrid fumes. It was dissolving. Gradually reducing itself to nothing more than a vile liquid that in turn began to boil and vaporise, the stench almost overpowered him.

The Werewolves had stopped their onslaught once the thing had become still and watched with interest as Reed had gone about his bloody work. Two of them returned to their human form, both men, both utterly naked but for all intents and purposes just two ordinary fellows caked in blood and grime. It happened in an instant and was unnoticed by the Sergeant such was his focus.

Bryson watched and waited. The others were safe, he would allow Reed his moment of revenge, he had earned it. He knew that he then had some explaining to do. Marga was at his side, unlike him she, like her friends, was once again stark naked and Bryson slipped off what remained of his jacket and gave it to her.

'*For the sake of the lad,*' he thought.

After a minute or so, once Reed's mighty arms relaxed at his sides and he stood within nothing more than a decomposing mess. Bryson called calmly called his name and placed his hand upon his shoulder.

'Reed.'

The sergeant turned and took in all of Bryson. The inspector was covered in blood, head to foot, a ragged shirt hung about him, his trousers hung open at the fly, torn to shreds below the knee.

'Are you a…?' Reed asked.

Bryson shook his head. 'No,' he said emphatically.

Marga stepped to him and placed a delicate hand onto his chest.

'It was temporary,' she said, 'something we,' she indicated the strange wolf creatures and bloodied humans that stood about them, 'could do to help both him and you.'

'How?' Reed said, 'how is that possible?'

'Blood,' Marga said plainly, speaking for Bryson as he seemed to have become overwhelmed by the situation now that his frenzy had abated.

'We gave him our blood. While it is in his system he ha strength, he has our…ability.' Marga said. 'His body will fight now and remove it. There will be no lasting effect.'

Reed took this in and accepted it, as there was really little more he could do. He had many other questions but as he made to speak to Bryson he saw Crowley near the Oak, and Lafferty levelling a pistol at him.

'Something's going on,' he said.

Bryson and Marga turned to see what Reed had seen.

'Good Lord!' Bryson said. 'Is Lafferty going to kill Crowley? What's happened?'

'I have absolutely no idea.' Reed began to run, Bryson immediately followed.

'Lafferty!' Reed shouted. 'What are you doing?'

'Drop the gun Lafferty!' Bryson bellowed, speaking and shouting felt strange to him after the shift from wolf to man but he had no time to consider it.

***

Crowley felt beads of sweat pouring from his brow. This was worse than when facing the High Priest. At least he had hated Benton. Dying to an enemy was fine, not particularly the outcome he ever wished for but far better than dying to someone he actually liked.

'*Aiwass, can you hear me? Can you help?*' he cast his thoughts into the Essence as best he could but he was useless at it, he could receive the projections of those who were strong but without his talismans, his totems and effigy's, without circles and drugs, lots of drugs, he was practically incapable of touching the realm that drove him to mind bogglingly these dangerous encounters.

Yet, while Aiwass was in no position to hear or help Crowley there was another Guardian close to hand.

'*He's going to kill you Crowley,*' the voice belonged to Penhaligon. '*I can't stop it. The Mokoi has him in its grip, too strong for me to loosen, too fast for anyone to stop it.*'

'*Bullshit*' Crowley projected his angry thoughts towards the source of the voice. '*How can a Guardian not be able to help?*'

'*Because I'm dead you fool.*' Penhaligon replied.

'*Oh…*' Crowley replied surprised. '*Sorry. My condolences.*'

'*Pevensy is too weak to aid you, your friends can do nothing and nor would they, they will not risk hurting Lafferty.*'

'*But they will risk hurting me of course…*'

'*Naturally.*' Penhaligon replied.

Crowley mentally scoffed. '*Naturally. Twats.*'

'*Help me save him Crowley. The Mokoi will tear Nigel's mind apart. Help me save him.*'

'*Save him, but not me.*'

'*I've told you, there is nothing I can do, you are going to die, but you can save the boy.*' Penhaligon began to form as an outline in Crowley's vision. He knew that only he could see him.

'*You have to take him through the gate Crowley, grab the boy and jump into the Gate. I'll hold him back, keep him anchored here in this reality, the Mokoi with have no aid and will be dragged in by you.*' Penhaligon had begun to sound clearer to Crowley, he was using his energy to create an almost physical form.

'*I'm really struggling to see what's in this for me.*' Crowley replied and heard his own voice starting to sound desperate.

'*You will save the life and hopefully the sanity of the boy, isn't that enough Crowley?*' Penhaligon spoke quite clearly now. Crowley could see a ghost like image of the Guardian at the side of Lafferty.

'*Do it Crowley. All your life you have done whatever you felt like doing, that has been the whole of the law to you. Be more than you have ever been for just this once man. Make someone else's life more important than your own.*'

Crowley let out a deep breath, his shoulders dropped and he looked to his right. He could see Reed, thundering towards them like some Swiftian giant. Inspector Bryson followed, he looked as though he had been through a shredder, but at least he didn't look like something that worried sheep. The girl was with them, the attractive red-head whose rather lovely legs were on full display, again.

Crowley looked back to Lafferty. The Mokoi was relishing its moment but he knew that it wasn't going to let anything get in the way of it killing him. Crowley wanted to go out with one last line, one final statement that he would be remembered by for all time in books and lectures.

But his wit and wisdom appeared to have dried up and instead he charged at the Mokoi. With the aid of Lafferty's gift for accurate shooting, the vengeful creature of the Shadow and Void delivered three accurate shots to Crowley's stomach and laughed.

The pain as the bullets entered his body almost caused Crowley to drop but his momentum kept him going just far enough to wrap his arms around Lafferty and hug him tightly. He had to spin, enough to make them face the entrance of the gate. The Mokoi wriggled, trying to free itself from Crowley's bear-hug but it was impossible. The occultist held him tight despite the crucifying pain in his abdomen.

With one final heave Crowley hurled them both towards the invisible portal. At this, Penhaligon used the last of his own power to hold Lafferty firmly in this world. As Crowley and the dark energy that allowed the Mokoi to exist on Earth passed into the gate Lafferty remained behind and collapsed to the floor.

Reed, Bryson and Marga reached Lafferty only moments after Crowley had vanished into the Gate.

Pevensy stumbled towards them. 'Move him, quickly. Move him away from the Gate,' he said.

Without hesitating to question the old man Reed and Bryson lifted Lafferty and ran with him towards the edge of the clearing.

Pevensy faced the Gate, sank to his knees and raised his arms high.

'Oh great and wise Oak, ancient Guardian of the forest, you have tolerated our impositions with grace, and shown mercy for to those who respect your valuable aid. I beseech you now to close this portal that you graciously opened at our request.'

As the Oak was the only thing in the forest whose ego might possibly match Crowley's it had to be handled carefully. Just like the occultist. Penhaligon was prepared to kiss its bark if required.

There was a shimmer in front of the Oak, as though a wave of heat had passed by, and abruptly, the gate was gone.

The Guardian's head dropped and he closed his tear filled eyes.

'It's over,' he said quietly, 'for now.'

The End

Epilogue

Kensington 2015

Terry woke from a deep sleep to the sound of both of his dogs, Freddy and Bazzer howling and barking with incredible volume.

They slept in his room, and although he wouldn't allow them to sleep on his bed he was sure they stealthily crept up and on to it when he was asleep. Labradors could be sneaky bastards. He kept the door to his bedroom open in case either animal wanted a drink of water in the night and so the heavy pounding upon the front door of his pub sounded clearly up the stairs.

'Shut it lads.' Terry shouted at the dogs. They did tone down the volume but still let out the odd warning bark to let him know that they were still on the case.

He looked at his alarm. Its bright green digital readout told him it was 2:46am.

'Who the bloody ell....'

He climbed out of bed, climbed into his jeans and pressed his feet into his slippers. Barry rushed to him and jumped up, pressing his paws against Terry's stomach.

'All right boy, alright.'

He almost opened the window to lean out and see who was knocking but remembered that since he had the porch built over the entrance to the pub he couldn't see who was down there anymore.

He grabbed his keys from the table and made his way downstairs. The pounding continued.

'ALRIGHT MATE. COMING.' Terry bawled as he made his way through the bar lounge area and to the door. 'Christ almighty... middle of the fucking night... no bloody rest,' he muttered along with other clichés concerning inconvenience.

He wasn't concerned at someone knocking at this late hour. He was a big bloke and handy with it. Eight years spent in the army and four years spent married to a woman who was possibly Satan's sister had hardened him, besides the whole place was on a multi-CCTV system, and he had a hefty snooker cue positioned carefully by the side of the door.

He blinked as he turned on the lights and cleared the sleep from his eyes. Barry and Freddy pattered around him, excited and a little bit scared.

He had been woken early by the police a few weeks ago. A car had skidded on a part of the road nearby that was slick with oil from a leaking vehicle. They wanted some tea for an old dear who was a passenger and knew that Terry was always happy to help out with this kind of thing. It was probably something similar tonight was what he was thinking as he twisted his key in the lock and unbolted the door.

His eyes widened as he opened it and before him, supporting himself with one arm on the doorframe and the other hand, that had been knocking on his door, holding his stomach, was a man he suddenly remembered.

'Hello Terry,' the man said. His voice sounded frail. Terry could see that blood was pooling at his feet, the hand that held his stomach was slick with it.

It was the same man. The exact same man that had knocked on his door three years ago wearing only a dressing gown and slippers.

'I know this is a bit of an imposition but I don't suppose you could get me to a hospital could you?' the man said.

He then tried to smile pleasantly but Terry could only think that in the weak light and shadows offered by the porch that it was more like the grin of a shark.

'Bloody ell... its Mr... Cowley, innit?'

'Crowley. My name is Crowley... How's it going Terry, how are you, how's it been? I see you've had some work done on the place. What nice doggies... could you get me a fucking ambulance please?'

Terry stared, unsure what to do until the man's eyes caught his in full and he felt compelled to get on with doing exactly what he had suggested.

'Uh... my phones on charge upstairs. I'll need to get it.'

'Well...off you go then.'

'Right... yes, uh... stay there... NO... er... sit, you need to sit, or lie down?

'I'll stay here Terry. Get your phone.'

'Right.' Terry replied. He turned and ran towards the stairs. Freddy chased after him while Barry sat and stared quizzically at Crowley. Crowley stared back at him.

'You know what, with the day I've been having I wouldn't be surprised if you suddenly turned into a policeman,' Crowley said.

Barry tilted his head and sniffed.

Crowley felt very weak and had to fight off the urge to close his eyes. He knew that if he did that he would sleep, and if he slept, he may never wake up. The thought occurred to him that it might not be such a bad thing, but his self-preservation would have none of it. It shook him by his psychological shoulders and slapped him across his psyche.

Terry reappeared. He already had the phone clamped to his ear and was talking to an emergency services operator.

'...some kind of stomach wound,' he said as he came towards Crowley, 'I dunno, in his sixties I think.'

'I'm fifty-five you twat,' Crowley snapped.

'Er... fifties,' Terry said. He nodded. 'Right... OK,' he said and brought the phone down from his ear.

'An ambulance is on its way. Shouldn't be long.'

Crowley let out a long breath. His stomach was on fire but the stabbing pains seemed to have eased. He wasn't sure if this was a good thing or bad but he was thankful for the respite at least.

'What happened Mr Crowley? Have you been attacked?' Terry asked, and the thought made him look beyond Crowley in case any possible assailants were still out there.

'You could say that,' Crowley replied. 'Look, I need you to do something for me. When they come and take me away I need you to make a call.'

'Uhm, yes of course. Your wife?'

'Hardly,' Crowley replied. 'Get a pen and paper.'

'Right,' Terry turned again and went to the bar. He leaned over it and picked up a pen from the side of the cash register and a receipt book. He returned to Crowley and prepared to write.

'I want you to call the British Museum...'

'The British Museum?'

'Look, I'm dying, if it doesn't sound like I'm stuttering then assume that what you hear is correct, alright?'

Terry nodded and said nothing.

'Call the Museum and ask for the Curator, but make sure you mention that there has been a problem with Perdurabo's membership to the *Algernon Braithwaite Memorial Society*, that's very important. Do you have that?'

'How do you spell...?'

'P...E...R...D...U...R...A...B...O,' Crowley drilled out the letters.

'Right...' Terry scribbled this down and then looked back to Crowley.

What does it mean?

'It means *I will endure.*'

'Oh...' Terry replied.

He could see a flashing light in the distance. 'They are coming Mr Crowley, won't be long now.'

'Good.' Crowley said.

He felt very weak, he felt the weight of his whole body upon his arm as he leaned against the doorframe and could no longer hold himself up. He began to slowly slide down to the floor, just as Benton had slid down the root that had spiked his body.

'Nigel…' Crowley said as the landlord came around to aid him, helping the occultist gently to the floor.

He thought that the old man must be losing it a little, what with the blood loss. He decided to roll with it, to keep him calm.

'Yes Mr Crowley.'

'Thank you for helping me,' Crowley said quietly. 'I do appreciate it you know. I don't blame you at all.'

'Er… no problem Mr Crowley,' Terry replied.

'Do what you will Nigel.'

'I'm sorry?' Terry said, unsure that he had heard correctly as Crowley's voice was fading.

'Do what you will Nigel. That is the whole of the law,' Crowley said, and closed his eyes.

Lightning Source UK Ltd.
Milton Keynes UK
UKOW04f0828021017
310244UK00002B/440/P